"This is a 3 [barcode] -
dimensional c [barcode] about
family and fin

—RT Book Reviews on *The Cowboy's Baby Bond*

"*A Baby for Christmas* is the best kind of sweet
and tenderhearted romantic read…a touching
inspirational story that readers will want to grab a
hold of."

—RT Book Reviews

"Plenty of action amidst a wonderful reunion love
story."

—RT Book Reviews on *Wagon Train Reunion*, 4.5 stars

Praise for Ruth Axell Morren

"Morren's latest historical is a must-read. [Her] flair
for the unexpected will keep readers turning the
pages. The ending is classic romance at its best."

—RT Book Reviews on *The Making of a Gentleman*

"A delightful read; Morren's characters are full of
life."

—RT Book Reviews on *A Gentleman's Homecoming*

"Morren does an extraordinary job of putting two
unlikely people together and showing us how love
and romance can flourish despite difficulties. This
exciting story has a wonderful climax, fast-paced
story line and just the right amount of spiritual truth
that leaves the reader feeling wonderfully satisfied."

—RT Book Reviews on *A Bride of Honor*

Praise for Linda Ford

beautifully crafted story with three

characters and uplifting lessons

ding one's place."

Book Reviews

Linda Ford
and
Ruth Axtell Morren

The Road to Love
&
Hearts in the Highlands

HARLEQUIN LOVE INSPIRED CLASSICS

If you purchased this book without a cover you should be aware
that this book is stolen property. It was reported as "unsold and
destroyed" to the publisher, and neither the author nor the
publisher has received any payment for this "stripped book."

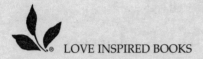 LOVE INSPIRED BOOKS

Recycling programs
for this product may
not exist in your area.

ISBN-13: 978-1-335-89587-5

The Road to Love & Hearts in the Highlands

Copyright © 2018 by Harlequin Books S.A.

The publisher acknowledges the copyright holders
of the individual works as follows:

The Road to Love
Copyright © 2008 by Linda Ford

Hearts in the Highlands
Copyright © 2008 by Ruth Axtell

All rights reserved. Except for use in any review, the reproduction
or utilization of this work in whole or in part in any form by any
electronic, mechanical or other means, now known or hereafter
invented, including xerography, photocopying and recording, or in
any information storage or retrieval system, is forbidden without
the written permission of the editorial office, Love Inspired Books,
195 Broadway, New York, NY 10007 U.S.A.

This is a work of fiction. Names, characters, places and incidents are
either the product of the author's imagination or are used fictitiously, and
any resemblance to actual persons, living or dead, business establishments,
events or locales is entirely coincidental.

This edition published by arrangement with Love Inspired Books.

® and TM are trademarks of Love Inspired Books, used under license.
Trademarks indicated with ® are registered in the United States Patent
and Trademark Office, the Canadian Intellectual Property Office and in
other countries.

www.Harlequin.com

Printed in U.S.A.

CONTENTS

THE ROAD TO LOVE   7
Linda Ford

HEARTS IN THE HIGHLANDS   283
Ruth Axtell Morren

Linda Ford lives on a ranch in Alberta, Canada, near enough to the Rocky Mountains that she can enjoy them on a daily basis. She and her husband raised fourteen children—four homemade, ten adopted. She currently shares her home and life with her husband, a grown son, a live-in paraplegic client and a continual (and welcome) stream of kids, kids-in-law, grandkids and assorted friends and relatives.

Books by Linda Ford

Love Inspired Historical

Big Sky Country

Montana Cowboy Daddy
Montana Cowboy Family
Montana Cowboy's Baby
Montana Bride by Christmas
Montana Groom of Convenience
Montana Lawman Rescuer

Montana Cowboys

The Cowboy's Ready-Made Family
The Cowboy's Baby Bond
The Cowboy's City Girl

Christmas in Eden Valley

A Daddy for Christmas
A Baby for Christmas
A Home for Christmas

Visit the Author Profile page at Harlequin.com for more titles.

THE ROAD TO LOVE

Linda Ford

This one thing I do, forgetting those things
which are behind, and reaching forth
unto those things which are before.
—*Philippians* 3:13

I am privileged and honored to have a special critique partner who encourages and challenges me. Without her, my struggles to map out my stories would be more painful and, at times, even fruitless.

Thanks, Deb. I couldn't do it without you. This book is lovingly, gratefully dedicated to you.

Chapter One

South Dakota Spring, 1933

The windmill stood tall and stately like a prairie light-house.

Kate Bradshaw shivered. She would sooner walk barefoot through a thistle patch than have to climb up there and grease the gears. But she had no choice. They must have water. She shuddered to think what would happen if the windmill quit and edged toward the ladder.

God willing, the drought would end soon, but the drifts of dust along the fence line reminded her how dry last year had been—and the two before that. She prayed the hint of spring green in the trees promised a better year ahead.

She'd put off the task as long as she could, hoping a friendly neighbor might happen by and offer to mount that high ladder and perform the dreaded task. None had.

The only sign she saw of another soul besides her children was a thin twist of smoke rising from inside the circle of trees across the road.

Another tramp, she suspected. One who preferred his

own company to hanging about with the bunch near the tracks. Wandering men were a sign of the times. The crash and the drought had left hundreds of men unemployed. Homeless. Desperate.

"Momma, hurry up. I want to see you do it." Dougie, her son, just barely seven, seemed to think everything was an adventure. He didn't understand the meaning of the word *caution*.

Which gave Kate plenty of reason to worry about him. More than enough dangers lurked about the farm. Yet she smiled at her young son, loving every inch of him. He possessed her brown eyes and brown hair but looked like his father. He'd grow into a handsome man.

Mary, her blue eyes wide as dinner plates, tugged at Kate's arm. "Momma, don't. I'm scared." A tear surfaced in the corner of each eye, hung there a moment then made parallel tracks down Mary's cheeks.

Kate sighed. This child, her firstborn, a fragile nine-year-old, feared everything. The animals. The machinery. The sounds in the night. The wind. If it had been the roaring, moaning wind that shook the house, Kate could have understood. But Mary hated even the soothing, gentle wind, as much as she did the distant cry of coyotes, lonely and forlorn for sure, but never scary. Mary would never admit it to her mother, but Kate felt certain her daughter feared her own shadow. Even as she wiped the tears from Mary's face, she shoved back the impatience this child's weakness triggered in her. And wondered how such a child could be flesh of her flesh, how two such different children could have both sprung from the same union, the same loins.

She patted Mary's blond head. "I have to, unless we want the whole thing to break down."

Dougie bounced up and down, barely able to contain his excitement. "I can help you." He headed for the ladder.

More out of protective instinct than necessity Kate lurched after him. Thankfully, she knew, he was too short to reach the bottom bar.

At her brother's boldness, Mary wailed like a lost lamb.

"Dougie, stay back," Kate said. "I'll do it. It's not such a big job. Your poppa did it all the time. Don't you remember?"

"No." Dougie's smile faded. His eyes clouded momentarily.

Mary's eyes dried as she proudly recalled having seen her father climb the windmill many times. "I was never scared when Poppa did it," she added.

Kate ached for her daughter. No doubt some of Mary's fears stemmed from losing the father she adored. Her daughter's screaming night terrors pained Kate almost as much as the loss of her husband. Hiding her own fears seemed the best way to help the child see how to face difficult situations so Kate adjusted the pair of overalls she had donned and marched to the windmill, grabbed the first metal rung and pulled herself up. *One bar at a time. Don't look down. Don't think how far it is to the top. Or the bottom.*

Be merciful to me, O God, be merciful unto me: for my soul trusteth in thee: yea, in the shadow of thy wings will I make my refuge, until these calamities be overpast.

The metal bit into her palms.

She hated the feeling that headed for the pit of her stomach as she inched upward, and continued as though the bottom had fallen out of her insides. But she had to ignore her fear and do this task.

She paused at the platform, loathing the next part most of all. Once she stood on the narrow wooden ledge…

Now was not the time to remember how Mr. Martin fell off while greasing his windmill and killed himself. She would not imagine the sound his body made landing far below.

A crow cawed mockingly as it passed overhead.

The Lord is my shepherd; I shall not want. He maketh me to lie down in green pastures: he leadeth me beside still waters.

There would be no water for the Bradshaw family or their animals if she didn't take care of this task.

She no longer missed Jeremiah with a pain like childbirth, no longer felt an emptiness inside threatening to suck the life from her. The emptiness still existed, but it had stopped calling his name. What she missed right now was someone to do this job.

Shep barked and growled. The dog must sense the man across the road.

"Be quiet," Dougie ordered. Shep settled down, except for a rumbling growl.

Kate mentally thanked the dog for his constant protection of the children.

The wind tugged at her trouser legs.

She clung to the top bar. This farm and its care were entirely her responsibility unless she wanted to give up and move into town, marry Doyle—who kept asking even though she told him over and over she would never give up her home or the farm. Which left her no option but to get herself up to the platform and grease the gears.

"Ma'am?"

The sound of the unfamiliar voice below sent a jolt of

surprise through Kate's arms, almost making her lose her grip on the metal structure. She squeezed her hands tighter, pressed into the bars and waited for the dizziness to pass before she ventured a glance toward the ground. She glimpsed a man, squat from her overhead view and with a flash of dark hair. But looking down was not a good idea. Nausea clawed at her throat. She closed her eyes, pressed her forehead to the cool bar between her hands and concentrated on slow, deep breaths.

"Ma'am. I could do that for you."

The tramp from the trees no doubt, scavenging for a handout. Willing to do something in exchange for food as most of them were. *But why, God, couldn't you send nice Mr. Sandstrum from down the road? Or one of the Oliver boys?*

"I can't pay," she said. Jeremiah had left a bit of money. But it had been used up to buy seed to plant new crops and provide clothes for the growing children.

"I'd be happy with a meal, ma'am."

A glow of gratitude eased through her. She'd feed the man for a week if he did this one job. But she hesitated. How often could she count on someone to show up and handle every difficult situation for her? She needed to manage on her own if she were to survive. And she fully intended to survive. She would keep the farm and the security it provided for her and the children, no matter what.

No matter the hot, dry winds that dragged shovelfuls of dust into drifts around every unmovable object, and deposited it in an endless trail through her house.

No matter the grasshoppers that clicked in the growing wheat, delighting in devouring her garden and making Mary scream as she ran from their sticky, scratchy legs.

No task, not even greasing the windmill, would conquer her.

"I can manage," she called, her voice not quite steady, something she hoped those below would put down to the wind.

"Certain you can, ma'am." After a pause, the man below added softly, "It's been a fair while since I had a good feed. Could I do something else for you? Fix fence…chop wood?"

Kate chuckled softly in spite of her awkward position. She wished she dared look down to see if he meant to be amusing. "Mister, if you chop all the wood in sight, there wouldn't be enough to warm us one week come winter. We burn coal."

The man laughed, a regretful sound full of both mirth and irony. "Don't I know it." he said.

The pleasure of shared amusement tickled the inside of the emptiness Kate had grown used to and then disappeared as quickly as it came.

He continued. "Makes it hard for a man to stay warm in the cold. Doubly hard to cook a thick stew even if a man had the makings."

Kate knew the feeling of unrelenting cold, hunkering over a reluctant fire, aching for something warm and filling to eat. Seemed no matter how long she lived she'd never get over that lost, lonely feeling. It was this remembrance that made her ease her way down the ladder.

She sighed heavily when her feet hit solid ground.

Shep pressed to her side.

Grateful for the dog's protection, she patted his head to calm him, and glanced about for her children.

Dougie bounced around the stranger, boldly curious while Mary had retreated to the shadow of the chicken house. Knowing how much Mary hated and feared the chickens, her choice of safety seemed ironic.

Kate faced the man.

He was taller than he looked from above, bigger, and lean to the point of thinness, his black hair shaggy and overly long, his skin leathered and brown from living outdoors, his eyes so dark she couldn't see the pupils.

But she liked the patient expression of his face. He looked the sort of man who would be unruffled by adversity. She mentally smiled. A roving man no doubt had his share of such.

His clothes were threadbare but clean.

It said a lot for a man that he managed to look decent under his present circumstances. And what it said made her relax slightly.

The tramp rolled a soiled cowboy hat in his fingers, waiting for her to complete her study of him. Suddenly, he tossed the hat on the ground and reached for the bucket of grease.

At first she didn't release the handle. She would have to do this job sooner or later. Then she let him take the bucket. Later suited her just fine.

He scurried up the windmill with the agility of a cat.

Kate watched his progress, squinting against the bright sun. Her chest tightened as he stepped to the platform and the wind tossed his hair. She shuddered when she realized he didn't hang on. She pulled her gaze from the man and grabbed Dougie's arm, putting an end to the way he bounced up and down at the ladder, trying to reach the first rung.

"Come on, the man is going to want to eat when he's done." If she didn't provide a decent meal he would no doubt leave one of those hobo signs at the gate indicating this farm provided mean fare. Why should she care? But she did. She still had her pride.

"Mary, come on. I need your help." Mary shrank back while Dougie tried to pull from her grasp. Seemed to be the way she always stood with them—holding Dougie back, urging Mary on.

She'd planned bread and fried eggs for them. Now she had to scrape together something for a regular meal. And she still needed to milk the cows, separate the milk, set bread to rise, a hundred other little tasks beyond measuring or remembering.

"Come, Mary." Her words were sharp. She sounded unforgiving. But she didn't have time to coddle the child.

Mary jerked away from the building and raced to her side.

As Kate shepherded both children to the house, she mentally scoured the cupboards for what to feed the man.

"Dougie, get me some potatoes." As she tugged off the coveralls and hung them on a hook, he hurried away, eager for the adventure of the dark cellar.

Kate smoothed her faded blue cotton dress. "Mary, bring me a jar of canned beef and one of green beans." Mary went without crying only because Dougie traipsed ahead of her.

Kate poured a cup of raisins into a pot and covered them with water to boil then scooped out a generous amount of her homemade butter and measured out half a cup of her precious sugar. She added the softened raisins, flour and spices then put the cake in the oven while the children did as she said.

Dougie brought back a basin full of potatoes, wizened and sprouted after a winter in storage.

Not much, but still she was grateful she had food for her children. She peeled the potatoes as thinly as possible so as not to waste a bit and set them to boil. She gathered the peelings in a basin to later take to the chickens.

Dougie watched out the window, giving a step-by-step description of what the man did. "He greased it. He's climbing down. Sure isn't scared like you are, Momma. He put the grease pail on the ground. He's watering the cows." The boy dashed out of the house.

"Dougie, wait." The skin on the back of Kate's neck tingled as she hurried to the door. She couldn't trust her child with a stranger.

Dougie raced to the man, spoke with him a minute and ran back to her. "Momma, his name is Hatcher. He says he'll milk the cows."

Hatcher? Sounded too much like hatchet for her liking. Was it his nickname? Earned by the deeds he did? She didn't like to judge a man prematurely but she'd sooner be overly cautious than have someone named Hatcher hanging around. "No. I'll do it," she said.

But Dougie grabbed the galvanized tin buckets and headed back outside before she could stop him. He rejoined the man who took the pails but stood watching Kate, waiting silently for her agreement.

Again she felt his quiet patience. Jeremiah had been like that. Slowly, she nodded, and her son and the man disappeared into the barn.

Suddenly a whole stream of worries assailed her. Was she foolish to let her son out of sight with a tramp? On top of that, she wondered if the man knew how to milk properly. Would she have to go out and strip the cows? She couldn't let them go dry. The milk fed herself, the children, the pig and the chickens. Besides providing their butter, the cream gave them the only cash they would have until the crop was seeded, and harvested. And that depended on having rain when they needed it, no grasshoppers to eat the crop and a hundred other things. "It's in God's hands," she whispered. "He'll take care of us. He's promised." She forced herself to dwell on these comforting words yet threads of concern knitted around the promise.

She stood in the doorway, torn between hurrying out to the barn and the need to prepare the meal. The cake was almost ready to come out. If she left it now, they'd have burned sacrifices for supper.

"Mary, sit on the step and watch the barn."

"What for, Momma?"

"Just watch it and let me know if anyone comes out." She shoved her daughter outside, ignoring the stark fear in her eyes. "All you do is sit here. I have to finish supper."

She tested the cake, put it back in the oven, pushed the boiling potatoes to a cooler spot on the stove and emptied the meat and beans into pots to heat.

Mary clattered inside. "Momma," she whispered.

"Ma'am?"

The deep voice, unexpected as it was, startled Kate. She jerked her gaze to the man standing in her doorway, two foamy pails of milk in his hands.

Dougie raced in behind the man.

Kate let her tense chest muscles relax knowing the boy was safe and sound.

The man carefully avoided looking at her as he set the pails on the worn wooden table next to the door and retreated.

"Supper is ready," she told him. "Make yourself comfortable while I dish you up a plate." She nodded to the step indicating he should wait there. When Dougie prepared to join the man, Kate called him inside. He reluctantly slouched indoors.

Kate dished up generous portions of food and carried the plate to the man.

He nodded. "Thank you, ma'am. Name's Hatcher Jones."

Kate hesitated then gave her name. "I appreciate your help, Mr. Jones. I'll bring you dessert in a few minutes." She ducked back inside, closed the door behind her, served the children and herself, all the time aware of Hatcher Jones on the other side of the solid wooden door. It made her feel awkward to sit at the table while he sat on the step, yet nothing in the world would persuade her to invite him inside the house. Most hobos were ordinary men on the move looking for work wherever they could find it but even without Mary's frightened look she became acutely conscious of the vulnerability of her two children.

Mary and Dougie finished and Kate deemed the cake cool enough to cut. She put a generous slice in a bowl, poured on thick, cool cream and took it outside.

Hatcher Jones handed her his spit-clean plate and took the bowl of dessert, his eyes appreciating the food as he murmured his thanks.

Kate hovered at the doorway, breathing in the pleasure of her farm. "Where are you from, Mr. Jones?"

"From nowhere. Going nowhere." He seemed preoccupied with the bowl of food.

"You must have belonged somewhere at some time." The idea of being homeless, having no roots still made her tense up inside. She couldn't stand the thought of someone out there, hunkered over a lonely campfire. Cold, wet, miserable, vulnerable to prying eyes. It was a too-familiar sensation she couldn't shake. Not even after all these years.

He shrugged. "Too long ago to matter."

"Going anywhere in particular? I hear a lot of men are heading toward the coast." She chuckled. "At least it rains there."

"Been there. Seems all it did was rain."

"So you didn't like it?"

Again he shrugged, a languid one-shoulder-higher-than-the-other gesture that said better than any words that he was short on opinions about such things. "Can get too much of even a good thing."

"You surely can't like this drought better'n rain. Even too much rain."

"Drought or rain. What's the difference? Man just has to make the best of it."

"A woman does, too."

He glanced over his shoulder to her. "It's not easy."

"No. It's not. But we do okay."

He nodded and looked across the fields. "How much land you got here?"

"Two quarters."

"How much in crop?"

"A hundred acres."

He grunted. "Planning to put it all down to wheat?"

How long had it been since anyone had asked her about her farm? Doyle's only question was when did she intend to get rid of it and marry him? Her answer was always the same. Never. This farm belonged to her. Lock, stock and piles of dust. She would never let it go or even take out a mortgage on it.

Even Sally, dear friend that she was, couldn't understand Kate's dedication to the land. All Sally could think was how fortunate Kate was to have a beau such as Doyle. Handsome, debonair, well-off, a lawyer with a big house. "You could quit working like a man," Sally said often enough.

Kate drew in a long breath full of spring sweetness. The smell of new growth. Who'd believe green had it's own scent? She'd once tried to explain it to Doyle and he'd laughed. Unfortunately the endless dust drowned out all but tantalizing hints of the freshness. So far this spring there hadn't been any blinding dust storms but no significant amounts of rain, either. What was the official total? .06 inches. Hardly worth counting.

She gathered up her shapeless plans for the spring work and put words to them. "I want to put in some corn. Seems to me it's pretty hardy once it's tall enough the gophers don't eat it off."

"No problem with blackbirds attacking it?"

"Some. But there's a bonus to that. They're good eating. 'Four and twenty blackbirds baked in a pie.'"

He straightened his shoulders inside his worn blue shirt, hesitated as if to consider her words and then grunted in what she took for amusement. "God's blessings often come disguised."

She stared at his back, saw his backbone edging at the faded blue of his shirt. A hobo who talked about God? Even more, about God's blessings. She couldn't keep herself from asking, "What blessing is disguised in being homeless?" She could recall none.

He lifted his head and looked out across the field. She wondered what he saw. Did the open road pull at him the way it had her father?

"There are certain advantages." He spoke softly, with what she could only guess was a degree of gratitude.

She rubbed at a spot below her left ear where her jaw had knotted painfully and tried not to remember how she'd hated the constant moving, the never knowing where home was or where they would sleep. Every time they settled, even knowing it was temporary, she hoped this would be the last time they moved. There was no last time for her father, still restlessly on the move. But a time came when Kate refused to move on. She felt no call to wander. No appeal of the long winding road.

Hatcher Jones considered her. "A hundred acres to seed this spring? Quite a job. You got a tractor by any chance?"

She gladly pulled her thoughts back to the farm—her home, her security. "I got me a tractor." She'd managed to limp it through last year with the help of the oldest Oliver boy whose ability and patience coaxed it to run. But since Abby Oliver headed north, she had no one to help her. "It needs a few repairs." She almost snorted. A few repairs. It was as pathetic as measuring .06 inches of precipitation and calling it rain.

Hatcher pushed to his feet. "I'll be moving on. Again, thank you for the meal."

"You're welcome. Thank you for taking care of the windmill." The rotary wheel hummed quietly on the tower. No more protesting squeal of dry gears. Another month before she'd have to brave the heights again.

Hatcher stood with his hat in his hand, looking as though he had something more he wanted to say. Then he jammed the blackened hat on his head and nodded. "Good food. Thank you."

Kate laughed. "Does that mean you won't post a secret sign at the end of the lane warning hobos away?"

She couldn't see his eyes, hidden under the shadow of his hat, but his mouth flashed a quick smile.

"No, ma'am. But I won't be letting others know how good a cook you are, either. Wouldn't want a whole stream of hungry men descending on you." He gave a quick nod. "Now I'll leave you in peace. God bless."

She watched him stride away, his long gait eating up the road in deceptive laziness and suddenly, she felt lonely. She thought of calling him back. She wanted to talk more about the farm. Ask him what he'd seen in his travels. How severe was the drought in other places? Did he really see God's blessing in the hardships he witnessed and experienced? She sighed deeply, pushing her useless longings out as she exhaled. Then she returned to the many chores still waiting.

She strained the milk and separated it.

"Mary, hurry out and shut in the chickens. Take out these peelings." She handed her the basin and ignored Mary's wide-eyed silent protest. "We can't afford to lose any of them." The child had to get over her unreasonable fear of chickens. "Dougie, go put the heifers into the corrals and make sure the gate's tightly latched." He was really too small to chase after the animals but she couldn't be everywhere at once. "Hurry now before it gets dark." She'd run out and help Dougie as soon as she finished the milk. And if the past was any indication, she'd end up dumping the basin of peelings. Mary never seemed to get any farther than the fence where she tried to poke the contents through the wire holes.

Kate prayed as she worked. *God, protect the children. Help Mary realize she's bigger than the chickens. Help me find a way to get my crop in.* She stilled her thoughts. As usual, her prayers seemed an endless list of requests. But she had nowhere to turn but to God who promised to provide all her needs. Seemed to her a God who owned the cattle on a thousand hills and held the waters in His hand could send a little rain to her area of the world. *Lord, help me be patient. I know You will provide for us. You've promised.* A smile curved her lips. *Thank You that I didn't have to grease the windmill.* A blessing in the form of a hobo. God must surely have a sense of humor.

She scoured the milk buckets and turned them upside down to dry, poured boiling water through the separator and cleaned it thoroughly.

Normally the work kept her mind adequately occupied but not tonight. One hundred acres to seed. A tractor that refused to run. And no help. She needed a hired man. One with experience. One with the ability to fix the tractor. One who didn't expect anything more than his keep. She knew no such person. She'd run an ad in a few papers but the responses were disappointing at best and downright frightening in the case of one man who made very inappropriate suggestions. Of course, as Doyle always pointed out, she had the option of selling the farm and accepting his offer of marriage.

As she dashed to the barn to help Dougie, pausing at the chicken yard to take the basin from Mary and toss the peelings into the pen, she wondered if she was being stupid or stubborn to cling to this piece of property. Probably both, she willingly admitted, but she wasn't ready to give up the only permanent home she'd ever known.

The sun sat low on the western horizon brushing the sky with purple and orange and a hundred shades of pink. At the doorstep, she turned, holding a child's hand in each of hers. As she drank in the beauty of the sunset she silently renewed the promise she'd made to herself after Jeremiah's death. Never would her children know the uncertainty of being homeless. Not if she had to pull the plough herself.

Chapter Two

Hatcher watched the blades on the Bradshaw's windmill turn smoothly as he headed down the road toward a nearby farm where he heard a man could get a bit job. All he needed was enough work to fill his stomach and a chance to bathe and wash his clothes before he moved on. He prided himself on a fair amount of work in exchange for a handout. Seems the meal Mrs. Bradshaw provided was more generous than the work he'd done. He'd have to fix that somehow.

As he shoveled manure out of the barn for a Mr. Briggs, he tied a red neckerchief over his nose and kept his mind occupied with other things than the pungent, eye-watering smell of a long-neglected job. Most men would be ashamed to let even a hobo bear witness to such slovenliness. Not that it was the worst job he'd ever done. Good honest work never hurt anyone. Long ago, he'd learned he could enjoy his thoughts as he worked at even the most unappealing job; his favorite way was to see how many Bible verses he could recall without stumbling. In the ten years he'd been wandering the back roads of this huge country, he'd committed hundreds to memory. From the first day the words from

Genesis chapter four, verse seven haunted his thoughts.
*If thou does well, shalt thou not be accepted? And if
thou doest not well, sin lieth at the door.*

He'd sought comfort and absolution in the scriptures.
He'd memorized the first nine chapters of Genesis, saw
over and over the failure of man to live as God intended.
A fact that surprised him not at all.

Today, as he worked, he interspersed his recitation
with plans on how to rectify his debt to Mrs. Bradshaw.
It would require he return to the slough where he'd spent
the previous night. Not often did he retrace his steps
but he couldn't move on until he adequately repaid her.

He finished working for Mr. Briggs, received a meager meal of one shriveled unpeeled potato and a slab
of side bacon that was mostly fat. It measured poorly
in comparison with the meal of the previous evening.
Mr. Briggs granted him permission to use the water
trough to wash his clothes and himself, which he did.
In his clean set of clothes, his wet ones rolled and tied
in a bundle, he returned to the slough where he hung
the garments to dry.

And then he tackled his project.

Next morning Hatcher headed up the driveway to
the Bradshaw home with the shelf he'd created from
willow branches. Nothing special. Hobos all over the
country made them. In fact, she probably had several
already. A woman who cooked a fine generous meal
like the one she'd provided him was bound to have received gifts before.

The big black-and-white furry dog raced out to bark
at his heels.

"Quiet, Shep," he ordered.

The animal stopped barking but growled deep in his

throat as he followed so hard on Hatcher's heels it made the back of his neck tingle.

Not a dog to let anyone do something stupid. Good dog for a woman who appeared to be alone with two kids.

The place seemed quiet at first but as he drew closer, he heard mumbled warnings. Seemed to be Mrs. Bradshaw speaking. Threatening someone.

He felt a familiar pinching in his stomach warning him to walk away from a potentially explosive situation but he thought of some of the homeless, desperate, unscrupulous men he'd encountered in his travels. If one of them had cornered Mrs. Bradshaw…

He edged forward, following the sound around the old Ford truck and drew to a halt at the sight of Mrs. Bradshaw standing on a box, her head buried under the hood of the vehicle, her voice no longer muffled by the bulk of metal and bolts.

"You good for nothing piece of scrap metal. Why do you do this to me? Just when I need you to cooperate, you get all persnickety." She shifted, banged her head and grunted. "If I had a stick of dynamite, I'd fix you permanently."

Hatcher leaned back on his heels, grinning as the woman continued to scold the inanimate object. After a moment, he decided to make a suggestion that might save both the truck and the woman from disaster.

"'Scuse me for interrupting, but maybe you should bribe it instead of threatening it."

She jerked up, crashed her head into the gaping hood and stumbled backward off the box, her palms pressed to the top of her head as she faced him, her eyes narrowed with her pain. "Oh, it's you. You startled me."

He regretted she had every right to be frightened of

him. Fact of the matter, she should be far more wary than she was. He tipped his head slightly. "My apologies." He slid his gaze to the dirt-encased engine behind her. "It's being uncooperative?"

She turned to frown fiercely at the bowels of the truck. "I've done everything. Even prayed over it."

He blinked in surprise and amusement at the way she glanced upward as if imploring God to do something.

"I might be able to help," he said.

She stepped aside, made a sweeping swing of her arm toward the truck. "It's all yours, mister."

He hitched up his pants, pretended to spit into his palms, rubbed his hand together, and imitating her gesture, glanced imploringly skyward.

She laughed, a snorting sound she tried to hide behind her fist.

He darted her a quick glance, not wanting to stare at the way her warm brown eyes flashed amusement yet his gaze lingered a second as a strand of her shoulder-length cinnamon-colored hair blew across her cheek and she flicked it aside. Nice to see a woman who still knew how to laugh. He'd seen far too many all shriveled up inside and out, worn down from fighting the elements, trying to cope with disappointment after disappointment and a mountain of work that never went away. Well, maybe he could do something to ease this woman's work and repay her for her kindness of two days ago. He bent over the hood of the truck and studied the motor. Sure could use a good cleaning. He checked the carburetor. The choke was closed. No wonder it wouldn't run. "You got a piece of hay wire?"

"Hay wire? You're going to fix my truck with hay wire?"

"Ma'am, ain't nothing you can't fix with hay wire and bubble gum."

She made that snorting sound of laughter again. "Sorry, I have no bubble gum but I'll get you some wire."

She sauntered away to the barn, chuckling and murmuring about the miracle of wire and gum.

He was glad to brighten someone's day. As he waited, he scraped dirt and bug guts off the radiator and tightened the spark plugs.

Her quiet chuckle heralded her return, the sound like the first rays of a summer day—warm, promising good things to fill the ensuing hours.

He quieted his soul with the words of scripture: *He that is slow to anger is better than the mighty; and he that ruleth his spirit than he that taketh a city.* He sought for the reference. Knew it was Proverbs but the sound of the woman at his elbow made him momentarily forget the exact location. He kept his attention on the motor until he brought his thoughts under submission. Proverbs sixteen, verse thirty-two. Only when he had it correct did he straighten.

"This do?" Her voice bubbled with amusement as she handed him a coil of wire.

"Just the thing." He bent off a piece and wired the choke open. "That should do the trick."

He cranked the motor over several times and it kicked to life.

Remembering her skyward pleas, grateful for divine assistance, he stood back, glanced up to heaven and nodded to thank God for His help.

Mrs. Bradshaw clapped. "Guess I just needed a prayer partner. And someone who understands motors. Can you show me what you did?"

"It's nothing. Just the miracle of hay wire." Side by side, they bent over the motor and he explained the workings of the carburetor and the function of the choke.

"Got it." She straightened and turned to lean on the fender that hinted at once being gray. Now it was mostly patchy black and rusty. "Trouble is, now I know that, it will be something else that goes wrong."

"Someone once told me, if you're not learning and growing, you're withering."

She chortled. "No doubt about it then. I'm growing." She grew quiet as she looked across the fields. "Though it seems my farm is withering."

"Your husband off working somewhere?"

She didn't answer.

Caution. That was good. Didn't pay to trust too quickly. He dusted his hands. "Brought you a gift." He retrieved it from beside the truck.

"A gift? Why?"

"To say thanks."

She took the shelf and examined it, ran her fingers over the words he'd cut into the front of the shelf. *The Lord is my helper.* "It's beautiful."

He heard the shimmer in her voice and lowered his gaze, tried not to let the tightness in his throat make itself known.

She cleared her throat and continued. "I'll hang it next to the door. But it's me who owes you thanks for getting the truck running. I have to get to town today and didn't know how I was going to make it there and do my errands before the children are out of school."

He'd made shelves such as that on two previous occasions. Once when a kind family had provided shelter from a raging snowstorm.

Another time after he'd helped an elderly woman bury her husband. He'd carved a verse in the top branch. Hebrews thirteen, verse five, *I will never leave thee, nor forsake thee,* hoping the object and verse would remind her she wasn't alone.

But Mrs. Bradshaw's gratitude for his poor offering gave him a queer mingling of regret and hope. He couldn't afford to luxury in either emotion. Backing away, he touched the brim of his hat. "Ma'am." He headed down the road. He got as far as the end of the truck when she called out.

"Wait. Mr...." She paused as if searching for his name, "Jones. I was planning to go to town and post a little advertisement for someone to help me. I can't run this farm by myself."

"Lots of men looking for work." He continued walking away.

She fell in step beside him. "I need someone who can fix my tractor and put the crop in. You seem like a handy kind of man."

"I'm moving on." Her steps slowed but his did not.

"Right away?"

"The road is long."

"And it calls? My father was like that."

He didn't argue but for him the open road didn't call. The back road pushed.

She stopped altogether. "I'm sure I'll find someone." Her voice rippled with determination. She turned and headed home. "Or I'll do it myself."

Hatcher faltered on his next step then marched onward. Before he reached the end of the lane, he heard her singing and chuckled at her choice of song.

"'Bringing in the sheaves, bringing in the sheaves. We shall come rejoicing, bringing in the sheaves.'"

The woman needed a whole lot of things to happen before she could rejoice about the sheaves. Not the least of which was someone to help her put the seed in the ground, but no need for him to worry about her. Within an hour of posting her little ad, she'd have half a dozen or more men to choose from.

Back at the slough where the flattened straw-like grass showed evidence of how long he'd camped there, he bundled up his now-dry clothes and packed his kettle away. He cocked his head when he heard Mrs. Bradshaw drive down the road.

He hesitated, thinking of her words *I'll do it myself*, and hearing her cheery voice in joyful song. She was the kind of woman who deserved a break. He would pray she got it and find a hired man who would be what she needed.

She'd never said if her husband was dead or gone looking for work elsewhere. Though it seemed the farm provided plenty of work. Maybe not enough income to survive on. Must be hard raising those two young ones alone and running the farm, as well. Hard for her and the kids. If only he could do something to ease their burden. Besides pray.

He thought of something he could do that might add a little pleasure to their lives. Another couple of hours before he got on his way wouldn't hurt. Regretfully resigned to obeying his conscience he dropped his knapsack and pulled out his knife, chose a nice branch and started to whittle. He stopped later to boil water and toss in a few tea leaves. When the tea was ready, he poured it into a battered tin cup, picked up his Bible, leaned against a tree trunk and settled back to read as he waited for the Bradshaws to come home. He calmed his thoughts, pulling them into a tight circle and stroked the cover of the Bible, worn now to a soft doe color, its pages as fragile as old onionskin. He'd carried it with him since he left home, knowing, hoping to find within its pages what he needed. He'd found strength for each day, a tenuous peace, and a certainty of what he must do, what his life consisted of now. Like Cain, he was a vagabond.

He opened the Bible, smoothed the tattered edges of the page with his fingertip and began to read.

Sometime later, he heard the truck groan up the lane, waited, giving the family a chance to sort themselves out then he headed up the dusty tracks.

The dog saw him first and barked. The little boy yelled. "Mom, it's Hatcher. He's come back."

"Dougie," a voice called from inside the house. "Stay here."

The eager child skidded to a halt and shuffled backward to the truck where he stopped and waited, bouncing from foot to foot as if still running down the road in his mind. The dog hovered protectively at his side.

Mrs. Bradshaw hurried out, saw her son was safe and shielded her eyes with her hand as she watched Hatcher approach. Her lips curved into a smile of recognition.

Something in his heart bounced as restless and eager as Dougie at the truck then he smoothed away the response with the knowledge of who he was and what his future held. He thought to warn the woman to spare her smiles for someone who'd be staying around to enjoy them. Pushed away that thought, as well. Settled back into his hard-won peace.

"Ma'am." He nodded and touched the brim of his hat, painfully aware how dirty it was. "I made something for the little ones, if you don't mind."

She studied him a moment. He could feel her measuring him before she nodded as if he had somehow passed an inspection.

A flash of regret crossed Hatcher's mind. For the first time his solitude seemed poverty-stricken. He needed to cling to the blessings of his life. One God had provided. One that suited his purpose.

He pulled a willow whistle from his pocket and held it out to Dougie. The child bounced forward and took it with loud thanks. He blew a thin sound.

Shep backed away, whining. The child looked at him and blew again. The dog settled on his haunches and howled.

Dougie blew. The dog howled in unison.

The boy stopped. The dog stopped. The boy blew his whistle. The dog howled. Both child and animal tipped their heads as if not quite sure what was going on.

Mrs. Bradshaw laughed. "Shep wants to sing with you."

Dougie giggled and blew several sharp notes. The dog lifted his nose and howled.

Hatcher's wide smile had an unfamiliar feel. As if he hadn't used it in a long time.

The little girl slipped out the door and pressed to her mother's side.

Hatcher pulled another whistle from his pocket. "One for you, too, missy."

The child hesitated. He understood her guarded fearfulness, respected it and waited for her to feel he meant her no harm.

"Go ahead, Mary," her mother said.

The child snatched the whistle from Hatcher's hand. He caught a glimpse of blue eyes as she whispered her thanks. The dog's plaintive howls drew the child away.

She blew her whistle. The dog turned toward the added sound and wailed. The girl laughed.

Hatcher nodded, satisfied he'd given both children a bit of pleasure. "Ma'am." He touched his hat again and retraced his steps toward the slough.

"Wait," she called.

He stopped, hesitated, turned slowly.

"Thank you."

He touched the brim of his hat. He'd done what he aimed to do—give a bit a pleasure he hoped would make the children forget for a few short hours the meanness of their lives.

"I'll make you supper."

He'd already been here longer than usual, longer than he should. "I have to be moving on."

"It's too late today to go anywhere."

She had a point. But he didn't want to hang around and...

Well, he just didn't care to hang around.

"Or did you find some game?"

He shook his head. He'd planned to snare a rabbit but he'd whiled away his hours whittling and reading. "I'm not the world's greatest hobo."

"Need more practice?"

"Don't think so." Some things just never got easier.

"Then please, allow me to share what we have. As thanks for the children's toys."

The youngsters had moved off, marching to their tunes, the dog on their heels, still adding his voice. Every so often the children stopped, looked at Shep and laughed.

"See how much fun you've provided them."

Hatcher's smile started in the corners of his mouth, tugged his lips to the centers of his cheeks and didn't stop until it nested in his heart. "That's all I wanted, ma'am. No thanks needed."

"Nevertheless, I insist." She spun around and headed for the door, paused and turned back. "Please."

The invitation, heartfelt and sincere, begged at his heart. He knew to accept it was to break his code of conduct. He didn't stay. He didn't go beyond kind and courteous. He couldn't. But her pleasant smile caused him to waver. One more meal and then he was on his way. "Very well."

She indicated he should wait. He leaned against the truck and looked around. A big unpainted barn, one door sagging. Breaks in the fences where tumbleweeds driven by the wind had piled up and then caught the drifting soil until the fence disappeared. A solid chicken house, the chickens clucking at the barren ground behind their fence.

A farm like many others. Once prosperous; now struggling to make it through each season.

He watched the children play. So happy and innocent. Maybe such happiness was reserved for the very young.

Chapter Three

Kate stood in the middle of her kitchen, a palm pressed to her throat, and tried to explain to herself why she'd insisted the man stay for supper.

Not that she regretted the invitation. She owed him for the gifts he'd given the children. It was pure joy to see them both laughing and playing so carefree. But more than that, he'd admitted he'd failed to catch a rabbit and she couldn't push aside the knowledge he'd go hungry if she didn't feed him. She'd learned at a young age how to snare the shy animal, had grown quite good at it for all it was a tricky business. But she recalled too well that rabbits were sometimes as scarce as hen's teeth. Hunger was not a pleasant companion. True, most times they were able to rustle up something—edible roots to be boiled, lamb's quarters—a welcome bit of greens in the spring but grainy and unpleasant as the season progressed. More times, her father got eggs or potatoes or even a generous hunk of meat in exchange for some work he'd done.

But although thankfully few and far between, Kate could not forget the days her stomach ached with hunger, when she'd gone to bed with nothing but weak tea to fill the emptiness.

No, she could not in good conscience turn a man back to an empty stew pot even if she had to scrape the bottom of the barrel to feed him. And although she'd used the last of her meat two days ago for the meal she prepared for Hatcher Jones she wasn't at the bottom of the barrel yet, for which she thanked God. And her farm.

Mr. Zimmerman at the store said he'd heard talk of setting up a butcher ring. She hoped her neighbors would do so. Mr. Zimmerman said the Baileys had something ready. Perhaps they'd take the initiative and start the ring. In a few weeks the yearling steer could be her contribution. But in the meantime, all she had to offer Hatcher was fried eggs and potatoes and something from the few items left from last year's preserving. As the eggs and potatoes fried, she raced down to the cellar for a jar of beet pickles to add to the meal for color. Everything ready, she went to the door and whistled for the children to come.

Mr. Jones jerked around and stared at her. No doubt he'd heard the same dire warnings as she about women who whistled. She smirked derisively. "I know, 'a whistling woman and a crowing hen are neither fit for God nor man.'"

He touched the brim of his hat. "Seems a crowing hen would taste just fine."

Her surprise at his answer gave her the sensation of missing a step, her foot dropping into nothingness, her stomach lurching in reaction. It took her a second to steady her breathing.

He touched the brim of his hat. "Ma'am," he added.

She was about to be ma'amed to death. "Name's Kate Bradshaw, if you don't mind."

"Good enough name far as I'm concerned."

At his laconic humor, she felt a snort start in the back of her mouth and pressed her fist to her mouth hoping to quell it, knowing she couldn't. She'd tried before. Tried hard. But she'd never learned to laugh like a lady. And with a willful mind of its own, her very unladylike snort burst around her fist. She expected to see embarrassment or surprise in Mr. Jones's face. Instead little lines fanned from the outside corners of his eyes easing the resigned disinterest dominating his expression so far.

Her laugh deepened as it always did after the initial snort. Her gaze stayed with him, fastened on his dark eyes as they shared amusement and, it seemed to her, a whole lot more, things too deep inside each of them for words or even acknowledgement.

The children marched toward her, Shep at their heels singing his soulful song and Kate escaped her sudden flight into foolishness and gratefully returned to her normal, secure world.

Dougie stopped at the steps. "Did you know dogs could sing, Momma?"

Kate shook her head. "I didn't know Shep could sing, though I've heard him howling at the coyotes."

Dougie turned to the man. "Hatcher, you ever hear a dog sing before?"

Mr. Jones nodded. "A time or two."

Dougie looked shattered, as if knowing another dog had the same talent made Shep less special.

Hatcher gave the dog serious consideration. "I never heard a dog sing as well as this one, though."

Dougie's chest expanded considerably. He looked at Mary, who retreated to the doorway. "See. I told you."

At that moment, Kate knew an inexplicable fondness and admiration for the man who'd returned her son's dignity through a few kindly, well-chosen words. She smiled at the children, including Hatcher in her silent benediction. "Get washed up for supper."

"Hatcher staying?" Dougie demanded.

"Yes, he is."

"Good." He faced the man. "Thank you for the whistle."

Kate turned Dougie toward the door. "Wash." As the children cleaned up, she dished a plateful for Mr. Jones and carried it out to him along with a handful of molasses cookies. They were dark and chewy. Not at all fancy but she had nothing else for dessert. "Would you care for tea?"

He hesitated before he answered. "Much appreciated." He waited until she headed indoors before he sat down and turned his attention to the food. At the door she paused. He seemed the sort of man who should share their table as well as their food. Yet, he was a stranger and a hobo at that.

She hurried inside, ate with the children then carried a cup of tea out to the man. He wrapped his hands around the white china cup, rubbing his thumbs slowly along the surface as if taking pleasure in its smoothness, causing her to wonder how long it'd been since he'd been offered a simple cup of tea.

He sipped the contents and sighed. "Good."

"It's just tea." She remained on the step, knowing she should return to the kitchen and get at her evening chores, yet feeling comfort in adult company. Not that she suffered for want of such. She'd stopped at Doyle's office while in town this afternoon and as always he seemed pleased to see her.

He'd smiled as she entered the office. "What a pleas-

ant surprise." He closed a folder and shoved it aside.
"I could use some fresh tea as could you, I'm certain,
before you head back to the farm. If you truly must
return." His pale blue eyes brimmed with adoration.
"Have you considered how convenient it would be for
both of us if you lived in town. In the best house, need
I remind you?"

She nodded, a teasing smile lifting the corners of her
mouth. "I've seen the house. I know how lovely it is."

"I decorated it and bought every piece of furniture
for you, my dear. All for you."

"So you've told me many times." His generosity
filled her with guilt. "Need I remind you that I didn't
ask for it?"

He rose and came around the desk to stand close to
her, lifted her chin so he could see her face as he smiled
down at her. "I know you didn't but everything is evidence of my devotion to you."

Again the uncomfortable twinges of guilt. She
openly admitted her fondness for Doyle. But one thing
stood irresolutely in the way of her agreeing to marry
him—the farm. But he must have seen her argument
building and tucked her arm through his.

"Some day I'll convince you but enough for now.
Let's have tea." He covered her hand with his protective
palm as he led her past his secretary, Gertie, a woman
with blue-gray hair and steely eyes that always made
Kate wonder what she'd done wrong. He left instructions as to where he could be found. They went to the
Regal Hotel, the best in town. Only and always the
best for Doyle.

Of course, it wasn't hard to be the best when, one
by one, the other establishments had hung Closed signs
on their doors.

Kate wondered again why he'd chosen her and why he continued to wait for her when other women would have been happy to be cared for by him.

He led her into the stately dining room, glistening with pure white linen and light-arresting crystal. As he ordered, Kate tried not to compare her simple farm life with the way Doyle lived—luxury, plenty of everything—a stark contrast to her current struggles. Even his clothes spoke of his tastes, a starched white shirt that the housekeeper must have labored over for hours, a perfectly centered tie, an immaculate black suit. She knew without looking that his fine leather shoes shone with a mirrorlike gleam.

He waited until the waitress in her black dress and crisp white apron had served them tea and scones with strawberry jam at the side then leaned forward. "I can offer you so much, Kate—you and the children. My holdings are growing daily. You would never want for anything."

She sipped her tea and watched him, fascinated with the way his eyes sparkled like the diamonds in the rings in Adam's Jewelers down the street where Doyle had taken her a few months ago, practically insisting she allow him to purchase a ring for her. She'd had a difficult time convincing him she wasn't ready to make such a decision.

She brought her attention back to what he was saying.

"This is a perfect time to invest in real estate. Land prices are sure to go up once this depression ends. Just this morning I bought up another mortgage which will soon make me the owner of the feed store." He pointed across the street. "Give me a year and I'll own the mercantile, the hotel—" He indicated the other businesses.

Kate was no financial genius but she understood what his good fortune meant. "Doyle," she said softly. "Doesn't it bother you that it means tremendous loss to the current owners? They'll walk away broke and defeated."

He shrugged. "I'm sorry for them, certainly. But I'm able to take advantage of the situation and if I don't, someone else will." His gaze grew intense. "It's all for you and the children." He leaned forward. She almost gave in when he stroked the back of her hand. "Doesn't it seem a waste for me to be alone in my house? You should be living there rather than me paying a house-keeper."

Kate studied their joined hands. She missed Jeremiah. Missed being a wife. Missed sharing all the challenges and rewards of her life with someone equally invested in the farm and the children.

He pressed his point and told her again of the lovely things in his house. "It's all ready and waiting for you to move in. Surely you can see how your children would benefit from the move."

That argument always made her wonder if she was doing the right thing. In town, Dougie and Mary would be close to school. They'd be able to play with their friends. They could enjoy a few conveniences. Even luxuries.

"What would I do with the farm?" she asked. They'd discussed this before and he always had the same answer.

"Sell it, of course. Maybe not right away. Not unless we can get a decent price for it."

"Doyle, if only you could understand what the farm means to me." She'd tried so often to explain it.

"You won't need the farm to have a home. You'll

have my home. A far better home. You won't have to struggle and work so hard anymore. I will take care of you. You can enjoy life."

"I need more than a fine home."

"You'll have much more. You'll have the best of everything."

She put on a gentle expression as she hid her disappointment. She'd have to accept her loneliness a bit longer because she couldn't let the farm go. Not yet. Maybe never. If he'd ever suggested she keep it…

But he was unwavering in his opinion of what should happen. He folded his napkin and placed it neatly beside his cup. "Besides, you can't manage on your own."

It was the final clincher. Little did he know this insistence convinced her to dig in her heels and hang on. She'd find a way to survive, manage on her own.

It was too bad because she liked Doyle. He was attentive and kind, accompanied her to church, and indeed, offered her a fine life. She was genuinely fond of him. Did she love him? She wasn't sure. She wasn't even sure she wanted that.

What did she want? *Consider the lilies how they grow: they toil not, they spin not; yet I say unto you that Solomon in all his glory was not arrayed like one of these. If then God so clothe the grass, which is to day in the field, and to morrow is cast into the oven; how much more will he clothe you, O ye of little faith?*

Yes, God would take care of her. She believed it with every breath she took. But she couldn't be content like the lilies with only the fields for her home. She wanted four solid walls and a roof. She wanted to be warm and dry, have food in her cellar or—thinking of the chickens and the meat and eggs they provided—on two squawking legs.

Certainly Doyle would generously provide for her, but it didn't feel the same as the security of her own piece of land and ownership of her own house.

She sighed from the bottom of her heart.

"Problems?" Hatcher asked.

His question brought her back from thoughts of her visit with Doyle. She realized what she longed for was someone with whom she could discuss her farming problems. To Doyle there was no problem. Or at least, a simple solution. Sell. She laughed a little to hide her embarrassment at being caught spending her time in wishing for things that might never be.

"You found a hired man today?" Hatcher asked.

"I didn't."

He glanced over his shoulder, a puzzled look on his face. "When I came through town there were at least a dozen men hanging about looking for work."

She shrugged, noting that today Hatcher wore a clean, unpressed shirt in washed-out gray. "I started to put up the ad." Her skin had tingled, her face grown hot at the men watching her, waiting to read the notice. "I changed my mind." She didn't need help that badly—to invite a stranger into her life. "I decided I can manage on my own."

He turned his attention back to his tea. "Hope all your tractor needs is an adjustment to the carburetor."

A sigh came from her depths. "My tractor has seen it's best days."

"No horses?"

"I had to trade the last one in the fall for feed to see the cows through the winter."

"Been tough all over."

She murmured agreement. "I'm not complaining."

"Me, either." He downed the rest of his tea, got to

his feet and handed her the cup. "You give me the milk buckets and I'll take care of the cows."

"No need."

"I never accept a meal without doing a job."

"It was my thanks."

He made no move toward leaving. "I 'spect the young ones need you." He nodded toward the interior of the house.

As she hesitated, torn between the truth of his statement and her reluctance to accept any more help from him, Dougie hurried out with the pails solving her need to make a choice.

"I'll help you, Hatcher."

The hobo patted Dougie on the head. "Good man."

Kate choked back a snort at the way her son preened and said, "Very well." But they didn't wait for her permission. She watched the man and boy saunter to the barn, smiling as Dougie tried to imitate Hatcher's easy rolling gait then she hurried inside. There seemed no end of work to be done. She needed to make farmer's cheese. The ironing had yet to be done and couldn't be put off any longer. Mary needed a dress for tomorrow and it had to be ironed. And most importantly, she had to have a look at the tractor and see what it needed to get it running. "More than a prayer," she mumbled.

"Momma?"

"Nothing, Mary. Just talking to myself. Now help me with the dishes then run and shut in the chickens."

"Momma. I hate the chickens."

"I know you do but what would we eat if we didn't have eggs and the occasional chicken?"

"I don't like eating chicken."

"I can never figure out why you object to eating an animal you'd just as soon see dead."

"I keep seeing the way they gobble up grasshoppers." Mary shuddered.

"But you hate grasshoppers."

"I don't want to eat anything that eats them." Mary shuddered again.

Kate shook her head. This child left her puzzled.

Hatcher returned with the milk, his presence heralded by Dougie's excited chatter.

"Your milk, ma'am."

"Thank you. Seems I'm saying that a lot."

"Won't be any longer. I'll be gone in the morning. My prayers for you and the family."

And he strode away.

Kate stared after him a moment, wondering about the man. But not for long. She had milk to strain and separate. She had to try and persuade Mary to actually enter the chicken yard and shut the henhouse door and then she needed to supervise the children's homework.

Next morning, as soon as the chores were done, Kate pulled on the overalls she wore for field work, dusted her hands together as if to say she was ready for whatever lay ahead, and pulled an old felt hat tightly over her head. It took her several minutes to adjust it satisfactorily. She recognized her fussing for what it was— delaying the inevitable. But the sooner she got at it, the sooner she'd conquer it. She gave her trousers a hitch, thought of the words from the Bible, *She girdeth her loins with strength,* and smiled.

"Here I go in the strength of the Lord. With His help I can conquer this," she murmured, and hurried out to the lean-to on the side of the barn where the beast waited to challenge her. Abby Oliver had parked it there last fall with dire warnings about its reliability.

Kate confronted the rusty red machine, her feet fighting width apart, her hands on her hips and in her best mother-must-be-obeyed voice, the voice she reserved for Dougie's naughtiest moments, said, "Could you not do the charitable thing and run? How else am I going to get the crop in the ground?" No need to think about getting it off in the fall. That was later. She shifted. Crossed her arms over her middle and took a more relaxed stance. "After all," she cajoled. "I'm a woman alone. Trying to run this farm and take care of my children. And I simply can't do it without your help." She took a deep breath, rubbed the painful spot in her jaw. *God, it's Your help I need. Please, make this beast run one more season.* She'd asked the same thing last spring. And again in the fall.

She waited. For what? Inspiration? Assurance? Determination? Yes. All of them.

My God shall supply all your need according to his riches in glory.

Well, she needed a tractor that ran. God knew that. He'd promised to provide it.

She marched around the tractor once. And then again. And giggled. She felt like one of the children of Israel marching around the walls of Jericho. If only she had a pitcher to break and a trumpet to sound…

She made a tooting noise and laughed at her foolishness.

She retrieved a rag from the supplies in the corner and faced the beast. "I will get you running somehow." She checked the oil. Scrubbed the winter's accumulation of dust off the motor, poured in some fuel and cranked it over. Or at least tried. After sitting several months, the motor was stiff, uncooperative.

She took a deep breath, braced herself and tried

again. All she got was a sore shoulder. She groaned. Loudly.

"Maybe Doyle is right," she told the stubborn beast. "Maybe I should sell everything and move into town. Live a life of pampered luxury."

"Ma'am."

Her heart leaped to her throat. Her arms jerked like a scarecrow in the wind. She jolted back several inches. "You scared me." Embarrassed and annoyed, she scowled at Hatcher. "My name is Kate. Kate Bradshaw. Not ma'am." She spoke slowly making sure he didn't miss a syllable.

"Yes, ma'am. Perfectly good name."

"So you said. What do you want?"

He circled the tractor, apparently deep in thought, came to halt at the radiator. "Want me to start her up for you?"

She restrained an urge to hug him. "I'd feed you for a month if you did, though I have to warn you, I've been babying it along for the better part of three years now."

Hatcher already had his hands in the internal mysteries of the machine.

"Do you need some hay wire?" she asked.

He didn't turn. "Going to take more than hay wire to fix this."

"I thought you could fix anything with a hunk of wire or wad of bubblegum."

"Hand me that wrench, would you?" He nodded toward the tool on the ground, and she got it for him, her gratefulness mixed with frustration that she couldn't do this on her own. And yes, a certain amount of fear. If she failed, they would all starve. She wasn't about to let that happen so some Godly intervention on her behalf would be welcome.

He tightened this, adjusted that, tinkered here and there. Went to the other side of the tractor and did more of the same. Finally, he wiped his hands on a rag Kate handed him, then cranked the motor. And blessing of blessings, it reluctantly fired up.

"I'll take it out for you," Hatcher hollered.

She nodded, so grateful to hear the rumbling sound she couldn't stop grinning. She pointed toward the discer and he guided the tractor over and hitched it up. The engine coughed. Kate's jaw clenched of its own accord. She rubbed at it and sighed relief when the tractor settled into a steady roar.

The discer ready to go, Hatcher stood back.

"Thank you so much. If you're still around come dinnertime, I'll make you a meal."

He nodded, touched the brim of his hat. "Ma'am."

Kate spared him one roll of her eyes at the way he continued to call her ma'am then climbed up behind the steering wheel, pushed in the clutch, pulled the beast into gear—

It stalled.

The silence rang.

"What happened?" she asked.

"I'll crank it." He did his slow dance at the front of the tractor. Again, it growled to life but as soon as she tried to move it, it stalled.

They did it twice more. Twice more the tractor stalled for her.

"Let me." Hatcher indicated she get down which she gladly did, resisting an urge to kick the beast as she stepped back. He got up, put the tractor into gear and drove toward the field without so much as a cough.

He got down, she got up and the tractor promptly stalled.

Her gut twisted painfully like a rope tested by the wind. She curled her fingers into the rough fabric of her overalls. "It doesn't like me," she wailed.

"I'm sure it's nothing personal," he murmured, and again started the engine and showed her how to clutch. She followed his instructions perfectly but each time the beast stalled on her.

Her frustration gave way to burning humiliation. What kind of farmer could she hope to be if she couldn't run the stupid tractor? How could she prove she could manage on her own when her fields were destined to lie fallow and weed infested unless she could do this one simple little job. Hatcher made it look easy. She favored him with a glance carrying the full brunt of her resentment, which, thankfully, as she sorely needed his help, he didn't seem to notice.

"I'll see what I can do." Hatcher changed places with her. The tractor ran begrudgingly but it ran, as she knew it would. *He* didn't seem to have a problem with it.

He started down the side of the field, took it out of gear, jumped down and she got back up. She did everything he had. She was cautious, gentle, silently begging the beast to run.

It stalled.

Tears stung the corners of her eyes. She blinked them away. She would not cry. Somehow she'd conquer this beast. "I have to *make* it run or I'll never get my crop in, but this thing has become my thorn in the flesh."

"A gift then."

She snorted. "Not the sort of gift I'd ask for."

"Two Corinthians twelve verse nine, 'My grace is sufficient for thee: for my strength is made perfect in weakness. Most gladly therefore will I rather glory in my infirmities, that the power of Christ may rest upon me.' And verse ten, 'When I am weak, then I am strong.' Guess it's when you can't manage on your own and need God's help, you find it best."

She stared, her jaw slack, not knowing which surprised her more, the challenge of his words or the fact of such a long speech from the man who seemed to measure his words with a thimble.

He met her startled gaze, his eyes bottomless, his expression bland.

She pulled away, looking at nothing in particular as the words of the Bible sifted through her anger, her frustration and fear, and settled solidly in her heart. She needed God's help. And He had promised it. When she needed it most, she got it best. She liked that idea.

In the heavy silence, she heard the trill of a meadowlark. The sound always gave her hope, heralding the return of spring. She located the bird with its yellow breast on a nearby fence post and pointed it out to Hatcher. "Can you hear what the bird is saying? 'I left my pretty sister at home.'" She chuckled. "Jeremiah told me that." He'd also told her to keep the farm no matter what. That way she'd always have a home.

Hatcher nodded. "Never heard that before. Jeremiah your husband?"

She listened to the bird sing his song twice more before she answered. Jeremiah taught her everything she knew about farming. But somehow she hadn't learned the mysteries of mechanical monstrosities. "He's been dead three years."

"Sorry."

"Me, too." She turned back to the tractor. "Would you mind cranking it again? I have to get this field worked."

He did so. The engine started up easily but as soon as Kate tried to make the tractor move, it quit.

"Maybe it just needs babying along. I'll run it awhile."

Kate stubbornly clung to her seat behind the steering wheel. "You were in a hurry to leave until you heard my husband is dead."

"I'm still leaving."

She stared ahead. She wanted to refuse Hatcher's offer. She didn't need pity. She wouldn't accept a man's sudden interest in the fact she was alone. Widowed. An easy mark. Desperate.

"Crank it again. I have to do this myself."

But nothing changed. The minute she tried to ease the tractor forward, actually make it do the work it was created for, the engine stalled.

This was getting her nowhere. The wide field seemed to expand before her eyes, and blur as if viewed through isinglass. She brushed the back of her hand across her eyes to clear her vision and jumped down. "Fine. See if it will run for you."

He started the temperamental piece of metal, climbed behind the wheel, eased it into gear and moved away.

She wanted to run after him and demand to drive the tractor, demand the tractor cooperate with her. Instead she stared after him. One, two, three…only when she gasped ten, did she realize she'd been holding her breath waiting for the beast to respond to Hatcher as it did to her.

It didn't. It bumped along the field as defiant as a naughty child.

At least Hatcher had the courtesy not to look back and wave.

He made fifty yards before he stopped, climbed down and plodded back to her. "I've got some spare time. I'll work until noon. By then I'll have all the kinks worked out of the engine."

Kate wanted to protest even though she was relieved to have a few more hours unchallenged by her stubborn tractor. She swallowed her pride. "Thank you."

He turned back and she hurried across the field to the house. He deserved some kind of compensation for doing this. She'd make cookies and biscuits to give him for his journey.

When noon came, she carried sandwiches and hot tea to the field and handed him the bundle she'd made of cookies and biscuits.

"What's this?" he asked.

She explained.

At first she thought he'd refuse, then he took the bundle. "Thanks. Appreciate it."

She'd been dreading it all morning but it was time to take over the tractor. She had no choice if she were to get the field prepared for seeding. And then what? But all morning she'd thrown up a barrier at the question, refusing to deal with the obvious answer—as soon as the field was worked she'd have to seed it and then— no, she wouldn't think that far ahead.

She climbed behind the wheel. The machine had run all morning. She'd glanced that direction often enough to assure herself of the fact. Hatcher had jumped down a few times and made some sort of adjustment then continued on.

But again, it stalled as soon as she tried to drive it. "Why can't I make it work?" she yelled.

He shrugged. "I'll finish out the day."

"Great," she muttered. She should be grateful and she was. But she was also on the edge of desperation. If he worked all day he wouldn't finish even one field.

Then he'd be on his way. And she'd be stuck with the beast. And two more fields that needed working. Suddenly marrying Doyle seemed like the most sensible thing in the world.

All afternoon, she considered her options. Marry Doyle and sell the farm. An easy way out, yet not one she was willing to take. Rent out the farm. But renting it out would mean they'd have to move. No man would want the farm without the house. No. There had to be a way she could make this work. If only the tractor would run for her as readily as it did for Hatcher Jones.

She had one option left. Somehow, she had to convince the man to stay. At least until she got the crop in.

She had hot water ready for him to wash in when he came in from the field. "Supper is waiting." She used her purchased tin of meat—a spicy loaf—mixed it with rice and tomatoes and spices. She'd made bread pudding for dessert, adding a generous handful of raisins. Not the best of fare but she'd done what she could with her meager supplies.

She waited until the children ate then took tea out to Hatcher. It stuck in her throat to beg, but she'd made up her mind.

"Mr. Jones, is there any way I can persuade you to stay around to put the crop in for me? I wouldn't be able to pay you much. But I could let you live in the settler's shanty on the other quarter."

Chapter Four

At her request, profound shock reverberated down Hatcher's spine and out through his toes. He felt the texture of the wooden step through the thin soles of his boots. His insides had a strange quivering feeling. For a matter of several heartbeats he could not pull together a single coherent thought. Then he heard the persistent buzzing of an anxious fly, sucked in air laden with the scent of the freshly worked soil and willed the crash of emotions away.

She had no idea what she asked; the risks involved in her asking. If she did, her request would be that he move along immediately.

Words of remembrance flooded his mind, words branded into his brain within weeks of starting his journey, put there by reading and memorizing passages of scripture pointed directly at him. *And the Lord's anger was kindled against Israel and he made them wander in the wilderness forty years, until all the generation that had done evil in the sight of the Lord was consumed.* Numbers thirty-two, verse thirteen, and verse twenty-three, *Behold ye have sinned against the Lord: and you can be sure your sin will find you out.*

He had sinned. For that he'd repented, but the scars, the burden and guilt of what he'd done could not be erased.

He was a wanderer. There was no remedy for that. "Ma'am, I'm a hobo. I never stay in one place."

She made an impatient sound. "I thought most of the men were looking for work. I'm offering you that along with meals and a roof over your head."

Silently he admitted the majority of men he'd encountered were indeed searching for a job, a meal and hope. He was not. He wanted only his Bible, his knapsack and forgetfulness. "Sky's my roof."

"It's been known to leak."

How well he knew it. They both looked toward the west, where clouds had been banking up most of the afternoon.

"Rain's a good thing," he said. "It 'watereth the earth and maketh it bring forth and bud, that it might give seed to the sower, and bread to the eater.' Isaiah fifty-five, verse ten."

She snorted. "Rain is good but not if you don't have shelter."

He thought to remind her of Psalm ninety-four, verse twenty-two, *My God is the rock of my refuge,* and point out God was his shelter but decided to save himself any possibility of an argument and said, "Got me a tarpaulin."

"My father had itchy feet. I've spent more than my share of nights under a tarp telling myself it kept off the rain. Trying to convince myself I wasn't cold and miserable and would gladly trade my father for a warm place to spend the night."

Her answer tickled his fancy. "That how you got this farm? Traded your father for it."

She made a derisive sound. "Didn't have to. I married Jeremiah and got myself the first permanent home I ever had."

He closed his mind to remembrances of his first and only permanent home.

She continued, not noticing his slight distraction. "I fully intend to keep it. I will never again sleep out in the cold and open. My children will never know the uncertainty I grew up with." She sighed. "As you already said, 'the rain watereth the earth and maketh it bring forth and bud,' but first the seed has to be in the ground. I can't put the crop in when I can't make the tractor run. Something you seem to be able to do."

Somehow he'd had the feeling she'd see the verse differently than he. He'd meant it as a comfort, she took it as a warning. "Never say never. Tomorrow will be different."

"You think the beast will run for me tomorrow?"

"I tuned it up best I could."

"I hope you're right. Somehow I doubt it." She turned to face him fully. "Is there any way I can persuade you to stay just long enough to get the crop in?"

Her persistence scraped at the inside of his head, making him wish things could be different and he could stay, if only for the season. But like Cain, he was a vagabond and a wanderer. "I've already overstayed my limit. Besides, you don't need me. There are plenty of willing and able men out there."

The look she gave him informed him she was only too aware of how willing some of the men were.

"I'll pray for you to find the right man for the job." It was all he could do.

She nodded, and smiled. "Thank you. I realize the prayer of a righteous man availeth much."

He didn't know her well enough to know if she appreciated his offer to pray or considered it a handy brush-off. He pushed to his feet, preparing to depart.

"Anyway, thanks for your help today," she said.

"Thank you for another excellent meal. And the cookies and biscuits." He stuck his hat on his head. "Ma'am." He strode down the road toward the slough. He'd broken camp three times now, had been on his way this morning when he heard Mrs. Bradshaw talking to herself again. One thing the woman had to learn, you couldn't fix a machine by talking to it the way you could persuade a horse to cooperate. You had to think differently. Listen to the sounds the machine made and learn what they meant.

He tried not to think of the woman's repeated failure to operate the tractor. And as promised, he prayed for someone knowledgeable and trustworthy to come along and help her.

He could do no more. The tractor was old. But if she treated it kindly...

A cold wind tugged at his shirt as he made his way to his usual spot. He scurried around finding deadwood and leaves for a fire. The grass picked bare, he searched the trees for dry branches. By the time he got enough wood to warm him, the wind carried icy spears. He pulled on the worn, gray sweater he'd had for ten years and a black coat he'd bartered for. The elbows were shredded, the hem frayed, but it had a heavy wool lining and had kept him relatively warm through many winters.

He pulled the canvas tarp out of his pack, wrapped it around his shoulders, adjusted it so the rip was hidden and hunkered down over the fire.

He opened his Bible and read in the flickering fire-light. But his thoughts kept leaving the page.

Mrs. Bradshaw had a huge load to carry. The farm was too much for a woman to handle on her own. He wished he could stay and help but it wasn't possible. He had to keep moving. He couldn't stay in one place long enough…

He shuddered and pulled the tarp over his hat.

Best for everyone if he moved on.

Mrs. Bradshaw could find a hired man in town. Like she said, most men were looking for work. And the majority of them were decent men, down on their luck.

He tried not to remember the few he'd met who were scoundrels. He was good at not remembering. Had honed the skill over ten years. But he couldn't stop the memory of one man in particular from coming to mind.

Only name he knew him by was Mos. A man with an ageless face and a vacant soul who had, in the few days Hatcher reluctantly spent time in his association, robbed an old lady of her precious groceries, stole from a man who offered him a meal, and if Hatcher were to believe the whispers behind other men's hands, beat another man half to death when Mos was caught with the man's daughter under suspicious circumstances.

When Mos moved on, Hatcher headed the opposite direction. He needed no reminders of violence.

The cold deepened. Rain slashed across his face. He shifted his back into the wind.

Mrs. Hatcher was a strong, determined woman. She'd find a way of getting her crop in. He'd pray Mos wasn't in the area. Or men like him.

She was right about one thing, though. No matter how long he spent on the road, he never learned a way of ignoring a cold rain. Worse than snow because you couldn't shake it off. It seeped around your collar and cuffs, doused the fire, left you aching for the comforts of a home.

He thought of his home. Something he managed to avoid for the most part. He had Mrs. Bradshaw and her talk of protecting her place to thank for the fact such thoughts were more difficult to ignore tonight.

But he must. The place he'd once known as home was gone. Now his home was the world; his father, God above; his family, believers wherever he found them, although he never stayed long enough to be able to call them friends.

The wind caught at his huddled shelter and gave him a whiff of cows and hay. Before he could stop it, a memory raced in. He and Lowell had climbed to the hayloft to escape a rainstorm. Lowell, three years older, had been his best friend since Hatcher was old enough to recognize his brother's face. Lowell had one unchanging dream.

"Hatch, when you and I grow up we're going to turn this farm into something to be proud of."

They were on their stomachs gazing out the open loft doors. Rain slashed across the landscape, blotting out much of the familiar scene, but both he and Lowell knew every blade of grass, every cow, every bush by heart.

"How we gonna do that, Low?" he asked his big brother.

"We're going to work hard."

Hatcher recalled how he'd rolled over, hooting with laughter. "All we do is work now. From sunup to sundown. And lots of times Daddy pulls us from bed before the sun puts so much as one ray over the horizon."

Lowell turned and tickled Hatcher until they were

both dusty and exhausted from laughing. "Someday, though, our work will pay off. You and me will get the farm from Daddy and then we'll enjoy the benefit of our hard work."

Hatcher sat up to study his brother and suddenly understood why Lowell didn't complain or shirk the chores their father loaded on him. "That why you work so hard now?"

Lowell nodded. "If you and me keep it up we'll have a lot less work to do when it's ours." Lowell flipped back to his stomach and edged as close to the opening as he could. "See that pasture over there? It could carry twice as many cattle if we broke it and seeded it down to tame hay. And that field Daddy always puts wheat in has so many wild oats he never gets top price for his wheat. Now, the way I see it, if we planted oats for a few years, cut them for feed before the wild ones go to seed, I think we could clean up the field."

For hours they remained in the loft, planning how to improve the farm. Hatcher remembered that day so clearly, because it was the first time he and Lowell had officially decided they would own the farm some day. As months passed, and he began to observe and analyze, Hatcher, too, came up with dreams.

But it was not to be.

If he let himself think about it he'd gain nothing but anger and pain and probably a giant headache. He determinedly shoved aside the memory.

Too cold and damp to read his Bible, he began to recite verses. He began in Genesis. He got as far as the second chapter when the words in his mind stalled. *It is not good for the man to be alone.* He'd said the words hundreds of times but suddenly it hit him. He was alone. And God was right. It wasn't good. Like a flash of light-

ning illuminating his brain, he pictured Mrs. Bradshaw
stirring something on the stove, that persistent strand
of hair drifting across her cheek, her look alternating
between pensive and determined. He recalled the way
her hands reached for her children, encouraging shy
Mary, calming rambunctious Dougie. He'd also seen
flashes of impatience on her face, guessed she was often
torn between the children's needs and the weight of the
farm work. He could ease that burden if he could stay.

It wasn't possible.

He shifted, pulled the tarp tighter around his head
and started reciting from the Psalms.

"Mr. Jones?"

Hatcher jerked hard enough to shake open his protective covering. Icy water ran down his neck. The shock
of it jolted every sense into acute awareness.

The voice came again. "Mr. Jones?"

He adjusted the tarp, resigned to being cold and wet
until the rain let up and he found something dry to
light fire to.

"Mr. Jones?"

He didn't want to talk to her. Didn't want to have her
presence loosening any more memories so he didn't
move a muscle. Maybe she wouldn't see him and go
away.

"Mr. Jones?" She was closer. He heard her footsteps
padding in the wet grass. "There you are."

He lowered the tarp and stared at her, wrapped in a
too-large black slicker. She held a flickering lantern up
to him. The pale light touched the planes and angles of
her face, giving her features the look of granite.

"It's raining," he said, meaning, *What are you doing
out in the wet?*

"It's cold," she said. "Your fire's gone out."

He didn't need any reminding about how cold and wet he was. "Rain put it out."

"I remember how it is. You must be frozen."

"I don't think about it." Dwelling on it didn't make a man any warmer.

Water dripped off the edge of the tarp and slithered down his cheek. It wouldn't stop until it puddled under his collar. He let it go, knowing anything he did to stop its journey would only make him wetter.

She remained in front of him. "I can't rest knowing you're out here cold and wet."

He'd rest a lot better if she'd leave him alone, instead of stirring up best-forgotten and ignored memories. "Been cold and wet before and survived."

"You can stay in the shanty."

"I'm fine."

She grunted. "Well, I'm not. I'll never sleep knowing you're out here, remembering how miserable the rain is when you're in the open." She began her laugh with a snort. "Though, believe me, I'm ever so grateful for the rain. It's an answer to prayer. Now if you'd accept my offer and get in out of the cold, I could actually rejoice over the rain."

He'd guess persistence was her middle name. "Shame not to be grateful."

"Then you'll come?"

The thought of someplace warm and dry or even one of the two, had him thinking. Still he hesitated. "You don't know nothing about me."

"I know what it feels like to be cold and wet. That's enough."

Still he remained in a protective huddle. "I could be wicked."

"That's between you and God. But right now, I'm getting a little damp. Could we hurry this along?"

"You're not taking no for an answer?"

"No."

She left him little choice. They could both be cold and wet to the core or he could give in to her obstinacy. The latter seemed the better part of wisdom and he pushed to his feet, disturbing his wraps as little as possible as he followed her through the thin protection of the trees, across the road and up a grassy path angling away from her house.

"Just tell me where," he said when he realized she intended to lead him to the shanty.

"I'll show you."

She'd be soaked to the gills by the time she made her way back home but he already discerned she was a stubborn woman set on doing things her way.

She stopped, held the lantern high to reveal a tiny shack, then pushed open the door, found another lantern on a shelf and lit it.

From under her slicker, she pulled out a sack of coal. "This should keep you warm." She held up her lantern high and looked around. "This hasn't been used of late. You'll probably have mice for company but there's still a bed here. Not much else."

"It's fine." Surprisingly, no water leaked through the ceiling. "I'll be warm and dry."

"Come up for breakfast."

Before he could protest, she closed the door and was gone.

He stood dripping. How had he ended up in the same place for more days than he knew was wise? His limit was two nights and he'd exceeded that.

His mind must be sodden by the rain. How else did

he explain being here in this house? He held the lantern high and looked around. A small shack of bare wood weathered to dull gray with one tiny window over a narrow table. Two wooden chairs were pushed to the table. From the drunken angle of one he guessed it missed a leg. A rough-framed, narrow bed and tiny stove completed the furniture and crowded the space. He couldn't imagine a family living here though he knew many had lived in similar quarters as they proved up their homesteads. But it was solid enough. And fit him like a long-lost glove, feeding a craving he refused to admit. Snorting at his foolish thinking, blaming the stubborn woman who'd insisted he stay here for his temporary loss of reason, he reminded himself he couldn't stay.

One night. No more.

He shrugged the tarp off, draped it over a coat hook on the wall and built a fire. As warmth filled the room, he pulled off his wet clothes, hung them to dry and donned his spare shirt and pants.

He tested the mattress. It felt strange not to feel the uneven ground beneath him. For all the comforts of the place, sleep eluded him. He rose and sat at the rough wooden table, opened his Bible and began to read. At Psalms chapter sixty-eight verse six, he pulled up as if he'd come suddenly and unexpectedly to the end of a lead rope. He read the verse again, then again, aloud this time.

"God setteth the solitary in families: he bringeth out those which are bound with chains."

A great yearning sucked at his insides until he felt like his chest would collapse inward. He longed to put an end to his solitary state. He wanted nothing more than home and family.

But it could never be. He had his past to remember.

He clasped his hands together on the open Bible and bowed his head until his forehead rested on his thumbs. "Oh God, my strength and deliverer. I have trusted You all these long years. You have indeed been my shelter and my rock. Without You I would have perished. You are all I need. You are my heart's desire." He paused. In all honesty, he could not say that. Despite God's faithfulness he ached with an endless emptiness for things he didn't have, things he knew he could never have. "God, take away these useless, dangerous desires. Help me find my rest, my peace, my satisfaction in You alone."

From the recesses of his mind came words committed to memory. *Delight thyself also in the Lord; and he shall give thee the desires of thine heart. Commit thy way unto the Lord; trust also in him; and he shall bring it to pass.*

"Psalm thirty-seven, verses four and five," he murmured out of habit. "But what does that mean for me?"

Long into the night he prayed and thought and planned then finally fell asleep on the soft mattress.

He'd considered ignoring her invitation to breakfast and eating a handful of the biscuits she'd provided but he didn't even want to guess what she might do. Likely tramp over and confront him. He smiled at the way he knew she'd look—eyes steady and determined, hands on hips—pretty as a newly blossomed flower. For the sake of his peace of mind it was prudent to simply accept her "offer."

He made his way across the still-damp fields to the Bradshaw house. The rain had been short-lived. Enough to give the grass a drink. Not enough to provide moisture for the soon-to-be-planted crops.

During the night, he'd come to a decision. One he

felt God directed him to and as such, not something he intended to resist.

He kicked the dampness off his boots and knocked at the door then stepped back to wait for Mrs. Bradshaw. She opened the door almost immediately and handed him a plate piled high with bright yellow eggs, fried potatoes and thick slices of homemade bread slathered with butter and rhubarb jam.

A man could get used to regular meals. "I'll stay long enough to put in the crop." He could do the spring farmwork and obey the verse filling his thoughts last night—*Pure religion and undefiled before God and the Father is this, To visit the fatherless and widows in their affliction.* James chapter one, verse twenty-seven.

So long as he stayed away from town and her neighbors, he'd be fine. And then he'd move on before anyone figured out who he was.

The woman grabbed his free hand, pressing it between hers, squeezing like a woman hanging on to her last dime. She swallowed loudly. "Thank you, Mr. Jones. Thank you so much."

He pretended the husky note in her voice meant her throat was dry and squirmed his hand free to clutch his plate firmly in front of him. "Don't thank me. Thank God."

Her smile filled both her face and his heart with wondrous amazement. "I most certainly do." She glanced toward the kitchen, hesitated as if afraid to let him out of her sight, fearing likely, and realistically, he might vanish down the road.

He tipped his chin toward the plate. "Food's cooling."

"I'll leave you to enjoy your breakfast." She patted his arm and backed away. At the door, she whispered, "Thank you. Thank God."

* * *

The ground would quickly dry under the hot prairie sun but until it did Hatcher tackled fence repairs. The woman insisted on helping.

"I can't tell you how much I appreciate this," Mrs. Bradshaw said.

Her continual gratitude weighed in the bottom of his stomach like a loaf of raw dough. He didn't want thanks for doing something he'd done because he felt he had no choice. "Then stop trying."

He grabbed a length of barbwire, twisted it together with the dangling end of the broken section and pulled it tight. He hammered in a staple to hold it on the post.

She let the hammer she held dangle at her side. "I can't help wondering what is it that makes men want to wander. I know many are hoping to find a job, maybe a better place to live but…"

The woman seemed to have the need to talk, perhaps wanting someone to hear the sound of her thoughts.

He himself didn't have such a need, no longer knew how to talk about things that didn't matter. And things that mattered to him would never be items of discussion. If they were he'd be on the move again.

She watched him work. "What is it that makes a man leave his home?"

Seems she wanted more than an audience—she wanted conversation. He wasn't used to listening to his thoughts on such matters but managed to find an answer to her question. "Every man has his own reasons."

"Like what? My mother said my father had itchy feet." She tapped at a staple, slowly driving it into place.

He could have done it in three blows. "Some have no place to go. No place to stay."

She stopped torturing the staple and carefully considered him. "Which are you?"

He shrugged, moved along the fence and pounded in three staples.

She followed after him carrying the bucket containing the fencing supplies. "Where did you start from?"

"No place."

"Are you expecting me to believe you were found under a pine bough? Or raised by wolves?"

The heaviness in his stomach eased at her comment and he smiled. "Why does it matter?"

"I'm just making polite conversation." Her voice carried a hint of annoyance then she grinned. "And maybe I'm a bit curious."

He grabbed the shovel and dug away the dirt burying the fence. "You have to keep the Russian thistle away from the fence line or you'll have the whole length buried." The thistles blew across the endless prairie until they reached an obstacle. In this case, a wire fence. They formed a tangled wall that stopped the drifting soil and buried the thistle and fence. He'd seen the whole shape of the landscape changed after a three-day dust storm.

"Are you from back East?"

Stubborn woman wasn't going to let it go. "Can't remember."

"Can't or don't want to?"

"Yup."

She planted her hands on her hips. "What kind of answer is that?"

The only kind he was prepared to give. He put his back into digging the fence out of the bank of dirt. "I'll finish this section then go back to working the field."

"Fine. Don't tell me." She dropped the hammer and

huffed away, got two yards before she stopped and laughed. "I admit it's none of my business." She returned, picked up the hammer and attacked another staple. "It's just that I'm so very grateful for my home and security and feel sorry for anyone who doesn't enjoy the same."

She was indeed blessed but he kept his thoughts to himself.

The next day, Saturday, Mrs. Bradshaw had the children to care for and Hatcher returned to riding round and round the field. At least she wouldn't bother him today with her need to talk and endless questions, which he'd refused to answer when they got personal. What she didn't know wouldn't hurt her.

The sun was unmerciful. Far too hot for this early in the season, sucking every bit of moisture from the ground before the seed was even planted. He studied the western horizon hoping to see clouds build up. Not a one. Not even as small as a man's hand. Didn't look like the drought was going to end this year.

He turned the corner of the field, squinted against the cloud of dust circling with him. Down the side of the ploughed ground, Dougie waited, a jar of water in one hand.

And another small boy at his side.

Hatcher's chest muscles tightened and his hands clenched the steering wheel. No one could know he was here. He didn't want to be forced to leave until he'd done as he promised.

He cranked his head around to look at the house. A second automobile sat beside the Bradshaw's truck. Another beat-up truck of uncertain color and lineage.

Hatcher pulled his hat lower over his face. He was far

enough from the house, hidden in dust. Even if someone looked at him with suspicious curiosity, they'd see
only a hobo doing a job. His thoughts hurried up, racing ahead of the slow-moving tractor. If he worked hard
and the tractor favored him he'd be gone in two weeks.
Two weeks was long enough for neighbors to be curious. But the work could not be made to go faster.

Dougie held out a jar of water, inviting him to stop
for a drink.

Hatcher thought to ignore the boy, keep his face hidden in dust but he couldn't bring himself to disappoint
Dougie. He pulled the tractor out of gear and jumped
down to wait for the boy and his friend to race across
the freshly turned soil and hand him the jar.

"Momma said you'd be parched by now," the boy
said.

"I am at that." He kept his face turned away. "Whose
your friend?" Better an enemy you knew than one you
didn't. Not that he thought the boy posed any real danger. But the boy had parents, protective, no doubt of
their son, and likely to ask questions even as Kate had.
Less likely to allow him to ignore them.

"This is Tommy."

"Where are you from, Tommy?" How close by did
the curious adults live?

"T'other side of town."

Not close enough to run back and forth daily. He
tipped the jar up and drained the contents down his
parched throat.

"My momma and Dougie's momma are real good
friends," Tommy said.

"Huh. I guess they see each other in town or at
church."

"Yup. We always sit together. And do other things

together. Me and Dougie like picnics the best. Or the ball games and—"

"Uh-uh." Dougie shoved his face into Tommy's line of vision. "I like it best when you come here and we play in the barn."

"Me, too. Race ya there."

The two scampered off, leaving Hatcher holding the empty jar and the knowledge it might prove harder to avoid the neighbors than he anticipated.

Chapter Five

"Who's driving your tractor?" Sally asked, her nose practically pressed to the window as she watched the boys hand Hatcher the container of water.

Kate stood at her friend's side. Her worry about the crop had been like a heavy necklace—a thing supposedly of adornment and pleasure, grown to be, if not resented then something first cousin to it, and now it'd been removed. She felt airy; her feet could barely stay still. "A hobo I hired to put in the crop."

Sally spun around. "He's one of those filthy, shiftless men?" She turned back to the window, straining for a better look. "Look how dirty he is. His hair sticks out around his hat. He needs a haircut. I don't know how you can stand there so calm about having a man like him just a few feet away. And to think you invited him to stay here? You might as well invite a rabid dog into your home. Kate, have you taken leave of your senses?"

Sally's reaction stole Kate's smile, killed thoughts of a happy dance. "Of course he's dirty. He's working in the field and I haven't invited him into my house. He's staying in the shanty. Besides, don't you think you're being a little dramatic?"

Sally shook her head. "I think you're being stubborn. Acting unwisely just to prove a point."

Kate spared her a warning glance that Sally missed as she concentrated on the activity in the field. There was nothing to see except the cloud of dust. "And what would that point be?"

"That you can manage on your own. I don't understand why you want to keep this farm. It's way too much work for you. You could live in the best house in town and have a maid to help with the housework yet you stubbornly hang on to this dried-out piece of land. Kate, give it up. Let it go."

Kate turned from the window, all pleasure in seeing her land being tilled lost by her friend's comments. Sally could not now or ever understand Kate's need for permanency and security. She'd always had a solid home, first with her parents and now with Frank. "You don't know what it's like. You've never been without a home."

Sally rolled her eyes. "Kate, what are you thinking? Doyle will give you a house."

The same question twisted through Kate's thoughts often. Why didn't she accept Doyle's offer of marriage? Why did it scare her to think of letting the farm go? "This is mine. I own it. No one can take it from me."

"What? You think Doyle wouldn't give you whatever you want. If his house isn't good enough, he'll buy another. What's the point in hanging on to the farm especially when you have to resort to hiring men like that?" She nodded toward the window where Hatcher worked.

Dougie and Tommy disappeared into the barn where they could play for hours. Mary sat under the spreading cottonwood tree Jeremiah had planted years ago, probably before Kate was born. It was one of Mary's favorite spots. She liked to read there or play with her dolls. Right now her two dolls sat on the ground facing her and Mary leaned forward, talking seriously to them. Such an intent child.

"Sally, let's have tea." She poured boiling water over the tea leaves and as it steeped set out a plate of cookies. She longed for her friend to understand her need for a home she actually owned, or if unable to understand, at least to support her. She waited until they both had full cups and each held a cookie before she broached the subject again. "You've been my best friend since my family showed up in town, probably as dirty and suspicious looking as you think Hatcher is but…"

"Hatcher? That his first or last name?"

"Hatcher Jones."

"What else do you know about him?"

"He knows how to keep the tractor running and how to milk a cow so she won't go dry."

Sally shook her head. "Who cares about that?"

Kate refrained from saying she did.

Sally continued. "Where's he from? Why is he on the road? Does he have family? What sort of man is he? How can you be sure he can be trusted? What about the children? Are they safe with him?"

Kate had asked many of the same questions but only because she was curious about the man, not because she felt he needed references. He hadn't answered her, yet she wasn't afraid of him. She'd seen something in the man's eyes when they laughed together, felt something solid when they'd worked side by side. But Sally's suspicions scratched the surface of Kate's confidence making her wonder if she'd been too eager to have him stay. She didn't thank Sally for filling her with doubts about the safety of herself and the children. "Would you feel better if I asked him? Or perhaps you'd like to."

"One of us should do it."

Suddenly exasperated by Sally's interference, Kate put down her half-eaten cookie and looked hard at her friend. Her pretty blond hair hung loose around her face, her hazel eyes had a hard glint to them. "Sally, I prayed long and hard for someone to help me. Hatcher is an answer to my prayer. He's only staying long enough to put in the crop. That's all I need to know."

Sally's look probed. "You're willing to do anything to keep this place, aren't you?"

Kate nodded. "So long as it isn't foolish, yes."

Sally grunted and shifted so she could look out the window watching Hatcher.

Kate thought of introducing her friend to the man. But if she did, he'd have to stop the tractor. The sooner he finished, the sooner he'd be on his way and the better Sally would like it. It was her sole reason for not introducing them. Not her petty anger at Sally's refusal to rejoice over Kate's blessing.

"I've potatoes to peel." Kate pushed away from the table and went to the basin Dougie had filled for her. She gripped the paring knife in her tight fist, ignoring the pain in her jaw she knew wouldn't go away until she relaxed. And she couldn't relax with resentment simmering inside her. Why couldn't Sally understand? "I remember when we came into town that night a dozen years ago. We'd been on the train three days and three nights. We hadn't been able to do more than wash our hands and face. The little boys had been sick all over Mother's dress. We were dirty, bedraggled and I'm sure most people looked at us with disgust and suspicion even though we were just good people looking for a kind word. Your mother took us in and cared for us.

Have you forgotten? Did you feel the same about us as you do about that man out there?"

Sally jerked away from the window. "Of course not. But that was different."

Kate refused to look at her, anger making every muscle in her body tighten. Her hand slipped. She barely managed to stop the knife before she sliced her finger. She stared at the blade. "How was it different?" She glared at Sally. They'd been friends since Sally's mother had taken care of them. They'd all been sick, one after another but the woman had never flinched at cleaning up after them, washing the bedding, making nourishing broth. She'd nursed them ten days before Father found a job and a little house for them all. During that time, she and Sally had become best friends.

She ploughed on with a whole lot more energy than she got from the old tractor. "Did we become friends just because your mother thrust us into your life? If she hadn't, would you have seen us a dirty, no-goods to shun?"

Sally gasped. "Katie, how can you even ask? You've been my dearest friend all these years." Her voice broke. "I could never have survived losing my baby without your help. Just think, I might have had a child the same age as Mary." She rushed to Kate's side and hugged her. "It's only because I care about you that I wonder about the man out there."

Kate received her hug reluctantly, her anger still not spent. "If you care then you know I have to do what I have to do."

Sally stepped back six inches and studied Kate. "Doyle has been more than patient with your putting him off. One of these days he's going to stop courting you. Then where would you be?"

"If Doyle isn't prepared to wait then he doesn't love me enough. And if he stops asking, I'll still have my farm. I'll still have my home."

Sally shook her head. "There is absolutely no point in arguing with you, is there?"

Kate smiled past the pain in her jaw. "So why do you try?" She squeezed Sally's hand. "I don't expect you to understand what it's like not to have a place you can call home. But it's a feeling I will never again have as long as I have my farm." Her resolve deepened. "My children will never know what it's like to be cold and dirty with no place to spend the night."

Sally didn't respond for a moment. "Does Doyle know he's here?"

Kate knew she meant Hatcher. "Not yet." Kate returned to the window to watch her land being prepared for planting.

"What will he say?"

For a moment she didn't answer then she smiled sheepishly at Sally. "Strange as it might seem, I never gave it a thought. But I suppose he'll be glad I have help."

Sally sighed. "I hope so."

Suddenly Kate had to get outside, touch the land that meant so much to her. "Come on." She grabbed Sally's hand and dragged her outside. She didn't stop until she got to the edge of the field. "Take a deep breath."

Sally did. "Now what?"

"Don't you smell it? The rich aroma of freshly worked soil? The heat rising from the ground, carrying with it all sorts of delicious scents—new grass, tiny flowers."

"You sound like Frank. He can't stop telling me how

good things will be once the drought ends. If it ever does."

Kate laughed. "It will and the land will always be here no matter what." She tipped her nose toward the trees. "Smell the leaves as they burst forth. All the signs and scents of spring. I love it." She swung her arms wide. "I love my farm. It's mine, mine, mine."

Sally laughed. "The smell of an overheated brain. The signs of rampant overimagination."

Kate laughed, too. "At least you didn't say rampant insanity."

"Doesn't mean I didn't think it."

"You didn't."

Sally looked away as if hiding her thoughts. "I'm not saying."

Kate chuckled, unable to stay upset with this dear friend for more than two minutes at a time. "I'll show you my garden."

"You've already got it planted?"

"No, but it's ready. I'll do it next week." When Hatcher had seen her turning the soil last night, he'd reached for the shovel.

"I'll do that."

She'd resisted. "I don't expect you to do everything around here."

He kept his hand on the handle waiting for her to release it. "I'm sure you have other things to do." His glance slid past her to the house.

Kate followed his gaze. Mary sat forlornly on the step. She'd asked Kate to help her with learning the names of the presidents. Kate explained she didn't have time but if she let Hatcher dig the garden she could help Mary. Yet she hesitated, found it hard to let go.

"I think someone needs her mother," Hatcher said softly.

If he'd sounded critical or condemning, Kate would have refused his help. But he sounded sad and Kate suddenly ached for Mary's loneliness. She'd neglected the child so often since Jeremiah's death. At first, Kate couldn't cope with anything but survival, then Dougie had been sick all one winter, and always, forever the demands of the farm.

"Thank you." She dropped her hands from the shovel and gave him a smile that quavered at the corners.

"My pleasure." The late-afternoon sun slanted across his face, making her notice for the first time the solidness of his jaw. He smiled and something soft and gentle filled his eyes.

She hurried back to the house, feeling slightly off balance from his look. It was only her imagination but somehow she felt he'd seen and acknowledged the loneliness she never allowed herself to admit.

As she helped Mary recite names she watched Hatcher make quick work of digging the garden. Finished, he put the shovel away and without lifting his arm, raised his fingers in a quick goodbye. She waved once, feeling suddenly very alone.

She wouldn't tell Sally about that. No need to start up her worries again.

Sally left two hours later. Caught up visiting with her friend, Kate had neglected meal preparations and hurried to complete them. Sally's husband, Frank, sent over some fresh pork so they would have meat for supper.

The potatoes had just come to a boil when she heard Mary's thin screech. Now what? A grasshopper? The wind? The child overreacted to everything. When was she going to learn to ignore the little discomforts of farm life? At least Sally hadn't pointed out the benefits of town life for Mary. It was the one thing capable of making Kate feel guilty. Her daughter would be much happier in Doyle's big house.

When Mary let out another yell, Kate hurried to the window to check on her and sighed. Chickens pecked around the child. Dougie and Tommy must have carelessly left the gate open when she'd sent them to get the eggs.

"Dougie," Kate called out the open window. No answer. And now he'd done a disappearing act, probably hoping to avoid a scolding. They had to get the chickens back in the pen before they wandered too far or laid their eggs in hiding spots. Kate needed every egg she could get.

She hurried to the stove, pushed the pots to the back, and grabbed the bucket of peelings.

Mary, wailing like the killing winds of summer, stood in the doorway.

"Help me get the chickens in," Kate said, heading outside.

Mary shrank against the wall, her eyes consuming her face.

Kate captured her hand and dragged her after her, ignoring the gulping sobs. "Mary, stop crying. I need your help." She struggled against Mary's resistance all the way to the pen before she released the child. "I'll go inside and toss out the peelings. Maybe they'll come on their own. If they don't you'll have to chase them this direction." She tossed out a few scraps as she called, "Here chick, chick, chick."

Mary hadn't moved. "Mary, do as I ask."

"Momma," Mary wailed. "What if they chase me?"

Kate sighed. "Chickens don't chase you. They run from you. You know that. Now go."

Mary stared at her, her mouth tight, her eyes so wide Kate feared they might explode from their sockets. She snorted. Now she was getting as fanciful as her daughter. "Mary, go."

Sobbing so hard her whole body quacked, Mary ran toward the cottonwood where most of the chickens clustered.

"And stop crying," Kate called after her. She had no time and little sympathy to spare over such silliness.

In the end, all Mary had to do was walk around the birds while Kate tossed out scraps. The chickens dashed for the food. Some, intelligent creatures that they were, ran full bore into the fence, squawking and shedding a flurry of feathers. "Mary, chase them around to the gate."

The child hesitated, gave Kate a look fit to boil turpentine then obeyed.

A few minutes later, the chickens all safely inside, Kate latched the gate securely. "That wasn't so bad, was it?"

"I hate chickens," Mary muttered, and stomped off.

Dougie sauntered out of the barn. He would have enjoyed chasing the chickens in, although he tended to overdo it and have them running in frantic circles. "Where have you been, young man?" For some reason she couldn't keep the sharpness from her voice. It seemed she always had too many things to do, too little time for it, and a mountain of needs. And now she had a man to feed. She took a deep breath. Now she didn't have to try and do it all, at least for a few days. Hatcher would put the seed in. She could relax and think about other things. Like supper, which was probably burning.

Half listening to Dougie describe the little farm he and Tommy had constructed in the back of the barn, she dashed for the house to rescue the meal.

As she and Dougie hurried into the house together, she saw the huge tear in his overalls and skidded to a stop. "Douglas Bradshaw, what have you done to your overalls?"

He sidled away, trying to cover the hole with his hand.

"Now I have to mend them. I repeat, what were you doing?"

"Nothin', Momma."

"Nothin' doesn't tear your clothes."

"Me and Tommy were playing. That's all." He continued to back away.

Kate felt anger boiling inside her, felt it flush her cheeks, saw wariness in Dougie's face, knew he heard it, sensed it and feared it. She took a deep breath. She would not explode. She fled to the kitchen. Her hand shaking, she grabbed a pot holder and lifted the pot lids without noting if the contents boiled or not. She turned away from the stove. Shaken, she leaned on the table. For weeks she'd felt ready to explode. Too much to do. A sense of the world caving in on her. But not until now had she lost control. She hated that her child had been on the receiving end. *Oh God*, she cried silently. *Help me. I do not want to feel this burning frustration. I do not want to punish my children for it. They don't deserve it.*

A verse came to mind. *Thou wilt keep him in perfect peace, whose mind is stayed on thee: because he trusteth in thee.*

She sucked in air and the power of God's promise. *I trust You, God. You sent me a man to put in the crop. I know You will meet my other needs, too.*

The panic subsided. She would manage with God's help and Hatcher to put in the crop. She would hold on to her farm and home.

She returned to the stove. A few minutes later she called the children and waved at Hatcher to come in for supper. Thanks to Sally, she wondered about him. She'd already asked questions he'd left unanswered, but whoever he was, wherever he was from, he'd promised to put the crop in. What did anything else matter?

She put out hot water for him to wash in and handed him a plate of food. She ate with the children then carried a cup of tea and a handful of cookies out to him.

He drained his tea and set the cup on the step beside him. "A couple hours yet until dark. I'll get back to work." He got to his feet and plunked his dirty hat on his head. He touched the brim and nodded. "Ma'am."

While she did the chores she listened to the rumble of the tractor and counted her blessings.

He worked until the light was gone then filled a pail from the well and strode off into the dark toward the shanty.

Kate relaxed when she could no longer hear his footsteps. The children were already asleep, bathed and ready for church the next day. She bowed her head to pray for safety for them all. *Thou wilt keep him in perfect peace, whose mind is stayed on thee; because he trusteth in thee.*

She trusted God. She had nothing to fear. Besides, Sally promised to pray for their safety. Kate would turn her energy to a different matter. *Lord, God, You have promised to meet all my needs. I needed someone to help with the farmwork. Thank You for sending someone to put in the crop. Please bless the land with rain this year.*

* * *

Preparing to head for the barn, Kate glanced up at the sound of boots on the step and saw Hatcher. She'd invited him to join them for breakfast but he'd refused, saying he had biscuits. Yet there he stood waiting.

Supposing he must have changed his mind, she opened the door. "Breakfast will be ready shortly."

"Didn't come for breakfast, ma'am. Came to milk the cows."

"I'm just on my way."

He reached for the buckets. "You have the children to care for. And you need extra time to prepare for church."

She chuckled. "Time is not something I'm used to having much of." Usually she rushed to pull off her cotton housedress or the old coveralls she often wore and hurried into her Sunday dress with minutes to spare. Not enough time to do anything more with her hair than slip in a couple of nice combs.

"Than maybe you'll let yourself enjoy it."

His choice of words startled her and he took the buckets from her as she stared after him. Let yourself enjoy it. Did she even know how anymore? Work seemed to be the shape of her life. What would she do with spare time? She thought of the neglected mending, the unwritten letters, the unpolished stove and laughed.

"Will you come to church with us?" she asked when he returned with the buckets full of milk and a pocket full of eggs.

He shook his head.

Disappointment like a sharp pin pricked her thoughts. For some reason she'd imagined him accompanying them, proving to Sally she could trust Kate's judgment. "But surely you want to worship with God's people."

"It's not a place for hobos."

She wanted to argue but after Sally's comments... "I could let you have some of Jeremiah's clothes."

"It's not just the clothes."

"I'm sure you'd be welcome."

"It's not the place for me. I'll worship God in His outdoor cathedral." He nodded and strode away.

Kate stared after him. Poor man, used to being an outsider. Perhaps she could help him realize he fit in so next Sunday he'd feel he could show his face inside a church building.

She had extra time to prepare for church and took pains with her hair, pinning it into a soft roll around her face. She wished, momentarily, her hair could be a rich brown instead of being streaked with a rust color. She dismissed the useless thought and pulled on white gloves.

She put Mary's blond curls into dangling ringlets and smoothed Dougie's brown thatch. She'd have to cut it soon.

The three of them climbed into the truck and headed for town and church. Doyle met them at the church steps.

"You look very nice this morning." He smiled his approval and Kate was glad she'd been able to spruce up more than usual.

Doyle pulled her hand through his arm and led her inside, the children following them.

She sighed. The familiar routine filled her with contentment.

He led her to the front pew, his customary place, and waited for the children to go in first so he could sit beside her. As always, attentive but circumspect, he limited his touches to a brushing of their fingers under the hymnal and a quick squeeze of her hand when the preacher announced Doyle had donated money for a bell in the belfry.

After the service, grateful parishioners surrounded Doyle thanking him for his generosity.

Kate stood proudly at his side, watching the way he accepted their praise—a kind man and handsome with his neatly groomed blond hair, his blue eyes and decked out in his dark, spotless suit. He noticed her studying him and reached out to pull her to his side. "Are you ready to go?" he asked.

She nodded. Dougie had raced away to play with Tommy and a couple other boys. Mary waited in one of the pews humming and swinging her feet. They collected the children and headed for the restaurant where they were given the best table, next to the wide windows looking out on Main Street. Mary sat beside Kate, as quiet as a mouse. Dougie fidgeted beside Doyle.

"Sit still, child," Doyle said and Dougie did his best to settle down.

Doyle ordered for them all—roast beef, Yorkshire pudding, mashed potatoes and gravy, carrots and turnips. It always seemed a bit extravagant to Kate to spend as much money on one meal as she spent on groceries in several weeks but she knew if she mentioned it, Doyle would say the same thing he said every time they were together—he could afford it and she deserved it. Besides the beef was excellent.

After ice cream they headed outside. Dougie raced ahead, loving the thunder of his boots on the wooden sidewalks, Mary skipped along in his wake. Doyle waited until they were out of earshot before he asked the inevitable question.

"When are you going to sell the farm and marry me?"

She laughed. "You know the answer."

"Be practical, Kate. You can't stay out there by your-self."

"I'm not by myself. I have the children."

"And too much work. Jeremiah had help when he was alive and here you are trying to do it all yourself. You deserve better. Let me give it to you."

"Doyle, you're sweet. And I appreciate it. I do." His attention made her feel like a woman. Made her feel cherished. "But I have help."

He slowed his pace and looked down at her. "Help? What do you mean?"

"I have someone to put in the crop for me." She hoped he wouldn't ask about the rest of the work and how she planned to get the crop off in the fall. One day at a time. That's all she needed.

"You hired someone?"

"Doyle, don't sound so surprised. It's what I've done the last three years."

"You hired the Oliver lad, but he's gone."

She smiled up at him. "He's not the only man in the country."

He didn't return her smile. "So who did you hire?"

She hesitated, sensing his disapproval. If she said a hobo, she knew he'd react even more strong than Sally. "What's the matter? You should be glad I have help. You just finished saying it was too much for me."

"When are you going to give up and marry me?"

He annoyed her, insinuating she would eagerly ac-cept his will for her. "I've never said I was."

"You're just being stubborn. You're a fine woman except for that."

She jerked her hand away from where it rested in his arm. "I am not stubborn. I am determined. And marrying you will not change that." She took two steps away. "Children, it's time to go home."

Doyle reached for her but she moved farther away. "Kate, be reasonable."

"How can I be? I'm stubborn, remember?"

"I'm sorry. I shouldn't have said that. Forgive me."

He had the sweetest smile but this time she wouldn't be affected by it. However, she couldn't refuse to grant him forgiveness. "Very well."

"Someday," he murmured. "You'll admit I'm right. You don't belong on the farm, struggling to survive. You and the children deserve better."

Consideration for the children always caused her hesitation. Maybe they would be better in town where they didn't have so much work helping her keep the farm going, where they'd surely get more of her time and attention. It bothered her how often they had to manage on their own while she did chores, or chased cows or tried to get the tractor to run, though with Hatcher's help the past few days, she'd been less rushed, less demanding of the children.

"Tell Mr. Grey thank you," she told her children. She added her thanks to theirs and climbed into her truck.

Doyle leaned toward the window. "When are you coming to town again?"

"I'm awfully busy right now."

He gave her a knowing look, which she ignored.

"Be sure and drop in at the office."

"Of course." She always did unless she had too many things to take care of. Which was often.

"Maybe I'll visit you. Make sure everything is what it should be."

"You're welcome anytime, of course. You know

that." Though he had no right to judge how things were. Not that he could. He didn't know oats from wheat from pigweed. And a cow was a smelly bulk of animal flesh, not the source of milk, cream, butter and meat.

She fumed as far as the end of the street then her attention turned to the fields along the road, several already planted. Soon hers would be, as well. And she again prayed for rain.

Monday, Hatcher ate a hurried breakfast at the house then headed out to start the next field. After the children left for school, Kate gathered up seeds and went to the garden. With little cash to purchase groceries, they depended on what they could raise.

She seeded the peas and turnips and carrots, paused to wonder if there would be another frost then decided to put in the beans. It was time-consuming, tiring work moving the string to mark each row, digging a trench for the seed with the hoe, measuring it out judicially then carefully covering it with soil, praying all the while for rain at the right time.

She had started tomatoes in early March but she wouldn't put them out for a week or two yet.

She paused long enough to make sandwiches to take out to Hatcher.

For weeks, she'd saved the eyes from peeling the potatoes. As soon as the children were home to help, she'd plant them. Then carry water to the many rows that would soon be green potato plants.

She didn't finish until suppertime. For once she didn't argue when Hatcher offered to milk the cows. As soon as the dishes were done she asked the children to help her carry water to the garden.

The three of them carried pail after pail, soon soaked to their knees despite efforts to be careful.

When Hatcher grabbed two pails and started to help, she didn't complain. She could see the children were worn-out. "You two go get ready for bed. I'll be in as soon as we finish this."

At first she kept up with Hatcher, but soon he hauled four pails to her two and then six.

"I'll finish," he said. "The kids are waiting for you to tuck them in."

She protested weakly. "This is my job."

"Nothing wrong with needing help."

"I have to learn to manage on my own."

"Yes, ma'am."

"Kate," she said. "My name is Kate."

"Yes, ma'am. Mine's Hatcher. Hatcher Jones."

"I know." About to say something more, the thought fled her brain as a slick gray automobile purred up the driveway. Doyle. What was he doing here? He never visited during the week. He was always too busy. But then, so was she.

She waved as he climbed from his car, half expected him to head to the garden but he waited for her in front of the house.

Wearily she headed his direction, acutely aware of her muddy state. Why did he pick a day to visit when she looked her worst? "What brings you out here?" she asked, as she drew near.

He let his gaze take in every detail of her state, managed to look pained, then smiled. "Maybe I miss you."

"I've been here for a long time and you've never before missed me enough to drive out during the week."

He didn't answer. His gaze went to Hatcher and stayed there. "That the hobo?"

"That's my hired man."

"Maybe I should introduce myself."

Before she could ask why, he headed toward the garden.

Chapter Six

Hatcher watched the man step from his fine car and adjust his charcoal-colored suit. He immediately recognized the type. Even dust from a stiff west wind wouldn't dare stick to him. The man looked his way. Even across the distance, Hatcher could read the censure in the man's gaze. The prissy man headed toward Hatcher with his nose so high he pranced. Ignoring his approach, Hatcher strolled back to the trough, hung the pails on a hook and headed toward his shanty.

"Wait up," the suited man called.

Hatcher pretended he didn't hear. He had nothing he wanted to say to or hear from any man. That man in particular. Fifty feet away he could smell the arrogance of him. Just the sort who would demand to know all about you as if it was his business.

"I say. Stop so I can talk to you."

His gut said hurry on. His breeding demanded politeness. He hesitated, slowed.

"Please wait," Kate begged.

The sound of her voice compelled him to stop. He had no desire to put her in the middle of a power struggle.

The suit fella breathed hard by the time he reached

Hatcher's side even though he'd only hurried the width of the farmyard. Hatcher had seen Kate chase across it many times and never show a puff. Then he grimaced at the dust on his shoes and shook each foot.

"So you're the ho…"

Kate shot the man a look that caused him to pause.

"You're the man Kate's hired for the season." He waited as if he expected Hatcher to suddenly sweep his hat off and pull his forelock.

Hatcher did no such thing.

The man harrumphed importantly. "My name is Doyle Grey. I'm the lawyer in town." He said it like Hatcher should be impressed.

He wasn't.

The man leaned back, full of his own importance. "As Kate and I are going to marry, I thought it prudent I check things out for her."

Kate pulled herself tall. "I've never said I'd marry you, Doyle."

He shrugged, gave her a look that said he knew he'd get what he wanted. He always did. "It's only a matter of time, as we all know." He turned away too quickly to see the woman he planned to marry tighten her jaw and glower.

Hatcher ducked his head to hide a smile. A man should know better than to try and force a woman like her to do his bidding. Her strong opinions needed consideration.

Aware of Doyle Grey's attentive study, Hatcher concentrated on wiping mud from the back of his hand. "Glad for both of you." He resumed his homeward journey.

"Didn't get your name," the lawyer said.

"Didn't give it." He lengthened his stride, determined to leave the man fussing without his participation.

"Why not? Is there something you're hiding?"

Hatcher ignored the man's challenging tone. A lawyer. Just the sort he did not want to talk to. For sure, he didn't intend to linger in his royal highness's presence.

"Come on, Doyle," Kate said. "I'll show you the garden. We were watering the potatoes."

"Why are you bothering with all this work? Why doesn't he tell me his name?" Mr. Lawyer couldn't seem to make up his mind which way to go. "Marry me and I'll take you away from this."

Hatcher eased out his breath when the man decided to follow Kate to the garden. He slowed his retreat so he could listen to her reply.

"I don't want to be taken away from this. I love the farm. I intend to keep it."

Hatcher grinned to himself. The man might be a lawyer but he wasn't very sharp when it came to Kate, his intended.

"What's the man's name? You must know it."

Hatcher stiffened. He couldn't hope to keep it a secret.

"Hat—" She broke off with a sigh. "How do I know if it's his real name or his hobo name?"

His feet grew lighter.

"I wonder if I've seen him somewhere," Mr. Lawyer said.

Hatcher's relief died as quickly as it came. *Be sure your sin will find you out.* Numbers thirty-two, verse twenty-three. He hurried to his quarters, yanked his shirt off the hook where he'd hung it to dry and dropped it in his knapsack. He would vamoose before Doyle Grey asked any more questions.

He ground to a stop as he stuffed his Bible in on top. He'd given his word to the woman. He said he'd put in the crop for her. He'd promised God, as well, and the Word said, *If a man vow a vow unto the Lord he shall not break his word, he shall do according to all that proceedeth out of his mouth.* Numbers thirty, verse two. He put his Bible back on the table. He'd leave as soon as he'd fulfilled his promise. Perhaps he'd get away before her lawyer friend dug up anything on him.

One thing puzzled him. Why hadn't Kate given his name? Her excuse that it might be a hobo name didn't hold a drop of water. Was she afraid of what Doyle would discover? Was she so desperate to get her crop in she'd protected him? Or had it been innocently unknowing?

The question still plagued him the next morning when he headed over for breakfast. He thought to ask her but as he reached the open door he saw Mary in tears as her mother tugged a brush through her hair. Kate looked ready to fry eggs on her forehead.

Dougie sidled up to him. "Mary's crying again."

"I hear."

"Momma's getting mad."

Kate shot her son a look with the power to drive nails and Mary choked back another smothered sob.

Hatcher ducked away to hide his smile and patted Dougie's head. "Might be a good time to pretend you don't notice."

"I guess."

"Breakfast is ready." Kate nodded toward the waiting plate as she continued braiding Mary's hair.

Hatcher grabbed the plate.

Dougie sat on the step beside him. "I'm glad I don't have to have my hair brushed and braided."

"Me, too," Hatcher said around his mouthful of eggs

and fried pork. "Course a man has to shave. That's not a lot of fun."

"I never seen anybody shave." Dougie sounded as if he'd lost Christmas and Easter all at once.

"It's not hard to learn. Only a nuisance." He didn't add especially if you couldn't get hot water and the only mirror you had was the size of your thumb.

"It's done," Kate announced and Mary shuddered a grateful sob. "What do you say, Mary?"

"Thank you, Momma."

"You're welcome and you look very nice."

Hatcher almost swallowed his food the wrong way. Mary didn't sound grateful and Kate didn't sound sincere. For some reason he found the situation amusing but seeing the tightness around Kate's eyes decided he best hide it. With thanks for the meal, Hatcher put his empty plate on the stand next to the door and headed for the tractor.

As he worked he chuckled often, remembering the scene. He guessed the two of them often struck sparks off each other. Kate, so strong willed, Mary, so uncertain of herself. No doubt they would eventually learn to understand each other.

He soon settled into the pleasure of the work. He enjoyed sitting on the tractor watching the field grow smaller and smaller as he went round and round. There was nothing quite like the smell of freshly worked soil. Or the beauty of birds swooping in after the discer, looking for bugs to eat. The fresh wind on his face blew the dust away on one side of the field, blew it in over him on the other. His eyes and nose and lungs filled with dust. The red neckerchief he pulled over his mouth and nose helped but it was always a relief to turn back into the wind. It became a game—struggle through the dusty length, enjoy the wind in his face until he turned the corner and again faced the dust.

Several days later he got off the tractor and stood proudly looking out at the last field. He'd worked the entire hundred acres. Now he could seed the crop.

Kate joined him. He didn't have to turn to know what her expression would be. He'd watched her day by day. Knew the sight of her in overalls so baggy she got lost in them. He'd chuckled at the way she wrinkled her nose as she mucked out the barn. He knew the look of her in her faded blue housedress, her arms browning from exposure to the sun, humming as she fed the chickens. And in her going-to-town outfit, a smart brown dress with a white collar. He'd learned her various expressions. The strained look around her eyes, her mouth set tight as she hurried to complete a task. Her maternal smile as she greeted the children returning from school. Fact is, he caught himself watching her more than he should, felt things budding in his heart he'd denied for years and must continue to close his heart to.

Yet for a moment, standing side by side, he allowed himself to share her enjoyment. He knew she'd be smiling with a touch of justifiable pride. She loved the land.

"It looks good," she said.

He heard the smile in her voice. Felt an answering smile in his heart and tucked it away into secrecy. "It does."

"Smells even better."

"Yup." But it wasn't the freshly turned sod he smelled, it was the warm faintly lilac scent of her. He wondered if she bathed in lilac-scented water or absorbed the sweet aroma from the bouquet of lilacs her friend, Sally, had given her and which now sat in the center of the white kitchen table.

"I can hardly wait to see the green shoots poking through the ground."

"I'll start seeding tomorrow." He headed back to the tractor.

"I think I'll make something special to celebrate." She laughed and ran toward the house.

Only then did he allow himself to watch her. Graceful, full of life and love. That Doyle was one fortunate fellow. Only she said she hadn't promised to marry him. For some reason, the thought brought a wide smile to his mouth.

The next morning, he headed over for breakfast. The woman was a fine cook. He had started to put on a little weight. And the rhubarb pie she'd made last night had been mighty fine. He wondered if there might be more of it left for breakfast.

He hadn't gone more than thirty feet when he heard cows bellowing, then a thin scream. Mary. And then Kate yelling. He couldn't make out the words but her panic rang clearly across the distance. Hatcher broke into a dead run. Soon he could make out her words. "Dougie, don't go that way. It's too far."

Hatcher didn't slow for the fence, cleared it without breaking stride and skidded around the corner of the barn. In a glance he saw it all—Dougie between a cow and her calf, the cow not liking it. Only the other cows milling around kept her from attacking him. The animals were restless, agitated. Something had spooked them.

Kate stood in the pen, trying to edge toward her son but the cows would have none of it.

Mary, crying, peered through the fence at her mother and brother.

Hatcher leaped over the fence and roared at the animals. He pushed his way through the melee, scooped up Dougie and spun away, letting the cow charge through to her calf. He jogged across the pen and dropped the boy to his feet across the fence then reached out, grabbed the woman by the arm and pulled her after him out of the pen. Mary clung to the rails, her eyes wide.

Kate hugged Dougie and scolded him at the same time. Her eyes glistened as she turned to Hatcher. "Thank you."

He touched his hat. "Ma'am."

She stood up tall, her son pressed to her side. "You've just rescued both me and my son. Don't you think it's time you called me something besides ma'am? Like my name."

In his mind he'd been calling her Kate for days but to say the word out loud threatened his peace of mind in a way he didn't want to think about, so rather than answer her question, he shifted backward to lean against the fence, realizing he still breathed hard from his little adventure. As much from the scare it gave him to see Kate and her boy in the midst of the snorting animals as from the physical effort of racing across the grass. He didn't want to analyze why his heart kicked into a gallop at the idea of either of them being hurt. He would hate to see anyone hurt, he reasoned, but it felt more like a mortal blow than normal concern for another human being. "Heard you folks as I left the shack. Ran all the way over."

"I'm very glad you did. But you're not changing the subject. I'm tired of being called ma'am." Her hard stare said she wouldn't be letting the subject go.

"Nothing against your name, ma'am."

She narrowed her eyes and edged forward until they were inches apart. The least movement would send some part of his anatomy into contact with her. Sweat beaded on his skin at the thought. He couldn't tear his gaze away from her demanding brown eyes.

"Not ma'am," she insisted. "My name is Kate."

"Know that already." Saying it would put him on the wrong side of a mental line—one he'd drawn for himself. A way to avoid getting close to people. Letting them get close to him. But she was a stubborn lady. He understood she wasn't prepared to let it go this time.

"Kate," she said.

He nodded, swallowed hard. "Kate." It sounded strangled and felt both foreign and sweet on his tongue.

She grinned. "Didn't hurt a bit, did it?"

Before he could say anything, not that he intended to, she turned to Dougie. "Now what happened?"

The boy had tried several times to break away from his mother's grasp but she wasn't letting him escape so easily. He refused to look at her. She squatted down until she was eye level with him and caught his chin, turning him to face her. "What happened? Something must have scared the animals. What was it?"

Dougie sent Hatcher a desperate help-me look but Hatcher couldn't help him. Whatever the boy had done caused a small stampede. Someone could have been badly hurt. His limbs turned watery at the idea.

"I didn't mean to, Momma," he whispered.

"What did you do?"

"I blew my whistle."

Kate shot Hatcher a surprised look then turned back to her son. "Why would that bother them? You two have been blowing those whistles nonstop for days."

Dougie studied his boots. "I snuck up behind them. Wanted to see if I could scare them."

Kate rubbed at a spot below her ear. "Well, you certainly did. And almost got trampled doing it. Dougie, I don't know what to do with you. Can't you see those cows are way bigger than you? Don't you understand how you could be hurt?" Kate stood and reached for the fence.

As the color drained from her face, Hatcher tensed, ready to catch her if she fainted. But although her knees bent for a second, she took a deep, noisy breath and stayed on her feet.

"Momma?" Mary slid closer, watching her mother anxiously.

"Ma'am?"

She shot him a warning look.

He relaxed. She wasn't too weak to object to the way he addressed her.

She held up one hand. "I'm fine."

Dougie began to slink away.

"Oh no you don't, young man," Kate warned. "I'm not done with you."

Dougie halted.

His mother studied him. "What am I going to do with you? You take far too many chances. One of these days you'll get hurt."

Hatcher watched and waited, wondering what she would do. The boy needed to understand the seriousness of his actions. He also needed to be shown a few things about being in a pen with cows and calves.

"Couple of pens in the barn need cleaning," he murmured, directing his words nowhere in particular.

No one responded.

"Not a big job. Really doesn't need a grown-up's time."

Kate looked at him a full thirty seconds then grinned. "Noticed that myself." She faced her son. "Dougie, after school you can clean out those pens. And while you're doing it, I want you to think about how foolish it is to tease the cows."

"Yes, Momma. Can I go now?"

Before Kate could answer, Hatcher clamped his hand on the boy's shoulder. "How be if I show you a few things every man has to learn about cows?"

Dougie preened at the idea of being considered a man.

"If your mother has no objections." Hatcher waited for Kate's nod.

He led the boy to the fence, waited for Dougie to climb the rails so they could lean side by side over the top one. "First, never get between a cow and her calf, especially if the animals are upset. Use your eyes and know where each animal is. It's a good idea to keep close to a fence. That way you can escape quickly if you have to. Now these animals are tame as pets but when they're frightened they're wild animals. Keep that in mind." He jumped over the fence into the pen of cows that had now settled down. They ignored his presence. He indicated Dougie should join him and step-by-step showed him how to handle cows. Where to touch them to get them to move without panic, how to turn them without shouting, and mostly how to remain calm yet alert.

"Think you can remember all that?" he asked the boy.

"I'll try," Dougie said.

Suddenly, Hatcher realized Kate remained at the

fence, watching him, listening to every word. Of course she would. Just being protective of her son. As Dougie ran to his mother, Hatcher backstepped past the cows, aiming for the barn.

"Thank you, Mr. Jones," she called.

"Name's Hatcher," he murmured, without looking at her.

"Thank you, Hatcher."

Her gentle voice wrapped itself around his resolve, threatened it in a dozen places at the same time. Made him forget. Made him want. Made him regret.

"Breakfast will be ready shortly."

Not until she turned away, the children at her side, heading toward the house did Hatcher realize he stood stock-still in the middle of the pen, his boots planted in a fresh, odorous cow pie.

He hurried out of the enclosure and scrubbed his boots on the grass. Something about Kate Bradshaw upset his equilibrium, his self-imposed indifference. Maybe it was her stubbornness. Her bravery at hanging on to the farm. Her protectiveness of her children. Didn't matter the whys. All that mattered was his handling of it. Best to keep his distance from the woman until the crop was in and then move on as fast and as far as he could.

Before the morning was half-spent, he realized his plan was doomed.

Kate wanted the wheat seeded first.

That made sense.

She wanted to show him where she'd stored the seed wheat.

Like he couldn't find it on his own.

She insisted on leading him to the seed instead of telling him. And she talked. Something inside her must have snapped for her tongue seemed to flap on both ends.

No way could Hatcher lose himself in his own thoughts. Not with Kate talking a mile a minute. And demanding his reply.

He headed for the drill to get it ready to go to work.

"I remember the first time I saw this farm," she said, skipping along at his side.

At least that didn't require a response. If the drill didn't require too much work, he would be out seeding before noon. Enjoying peace and quiet.

"I was sixteen years old. Jeremiah needed someone to do some housework and cook his dinner. At first, I seldom saw Jeremiah. And the work wasn't too hard so I had time to explore. I couldn't believe one man owned all this. Course I knew about big farms. Father had worked on a few, but this was different."

He expected she would tell him how this land was different without him asking and he opened the drill boxes. Someone had neglected to clean them properly. He dug out the sprouted seeds and tossed them on the ground.

Kate reached in and helped.

It amazed him she could work and talk so fast at the same time. He began to wonder how much coffee she'd had for breakfast. She'd only offered him one cup.

"Jeremiah said I was welcome to do whatever I wanted. Go where I wanted. And I did. My favorite spot was the barn loft." She paused long enough to take a breath and glance at the barn.

Long enough for his unguarded thoughts to rush back to a familiar loft where he and Lowell had spent so many hours. He mentally squeezed the memory away.

"I could sit in the open door and see for miles," she

continued. "I dreamed about someday having a house like Jeremiah's. Owning my own land. My father never owned a thing except the clothes on his back." She chuckled. "And the tarpaulin that was supposed to keep us warm and dry when we were on the road."

Long-denied memories of Lowell and the home they'd shared burst full bloom into his head.

Hatcher grabbed a wrench and checked each bolt, tightened the loose ones.

Speaking of loose—Kate's tongue continued to flap nonstop.

"I knew it wouldn't last. None of my dreams would come true but you know what happened?"

He locked his mind tightly to dreaming of possible answers. "Nope." He walked around the machine, Kate tripping on his heels.

"As always Father decided to move on. I cried when he told me. I was sick and tired of moving. I dreaded telling Jeremiah. When I did, you know what he said?"

"Nope." Some grease here and there and the drill would be ready.

"He offered to marry me."

She left a space between her words. Looked at him to fill it.

"Huh." Best he could do. After all what does a man say about such a thing?

"I wasn't sure at first. You see Jeremiah was fifteen years older than me. He'd been married once a long time before. She'd died of influenza after they'd been married only three months. Isn't that sad?"

"Uh-huh. I'm going to get the tractor now and hook on." He strode away.

She stayed at the drill.

He breathed in the quiet. Even the roar of the tractor

had its own peace. A peace that lasted until he'd pulled the drill over to the granary of seed wheat.

Kate followed him and helped fill buckets with wheat. She picked up her story just like she'd only taken a breath, not waited half an hour between one sentence and the next. "I'd never thought of marrying Jeremiah. He was kind and gentle and I really liked him but with him being so much older…well, you understand what I mean, don't you?"

He didn't have the least idea, marriage being an unfamiliar notion for him. Though he supposed being married to a woman like Kate might be kind of pleasant. He blinked at the waywardness of his thoughts and again slammed a door in his mind. "Uh-huh," he muttered, when he realized she waited for him to answer. One safe way to keep his thoughts where they belonged— focus them on something safe. He mentally calculated how many bushels were in the granary and figured out how much he could seed per acre. "You want to use up all this seed?"

"It's enough, isn't it?"

"Looks about right."

"Jeremiah said I'd never have to move again if I married him. I know that's not reason enough to marry a man but after I thought about it awhile and prayed about it, I knew I didn't want to leave. I wanted to stay with Jeremiah and take care of him. Does that sound foolish to you?"

"Uh-uh." People got married for less reason than that.

"It was the best decision of my life. We had a good few years together before he died."

He handed her the empty buckets. "What happened?" As soon as he spoke he wished he could pull back the words and stuff them into the pail with the grain. He already knew more about this woman than was good for him—the sound of her laugh, the shape of her smile, the color of her eyes when she laughed—

"To Jeremiah?"

"Uh-huh."

"He got a chill that last winter. Couldn't shake it. Eventually it turned into pneumonia. He died in May after struggling for months."

"Sorry." And that left her to cope on her own. She was rail thin, proof of how hard she worked to keep the farm. Once she married the lawyer fella she wouldn't have to work so hard. The idea should have felt better than it did.

"So here I am. Twenty-eight years old with two children to raise but with a house and farm that belong to me." Her voice filled with pride. Or was it determination? Probably both.

They again exchanged buckets. She held the handle of one, waited until he glanced at her to see what was wrong.

"How do you do it?"

He lifted his eyebrows. "What?"

"How can you wander around without a place to call home?"

He took a full bucket from her. He would prefer to ignore her question but he felt her waiting. Knew she would prod and poke until he answered. Maybe build her own reasons and then, no doubt, want to discuss them in detail right down to the dot at the end of her sentence. "Home is where the heart is." That would surely sound philosophical enough to stop any more questions.

"You're saying you need nothing but what you carry on your back to be happy?"

Sounded about right to him so long as he didn't let any more wayward thoughts escape. "Uh-huh."

"How can you be content like that? Never knowing where your next meal is coming from, where you're going to sleep. Having to endure cold, wet, unkindness from people. I just don't understand it. Never have."

They stared at each other. Her brown eyes flooded with distress, her lips tightened with worry.

He practically fell backward as her concern shredded his indifference. He had to do something to bring back her joy. "I am not alone. I am not afraid because I know God is with me. That's all I need." He suddenly felt the need to protect himself with words. "Psalms one hundred thirty-nine, verse seven says, 'Wither shall I go from thy spirit? or wither shall I flee from thy presence? If I ascend up into heaven thou art there: if I make my bed in hell behold thou art there. If I take the wings of the—'"

She cut him off before he finished and he wondered why he had thought he wanted to quote the entire Psalm. "I never found God's presence kept me warm. I suppose I don't trust enough. Or believe big enough."

"Believing isn't the same as feeling. Even if you believe, you can have all sorts of feelings, including hunger and cold. Don't change who God is."

She stared at him, her eyes revealing her struggle with his words. "'Believing isn't the same as feeling.' I like that." Suddenly, the inner light returned to her eyes, leaving him relieved almost to the point of silliness.

He wanted to click his heels together and salute the heavens. He did neither. Just grabbed the empty pails and stowed them in the granary.

"Yes, I like that," she murmured again, her smile as bright as the sunlit sky.

The drill box was full, ready to go.

"I'm thirsty," she said. They both headed toward the well for a drink.

"Don't you ever get lonely?" she asked, as she wiped the trail of water from her mouth.

Her words shocked him as if he'd fallen into the trough full of cold water. His gut twisted like a summer tornado, a tumult of emotions. He steadied his hand, stifled his thoughts as he filled the dipper and tipped his head back to drink.

He wouldn't tell of the nights he lay awake staring up at the stars. He wouldn't even allow himself to think about them. Or how he wondered what his life would be in another ten years. Would he still be alive? Would he be someone normal people ran away from? Like the man in the Bible who inhabited the tombs?

A person couldn't think too far ahead. It might drive him to desperation.

"'God is our refuge and strength; a very present help in trouble.' Psalm forty-six, verse one." Now why had he said that verse? Made it sound like he needed to be comforted. Feared danger. He tried to think of a more reassuring verse. "'I am with you always, even unto the end of the world.' Matthew twenty-eight, verse twenty."

She rocked her head back and forth. "I wish I had your faith. Then maybe I wouldn't find it so hard to think of letting the farm go. I wouldn't be so afraid of being homeless."

Hatcher didn't argue. She had it wrong, though. His faith sustained him but it was his fear that kept him homeless.

Chapter Seven

Kate drank again of the cold refreshing water. If only she could be as relaxed as Hatcher about home and belonging and safety and all the things this farm meant to her and her children. "I know I should trust God more. He's promised to meet all my needs. Yet, I can't let go of what this farm is. You know what I mean?"

Hatcher hung the dipper and wiped his mouth. "Sort of."

He met her eyes. A flash of pain, dark and heavy filled them. She knew then they shared the same weight of disappointment and hardship. She couldn't guess the source of his, but in that moment, before he lowered his eyes, she felt a connection, a kinship. She wondered if he realized how much he'd revealed in those fleeting seconds.

She jerked her head up and stared across the familiar yard, startled to realize she'd told him more about her farm, her dreams and her fears than she'd shared with anyone. More than she'd ever admitted to Sally and certainly more than Doyle knew or cared to know.

"So you once had the same thing—farm, home, belonging. What happened, Hatcher? How did you lose it?"

"I didn't." He touched the brim of his hat, avoided meeting her gaze and headed for the tractor. He didn't appear to hurry yet his strides ate up the distance and within minutes he headed for the field.

What secrets hid behind his words, his withdrawal? Perhaps she would never know. He was here such a short time. She crossed her arms over her stomach and tried not to think how alone she would be when he left. Even worse than before, because until he came she'd never really had anyone to share her thoughts with.

She rubbed at her jaw. She would not allow herself to think about it.

She watched for a while, smiling as he planted her crop. Her gaze shifted from watching the furrows behind the drill, to the mysterious man driving the tractor. Both Sally and Doyle had warned her of the dangers of associating with a hobo but she'd seen enough to be convinced of a number of things:

He knew farmwork, seemed as familiar with it as if raised on a farm.

He was honest. If he'd wanted to steal anything, he could. She never locked anything up.

He was gentle and kind with both her children.

And if someone asked, and she answered truthfully, she'd have to admit his quiet strength meant something to her.

She snorted. Some would say she exhibited signs of a lonely widow woman, looking for manly attention that didn't exist simply to persuade herself she might yet find another man to marry.

For another moment, she watched Hatcher, relaxed looking despite the bounce of the tractor. Yearning filled her soul. She didn't want a man just to have a man. But she ached to share with someone. Be able to reveal her deepest feelings without fear of ridicule or condemnation. Hatcher, with his quiet patience, had allowed her that if only for brief periods.

For several days, Hatcher seeded wheat. Kate rejoiced in every acre planted and continued to pray for the desperately needed rain.

Today they were going to plant corn. First, they had to go to the Sandstrums and pick up the seed she'd traded some seed wheat for.

She let Hatcher get behind the wheel of the truck. She settled on the stiff seat beside him. He had long fingers, as brown as the soil of her farm, yet his nails were neatly trimmed and surprisingly clean.

She forced her gaze straight ahead and pointed him in the right direction.

Mr. Sandstrum, out seeding, saw them approach, stopped the tractor and crossed the field to greet them as they pulled up to the bin where Kate knew he kept his corn.

"Kate, I been wondering when you'd come."

"Mr. Sandstrum. This is Hatcher Jones. He's putting in my crop for me."

The men shook hands. Mr. Sandstrum pushed his dusty hat back on his head, revealing a white forehead as he gave Hatcher a long, hard look then nodded.

Kate wondered if that signified approval.

"'Bout time you found help." He threw open a bin. "It's bagged and ready to go."

Kate stood by, wanting to help, but Mr. Sandstrum waved her toward the house.

"Not woman's work. You go visit the missus."

She wanted to argue but caught a sudden flash of a smile on Hatcher's lips. "We'll manage," he murmured.

Knowing they would and she would only be in the way, she nodded. She'd wanted to see Alice and the new baby anyway.

At her knock, Alice called for her to enter. Alice sat in the kitchen, her blond hair in tangled disarray, her hands hanging limp at her side. Unwashed dishes stood on the table, the floor was unswept and dirty.

Kate rushed forward. "Alice, you look ill. What's wrong?"

Alice swung her gaze toward Kate, stared without recognition then blinked her eyes into focus. "It's not me. It's the baby. She never stops fussing."

Kate heard a weak mewling from the other room and hurried to get the baby. The infant needed clean diapers. Her little bottom was red and sore, her legs so thin tears stung Kate's eyes. She cleaned up the baby and took her to Alice. "Are you nursing?"

"Trying." As soon Alice put the baby to her breast, Kate knew what the problem was. Alice had no milk.

"Alice, you have to give the baby a bottle. Do you have any cow's milk?"

"Axel let the cows go dry."

"I'll bring some from home." When she did, she'd come prepared to spend the day. Let Alice sleep a few hours while she cleaned the house and bathed the poor wee mite of a baby.

While she waited for Hatcher to load the corn, she boiled water and washed dishes.

"I'll return," she told Alice as she heard the truck approach.

Alice nodded wearily, too exhausted Kate knew, to care about anything. Even her baby.

"I have to get right back," she said to Hatcher as soon as she closed the truck door behind her. "The Sandstrums have an eight-week-old baby who's starving to death. I'm going to take milk over. And I'm going to stay to help. You don't need me anyway."

Hatcher grunted. "Think I can figure out what end of the seed to plant first."

"You don't have—" She broke off, knowing he was teasing her, and laughed. "I'm sure you can."

"Will the little one be all right?"

"I hope so. She's awfully weak. I just hope I can get her to take a bottle. I'll need to pray really hard. Will you, too?"

"Certainly."

"Right now? I'm afraid it's almost too late for the baby."

Hatcher looked startled, surprised, uncomfortable then resigned as if he couldn't be bothered to argue with her. They approached the driveway to her farm. "Okay if I drive to the house first?"

She laughed, felt a quick release of the tension knotting her stomach since she'd seen the sickly baby.

He stopped the truck in front of the house.

Neither of them moved. She could hear his breath rasp in and out.

The silence between them grew awkward.

She stared out the window. She couldn't believe she'd asked him to pray with her. She hadn't prayed aloud with anyone in her entire life. For one shaky moment, she thought to withdraw her request. Then she remembered how weak the infant was, faced him and grabbed his hand. "I'm really worried about the baby. I need some of your strength to go back and care for her." Her voice dropped to a whisper. "I'm afraid the wee thing will die. Please pray I'll know what to do and the baby will live."

He hesitated, a hard, unreadable expression on his face. Was he uncomfortable praying aloud? But she knew he was a Christian; he must have been called upon to pray aloud before this. Was he embarrassed to pray for a tiny baby? Somehow she didn't think that could be the reason. Perhaps it was simply because they didn't know each other well.

He slowly bowed his head.

Relieved to see he meant to comply with her request, she did the same.

"Heavenly Father," he said, his voice thick. "Touch the Sandstrum baby and make her well. Amen."

Kate took a deep breath. "Lord, don't let it be too late. Please. And help me know what to do. Amen."

His hand lay warm beneath her palm, his fingers curled away in a hard fist.

She jerked away, heat stinging her cheeks at her boldness. Immediately she missed the contact. Felt an emptiness that knew no beginning, no end.

He shifted, slipped his arm up the steering wheel as if to make sure it was out of her reach.

At his obvious withdrawal, tears stung Kate's eyes. She grabbed for the door, intent on escape. What had she expected? That he'd protest and reach for her hand again? Of course not. She sucked in a calming breath. It would not be good, she warned herself, to get used to sharing her burdens with a man who couldn't wait to leave.

Shoving stubborn resolve down her limbs, she looked in the window. "I'll get things ready—" she said, her voice mercifully calm "—while you unload the corn."

He sent her a quick smile. "I've no doubt you'll know how to handle things."

The threatening tears of a moment ago turned to liquid surprise. She dashed at her eyes with fingers that seemed suddenly stronger. How long had it been since anyone believed in her?

She hoped her eyes wouldn't reveal her gratitude and longing and aching. "Thank you."

She studied his strong, calm face, felt a sudden urge to kiss him, she was that grateful. She hurried to the house before she made a fool of herself and concentrated on the tasks she must complete.

She made enough sandwiches for Hatcher and the Sandstrums, noted she'd have to mix up more bread when she got home, gathered together supplies for the baby and a clean towel for the poor little thing's bath.

Hatcher brought the truck to the house and she handed him his lunch. Thankfully, he seemed oblivious to her weakness of a few minutes ago in the truck. Or else, she suspected, more likely he chose to ignore it.

He helped her carry the supplies to the truck.

She paused before she got behind the wheel. "Please continue to pray. I'll be back when the children get home from school. Or as soon as possible." She hesitated. Would the children be all right if she happened to be late?

"I'll watch for them," Hatcher said.

Knowing he'd be here, she gladly let that worry go.

Axel Sandstrum was working out in the field when she returned. Kate wondered if he'd given the baby or his wife more than a glimpse. Surely if he did, he'd be in the house tending them instead of his fields.

But she didn't have time to wonder about his lack of concern. She pushed into the house without knocking.

Alice slumped in the same chair, in the same position as when Kate left, her cheeks pale hollows, dark shadows circling her eyes. Kate wondered if the woman was more than just tired and touched her brow. She didn't seem feverish.

"Alice, honey, go rest. I'm going to feed the baby and take care of things for a while."

Alice stared at her.

"Come on." Kate helped her to her feet and urged her toward the bedroom. She edged her to the side of the bed where Alice collapsed. Kate helped her stretch out, covered her with a quilt and left.

She prepared a bottle of milk and went to the cradle where the baby lay motionless, her eyes wide. It frightened Kate that the baby didn't cry or respond when Kate bent over and cooed at her. She scooped up the infant, checked her diaper, found it still dry. Knew that wasn't a good sign. She wrapped a tiny blanket around the little thing and cuddled her close.

"Come on, baby, you have to eat." She edged the nipple into the tiny mouth. The baby made no effort to suck and when milk dripped out of the nipple it ran out the sides of the pink mouth. The baby never even tried to swallow.

Axel stomped into the house. "Where's Alice? Where's my dinner?"

"Alice is resting. I brought some sandwiches." She pointed to them. "I'm going to stay and help Alice this afternoon. She's wore right out."

"The baby's been real fussy."

The baby didn't have the strength to cry. Pity and anger mingled that her father hadn't noticed. "The baby is starving. You need to get a milk cow. I can bring milk over for a few days until you do." Kate refrained from saying what was uppermost in her mind. If this little bitty girl didn't start eating, the Sandstrums wouldn't need a cow. *Please, God, help her swallow. Don't let me be too late.*

Mr. Sandstrum glanced at the baby in Kate's arms. "Not a hearty baby."

"She's starving. You'll be surprised at the difference if we can get her to take this milk." But instead of sucking, the baby fell asleep in her arms.

Kate sat in the wooden rocking chair in the tiny living room and swayed back and forth. The chair listed to one side but she ignored it and sang every lullaby she knew as the baby slept.

An hour later the baby stirred and Kate prodded her awake, tried again to get her to swallow and suck. The infant lay practically lifeless. "Come on, baby," she whispered, wishing she could remember the little girl's name. "You have to fight. You don't want to give up. There are too many delights in this world to leave it without enjoying them. You'll get so much fun out of discovering how soft a kitten is, hearing a bird sing, watching it fly from branch to branch, seeing your first newborn calf, learning to read and write and sing. Come on, baby." As she murmured to the baby, she silently prayed. And then her prayers and baby conversation twisted together. "Come on, baby. *Please, God, give her the strength to suck.* One of these days you'll fill your hands with dandelions and bring them to your momma. *Please, God, don't let this precious baby die.* All it takes is for you to start eating. *Just one swallow, God. I'm sure once she starts she'll be on her way.* You'll learn about God and His love. *God, I know You love her but it's too soon to take her back into Your arms. Alice needs her. Restore Alice's strength, too, please, God.*

She stroked the baby's cheek trying to trigger the sucking reflex. She lost track of how long she sat there praying and trying to get the baby to swallow. She grew weary, discouraged, thought of admitting defeat, then remembered Hatcher's promise to pray, felt his quiet strength uphold her.

The sun came around and shone in the west window, falling across the baby's face. The infant blinked, sneezed and swallowed. Her eyes widened as the milk slid down her throat and warmed her empty stomach. She drew her cheeks in and tried to suck. Slowly, she managed to down two ounces then fell asleep.

"Thank you, God. Thank you." Tears streamed down Kate's face. She held the baby longingly. But the afternoon was slipping away and she had much to do. She put the baby in the cradle, covered her warmly and headed to the kitchen. She swept the floor and washed it, changing the water twice before she got to the end of the room.

The baby needed to be fed every two hours until she gained strength. Kate put away the cleaning supplies and prepared another bottle. This time the baby knew what to do when the bottle went into her mouth. Again, she fell asleep after two ounces. She had wanted to bathe the baby but feared she was too weak. Far more important to get her to eat and gain some strength.

Kate glanced at the clock. She needed to get home to her children. But she didn't want to leave the baby until Alice woke up. She tiptoed into the bedroom. Alice looked so peaceful. So thin. She hated to wake her but Dougie and Mary could not be left alone.

"Alice." She touched the woman's shoulder. "Alice, wake up."

Alice dragged herself from sleep and stared at Kate. She struggled to sit up. "How long did I sleep?"

"All afternoon. Are you feeling better?"

"I think so. Where's Annie? I don't hear her." She scrambled to her feet and swayed.

"Annie's just fine." The perfect name for such a fragile baby. "I got her to take a bottle. You keep her on cow's milk and I expect she'll do fine."

Kate made Alice tea and left with instruction to feed the baby every two hours. And then she hurried home, already late.

She didn't see the children as she pulled to a halt before the house. The tractor stood idle at the edge of the field. She raced into the house. "Dougie. Mary." Nothing but nerve-scratching silence.

She dashed outside, headed for the barn, spared a glance at the windmill ladder as she ran past. Thankfully no children clung to its rungs.

She called their names in the musty silence of the barn and got only the rustling of mice overhead for answer.

Her heart pounded against her ribs. She struggled to fill her bursting lungs as she raced from the barn. The cows grazed placidly in the pasture.

"Dougie. Mary," she called.

"Over here." It was not a child's voice. She turned toward the sound and hurried past the corrals. Hatcher and the children hunkered down in a tight circle.

"Momma, we found a baby rabbit," Dougie called.

"I didn't know where you were. You should have stayed where I could find you." She scowled at Hatcher. Her fear and frustration made her sound cross. Well, she was. It had been downright frightening to have her children missing if only for a few minutes. After an afternoon spent fearing baby Annie would die in her arms, she'd panicked. "What was I to think?"

Hatcher pushed to his feet, dusted his knees and

straightened. "Thought it best to keep them occupied until you got home. How's the baby?"

"She started to suck. I think she'll make it."

With a quick nod, Hatcher headed for the tractor.

Kate thought to call him back, tell him more about the baby, thank him for watching the children, but she sensed from the set of his shoulders that he didn't want to listen to her chatter at this moment.

"Look, Momma," Mary said.

Kate stared at her daughter holding the tiny rabbit. "You aren't afraid of it?"

"No, Hatcher said it was scared so I needed to calm it down."

"Can we keep it?" Dougie asked.

"Wild young things don't like to be caged up."

"But Momma," Dougie pleaded. "If we let it go who will take care of it? It's just a baby."

"You have to take care of babies," Mary said in a voice wise beyond her years.

"Where would you keep it?" Kate asked, already half-swayed by their arguments.

"We could use one of the broody houses," Mary said, speaking of the little houses where Kate put the hens with eggs to set. Two of them were in use right now but there was a third she didn't need.

"I suppose you can if you both promise to make sure it always has feed and water."

"We will," they chorused.

Permission granted, they hurried to take care of the rabbit.

Kate stared at Hatcher on the tractor. She'd been rude to him when all he'd done was watch the children and she guessed her comments would feel like an attack on him.

She must apologize.

But when she waved at him to come in for supper, he circled his hand to indicate he'd make another round.

She dropped her hand and watched, a little worried she'd offended him so badly that he felt the need to avoid her.

She set aside a plate of food for him. She ate with the children, only half-aware of their conversation as she listened for the tractor to stop. They finished but still he didn't come to the door.

She cleaned up the kitchen, paused several times to glance outside. He continued going round and round. Was he trying to finish the field, or trying to think up an excuse to explain how he had to leave?

She grabbed milk pails and headed for the barn. She'd apologize, explain her alarm over the children, make him see he didn't deserve her anger.

She milked the cows to the rumble of the tractor. Did he plan to work right through till dark? She should be happy if he did. Glad her crops would soon be in the ground. Glad, however, was not how she felt.

She hurt for the unkindness she'd spoken, worried he might leave because of it.

She did not want him to leave. And it had nothing to do with her crop. He would go. She would stay. That was the plain and simple fact of it. She pressed her head into the cow's warm flank and took calming breaths.

She carried the milk to the kitchen, left some not separated to take to baby Annie in the morning. Still the tractor growled on. Hatcher's food grew cold and sticky on the plate.

The children hurried through their chores so they could spend time with their rabbit. She let them play later than usual.

The western sky streaked with orange and purple and gold then turned navy before the tractor finally stopped its incessant roar.

Kate scraped the food off the plate into a fry pan and set it to warm. Through the dusk, she saw Hatcher head to the pump where he drank deeply then splashed water over his head and scrubbed his hands and face. Sally had said hobos were dirty but Hatcher wasn't. He was almost meticulous in washing before he ate. And each day he wore a clean shirt and trousers. He had a spare of each, which he washed out at night. He'd consistently refused her offer of Jeremiah's things.

His meal warmed as he finished washing. She hung a towel outside the door for him and as he dried, she scooped the food back to the plate.

"It looked more appetizing a few hours ago," she said as she handed it to him.

"Wanted to get in a few more rounds."

"I appreciate it but you don't have to work so hard."

He sank to the step and ate with the dedication of a hungry man.

She sat on the step beside him. "Hatcher, I want to apologize for being cross when I got home this afternoon. I wasn't angry at you. I appreciate that you kept an eye on the children until I got home. I was just worried about them. Truly, I'm sorry I spoke the way I did."

"Not a problem."

She settled into an uneasy silence. He'd readily, quickly accepted her apology. Almost dismissed it. What had she expected? She didn't know, only knew she wanted more. So much more that it parched the inside of her stomach.

"Glad to hear the Sandstrum baby is doing better."

"I couldn't get her to suck for the longest time. I

thought—" Her voice caught on unshed tears. "I thought she was going to die." A sob escaped.

Hatcher put his empty plate down. "But she didn't?" He smelled of good earth, the fumes from the tractor and the fried pork she'd cooked for him.

"No." Suddenly she had to tell him about her afternoon. She began with her concern about Alice and continued until she shared her excitement when Annie started to swallow. "I prayed and prayed and finally she took a swallow and suddenly seemed to realize she was hungry. I think you must have been praying, too."

She should go inside but she remained seated beside him. She wanted this moment of comfort to continue.

"I was praying." His words were soft.

Shep sprang to his feet and barked.

She stared down the road at an approaching vehicle. "Doyle," she murmured. That put an end to a peaceful moment. "What's got into him that suddenly he starts driving out here midweek?"

"Maybe afraid you're managing too well without him."

She snorted. "He'd like me to be the lady of his castle. He wants me to sell my farm."

"Is that going to happen?"

Suddenly everything was clear as the sky above them. "No." She was genuinely fond of Doyle but not so much as to give up the security and safety of her farm. If he would offer to let her keep it, perhaps let someone else run it… But for Doyle life fit into neat little cubbyholes. There was no slot for his wife owning a farm of her own.

Doyle stopped his car behind Kate's truck and climbed out. "Isn't this cozy?"

Hatcher and Kate pushed to their feet. "Hello to you, too, Doyle," Kate said.

Hatcher started to leave. Doyle said, "Hatcher Jones, you should probably stick around for this."

Kate's spine stiffened at the way Doyle spoke to Hatcher but before she could protest, Doyle spoke again.

"I thought there was something familiar about you. You're that man from Loggieville, aren't you?"

Hatcher stared out at the seeded field.

"I remember the case well. Don't suppose you thought it would catch up to you here. You didn't take into account that lawyers all over the country watched the proceedings with keen interest. Would you get away with it or not? I didn't think you would, but you certainly proved me wrong."

Kate watched the stiffness return to Hatcher's shoulders. She hadn't even realized it was gone until now. "What's this all about, Doyle?"

"Your hobo is a murderer."

Anger bolted the full length of her body at Doyle's cruel accusation. "If that's the case, why is he walking around a free man? I thought there was a death penalty for murder."

"He weaseled his way out of it."

She ground her words past the anger twisting her throat. "I see. What you're saying is a court of law found him not-guilty?"

"Couldn't convict him when no one was willing to tell the truth. They were all afraid of him. Afraid he'd get to them and make them pay if they spoke out."

"But, Doyle, you're a lawyer. Don't you believe in the justice of our legal system?"

Doyle laughed. "It has certain flaws."

"Yes, but if he was convicted of murder, wouldn't his

accusers know they'd be safe? After all, he'd be dead."
She shuddered at the idea.

"Things can happen."

"Men can be innocent."

Doyle stepped closer to Kate. "Are you saying you
believe he's innocent? You don't even know what happened?"

"I don't need to. I've seen Hatcher."

Doyle was inches away. "What has he done to you?
Kate, you pack your things right now. And the children's. You're moving into town. You can sell the farm
immediately. Just yesterday, someone was asking about
land. Willing to pay handsomely for it. Hurry now. I'll
wait here."

Kate crossed her arms across her chest. "I'm not
going anyplace. I'm perfectly safe here. And it's time
you got it through your head that I do not intend to sell
the farm. Ever."

"Kate, be sensible. Now is not the time to be stubborn."

She leaned forward. "Doyle, you picked the wrong
time and the wrong place to order me about."

Doyle backed up, held up his hands. "I guess I came
on a bit strong. But I'm worried about you and the children. This man…" He turned to glower at Hatcher.

But Hatcher was gone. Kate caught a glimpse of him
disappearing around the barn. "Hatcher," she yelled.
"I've got fifty acres to seed yet." She started after him,
needing to persuade him to stay but Doyle grabbed
her elbow.

"He'll be on his way now that I know who he is."

Her anger seemed to know no bounds. It clawed at
every muscle. Her legs vibrated as she spun around to
face Doyle. "And where does that leave me? Having to
find someone else to help? Is that what you want?" She

watched a play of emotions across Doyle's face. Triumph. Caution. And then his beguiling smile.

She did not smile back. "You're hoping I can't manage on my own. You think I'll be forced to give up my farm." She stared at him. "You did this for the sole reason of trying to make me marry you. Even knowing how much the farm means to me..." She couldn't look at him anymore. Couldn't believe his treachery. If Hatcher left...

Please God, make him stay. I need him.

She added, *For the farm.*

Chapter Eight

Hatcher's breath scalded in and out as he consumed the distance to the little shack. Tension grabbed his shoulders as if the skin had grown five sizes too small.

He wasn't surprised at Doyle's revelation, knew it was inevitable. He was angry at himself. He'd forgotten who he was, what he'd done. For a few days, he'd allowed himself to pretend he could belong, if only for a short time.

He threw back the door and reached for his knapsack. His elbows had a wooden quality about them, reluctantly doing his will as he rolled his trousers and shirt and stuffed them in the bag. He pulled other items from the nails, startled to see the evidence of how much he'd let himself feel at home here. Not often he left anything out of his pack except to use it.

The Bible went on top as always. "'I will set my face against you, and ye shall be slain before your enemies, they that hate you shall reign over you; and ye shall flee when none pursueth you.' Leviticus twenty-six, verses sixteen and seventeen. Lord," he groaned. "It's nothing more than I deserve. I know the sin that filled my heart." Even if a jury had dismissed the charge, it did not take away his guilt.

He slung the pack over his shoulder and headed for the door. He could make a mile or two even in the dark.

He paused for one last glance around the small, meager cabin that had been the closest thing to a home in years, thanks to Kate's generosity.

Suddenly, he pictured Kate as she met Doyle's confrontation so fearlessly. Spunky little lady. So determined to keep her farm. Seems Doyle was equally determined she should give it up to marry him. He couldn't imagine what kind of life she'd have if she did. Doyle would always want Kate to do his bidding.

He laughed out loud, the sound as unexpected as nightfall at noon.

Maybe he should feel sorry for Doyle if he tried to order her about. You'd think the man would have figured out Kate was his equal. More than his equal.

Hatcher rubbed his chin. Why hadn't she ordered him off her place once she heard the sordid story? She sounded like she believed his innocence.

Even his own father hadn't.

"Son," the older man had said after Hatcher had been arrested. "This here's been a long time coming. You got yourself a wicked temper and it seems you're always looking for a reason to vent it. Don't seem to matter on who or where." Course his words were so slurred Hatcher had to guess at much he said.

Hatcher, still young and volatile, had risen to the accusations. "Maybe you should ask me why I got this problem. And when? Or better yet, ask yourself."

Muttering about his son's rebellious ways, his father left Hatcher to stew in the sordid jail cell.

He never visited again, though he sat in the very back

row of the courtroom during the trial. Sat like a curious spectator come for the entertainment. Never once did the man offer a word in Hatcher's defense.

And his reaction when Hatcher had been declared not guilty? Just a few words that burned themselves into Hatcher's brain.

"Son, I think it's best for everyone if you leave."

Hatcher finally found something he and his father agreed on. And he'd never turned back.

But Kate had called after him. Reminded him of his promise to put in the crop. As if she expected him to stay. Even wanted him to stay.

She was the first person in an uncountable length of time who acted like she trusted him.

He thought of the times she'd confided in him. She told him she worried how she'd be able to keep the farm if this drought continued.

He'd wanted to offer her reassurances. Instead he'd quoted scriptures, his way of avoiding saying what he really thought—that no one knew how long the drought would last nor how much it would cost her before it ended.

One time she'd confessed she didn't love her husband, but was grateful for his protection and for the children he'd given her. He didn't want to think about her in a loveless relationship, though she didn't seem to have any regrets and spoke of Jeremiah with real affection.

And just before Doyle had shown up trying to order her about, she'd stated she wouldn't give up the farm to marry Doyle. He wondered if she'd meant to say more before they'd been interrupted.

For certain, she'd need help if she intended to keep the farm. A woman like her deserved a helping hand. He'd given her his assurance he'd put the crop in. She'd been counting on it no doubt. He dumped the contents of his pack onto his bed. He'd fulfill his promise. She already knew the truth. And no doubt so would everyone in town before another day passed but another few days wouldn't change things. Then he'd be on his way to where no one knew him or his wretched past.

Kate smiled when he showed up for breakfast. "Thought you might have left."

He let her smile ease the tension that built as he walked across. All night he wondered if she'd come to her senses, or been convinced by Doyle, yet here she was smiling a welcome and here he was, ready to fulfill his promise. "Thought I might have, too."

"So what made you stay?"

His heart near exploded with the truth. *You, Kate. You with your trust and stubbornness. You made me stay.* But he stilled his emotions, smoothed his face and replied. "I said I'd put the crop in and I will."

"Then you'll be gone?"

The words cut like a thorn. He didn't want to leave. But he must. He had to spare her the censure and shunning that came with knowing him. He nodded.

"Hatcher, what really happened?"

He took the plate of food from her hand and ate it hurriedly without answering. "I'll get right at the seeding," he said, handing back the empty plate.

"Fine. Don't tell me. But…"

He slid her a glance, saw her eyes gleaming like earth warmed by the hot sun, felt the same warmth wrap around his heart. He envied the man who'd enjoy that glance day after day. He only hoped it wouldn't be Doyle. She deserved better.

"Someday, you'll tell me the truth, Hatcher Jones."

He laughed mirthlessly. "Someday will never come."
He grabbed the milk pails. "It's best not to know everything." He headed for the barn.

He sat with his head against the warm flank of the
Jersey cow when he heard her approach. He should have
known she wouldn't let the whole thing rest. She'd work
at it like a farmer preparing the soil.

She poured some oats into the trough for the cows,
wondered aloud whether or not the supply would last
the summer but Hatcher wasn't fooled. She vibrated
with curiosity.

"Hatcher, do you have parents?"

Her question, coming out of left field like that, startled him. It did him no good to think of his parents. Any
more than it served any purpose to remember what had
happened. "Nope."

"They're both dead?"

He couldn't lie. Knew she'd guess it if he did. "Why
do you want to know?"

She stood beside him, her presence crowding his
body and his thoughts. "When was the last time you
saw them?"

"You planning to write a book?"

She chuckled. "Are you saying there's a story here?"

"Nope." There'd been far too much written about
it already. He wanted only to erase it from his mind.

"I just keep thinking what it would be like for me
if it was Dougie or Mary. You know I have two brothers. Ted is eighteen now and he's working on a ranch
in Montana. He came to visit two years ago, before he
started work there. Ray's older. He's like Dad. Always
on the move. I haven't seen him in four years. Got a
letter last Christmas. He was in California then. Don't
expect he still is."

Hatcher wondered where she was going with this tale. He finished the Jersey cow and moved on to the big Holstein.

Kate turned the Jersey out and returned to his side. He could only dream she'd feel the need to go bake cookies, or whitewash the walls or something. Anything but push at his memories with her talk of parents and brothers.

"Do you think it's fair to my children to keep them on the farm?"

He blinked, grateful he was bent over the cow's flank and she couldn't see how her question surprised him. Talk about a sudden switch. Before he could figure out where she was going with this, she hurried on.

"Maybe they'd be better off in town. After all, they have so many responsibilities here. I need them to work, especially when I don't have help. Seems I never have time for them." She backed away. He hoped she'd give him room but she only lounged against the rough wood panel, settling down for a long, intimate talk.

Not far enough away he could breathe without inhaling her presence.

"Mary would almost certainly be happier in town," she mused. "She's afraid of the chickens, the cows, almost everything."

Hatcher sprang to the child's defense. "Best thing is she faces her fears, realizes what's real danger. She'll be stronger for it."

"Never thought of it that way. I suppose you're right. But Dougie worries me. He's reckless."

"He's a boy. Just needs to learn to measure things. You wouldn't want him to be afraid of risks." Not that it was any of his concern what she did with her two kids.

"Don't see how moving them into town will change who they were or how they need to grow."

"But I'm so busy. If I lived in town I'd have more time to spend with them."

The woman was more persistent than a newspaper reporter. He finished milking and jerked to his feet. "Ma'am, if you want to spend more time with your kids, you'll just do it. Whether you're on the farm or in town."

She stared at him as if he'd announced the cow had gone dry.

He continued. "Sure, life in town might be easier. Or just different. It's got nothing to do with what you're talking about. Seems you've just forgotten how to have fun."

He headed for the house with the milk, not surprised when she wasn't on his heels. Couldn't expect a woman to be happy about having a few truths thrown in her face.

But he'd only set the pails inside when she bounced up and down at his back apparently ready to overlook his interference.

"I need to take some milk to the Sandstrum baby."

He'd left most of the bags of corn in the back of the truck. Made it easier to get it to the field. "I'll fill the drills."

A little while later, he watched her drive away and prayed the baby would be stronger today. Then he lost himself in the roar of the tractor, the need to concentrate on following the previous track and the wind alternately at his face, his back, on one cheek or the other.

Only his thoughts wouldn't be lulled. Thanks to Kate and her persistent questions, he kept thinking of his father, wondering how he was, missed his mother, wished he could see Lowell just one more time. He didn't need such thoughts or their accompanying memories. They only made his stomach ache the way it had when he was a child. He rubbed at the chicken pox scar on his wrist.

"Hatch, honey, don't scratch, you'll get infection." His mother caught his wrist and examined the sore. "I'll put on some more chamomile lotion."

Her eyes had the special look that made him feel loved and important.

"How come I gotta be so sick when Lowell wasn't?" His brother had four chicken pox and spent the time at home reading and playing. Hatch had spent his days feeling miserable and wanting to scratch every inch of his skin.

His mother rubbed his hair. He didn't mind that she made a couple spots itch. "Would you feel better if your brother felt as bad as you do?"

"Yes." At her saddened expression, he'd instantly repented. "I guess not. No use both of us wishing we were dead."

His mother's hands stilled.

He knew he'd disappointed her. "I didn't mean it, Ma." At ten, he thought talking tough proved he was grown-up.

His mother took both his hands, gently avoiding the sores. "Hatcher William Jones, I pray you will never feel desperate enough to mean those words. No matter what happens there is something about life that makes it worth living. Promise me you'll always remember that. Promise me you'll never say those words again or contemplate such a thing."

"I promise." But there'd been times he'd wondered if she'd been wrong in saying there was always something about life that made it worthwhile. Sometimes all that kept him going was the promise he'd given her.

Until Kate.

He groaned. He'd be leaving in another day or two. It would be the hardest thing he ever had to do.

Kate returned at noon. He waited until she waved from the kitchen door before he stopped and headed for the pump where he stuck his head under the gush of water to wash off the dirt. He used the time to deny the strong feelings growing toward this woman. Years of hiding his emotions enabled him to push them away.

He shook the water from his head, scrubbed his hair back and wondered if Kate could lend him scissors so he could cut it then sauntered to the step where Kate waited with sandwiches and cookies.

All his practice at denying his emotions seemed wasted. He couldn't look at her without his heart bucking like an unbroken horse. He clutched at the safest topic that came to mind. "How's the baby?"

"Improving. I think she'll make it."

"Good."

"I can't imagine losing a baby. Or a child."

He ignored her expectant look. Knew she wanted to hear about his parents, his family, how he'd been arrested for murder.

He gulped his food and escaped back to the field, where his thoughts would still haunt him but at least he'd be alone with his torture.

It was Saturday. Hatcher watched the activities around the house as he bounced along on the tractor while Kate and the children housecleaned. Dougie shook out the floor mats, banged them on the step, laughed as the dust rose in a cloud.

Hatcher's throat tightened for so many reasons. The family he'd left behind, lost. The times he'd done the same thing for his mother. The laughter he'd shared with Lowell.

And the knowledge he'd soon be saying goodbye to Kate and the children. The ache inside his chest yawned like a bottomless cave.

Mary carried water from the house and poured it on the rows of potatoes, some already poking through the soil. Hatcher guessed it was wash water. He imagined the floors gleaming. Floors he'd had glimpses of when he handed the milk to Kate each day. The first day he'd seen inside, the house had a slightly neglected air—jackets tossed helter-skelter, dishes stacked on the sideboard as if she didn't have time to put them away. Over the days, the interior took on a distinctly different air—it smelled fresh, it looked renewed. Every surface was clean and tidy.

Kate stepped outside and shook a floor mop. She glanced toward him and waved.

Ah, sweet Kate. My world will be the sweeter for having known you, the sadder for having to say goodbye. He acknowledged the truth of his mother's words—there was always something that made life worthwhile. Having known Kate for even such a short length of time would make the rest of his life worth the living simply for the pleasure of remembering her.

He lifted his hand in a quick salute. She continued to watch him until he grew wary. She was scheming something. Likely figuring out how to persuade him to tell about his past. She was wasting her time. A shame considering how busy she was.

She still watched as he turned a corner. He told himself he didn't care if she stared at his back. No matter to him. But didn't she have better things to do?

Come noon, he considered skipping lunch. Except his stomach rebelled. And he couldn't deny a little curiosity to see what all the running to and fro meant.

He didn't have to wait long as Dougie ran out and met him halfway across the yard.

"We're taking a little holiday."

The yard suddenly seemed too full of space as though something had dropped out of his world. They were going away? Well, he'd been alone before and would soon have to get reacquainted with that state. "That a fact?"

"Momma says we deserve it for working so hard this morning. We cleaned the house from one end to the other. Momma says it hasn't been so clean in a long time."

No reason for them not to enjoy themselves. In fact, he was happy for them. Less so for himself as he envisioned the emptiness when they left. "Uh-huh."

Mary joined them, her usual restrained, sedate self, or so he thought until she stopped dead center in front of him and giggled. "Guess what we're going to do?"

"Maybe take a holiday?"

She wilted. "Dougie already told you."

"Yup."

"Bet he didn't say what we're going to do."

"Nope." He squeezed Dougie's shoulder before the boy could shout it out. "Let Mary tell."

"We're going to the coulee to find violets." The girl grinned so wide Hatcher knew this must be something special.

"Momma says she used to go there every spring," Mary added.

"Before Poppa died," Dougie said. "Before she got too busy," he added in a sad tone.

Hatcher chuckled. The two of them sure could be dramatic.

"You're coming with us, aren't you?" Mary asked.

His heart leaped to his throat. He faltered on his next step. He'd once been part of a family, part of their outings. He and Lowell had favorite escapes. One, a grove of trees where they could play for hours. Lowell had spent much of his time building a tiny log shelter.

"If we didn't already have a farm, I'd say let's move west and build us a log cabin," Hatcher had said, fascinated by the construction.

If only Lowell could see these flatlands where the trees were no bigger than a sapling, he'd be disappointed to say the least.

Hatcher shoved aside the thought, dismissed the memory, ignored the way pain tore through his gut.

"I have to work." They reached the steps where Kate waited with his lunch in hand.

"No, you don't. I've declared the afternoon a holiday for the whole farm," she said.

Dougie cheered. "Now you can come, too."

Hatcher kept his gaze on the plate, though for the life of him he couldn't have said what the food was. Surely she didn't mean to invite him.

"We're going as soon as we finish dinner," Mary said. She looked happier than Hatcher had seen her.

"That includes you," Kate said softly.

To his credit, he didn't flinch. He didn't have to look to know her eyes would be stubborn and gentle at the same time.

Common sense returned. The children would no doubt tell of their adventure. People would soon realize he'd accompanied them. Doyle would have a royal snit. "Ma'am, I don't think that would be a good idea."

"I refuse to take no for an answer. Besides, do you want to disappoint the children?"

"Please say you'll come." Dougie practically bounced off the ground in his excitement.

Hatcher had to wonder when Kate had last taken the children on a fun outing.

He knew he shouldn't do this. It was way over the line. Someone would end up paying for it. Probably all of them. Yet he allowed Dougie's words and Mary's eager look to override his internal protests.

He met Kate's eyes then. The triumph in her expression let him know she realized his predicament.

He nodded slightly. Just enough to let her know he realized he'd been set up. He couldn't spoil the children's fun, though if he gave himself a chance to think it through, he would admit there was no point in them getting used to having him around. It would end soon.

"Very well," he murmured.

"Let's eat." Kate shepherded the children inside leaving Hatcher with his uneaten lunch and undigested thoughts.

He didn't know how they managed to eat and clean up so quickly but they returned before he'd choked down his own lunch or figured out a way to escape the afternoon.

"Come on." Dougie stood in front of him, rocking from one foot to the other as he waited for Hatcher to join them.

Kate smiled as he slowly got to his feet and followed the children.

He'd pleased her with his decision to join them. He briefly allowed himself a taste of pleasure at her nod of approval, all the time aware of warning tension in the back of his head.

He should not be doing this.

Chapter Nine

The coulee with its constantly changing array of flowers was Kate's favorite place away from the farm site. Yet she hadn't been there since Jeremiah died. She hadn't had time. The farm took every minute of her life and all her attention, demanding even more than her children received. But today she intended to make up for all the times she'd been too harsh, too hurried, too distracted. Today they were going to enjoy themselves. Hatcher included.

She shuddered as she recalled the way Doyle's announcement speared through her like a well-aimed pitchfork. Her quick defense of Hatcher had been automatic, the accusations against him as unbelievable as someone naming Dougie a gunfighter. Not that Hatcher denied it. Something had happened, and Kate, curious, wished Hatcher would tell her. But whether or not he chose to wouldn't change her conviction, her unquestioning knowledge of his innocence.

Once her initial shock died away, her throat practically pinched shut. She couldn't begin to imagine what it felt like to be accused of such a crime. How had he been involved enough to receive such a terrible charge?

But whatever happened had to have been an accident or a mistake.

How she ached for the pain and shame he'd faced, continued to face. She'd seen his resigned look when Doyle delivered his information. The wary guardedness in his eyes. Knew he'd experienced rejection because of the murder charge. It explained his hobo lifestyle.

She wanted nothing more than to ease that pain, erase the guardedness, comfort his sorrow. She longed to hold him close but the best she could do was include him in this outing, prove to him she didn't believe he'd done wrong. Remind him of all the good things life offered.

She laughed from the pure joy of an afternoon free of the demands of work. She wanted to run and jump and holler like Dougie did. And laugh and dance like Mary. Instead she held her excitement at bay. But it swelled until her heart and lungs and stomach couldn't take any more. For a moment she thought it might erupt uncontrolled, unfettered, unmanaged. But she metered it out in little laughs and wild waves of her hand as she pointed out the nearby farms to Hatcher.

"Listen," she said, and they all ground to a halt and turned toward the sound of the train whistle as it passed through town five miles away. She and the children laughed and Hatcher looked amused, whether at hearing the train in the distance or their exuberance, she couldn't say. Nor did it matter. For the first time in months she felt young and full of life. Today was for enjoying with her children and Hatcher.

She stole a quick glance his direction, confused at all the things his presence made her feel. She knew if he'd stayed at his work this afternoon he'd be close to finished. She'd purposely taken him away to delay the inevitable—he'd be gone once the crop was seeded.

She stopped the direction of her thoughts. She wouldn't mar this day dreading the time he'd walk down the road without a backward look. She wouldn't admit the hollowness in her middle at how lonely she'd be. Instead, she turned her attention back to the beauties of nature—the satin-blue sky, the rolling sweep of the buff-colored prairie.

"There it is," she called, pointing to the dark line indicating the coulee. Dougie raced ahead. "Be careful," she called. Then promised herself not to ruin the day with worries.

"There. Look." She pointed toward the perfectly round hollow three or four feet in the ground solidly paved with purple flowers crowded in so thick they hid their own leaves. "Your father—" she told Mary "—said this was a buffalo rub. I guess that's why the violets do so well here." The air was sweet with the smell of spring. "Impressive, don't you think?" she asked Hatcher.

Hatcher shifted his gaze from studying her to the flowers. "Lots of them."

She'd caught a look in his eyes making her throat suddenly refuse to work. Tenderness? Longing? Or was it only a reflection of her own emotions? No. She knew what she'd seen. But what did it mean? That he wanted something more than his past provided? Did he need her to convince him he didn't need to keep running?

"Hatcher—"

"Look," Dougie called. "A hawk's nest."

"Can I pick some?" Mary asked, standing at the edge of the mass of flowers.

She jerked her attention to her children, her cheeks

stinging. Did she think all he needed or required was her permission to stay? If it needed only that, he would have stopped running before the first year on the road ended. Something stronger than the wrongful murder charge drove him.

Grateful her children had saved her from making a fool of herself, she turned to her daughter. "Let's get some on the way home."

Mary nodded and raced toward Dougie and the hawk's nest.

Kate took a step to follow them, stopped, turned her gaze first to the sea of purple then gathering her courage, faced Hatcher. "I hope you can let yourself enjoy the afternoon. I want everyone to have a great time." She wanted them to have an afternoon full of sweet memories for the future. For a few short hours, she'd let nothing interfere with the joy of sharing this special time with Hatcher.

His eyes, dark as a moonless night, revealed nothing, his flat expression gave no insights into his thoughts but then his lips curved slightly at the corners.

It was enough. A quiet whisper of hope brushed her thoughts and she laughed. "Shame to miss what life has to offer." She held his gaze for a moment.

He shifted, looked past her, putting a wide chasm between them as effectively as if he had jumped to the far side of the coulee.

Her pleasure and hope were snuffed out like a candle extinguished.

"'The earth is the Lord's and the fullness thereof; the world and they that dwell therein. For he hath founded it upon the seas, and established—'"

She cut him off before he could quote the whole book

from wherever the verse came. "Stop trying to hide behind your recitation."

She knew a wave of gratification when he looked shocked.

He hesitated only briefly. "Psalm twenty-four."

She pursed her lips. "I'll be sure and check it out."

He flashed a glance at her, managing to look both surprised and a tiny bit offended.

She smiled, her lips taut across her teeth. How she'd like to shake him from his incredible composure.

"Momma, look."

Dougie's call turned her attention away from Hatcher.

Her son hovered close to the edge of the bank, peering over the edge at a nest in the tree below. Suddenly he dropped from sight. Mary screamed. Kate gasped and Hatcher raced forward, Kate at his heels.

She skidded to a halt at the edge of the cliff, as breathless as if she'd run a mile rather than a few steps.

Dougie clung to bushes four feet down. Solid ground lay twenty feet below.

Her heart trembled. "Hang on, son," she called. "I'll get you." She stepped closer, swayed at the nothingness below her. She flung her head around looking for something, anything to aid her. A bush, even a good clump of grass to cling to. Saw nothing but dried blades of grass. She could slide down to his side. But how would she get him up. She teetered forward, gasped and leaned back. What if she caused him to fall the rest of the way? She closed her eyes as fear burst through her veins, erupting in hot spots at her nerve endings.

Hatcher grabbed her elbow and pulled her back. "I'll get him."

The pulsing need to rescue her son wouldn't let her relinquish the job to another. "He's my son."

"Yes, ma'am. You stand back and let me help him."

She turned, saw the dark assurance in his gaze. She trusted him completely. She was safe with him. Her son likewise safe. She nodded.

Hatcher flopped on his stomach and reached for Dougie. Eight inches separated his hand from Dougie's. Hatcher edged forward, still couldn't reach him.

Kate gasped as Hatcher started to slide. He was going over the edge, too.

He edged backward to safety.

"Momma," Dougie cried, his voice thin with fear.

Instinctively, Kate knelt at the edge reaching toward him.

"Stand back," Hatcher ordered.

Automatically she obeyed his authoritative voice.

"I don't want to have to pull you up, as well," he said in a softer tone.

Her limbs felt as if they'd been run through the cream separator as she watched her son struggling to hang on.

Hatcher sprang to his feet, found two rocks, wedged them solidly into the embankment then dropped to his stomach again.

When she realized his intentions, her legs gave out and she sank to the parched ground.

He wormed forward until his shoulders rested on the rocks. As he reached toward Dougie, one rock shifted.

Mary screamed.

The sound shredded Kate's nerves. "Quiet."

She didn't let her breath out until the rock dug into the sod and held.

Hatcher's hand reached Dougie. He wrapped his fingers around the boy's wrist.

"Grab hold as hard as you can," he grunted, the sound struggling from compressed lungs.

Dougie grabbed on and Hatcher began to edge backward.

The air closed in around Kate, suffocatingly hot, impossible to breathe. Her heartbeat thundered in her ears as she watched Hatcher pull her son up, inch by inch.

"Please, God. Please, God. Please, God." She murmured the words aloud, unable to pray silently.

Hatcher reached level ground and jerked Dougie over the edge of the embankment to safety.

Laughing and crying, she grabbed her son, wrapping herself around him. When she could speak, she said, "What were you thinking? You can't just throw yourself over a cliff and expect to survive."

"Momma, I fell."

Kate hugged him close. "I know you did but you scared me so badly." She sank to the grass and pulled Dougie to her lap. Sobs racked her body.

Tears streaming down her cheeks, Mary threw herself on top of them. They tipped over in a tangle of arms and legs. Tears gave way to laughter.

Kate hugged both children and looked up at Hatcher. "How can I ever thank you?"

He smiled. "You just did."

At first she thought he meant her words, then noticed his dark eyes sparkled with laughter and realized he meant the amusement of watching the three of them tumbled in a heap.

He sobered but didn't blank his expression as he usually did. His dark gaze held hers with unwavering intensity as something eternal occurred between them.

He shifted, broke the connection. When his gaze returned he had again exerted his fierce mental control.

Her stomach ground fiercely. She'd wanted to shake him from his composure. It had taken Dougie's accident to succeed in that. She didn't know if she should rejoice in his momentary lapse or mourn the fact it was so brief.

One thing she knew, she didn't want her son to repeat the episode for any reason, not even to bring about a break in Hatcher's reticence. She scrubbed Dougie's hair with her knuckles and kissed Mary's head.

"I don't think I'm going to let you out of my sight for the rest of the day," she warned her son.

"I'll be careful," he promised, leaping to his feet. "Did you see the nest?" He ran over for another look.

Her heart leapfrogging to her throat, Kate pushed Mary aside and gained her feet in a rush. But Hatcher had already corralled the boy and gently guided him to a safe distance.

"A man always keeps his eye on what's ahead, making sure he won't step into something dangerous."

He twitched as if the words had hit a target in his mind.

He was teaching her son to think before acting but did he think to apply his words to his own life, his past and the crime he'd been accused of, the present and her little family or the future and the open road?

She glanced around. Her children were safe. Thank God and Hatcher. The sun was warm. The sky blue. The prairie dotted with flowers of purple and yellow. Hatcher chuckled at something Dougie said. If only she could stop time, keep life locked on a day like today, only without Dougie trying to scare her out of ten years.

If only she could persuade Hatcher to stay.

Her eyes locked hungrily on him as he played with the children. His hair sorely needed cutting, yet it didn't detract from his rangy good looks. A man with unquestionable strength. The sort of man she'd gladly share the rest of her life with.

She gasped and turned away from the sight of him as the awful, wonderful truth hit her.

She loved him.

She breathed hard, stilling the rush of emotions reverberating through her veins. She knew with certainty she had never before been in love. She'd cared deeply for Jeremiah. She had a certain fondness for Doyle. But never before had she felt the power of a merciless, consuming love.

And foolishly, she'd made the mistake of learning the depths of her heart by falling in love with a man who would never stay.

She leaped to her feet, a boundless energy begging for release. "Let's play tag," she called. "Not it."

The children quickly called "Not it" and danced away from Hatcher. His expression shifted—surprise, refusal and then mischief. He turned away to stare down the coulee. "Who said I wanted to play?"

Dougie sidled up to him. "Aww, come on. Play with us."

Kate saw it coming and laughed as Hatcher spun around and tagged Dougie. "You're it."

Dougie looked surprised, swallowed hard then headed for his sister but Mary had guessed what was coming and raced away, then turned and headed toward Kate. Squealing, Kate broke into a run, Dougie hot on her heels. When had her son learned to run so fast?

He tagged her easily.

She leaned over her knees, catching her breath. Waiting until they all moved in, teasing and taunting her. She continued to pretend to be out of breath until she saw Hatcher out of the corner of her eye. She waited, gauged the distance then sprang at him. He leaped away but she tagged his elbow. "You're it," she gloated.

"Cheater," he growled. "You were faking."

"Part of the game."

Hatcher headed for Mary, who screamed and took off at an incredible pace. Kate shook her head. Both her children had grown so much and she'd hardly noticed except to buy new clothes. Dougie bounced around at what he considered a safe distance but suddenly Hatcher veered to his right and lunged at the boy, tagging him before he could escape.

They played until, breathless from running and weak from laughing, Kate called a halt. "I'm going to melt into a little puddle soon." She flopped on her back. "Wish we'd brought some water."

The children joined her, one on each side and Hatcher sat a foot away, his arms draped over his bent legs.

"We should take more holidays," Dougie declared.

"You are absolutely right." Kate promised herself she wouldn't let so much time pass before she played with her children again. She blew out a sigh. "I suppose it's time to go home."

"Aww," the children chorused.

"Soon," Kate said, as reluctant to end the day as they. She sat up. "Days like this remind me why I like the prairie."

"I hate the wind," Mary murmured.

"It's okay as long as it isn't blowing all the dirt around," Dougie said.

Kate glanced at Hatcher. Saw her worry reflected in his eyes. It hadn't rained for days. And then barely enough to settle the surface. All it needed for a dust storm was a hot dry wind. Her hair tugged at her scalp. Had the wind increased as they enjoyed the spring day?

She pushed to her feet. "We better go."

Before they reached the shelter of the farm, a black

cloud appeared in the south. Mary started to cry. Kate grabbed Dougie's hand; Hatcher grabbed Mary's and they broke into a hard run. Dust stung their eyes as they raced for home. They veered around the barn, found a pocket of wind-free shelter, took in a deep breath and made the last dash for the house. They burst in, pushing the door closed behind them.

Kate didn't slow down. "I have to plug the holes." She grabbed the pail of rags and began dampening them, stuffing them around the window frames. "Here." She tossed Hatcher a thick rug. "Put this under the door."

He looked at the rug, looked at the door, looked at her. "I should go."

"Not in this." The room darkened. The wind screamed like a demented animal. Dirt rattled against the window like a black snowstorm.

Mary huddled on the chair farthest from the window and sobbed. Kate didn't have time to deal with her right now.

Hatcher took a deep breath, glanced around the room as if he thought he'd find some other means of leaving then dropped to his knees and started pushing the rug under the door where fine, brown dirt already made its way in, sweeping across the floor like a stain. "Can't seem to get it in right. Mary, do you know how to do it?"

Kate, busy trying to stop the dirt from finding a way in, spared little attention for the others but turned at his request.

Mary hesitated then slowly went to his side. "It's easy. Like this." She knelt beside Hatcher showing him how to push the rug under the door.

Hatcher glanced up, caught Kate's gaze on him and managed to look embarrassed and triumphant at the same time.

She mouthed the words, *thank you.*

He shrugged.

The children would miss him when he left.

Her eyes stung and she turned away to hide the heat of her love.

Kate finished and looked around. "It's the best we can do." Still dirt sifted across the floor. She would find it in her cupboards, her closet, her shoes.

Hatcher stood with his back to the door. He twisted his hands, his eyes darted from object to object, everywhere but directly at her.

"Hatcher." She kept her voice calm and low. "You'll stay here until the storm is over."

At the reminder of the weather, Mary sobbed.

Kate grabbed the lantern. "No point in sitting in the gloom. Who wants to play a game?"

Dougie, at least, looked interested.

"Do you remember how to play Snakes and Ladders?" Dougie shook his head. Had it been that long since they'd played games together?

"I do," Mary said, her tears gone. "Poppa used to play it with us."

"That's right. Your father loved to play games of any sort. It's still in the hall cupboard." She went to the hall and found it under layers of coats and blankets. She pressed the box to her nose, remembering Jeremiah's smell, his delight in games, his competitiveness. She could never beat him and if, occasionally, she did, he insisted on a rematch. She soon learned to let him win so they could go to bed.

She carried the game to the kitchen table and opened it. "Come on, Hatcher. Join us."

He hovered at the door.

Dougie pushed a fourth chair to the table. "You can sit by me."

Hatcher hesitated then hung his hat on a nail and shuffled over.

Kate stifled a smile, amused at his inability to refuse any reasonable request from the children, rejoicing to have him at her table, if only briefly. She'd have the scene to help sustain her in the future. She handed him a game piece and they began.

Mary quickly recalled how to play. Dougie needed a few instructions but the game was simple enough for even younger children.

Hatcher, at first, was quiet, stiff. But after he hit a snake and fell back three rows and Dougie laughed, he grew intense, acting like he had to win. She soon realized it was pretense. Mostly he tried to give the children a good time.

She loved him the more for his goodness to her son and daughter.

Mary forgot the dark sky, the sharp wind until something solid hit the wall. She jerked forward in her chair. "What was that?"

Hatcher shrugged. "Someone's outhouse?"

Kate laughed. "I hope it was unoccupied."

Mary looked startled then offended before she laughed. "You're teasing me."

"Might as well laugh as cry," Hatcher said.

Mary blinked. "I guess I'll laugh then." And she did.

It was Dougie's turn to play. He moved five places, hit a snake and returned to the start. "That's the third time I got sent back." He leaned back and stuck out his lips.

"Be a good sport," Kate said.

Hatcher's turn followed. He hit a snake and returned

to the third square. He sat back on his chair. "I've been here three times already." When he imitated Dougie's pout, Kate laughed.

Mary was next. She moved, hit a ladder, advanced three rows and smirked.

It was Kate's turn. She let out a huge sigh when she hit neither snake nor ladder.

Hatcher winked at Dougie. "Your turn. You've got nowhere to go but forward."

Cheered by the idea, Dougie abandoned his pout.

They played for more than an hour while the storm continued. Finally Kate shoved away from the table. "I'll have to make supper."

Hatcher jerked to his feet. "I'll go milk the cows."

She stopped him with a hard look. "Wait until the storm ends. Besides the cows will have found shelter and will refuse to move even to get milked."

She fried up potatoes and the last of the pork. Mr. Sandstrum had given her carrots from his root cellar in return for the milk she took over so they had cooked carrots. "Time to put the game away."

Mary packed it away carefully then helped set the table.

Kate served up the meal, indicated Hatcher should remain where he was.

He looked ready to leap up and let the wind carry him away.

Happily, she'd stopped all the holes and he couldn't escape.

She sat down. "Will you say the blessing, Hatcher?"

He blinked, looked at each one around the table, then bowed his head and prayed. "Heavenly Father, thank You for Your many blessings and especially the gift of food. Amen."

As he prayed, she imagined him at the head of her table, day after day, offering up prayers of gratitude, surrounding the family with love and support. Kate kept her head bowed a second after his "amen," pulling her futile wishes into submission.

"Help yourself." As she passed him the meat, their gazes connected.

"I should not be here." He spoke softly as if he didn't want the children to hear.

She thought he meant because of what Doyle had said, the stigma of his past.

"You have neighbors," he murmured.

Realizing what he meant, her eyes burned. People would consider Hatcher's presence inappropriate.

"I'd send neither man nor beast out in this weather. It will surely end soon, though I can't imagine how much damage it will have done. Last time we had a blow like this, it brought down the board fence next to the barn and the cows got out and moved with the storm. They ended up at the Olivers. They could have just as easily missed the barn and ended up in the next state. You never know with cows." She clamped her mouth shut to stop her babbling and turned to serve Mary potatoes.

Not until Mary's protesting, "Momma," did she stop.

"Oh dear." She'd scooped half the bowl onto the child's plate. What was she thinking? She took most of it back.

She closed her eyes and filled her lungs slowly. There was no reason to be all twisted up inside. But she couldn't get Hatcher's presence out of her senses. People would certainly talk if they could read her mind and see how desperately she wanted him to stay.

"Momma, did I ever play Snakes and Ladders before?" Dougie asked.

Thankful for his distraction, Kate pondered his question a moment. "I don't suppose you did."

"Hatcher, you ever play it before?" he asked the man.

Hatcher stared at his plate, the food untouched.

"Hatcher?" Dougie asked, puzzled that his question wasn't answer.

Hatcher shook his head. "Sorry. What did you say?"

Dougie repeated the question.

Hatcher picked up his fork. "Used to play it with my brother." He put his fork down again and stuck his hands beneath the table.

"You have a brother?" Kate stared. It was the first bit of information Hatcher had ever revealed and she knew he hadn't intended to.

"Used to have."

Mary gasped. "He's dead? Like my Poppa?"

Hatcher kept his head down. "Not so far as I know."

"What happened to him?" Mary demanded.

Hatcher looked at the child, pointedly avoiding Kate's wide-eyed curiosity.

"Nothing. I expect he's fine. I just haven't seen him in a long time."

"Why not?"

His shoulders crept toward his ears, his eyes grew dark. Kate felt sorry for him. The more he tried to extricate himself from the hole he'd stepped into, the deeper he got. She was every bit as curious as the children. She wanted to know more about this man.

"I haven't been home in a long time."

Both children watched him now. Kate could feel their curiosity, their sadness that anyone should be away from home too long. She shared their concern. Home meant comfort and safety to her. But she wasn't sure what it meant to Hatcher. With the accusations he'd faced, perhaps home meant other things to him.

"Don't you want to go home?" Mary asked.

Hatcher's expression grew tighter with each passing moment. Kate couldn't stand any longer to witness his discomfort. "Children, enough questions. Eat your supper."

He sent her a brief look of gratitude then turned his attention to the plate of food before him.

But Mary continued to stare at him, her blue eyes swimming in tears. "You can stay with us."

Kate stared at her daughter. "Mary, what a thing to say."

Mary blinked back her tears and gave her mother a defiant look. "Why can't he stay? Everyone needs a family."

Kate's shock softened. "You're right."

"Don't you *want* to stay?" Dougie asked.

Hatcher's eyes turned to liquid coal. "I can't think of any place I'd rather be." He gave each child a gentle look. "But I can't stay." He raised his eyes to Kate and smiled—regretfully.

Her heart sang. He didn't want to leave.

If she could stop time it would be at this moment—this tender, fragile moment when the four of them shared a common place, acknowledged a single wish.

How would she manage when he left? To still the pain that didn't have the kindness to wait until he left to make itself known, she forced her thoughts to the farm.

The seed would be in the ground but then there was haying and eventually, God willing and with the gift of rain, the crop to harvest. She could hire someone with a threshing machine. But she didn't want to go back to what she was before he came—driven to do it all, driven to keep the farm at all costs. The one cost she hadn't thought about, had overlooked, was her children.

Yet it was for them that the farm had to remain intact. Never would she allow them to experience the fear and cold and misery of not having a solid roof over their heads. Never would they know the feeling of stomach-clenching uncertainty about the future.

Jeremiah told her as long as she held on to the farm, they would be safe and sound. It had been harder than she imagined, more work, more responsibility.

If only Hatcher would stay…

Together they could manage nicely. But it wasn't for the sake of her children or the farm she wanted him to stay. It was for her.

She hadn't been lonely since Hatcher came. She could look out the window any time of the day and see him, slouched into a comfortable posture on the tractor, or heading to or from the barn, milk pails swinging from his hands, or striding across the prairie on his way from the little shanty.

How could she, in such a short time, have grown used to seeing him? Anticipated looking up and glimpsing him nearby. Felt settled and safe by his very presence.

How ironic. She'd never before felt safer and it was with a man accused of murder, though Hatcher could no more murder someone than Mary could. It just wasn't in him.

"Is there any way I can persuade you to stay?" she asked.

The lines around his eyes deepened. His lips flattened as he met Kate's begging gaze. "I can't."

She nodded, ducked her head to hide her disappointment. "Finish eating," she murmured to the children. "There's chocolate cake for dessert."

They ate in silence. Silence? "The wind has died down."

Everyone cocked their head and listened then resumed eating without comment but even the cake didn't excite them. The children were saddened at the idea of Hatcher leaving.

They finished up. Kate offered tea. Hatcher refused and pushed from the table. But before he could escape, an automobile growled into the yard. Kate glanced out the window and groaned. "Doyle again?" She hurried to the door at the sound of his knock.

"Hello, Doyle. Have you come to make sure we weathered the storm?"

"I knew you'd be fine." He peered past her shoulder. "What's he doing in your house? I thought he'd be gone."

Chapter Ten

Hatcher's gut twisted so he wished he hadn't eaten. He'd hoped this moment wouldn't come. He knew better. He never allowed himself get close to people. It carried too many risks.

This time saying goodbye would hurt even worse than his father's goodbye.

Yet knowing that, he'd spent the afternoon in the luxury of feeling things, thinking things, wishing things that could never be his.

It was time to accept the inevitable; he was destined to be a wanderer and a vagabond.

*The Lord's anger was aroused that day and he swore this oath: because they have not followed me wholeheartedly, not one of the men twenty years old or more who came up out of Egypt will see the land I promised on oath...*he continued reciting the passage until he reached the verse that seared his brain. *He made them wander in the desert forty years, until the whole generation of those who had done evil in his sight was gone.* Numbers thirty two, verses eleven through thirteen.

His desert included the ocean, the mountains and the parched prairie.

And for a few days, this oasis of longing and belonging, hope and despair.

It was time to return to the desert. That solitary, desolate place. He'd be more alone than he'd ever been but he didn't regret one minute of the time he'd lingered here. Memories of Kate and her children would be his companion in the days to come.

He'd move on as soon as he did the thing he'd promised Kate—put in the crop. In the meantime, he would help with the chores and he grabbed the milk buckets. "I'm just leaving." But when he tried to push past Doyle, the man blocked the door.

"Exactly where are you going?"

Hatcher understood the man's unspoken order. But he wouldn't allow Doyle to tell him when and where. "To milk the cows."

"Think again. You need to be gone for good."

Hatcher grinned, knowing it would annoy the other man. "I'll go when I'm done."

Kate's angry look should have warned Doyle, but he ignored her. "Doyle, he's putting in the crop. You know that."

"He's a mur—"

Kate clapped her hands. "Children, go outside and see how Shep is. Check on your bunny and make sure it's safe. Don't come back until I call you." She jerked Doyle from the door so the children could leave. Mary hurried out as if she couldn't get away fast enough.

"Momma." Dougie started to protest, sensing he was about to miss something and not wanting to.

"Go." She pushed him after his sister.

Hatcher tried to slip out after them but Doyle stepped in front of him.

"Like I started to say, murderers are not welcome here."

Kate leaned back, her eyes burning. "Doyle, we've been over this before. Obviously Hatcher isn't a murderer or he'd be in prison. Besides, I say who is welcome here."

Doyle stared at Hatcher, his washed-out blue eyes snapping with dislike.

Hatcher returned his look. He had long ago learned to deny any emotion but this man's dictatorial attitude toward Kate made Hatcher's skin prickle. Did he think he could order the woman around and she'd meekly obey? He squelched the emotion. Replaced it with studied indifference. Gave the man a look that said his opinion carried as much value as fly guts.

"Is this your mode of operation? You worm your way in with a widow and then take advantage of her. And if anyone interferes, they mysteriously die? I wonder how many people you've murdered since Loggieville."

Some people wanted to believe the worst about others because it somehow made them feel superior. Hatcher had seen it time and again. Not that anyone had before accused him of repeated murders. But he'd seen the quick judgments men often passed. A man refused to offer a job and suddenly becomes a Commie. Someone hoards his last bite of food and he's accused of stealing it. As if calling a difference of opinions something evil didn't brand both the accused and the accuser. *Judge not, that ye be not judged. For with what judgment ye judge, ye shall be judged: and with what measure ye mete, it shall be measured to you again.* Matthew chapter seven, verses one and two.

Hatcher knew how to deal with people like Doyle. Walk away. Don't give the satisfaction of letting them see their words mean anything. But he wouldn't walk away and leave Kate to deal with this man. Even if she intended to marry him. He stood his ground, staring at the man hard enough to burn a hole through his skin.

Kate surged forward. "Doyle, I will not allow you to make such vile accusations in my house." She planted her hands on Doyle's chest, glowering as she pushed him out the door.

Doyle looked startled. Maybe even a little scared. Then he took a step back and straightened his suit jacket.

Hatcher repressed a smile. Silly little man. Unsure of himself, he accepted no limits in the quest to prove to himself and everyone else his importance—the most dangerous sort of person.

Doyle gave Hatcher a look that reminded Hatcher of a rabid dog he'd once seen—full of hate and meanness. "You might fool Kate but you don't fool me. I know you're up to something. And I intend to find out what it is."

Hatcher shrugged and stepped past the man. "Come along and you can see for yourself. I'm just going to milk the cows." He took his time as he headed toward the barn, shamelessly listening to the conversation between Kate and Doyle.

"How dare you act like that on my farm? Who do you think you are? You don't own me. Or my farm." He could hear the anger in Kate's voice, imagined the way her eyes would bore into the man.

"Kate, it's for your own good. He's a murderer."

Weaselly little whine.

"If you really believe that, tell the sheriff. Have him arrested."

"I told you. Everyone is afraid to testify against him. Afraid of his violent anger."

Kate snorted. "I've seen him handle things without ruffling a hair. In fact—"

Hatcher glanced back to see Kate jabbing her finger at Doyle's chest and he grinned. Doyle had pushed too far and he would soon discover the depth of Kate's spirit—something he thought a man who planned to marry her should already be acquainted with.

She stuck her face close to Doyle's. "I've seen more anger from you in the last five minutes than I've seen from Hatcher his entire stay."

"Kate, trust me. He's a danger to you and the children."

Kate snorted. "I can't imagine where you're getting this information. I know it isn't true. Maybe you should look for the facts instead of believing falsehoods."

"I don't know how he's done it but he's duped you. You need to trust me on this matter. I understand these thing far better than you."

"I admit I don't know legal terms but you don't know people like I do."

Hatcher grinned as he ducked into the barn where he could no longer hear the conversation. Kate was right about knowing people better than Doyle. Doyle didn't even know Kate.

But she didn't know him—Hatcher. He did have murder in his heart when Jerry died. His anger ruled his actions. It was judged accidental but he'd been running from his anger since his release, afraid of its evil power.

As long as he didn't let himself get close to anyone, as long as he didn't care about anything, he could control his anger but he'd been here long enough to start caring about Kate. About her children. He'd crossed his mental line. He had to leave before anyone got hurt.

Yet part of him wanted to stay and protect her, care for her.

He pulled a stool up beside the patient Jersey and milked her. A man could find satisfaction in regular chores like this.

It wasn't possible. One more day and he'd be done the seeding and on his way.

When he took the milk to the house, Doyle and his fancy car were gone.

Kate met him at the door. "I'm sorry for what he said. You have to realize he doesn't speak for me."

Hatcher let himself look into her eyes. They had none of the fire and anger he'd seen when she challenged Doyle. He felt his resolve swirling in their warm brownness.

"You believe me, don't you?" she asked.

He jerked his gaze away. Stepped back three feet. "I believe you." He wouldn't look at her, wouldn't allow himself to be tempted by the welcome in her eyes.

He remembered the way she'd smiled at him earlier this afternoon out on the prairie, a smile full of warmth and caring. Welcome even? He'd let himself believe so for a bit. Even let himself respond to it.

Only years of practice enabled him to successfully bury the thought.

"He's not the sort of man you should marry." He jerked his chin back. He should not have spoken the words aloud.

Kate looked equally surprised at his statement. Then she grinned, making him forget he'd moments ago forbidden himself to think how ferociously beautiful she was when she smiled, how her eyes widened as if surprised then softened unexpectedly, how the sun kissed her skin with uncommon warmth.

She snorted, signaling laughter that filled his heart with a waterfall of pleasure. "I'm not going to marry him. Truth is, I'm not sure the offer is still open."

She sobered, pinned him with a demanding look. "Hatcher, I know you didn't murder anyone. What really happened? What are you running from?"

"You know nothing about me." His voice grated past the tightness in his chest. "You don't understand the damage my anger can do."

What would she say if she knew the truth? He wanted to tell her. Perhaps she deserved to hear what happened after her defense of him. Even as he excused himself, he knew it wasn't for her he wanted to tell. He ached to share the whole sordid story with someone who would not condemn him. But would telling change her faith in him? More importantly, would it change him? He knew it wouldn't.

"Hatcher, I want to know because I care about you, but if it's something you don't want to talk about, I understand."

The sweet softness of her voice proved his undoing. He edged back as if the movement could put a safe distance between Kate and his past. "I was known for my quick temper. I would fight at the drop of a hat." He snorted. "Or the drop of a shirt or a teasing word. Anything set me off. It was inevitable that one day the anger in me would hurt someone." He watched her closely to see when her expression would grow cold, shocked, condemning. To her credit she continued to look concerned.

"And that someone was…"

"Jerry Wilson."

"You didn't kill him."

Her unwavering faith shook him as though he stood

outside in a raging dust storm. For a moment he couldn't speak. Could barely breath.

"So what happened?"

"We fought. I knocked him down. He struck his head and died."

"So it was an accident?"

"I had murder in my heart. 'But I say unto you, That whosoever is angry with your brother without a cause shall be in danger of the judgment: and whosoever shall say to his brother, Raca, shall be in danger of the council: but whosoever shall say, thou fool, shall be in danger of hellfire.' Matthew chapter five, verse twenty-two."

"Why were you so angry?"

She put it in the past tense as if it no longer existed. He didn't intend she'd get the chance to be proven incorrect.

"The reasons don't matter." He could no longer face this woman. He turned on his heel and headed for the shanty.

She called after him, "'And the Lord said unto her, Neither do I condemn thee.'"

Her words offered hope that didn't belong to him and he shut his mind to her voice.

Chapter Eleven

Kate braked to a sudden stop in the churchyard, climbed from the truck and smoothed her dress as best she could. The heat and dust of the drive hadn't improved its appearance.

"Hurry, children. We're late."

Hatcher hadn't shown up to help with the chores and she'd grown slack about getting things done in a hurry. She'd barely had time to change and settled for tying her hair back with an ecru ribbon.

They hurried inside. Doyle sat in his customary place, room beside him for the three of them. She wondered if he'd save her a place after his parting words yesterday.

"I expect you to come to your senses by tomorrow."

Thankfully, she had.

They slipped in beside him. He met her gaze briefly, his too-blue eyes sober, inquisitive. As usual, he was immaculate, not a hair on his head out of place. She felt his quick look of disapproval at her rumpled, windblown look. She flashed a quick, nervous smile, mouthed, "sorry," wanted to explain life didn't always leave time for meticulous grooming.

But the service began and he pointedly turned his attention to the front.

She sank beside him, shushed the children and tried to concentrate on the proceedings, but the sun trumpeted through the windows, baking the inhabitants. The discordant music grated her nerves to rawness. The sound had never before bothered her. Today she was too tired to ignore it. She hadn't slept well at all. If she wasn't angry with Doyle for his inexplicable dislike of Hatcher, she fretted over Hatcher's situation. Seemed the man carried a dreadful burden of guilt. One he needed to get rid of. God surely didn't expect him to swelter beneath it.

But mostly she dreaded the awful loneliness that would consume her after Hatcher's departure.

She shifted, wished she could dab at the perspiration soaking the back of her neck and jerked her head toward the sound of a fly banging into the window.

Doyle stiffened. She could feel his silent warning to sit still and she hid a sigh as she fixed her eyes on the preacher.

Suddenly, the words of the sermon broke through.

"We worry about things we shouldn't worry about. Things we should leave in God's hands." The preacher paused and smiled around at the congregants.

"I think this story illustrates the point. There was once a man struggling along the road with a heavy load. His back bent from the weight, his steps grew smaller and smaller. He wondered if he'd make it to town. But then a wagon pulled up beside him. The driver called, 'I'll give you a ride, friend.' Gratefully, the man pulled himself to the seat and the driver flicked the reins and continued his journey. After a few minutes, the driver turned to the man. 'Friend, why don't you get rid of that

heavy load? Put it in the wagon box.' The man shook
his head. 'I couldn't do that. It's enough you give me
a ride. You shouldn't have to carry the pack, as well.'"

Light laughter filled the pause.

"We need to give God our burdens and trust Him
to carry them."

Kate sighed. If only Hatcher could have heard this
message. What was she thinking? No finger-pointing.
As Jeremiah often said, you point a finger at someone
and three point back at you.

She readily admitted she needed to hear this message. She worried about her farm, having a home, so
many things. She needed to trust God to take her burdens.

The service ended, rustling filled the church as people prepared to leave.

"Doyle," she whispered.

"We'll talk outside." He sounded pleased with himself.

He'd be less pleased with her when she'd had her
say. She stood, smoothed her Sunday dress, hoped her
collar was straight.

Doyle stepped aside for her and the children to go
ahead. They marched down the aisle like cattle driven
to pasture.

"Over there," he murmured, jabbing his finger past
her to indicate the corner of the churchyard farthest
from the little graveyard.

"Children, run and play until I call you."

They crossed the yard. She turned to confront Doyle
but he spoke first. "Is he—"

She cut him off. "Doyle, I have something to say
to you."

He was a fine-looking man. Perhaps a bit too fine.

He could use a few wrinkles, a smudge or two to make him real. He wore an expectant look of self-satisfaction.

"Doyle, I can't marry you."

His eyes flashed brittle blue. His mouth flopped twice before he could speak. "It's because of that man, isn't it?"

She wished it were. "I realize I don't love you and I can't marry a man I don't love."

He studied her with narrowed eyes.

She hoped her smile was gentle, conciliatory.

"Did you love Jeremiah?" he demanded.

The question sliced through her. No, she hadn't love her husband with the heart-exploding kind of love she felt for Hatcher. Guilt tinged her thoughts. "I respected him greatly." Let him come to any conclusion he wished. But she didn't respect Doyle. Not after his recent behavior.

He drew himself up, stepped back, his nose curled as though she'd developed a strong odor. "You will never keep your farm. When it goes to the highest bidder, I'll buy it and sell it at profit. Something you know nothing about."

She hadn't expected him to be overjoyed at her announcement, but neither had she expected him to be vindictive.

"You'll come crawling to me on your hands and knees."

She could only stare. She grew aware of people glancing their direction. Sally hovered nearby, her face awash in concern. She turned back to the man. "Doyle, I wish you all the best."

He shot her a look that would wither the trees around the graveyard and spun around, practically mowing Sally down.

"Maybe you can talk some sense into your friend. Convince her it's foolish to keep company with a murderer."

Kate's knees melted, tears stung her eyes. She ordered her legs to straighten and sniffed back the tears. She wouldn't wipe at them in front of everyone.

Sally hurried to her side.

Kate wanted to throw herself into her friend's arms but again refused to fuel her neighbors' curiosity. Instead, she edged around so Sally blocked their view.

Sally grabbed her hand. "A murderer—what did he mean?"

Kate shuddered back a sob.

"Are you okay?" Sally demanded.

Kate managed a nod. "He's angry because I told him I couldn't marry him."

Sally yanked her arm. "Are you completely crazy? Marriage to Doyle would be the best thing for you."

Kate stiffened her spine. "I don't love him."

"He can offer you a life of luxury and ease."

Her jaw began to ache. "That's not what I want."

"You *are* crazy."

Kate looked over Sally's shoulder to where Frank stood, shifting from foot to foot, glancing back and forth from his wife to Doyle, who strode rapidly away. Kate smiled. Frank would chase the man down and pummel him if he threatened Sally. "Are you saying you'd give up your life with Frank for a life of ease with a man you didn't love?"

Sally's expression hardened. "I might."

Kate's gaze raced back to her friend. "You don't mean that."

"I suppose not." There was a shrug in her voice. "But

I get dreadfully tired of the work and worry and futileness of trying to survive on a dirt farm."

Kate's mouth cracked at the corners of her smile. "At least you have a home."

"At least I have a home." Sally sighed, looked unsatisfied, then brought her gaze back to Kate and studied her with narrow-eyed concentration. "Who is the murderer?"

Kate shook her head. People seemed reluctant to leave, waiting to discover the same thing. Their murmured curiosity scratched at her senses.

"It's that hobo, isn't it? I told you he was no good. You should have listened to me from the start."

A sigh as big as the sky filled Kate's lungs and escaped in a hot blast. "He isn't a murderer."

"Doyle made up a lie?"

"Not exactly."

Sally shook Kate's arm. "Then 'exactly' what did he mean?"

"He had no right to say anything. The man deserves to leave his past behind. He shouldn't have to run from people's cruelty for something he didn't do." Her words blasted as hot as the scorching sun.

"What didn't he do?"

"He didn't kill the man. It was an accident. The courts said so. Don't you think it's time he was allowed to start anew?" She hadn't meant to sob the last word.

"You've fallen in love with him." Sally's words rang with disapproval.

Kate faced her friend squarely, thought to deny it but suddenly couldn't keep it a secret any longer. She put her arm through Sally's and pulled her close, led them toward the fence. "So what if I have?" She meant to sound defiant but couldn't stop the sob that accompanied her words. "He's leaving as soon as the crop is in unless I can persuade him to stay."

"Kate Bradshaw. How can you even think such a thing? Listen to me. Get rid of him immediately. As soon as you get home. Then go to Doyle and tell him you were wrong. Marry the man while you can."

Kate jerked away, put several feet between them. "I have to get my crop seeded." She didn't care a hair about the crop but surely Sally would appreciate the need.

"I'll get Frank to finish your crop. Just get rid of that hobo. A murderer." She shook her head. "I knew the first time I saw him he'd be bad news for you."

Kate stopped walking. "I thought you of all people would understand."

"I understand you are making a huge mistake."

"You don't know the first thing about him, yet you're willing to condemn him. Doesn't seem very Christian."

"It's common sense. A God-given quality you seem to have lost."

Kate gulped back a sadness that ached like forever. Never had she felt so alone. Abandoned by everyone she thought she could count on.

She spun away. "I have to go." She called the children, got them into the truck without anyone sidling up to her to demand answers. Silent and broken, she turned the vehicle toward home.

Mary, seated in the middle, stared straight ahead. "Momma, what did Mr. Grey mean?"

The brittle sun stung Kate's eyes and she blinked hard to clear her vision. She wanted to spare Mary's feelings, protect her from the awfulness of that ugly word. "He spoke in anger."

"But he said…did he mean Hatcher?"

Dougie turned from peering out the window. "What about Hatcher?"

"Mr. Grey said—"

Kate interrupted her daughter. "Don't say it, Mary." Mary's face crumpled. Tears flooded her eyes.

"Honey, I'm sorry you had to hear that. It was unkind of Mr. Grey to say it." Doyle would excuse it as the truth, but sometimes the truth didn't need to be so brutal.

"What about Hatcher?" Dougie demanded.

"He's leaving soon." If he hadn't already. It hurt to say it out loud. She could understand him not wanting to face the cruel curiosity of others, but how awful that unkindness should drive him away. She groaned.

"Momma?" Mary's worried voice made Kate realize she must hide her feelings better. She would not let her children suffer any more than she could help.

"We'll soon be home." Maybe Hatcher would still be there, and they could enjoy his presence for a few more hours. She swallowed her agony as she faced the reality of tomorrow. He'd finish seeding and leave. If he hadn't already.

She forced her attention to the struggling crops of the neighbors. The plants that survived yesterday's dust storm wilted under the brassy sun.

As she turned up the driveway, she glanced toward the shanty. The door stood open.

There was no sign of Hatcher.

Dougie bounded from the truck. "Can I go see Hatcher?"

"No. He might be gone already. We all know he's going, don't we?"

"Yes, Momma," they chorused in sad alto voices.

"Then we might as well get used to it." How easy the

words, how difficult to make her heart accept them. He *could* stay. That's what hurt the most. He could face the pointing fingers, the whispers and prove he was innocent. Didn't running make him look guilty?

She flung into the house. "Get changed and play outside. I'll call you when dinner is ready." She hurried to her room to shed her hot Sunday dress.

Let him leave. It didn't matter to her. She'd manage. She wouldn't miss his slow smile, his steady kindness, the dark flash in his eyes when he didn't know she saw him watching her.

Moaning, she sank to the edge of the bed.

Yes, she'd survive. She'd manage. She just didn't know how she'd mask the pain.

She lowered her head to her hands. "God, if it's possible, persuade Hatcher to stay. If he won't, if it's best for him to move on, give me the strength to handle it." Remembering the morning's sermon, she added, "You can carry my concerns as easily as you do me."

When thou passest through the waters, I will be with thee: and through the rivers, they shall not overflow thee: when thou walkest through the fire, thou shalt not be burned; neither shall the flame kindle upon thee. For I am the Lord thy God, the Holy One of Israel thy Savior.

"Thank you, God."

Hatcher would know where to find the verse. Smiling, she picked up her Bible and began to look for it. After a few minutes she located it. "Isaiah chapter forty-three." She'd be prepared if she got a chance to tell Hatcher about the verse. Feeling more peaceful, she returned to the kitchen and sliced bread to make sandwiches for dinner.

Mary raced into the house and grabbed the pail of scraps.

"What are you doing with that?"

"The chickens are out."

Kate groaned. She didn't want to face the blazing hot sun again especially in the middle of the day. "Where's Dougie?"

"I can do it. Hatcher's going to show me how to trick the chickens."

Kate stared at her departing daughter. This was Mary? The child who both hated and feared chickens? Hatcher was still here? She rushed to the window.

Yes, Hatcher stood at the chicken house talking to Mary, pointing first at the pail of peelings then the chickens.

Mary nodded several times then with Hatcher watching, marched into the chicken yard. She stopped at the far side, tossed a few peelings on the ground and chanted. "Here, chicken. Here, stupid chicken. Come and eat. Cluck, cluck."

At the sound of food, the chickens headed for the gate. Some, as usual, ran into the fence, squawking and shedding a flurry of feathers.

Kate blinked when Mary laughed. Mary continued to call the birds, tossing out handfuls of peelings as she backed away. As the last bird raced in for a snack, Mary dashed out and threw the gate shut, leaning against it, her triumphant smile gleaming. Hatcher patted her shoulder.

Kate watched them through a blur of tears. The children needed him as much as she did. Would that argument convince him?

Hatcher saw her watching from the window, kept his gaze locked on hers as he straightened. Across the distance, through the dusty glass, his gaze burned away every doubt. Her heart skittered in her throat. He felt something. She knew it. Surely she could convince him to stay.

She lifted her hand, waggled her fingers and mouthed, "Come for dinner."

He shook his head, spoke to Mary again then strode toward the shanty.

Kate leaned over the windowsill as pain sliced through her. She pulled herself together and called the children for dinner.

"Did you see me, Momma?" Mary asked. "Hatcher said chickens were the stupidest thing God made apart from rocks." Mary giggled before she went on. "Said I could trick them because I was tons smarter. He said if I threw the food away from me instead of at my feet, the chickens wouldn't even come near me. He was right, wasn't he, Momma?" She sobered. "He's smart, you know."

Kate stared at her shy, nervous daughter. The man had helped her in a way she, the child's mother, hadn't. And it was so simple. Why had she never thought to give the child coping skills instead of hoping she'd outgrow her fears?

Couldn't he see how badly they all needed him?

The sun continued its journey westward in the brittle blue of the sky. Kate sat in the shade of the house, fanning herself as she tried to read. Her mind wandered over to the shanty. What was Hatcher thinking? Feeling? Did he dread the parting as much as she?

Suddenly she remembered something.

"Mary." Her daughter sat on the ground beside her, playing with a doll. Dougie had gone to play in the barn. Seems they had all sunk into the stupor of the day. She blamed it on the heat, though there seemed no point in pretending they didn't all feel at odds because of Hatcher's impending departure. "Mary, did you see any of the Sandstrums at church?" Kate hated to admit she'd been so wrapped up in her own drama she couldn't say if they'd been or not.

"No. I looked for them. I hoped Mrs. Sandstrum would bring the baby. I so want to see her. But not even Mr. Sandstrum was there."

Axel had come every Sunday, even when Alice couldn't. A terrible thought bit at Kate's mind. Had the baby worsened? Died? Or was Alice sick? She'd have to be awfully sick to make Axel break his routine.

"Run and get your brother. We're going over to see them."

Mary dashed away, cheering.

Kate could only pray. *God, may they be safe.* She reached for the box of baby things she's sorted for Annie then hesitated. What if they were no longer needed? She wouldn't take them until she knew for sure.

The children climbed into the truck, but Kate hesitated. She didn't want them to be in the Sandstrum house if…but she didn't want them waiting out in the sun or playing unsupervised. She could imagine the mischief Dougie would find.

Her gaze shifted to the shanty. "Wait in the shade." She marched toward the shack, the dry grass brittle under her feet, grasshoppers flying before her.

Hatcher sat in the doorway, tipped back in one of the old chairs, his feet propped on the doorjamb, his Bible on his lap. When he saw her, he dropped the chair to all fours and leaped to his feet in one swift movement. "What's wrong?"

"I hope I'm worrying needlessly, but Axel wasn't at

church today. He never misses, even when Alice is sick. I'm going over to check on them."

"Can I do something?"

She smiled. "I hoped you'd ask. I want you to come along…." She didn't want him solely for the children. She wanted his strength to lean on if… "Just in case."

He drew back, looked stunned. He opened his mouth, closed it again, shook his head. "I can't."

"I don't want the children—"

"You could leave them here."

She could but no way could she face the dreadful possibility that lay across the fields. "I already told them they could go and Mary is hoping to see the baby." *God, let the baby be well. Let Mary get to hold a live baby.*

He dropped his Bible to the chair and accompanied her with all the enthusiasm of Dougie on his way to bed.

She let him drive, holding Dougie on her lap as they headed for the Sandstrums. She needed the comfort of his warm, vigorous little body.

Axel came to the door as they drove in. At least he was well and accounted for.

She jumped from the truck. "Stay here—" she told the children "—until I call you."

"They'll be okay with me," Hatcher said.

She clung to his steady gaze for a moment, wanting to point out how much they all needed him. Then she took a deep, fortifying breath and went to Axel. "Alice and Annie?"

"Inside." He tilted his head to the house. "Little one is starting to grow."

"Thank God." She rushed into the house to see Alice looking so much better than a few days ago, feeding Annie her bottle. She grabbed a chair and sank into it. "When none of you were in church, I feared the worst."

Alice laughed. "We're fine, thanks to you and your help, but thanks for worrying. When Axel went out to start the truck he discovered he had a flat tire. He knew he'd never fix it in time so decided he might as well stay home."

"Kate?" Hatcher stood in the doorway.

She smiled. "Tell the children to come and meet baby Annie."

Alice let the children hold the baby, invited them all for tea. Hatcher hesitated but Axel drew him outside to look at the crops.

A short while later, they headed back home.

As they neared the driveway, a gray car drove out and headed for town.

"Doyle," Kate muttered. What did he want? She never expected to see him on a personal basis again. Couldn't think she'd want to.

Kate let the children out at the house. "Thank you for coming with me," she said to Hatcher.

"I'm glad you didn't really need me."

But I did. I do.

"Unfortunately you missed your lawyer friend."

"I can't imagine what he wants."

Hatcher jerked his head in what might have been a nod and headed toward the shanty.

Chapter Twelve

Hatcher was up before dawn the next day. By the time the sky turned silvery and pink, he'd filled the drill boxes for the last time. As the sun broke over the horizon, he started around the field.

Kate came to the door and stared in his direction. He couldn't see her expression but guessed at her surprise at him starting work before dawn. He drank in the sight of her, cinnamon-colored hair tied back neatly, wearing a familiar cotton housedress—a mixture of pink and brown flowers. He knew he would never drink his fill of her, yet he wanted to store up memories for the future.

When she waved him to come for breakfast, he shook his head. He intended to finish this job without spending any more time with her. He hadn't planned to go over yesterday, either, until he saw Mary open the gate of the chicken pen and clap her hands until the birds scattered across the yard.

He'd crossed the yard then. "What are you doing, Mary?"

"Chasing the chickens." Her tone suggested he should be able to see that for himself.

"Why?"

"Mr. Grey said a bad word about you."

Hatcher sighed. Everyone he knew and cared about was bound to be hurt simply because he had stayed too long. "You shouldn't pay any attention."

Mary's eyes were awash in tears. "I don't want you to leave."

"I must. Someday you'll understand that it's for the best."

She stomped her foot. "I'm tired of being told that."

He chuckled. "Can't say as I blame you. But this time it's true."

"Then I don't want to stay on the farm." She waved her arms, laughing mirthlessly when the nearby chickens squawked and flapped away.

"But where would you go?"

The child didn't answer.

"Didn't this farm belong to your poppa? What would he want you to do?"

Still no answer.

"Do you want your mother to marry Mr. Grey?"

"No. I don't like him. He just pretends to be nice to Dougie and me."

"Then maybe the farm is a better place to be."

"Maybe."

"Do you think you should get the chickens back in the pen?"

She shuddered. "I hate chickens."

"They're the dumbest thing God made except for rocks."

She'd laughed and let him show her how to outsmart the birds.

He would miss the children.

He clamped his jaw tight. No point in thinking such things. *But whoso shall offend one of these little ones which believe in me, it were better for him that a mill-stone were hanged about his neck, and that he were drowned in the depth of the sea.* Matthew eighteen, verse six.

She'd already been offended once because of him. It wouldn't happen again. He was prepared to sit on the tractor until he finished this field and then move on. Leave them all in peace.

Only when he turned the corner closest to the house, Kate stood at the furrow. He should have known she wouldn't let him be. Obstinate, headstrong woman. Pity the man who married her.

No way he could ignore her unless he wanted to run over her. He stopped the tractor and waited as she marched toward him.

"I brought you breakfast, seeing as you wouldn't stop." She held out a towel-covered plate.

"Not particularly hungry."

She didn't withdraw the offered plate. They did battle with their eyes, no words necessary for her to make her message plain. She didn't plan to take No for an answer.

"You started early today," she said.

"I'll finish today." He left the rest unsaid. *Then I'll move on*.

The egg yolks were runny. Just the way he liked them. The bread, freshly baked, soaking up butter. He concentrated on the food, one of the pleasures of life. Good food, good weather, a dry place to lay his head. Simple, everyday things he would find on his travels. What more did a man need?

"I saw how you helped Mary yesterday." Kate's voice carried expectation.

He nodded. "Big job to chase chickens." He knew it

wasn't really what she wanted to talk about, but he offered nothing more.

"You're good with the children. You've taught them
a lot." A long, waiting silence that Hatcher didn't intend to fill.

"Hatcher, don't you see how much we need you?
The children?" Her voice dropped to a whisper. "Me?"
She sucked in air as if she'd run a mile head on into the
wind. "You don't need to leave."

She thought she wanted him to stay, but she didn't
know what it meant. The name-calling, finger-pointing,
blaming. And that was the least of it.

He'd learned to keep his anger contained by walking
away from situations and people. The longer he stayed,
the more he let himself care, the more likely his anger
would escape his control. One man had already died,
others had been hurt in different ways from his vicious
anger. He would never put Kate and her children at risk
of such ugliness.

He gulped the rest of his breakfast and handed the
plate back. "Thank you." He headed the noisy tractor
down the field without a glance at Kate.

It took a great deal of concentration to recite Bible
verses throughout the morning, but he would not let his
thoughts dwell on anything else.

The hot sun hung straight over his head baking the
soil when he saw two cars approach. He recognized
Doyle's. Watched as the man climbed from his vehicle
and stared in Hatcher's direction. He recognized the
look. A warning to Hatcher that Doyle had taken control of things.

Why didn't the man let Hatcher finish so he could
be on his way?

Then he saw the insignia on the door of the second

vehicle. The law. Was it about to start all over? But he'd done nothing. Hadn't left the farm except to go to the Sandstrums.

A uniformed man stepped from the second vehicle. The men spoke to Kate, who'd come to the door, then headed toward Hatcher. Kate followed, talking, being ignored as the men strode across the field. The sheriff waved him down. Hatcher stopped the tractor and waited.

"Mr. Jones? Hatcher Jones," the lawman said.

"That's me."

"Would you step down?"

Hatcher hesitated. Whatever it was, he hadn't done it but from the look on both men's face, he guessed they wouldn't believe him. He jumped down and faced the sheriff. "What can I do for you?"

"You're under arrest."

"For what?"

"Robbery and vandalism, to start with."

Who had been robbed? Of what? But he kept his mouth shut. He was a hobo. Had been in jail before. Been accused of worse than this. And one thing he knew, his previous experience would be counted against him.

The sheriff clamped on handcuffs.

"He never left the farm. How could he have done it?" Kate protested.

"We have an eyewitness."

"Who?" Kate demanded.

"The storekeeper remembers him stopping there before."

"Did you?" Kate asked Hatcher.

She wondered if he was guilty? If she had any doubt

she'd already convicted him in her mind. "What is it I'm supposed to have done?"

Kate answered before the sheriff could explain. "They say you robbed Mr. Anderson's store."

"Did a pile of damage at the same time," the sheriff said, pushing Hatcher ahead of him off the field.

"Did you stop there at any time?" Kate asked, keeping at his side.

"I went by when I first came to town." The one and only time. He and three other hobos had picked through the garbage in the alley hoping to find something useful. Preferably edible. The owner had chased them away. He hadn't been to town since.

He hadn't even known the man's name. Mr. Anderson, huh? Wonder what he was supposed to have taken. And what he'd damaged.

"I understand you've been staying in that shanty over there. Let's have a look." The sheriff pushed Hatcher in that direction.

Kate continued to hop at Hatcher's side, trying to look at him and keep up. She fired questions at him and the other men. "Whose accusing Hatcher? What proof do you have? This is all wrong."

Hatcher ignored her. Would they need or want proof? He knew Doyle wasn't interested in the truth. He just wanted to get Hatcher out of the way. Punish him because Kate had defended him. And he couldn't say whether the sheriff wanted the truth or an easy scapegoat.

They reached his tiny quarters. Doyle burst through the door first.

His hand on Hatcher's handcuffs, the sheriff followed.

Kate remained at Hatcher's side. Doyle stepped to one side and waited for the sheriff to do his job.

Hatcher's belongings were rolled into a bundle.

"Were you planning on leaving, Jones?" the sheriff asked.

Hatcher didn't answer. The less he said the better. Besides, it was obvious he intended to move on.

But Kate had no such qualms. "It's no guilty secret he meant to leave as soon as the crop was in. He would have finished today if you hadn't interrupted his work."

"So he had it planned. Maybe meant to leave without finishing but couldn't leave the pretty lady," the sheriff mocked as he flipped open Hatcher's belongings and started to paw through them.

A jangle of coins and a wad of money rolled out.

The money wasn't his, though Hatcher didn't expect anyone to believe him. Someone had planted it. But who? Doyle? Was that what brought him to the farm last night? But why? He knew Hatcher was leaving. He posed no threat to the lawyer.

"What do we have here?" the sheriff demanded. "Care to explain this?"

Hatcher glowered at the man. He wouldn't say anything. He wouldn't lay the blame where it seemed most likely to belong—at Doyle's feet. Not when Kate seemed bent on marrying him no matter how much she said to the contrary. He couldn't ruin her chance of happiness. Not that it mattered. No one wanted the truth. No one would believe his innocence. He tried not to see the shocked look on Kate's face. She'd have to believe whatever she wanted.

"You can try explaining it to the judge." The sheriff jerked him around and not caring how the cuffs dug into his wrists.

He let the sheriff push him roughly into the back of the car and rode silently back to town, where he gave nothing but his name in way of a statement before he was shoved into a cell. The door locked behind him.

He stood behind the bars of the six-by-six-foot cell and stared hard.

Verses he'd memorized raced through his brain. *Surely the churning of milk bringeth forth butter, and the wringing of the nose bringeth forth blood; so the forcing of wrath bringeth forth strife.* Proverbs thirty, verse thirty-three.

He'd let his anger break forth too many times. It had caused strife. Death. *Be ye angry and sin not.* Ephesians four, verse twenty-six.

But his anger had led to sin. Even before it led to the death of another man. *For the wrath of man worketh not the righteousness of God.* James one, verse twenty.

God demanded repayment for Hatcher's anger and the death he'd caused. He'd known for ten years he would pay. Now was the time. He'd prepared himself for it. Just didn't think he'd care so much.

That was his mistake. He'd let himself care about Kate, her children, her happiness. After Doyle's first visit he knew he should move on. But he'd let his caring get in the way.

He rubbed his sore wrists and spun around. The narrow cot with its thin mattress would be hard and uncomfortable but he'd spent ten years getting used to sleeping on everything from rocky ground to wet snow. He stretched out and closed his mind.

"I want to see him."

Hatcher kept his eyes closed as Kate's demanding voice rang through the jail. Keys rattled and she was admitted to the cell block.

He heard her firm, hurried steps stop in front of the bars confining him. But he didn't stir, kept his breathing deep and slow.

"Hatcher, we have to talk."

He didn't move a muscle or a hair.

"Come on. Stop faking it and pay attention." She waited but when he refused to acknowledge her presence, she didn't let it deter her. "I know you didn't do it. I've seen the way you handle yourself. Whatever happened back when you were accused of murder, I know you didn't do that, either. You wouldn't hurt anyone. The court was right when it declared you innocent. Same as I know you didn't rob the store or anything else they say you did."

"Shouldn't you confine yourself to the facts," he murmured, without opening his eyes.

"What are the facts?" she asked, quietly pleading for an explanation. She waited a few seconds for him to answer.

But he wouldn't. The less she knew, the better.

"I am going to find out what really happened in Mr. Anderson's store."

He leaped from the cot, took the two steps that brought him to the bars and grabbed one on either side of her curled hands. "I don't want you getting involved. Find someone to finish putting in the crop. Go home and look after the children. Stay away from me."

She jerked back, her eyes wide. Surprised. Hurt.

Good. Better she should accept the truth about him and leave him alone.

Then her expression softened. Her eyes smoldered and she gripped the bars tighter, jammed her fists against his.

He stilled himself to keep from jerking back but he wouldn't let her see that her touch meant anything.

It didn't.

He wouldn't let it.

"Hatcher. I am going to find out what really happened." She stepped back totally unaffected by his best scowl. "You won't be able to do anything about it." She tapped the bars. "You'll be busy here."

And she left. Left him fuming. Powerless to do anything. Just like she so joyously pointed out.

Stubborn, stupid woman. She had no idea what she was getting into.

Chapter Thirteen

Kate drove home.

The scenery passed in a blur of old yellow from the dry pastures and sifted brown fields against a mockingly bright sky. A blackbird whistled, oblivious to the realities of life, content with his waving reed. Dust swirled in the open window and caught in her lashes, made her eyes water.

She gripped the steering wheel, welcomed the rattle of the old truck vibrating up her arm, jarring her spine. She reached the driveway, jerked too hard on the wheel as she turned, skidded, overcompensated and swerved toward the opposite ditch. Clamping down on her jaw sent a spasm up the side of her face. She held the wheel straight and bounced up the dusty trial to her house.

Shaking, she stopped, found she couldn't let go of the steering wheel, pressed her forehead to her hands, smelling oil and gas fumes and let the dust wash from her eyes.

Her insides knotted so painfully she couldn't breathe. Perhaps she had something wrong with her—an infection, a tumor. Only her agony wasn't physical. It came from deep in her soul. It began as something small when the sheriff cuffed Hatcher, grew when he drove Hatcher away in the back of his car, expanded as she followed in her truck.

But seeing Hatcher in jail, resigned and accepting, not speaking a word in his defense, making it clear he didn't intend to—

Even childbirth hadn't been as difficult to bear.

She straightened, scrubbed at her eyes with aching fingers and stared at her house and the newly planted fields. The earlier seeded ones should be showing green by now. But the seed wouldn't germinate without rain.

Somehow she could think of another crop failure, even the loss of her farm, with detachment. It's significance paled in comparison to Hatcher's situation.

He wouldn't tell the truth.

It was up to her to discover it and make it known.

The children would be home soon. She needed to wash her face, compose her expression and pray they hadn't heard about Hatcher's arrest.

Dougie burst through the door first. "Momma, where's Hatcher? Tommy said he got 'rested. Did he?"

Kate reached for her son. Glanced past him to Mary, who moved like a broken toy, her face pale and streaked from crying. She held her arm out to her daughter.

"Is it true, Momma?" the child whispered.

She held the children close and prayed for the right words to explain this and to comfort them. "I'm afraid it's true. But it's an awful mistake."

"What did he do?" Dougie asked.

"Is it about what Mr. Grey said?" Mary's words caught in her throat.

"Listen to me and listen good. Do either of you think Hatcher would do something bad?"

Mary shook her head emphatically but Dougie

looked doubtful. "I heard Teacher whispering to Mrs. Mackenzie. They didn't know I could hear them. They said—"

Kate took her son's chin and turned him to look full into his eyes. "People say things they shouldn't and others are too willing to believe them without bothering about the truth. Hatcher has been accused of something he didn't do."

Dougie's expression cleared. "I didn't think he'd do something bad. He told me a man was only as good as his word and should never give anyone reason to doubt him." He puffed out his chest but he quickly again deflated. "But Tommy said he's in jail."

"Yes, he is."

"But why, if he didn't do anything wrong?"

Kate hugged the children tight wishing she could explain the mistake, assure them it all would work out. "I intend to see he's out soon. But there's something you can do to help."

They both looked eager.

"We need to all pray for him." She bowed her head, held the children's hands and prayed as earnestly as she ever had. "Heavenly Father. We need Your help so badly. So does Hatcher. Help us know what to do, and most of all, keep Hatcher safe. Amen."

"I'll pray for him at bedtime," Dougie announced.

"I'm going to kneel beside my bed right now and pray," Mary said.

The two of them went to change their clothes and Mary, at least, to raise her own petition to God.

After three fruitless, frustrating days, Kate discovered trying to uncover the truth was tougher than she anticipated. At least the truth she wanted. She didn't believe Mr. Anderson's insistence he'd seen Hatcher lurking about the store several times. Kate knew Hatcher had been at the farm. Even with the sheriff pointing out there were plenty of opportunities for Hatcher's absence—when she went to town or visited the Sandstrums—Kate knew it didn't add up with the amount of work Hatcher did while she was gone.

But the sheriff smiled benignly as if to say as a woman she couldn't know for sure. Or perhaps his smirk meant he thought she was emotionally involved with Hatcher and prepared to lie for him.

She returned to the farm after another day of trying to ferret out the truth. She stared at the tractor in the middle of the field. She should try and put in the last few acres of seed but she couldn't think of the farm while Hatcher sat in jail. Nor could she bring herself to challenge the beast.

She moaned. If only she could see Hatcher. Take him something to eat. Assure herself he wasn't suffering physically. She couldn't imagine his mental suffering. But he refused to see her again. It was the sheriff who let it slip that Hatcher hadn't tried to get a lawyer.

She'd seen the resignation in Hatcher's expression, knew he wouldn't defend himself. He didn't expect a fair trial. She wondered if it even mattered to him.

Well, it mattered to her. He had to have a lawyer. A good lawyer would point out the discrepancy in the stories, insist on presenting the facts and not conjecture.

Besides Hatcher was a man of the open like her father. He would wither and die in prison. She could not allow that to happen. If he wouldn't hire a lawyer to defend himself, she would. She knew only one lawyer. Doyle. He had a reputation as a fighter for justice.

She pushed to her feet. There was time before the

children returned from school to pay a visit to Doyle's office. She smiled at the irony of it. He'd predicted she'd come begging on her hands and knees. She'd crawl on her belly if that's what it took to get him to defend Hatcher.

She changed into a pretty dress she seldom wore because she found it stiff and uncomfortable, a grey one with white collar and cuffs that Doyle had commented looked very becoming on her. She pulled her hair back and pinned it into a roll instead of letting it hang loose as she preferred.

Tucking a pair of clean white gloves into her pocket to slip on just before she entered his presence, she started the truck and headed for town.

Doyle's secretary greeted her coldy and slipped to the inner office to announce her.

Doyle strode out. "Well, well, well, so you've changed your mind?"

She lowered his eyes to hide the truth, hoped he'd think she was only being demure.

"I've come to talk business." She peeked up to see his reaction.

His eyebrows reached for his hairline. "Very well." He waved her into his private office, held a chair for her to sit facing his desk then went around and sat on the other side of the wide, polished surface. "Let me guess. You're ready to sell the farm and would like me to act as your agent?"

"I want to hire you."

He nodded. "That man I mentioned some time ago is gone but I'm sure we can quickly find someone else interested in buying the farm."

"Not to sell my farm."

His eyebrows shot up again. "Then what can I do for you?"

"I want to hire you to defend Hatcher."

He guffawed. "Surely you jest."

"You're the best lawyer I know." Only one but she figured adding that would defeat her purpose. "You believe in the justice system. Surely you want to see him given a fair trial."

"Why do you want to help him?" He studied her so intently she pretended she needed to fuss with her gloves.

"Because I know he's innocent."

"There's more to it than that."

She shrugged. "I guess he reminds me of my father." It wasn't the biggest reason, but one he might find acceptable.

Doyle's eyes narrowed as he continued to study her.

Her heart drummed against her ribs as she met his gaze, waited for his answer. He was Hatcher's only hope. She prepared to beg.

But he suddenly jerked his head decisively. "On one condition."

She nodded, prepared to agree to almost anything.

"You marry me."

Her mouth opened, but no words came out. She clamped it shut, swallowed hard, almost choked on her dry throat. She didn't love him. She didn't even care much about him any longer. She certainly didn't want to marry him.

But she knew if—no, when—Hatcher was released, he'd want to be on the road. There was no room for a wife and children in that sort of life. She would never make the mistake her mother had, following a man back and forth across the country, dragging her children through the cold and snow, never letting them stay in one place long enough to make friends, get an education, feel like somebody.

And if it meant Hatcher's freedom…

"Agreed."

"You'll sell the farm and move into town."

She could learn to like town. She'd have a nice house. Lots of nice things. The children would enjoy the benefits. Besides what difference did it make where she lived? God was with her the same on the farm or in town; owning her own home or ensconced in her husband's. God would be with her wherever she went. Besides, it wasn't the farm that mattered. It was Hatcher's freedom. "Will you let me bring Shep and the bunny?"

His lips curled so slightly. "As long as they're kept in the backyard."

"Then I agree."

They shook hands like business partners. Then he came around the desk and hugged her. She forced herself to return the embrace.

Back on the street, she leaned against the wall, took several cleansing breaths, stared at the jail across the street then headed home.

Not until she'd reached the safety of her own house did she collapse in a panting, panicked ball in the middle of her bed. She'd just promised herself and her farm to a man she didn't love in exchange for freedom for a man she did love. She would do it again. Gladly. Yet she shivered at the cost.

A vehicle rumbled into the yard.

She curled up tighter. She didn't care for a visit from anyone. Couldn't imagine who'd come calling unless for the purpose of asking nosy questions.

The motor died.

A visitor was inevitable. Kate scrambled to her feet, did her best to smooth the rumpled grey dress, wiped her eyes on the corner of the cotton dress laying discarded on a chair, scrubbed at her cheeks to hide any paleness and hurried from the room.

She glanced out the window, saw Sally climbing from her truck. Come to gloat, no doubt.

She waited for her friend to knock before she crossed the room and opened the door, determined to give Sally no reason to suspect her distress. "I expect you've come to say 'I told you so.'"

Sally remained on the step. "I came to see if you're still speaking to me after the way I acted."

The two faced each other, their argument making them wary and uncertain of how to proceed.

Sally lifted a hand, dropped it again. "I should have come sooner, when I heard what happened to Hatcher… but I was pouting. Kate, I am so sorry for the things I said." Her voice trembled.

Sally had been her friend and confidante too many years for Kate to harbor unforgiveness. She stepped back and indicated Sally should join her then turned to make tea.

"I've heard so many things," Sally said, her voice guarded as if fearing Kate's reaction. "What really happened?"

Kate put the tea to steep and sat down to face her friend. "At least you're asking for facts this time but do you really want the truth?"

"Of course."

"Hatcher has been falsely accused of robbery." She repeated the details.

"Are you certain it's a false charge?"

Kate gave her friend a look that dared her to question. "He was never in town. I've tried to get to the truth but everyone treats me like I'm some kind of weak-brained imbecile. However, I've done the best I can to help him." Despite her resolve to be strong and brave and not count the cost to herself, her voice cracked and to her utter amazement, tears washed her cheeks.

Sally sprang to her side, wrapped an arm around her shoulders. "Kate, I'm sure you've done all you could. It's in the hands of the authorities. The truth will be revealed."

Kate sobbed in great shudders.

Sally continued to try and comfort her. "Everything will work out. You'll see. Don't upset yourself about it."

Kate drew in a long draft of air, held it until her sobs subsided. "I expect things will work out now that I've arranged for Doyle to represent him."

Sally dropped to the nearest chair. "Doyle? And he agreed?"

Kate looked out the window. "With certain conditions."

"Such as?"

She jerked her gaze back to Sally, her eyes stinging with tears she would not release. "You'll be pleased to know I've taken your advice and agreed to marry Doyle. I've agreed to sell the farm." She clamped her lips shut, widened her eyes. She didn't want Sally to know how helpless she felt.

Sally gave her narrow-eyed study. "You agreed to marry him so he'd defend Hatcher?"

Kate nodded defiantly.

Finally Sally looked away, glanced upward as if exasperated.

Kate allowed herself to relax enough to sucked in a full breath.

"I wanted you to marry him," Sally said, "because I wanted you to be happy." Her voice fell to a whisper. "I don't want you to be miserable."

Kate blinked back tears. "I'm sure I'll appreciate the finer things of life."

Sally nodded. Suddenly she laughed. "I plan to be the first to visit you in your big house. You could serve me tea in the garden."

Kate pasted on a smile. "Won't that be fun?" But her gaze went to the vegetable garden she had labored over, the emerging potato plants to which she'd carried bucket after bucket of water. How often Hatcher had shown up to help her. She'd let herself dream of sharing the harvest with him.

Now she would likely have to abandon the garden. She couldn't imagine Doyle thinking it worth his time or hers to tend it. Perhaps new owners would reap the benefit.

She lifted her teacup to her mouth but couldn't swallow the liquid.

Chapter Fourteen

"Someone wants to see you." The deputy called through the closed door.

Hatcher lay on the hard cot counting again the cracks in the ceiling and reciting scripture. "Not entertaining today." He'd informed the sheriff he didn't care to see Kate. He didn't want her coming in, pushing at his disinterest, making him think of things he might want if he had a different life. He wanted to be left alone so he could forget. But Kate was a stubborn woman. Every day she came, demanding to see him. Every day he steadfastly refused. He'd learned to cover his ears against her pleas through the heavy door but despite every effort to be unaffected by her visits he couldn't help smile at the sound of her alternately arguing and begging the sheriff to let her in.

"It ain't your lady friend and it's 'extremely important.'"

"Not interested." He lifted a lazy hand and squished a bug on the wall.

A scuffle sounded on the other side of the door and then Kate's friend, Sally Remington, pushed her way in. He'd seen her a few times when she visited Kate.

Met her once when she accompanied Kate to the field with cold water for him.

"She wouldn't take no for an answer." The portly deputy stood helplessly in the open door.

Hatcher sighed as quietly as the spider climbing toward the window ledge. The deputy didn't know how to handle forceful women but at least he'd never been on duty when Kate stormed the place. Otherwise she would have bowled right over him. He could thank God and the sheriff that hadn't happened. Seeing Kate would make his self-control scramble like the fly buzzing in crazy circles over his head. *He that hath no rule over his own spirit is like a city that is broken down, and without walls.* Proverbs twenty-five, verse twenty-eight.

He figured Kate had sent her friend and flicked a blank look her direction. "Sorry, can't offer you a chair."

"This won't take long."

He snorted. "Good. 'Cause I'm short on sociability, too." But long on time which was proving to be his undoing. He'd spent many hours and years with no company but his own thoughts. He'd filled them with observations of nature and his fellow man. He'd filled them with God's word. It had been pleasant enough. Not so this time. With nothing to do but think, he couldn't keep stop himself from remembering every minute he'd spent with Kate. He could recall every gesture—the way she rubbed a spot on her cheek when she was stressed, the way she looked over the land with such pride and sometimes worry. The way she smiled at her children, her eyes brimming with love. He knew her scent whether hot and dusty after doing the chores or sweet with lilac-scented toilet water as she left for church. He knew the way her eyes lingered on him.

Knew what she wanted. How she'd built him into her dreams.

It could never be. *Flee also youthful lusts: but follow righteousness, faith, charity, peace, with them that call on the Lord out of a pure heart.* Two Timothy two, verse twenty-two. He would flee the rest of his days in order to ensure Kate lived a life of peace.

Mrs. Remington cleared her throat, brought him back to the here and now. "I'm not here for a social visit."

"Now that we've got that straight."

She stared at him long enough for him to wonder what she wanted and how long he'd have to wait until she told him.

"What do you think about Kate?"

He managed to hide the surprise jolting through his veins. What kind of question was that? "I think she's hardworking, determined and a good mother."

"That's not what I asked. What do *you* think of her?"

He closed his eyes, thought to be grateful the woman couldn't see his face. Stilled his features to reveal none of the pain scrapping his insides. The things he thought of Kate couldn't be expressed in simple words; they would require the whole sky as parchment, the oceans full of ink to even contain a fraction of what he felt. "She's hardworking, determined and a good mother." His hard-edged words scratched his throat in passing.

"Hatcher, I have to know if you care about her."

Care? A word too small to carry what he felt. "Why?"

"Would you stand by and let something or someone hurt her?"

He'd face two grizzlies and a mountain lion all at the same time if they threatened her. He stared at the pocked ceiling. Reality was, his situation wasn't conducive to bear wrestling. He snorted. "No. I'd walk out of here and stop them. Right through the bars. Quick as could be." He laughed, a bitter hollow sound.

"Well, she's done something really stupid and as far as I can see, you're the only one who can stop her."

"Right. Step aside. I'll be on my way." But his nerves tensed. "What did she do?"

"She's so determined to see you get a fair trial, she's hired a lawyer."

The skin on the back of his neck tightened. "Who?"

"Doyle."

He made an explosive sound and turned toward the wall. How would that insure a fair trial? He had been set up by the man.

"That's not the worst of it."

He continued to stare at the wall.

He didn't want to hear.

He couldn't stand not to know.

He wanted to forget Kate, forget he'd ever met her. Forget how she'd made him feel alive and whole. Made him briefly forget the specter of his past.

But he would never forget her. And in order to have even a pretense of peace, he had to make certain things were well with her.

"Tell me."

"She promised to sell the farm and marry him if he would."

"She what?" He jerked to his feet and in two steps faced the woman, wished he could bend the bars and walk out, put an end to Kate's stupidity. What a crazy, stubborn, adorable woman. "That's the stupidest thing I ever heard."

Sally nodded vigorously. "I agree, even though I used to think Doyle was the man she needed. But she's miserable. Doing her best to hide it because she's prepared to go through with it for your sake. What can we do about it?"

He ground around, strode the two steps to the wall and slammed his palm into the cold surface. He let his head drop and stared at the floor. By hanging around too long he'd brought this upon her. This was exactly the reason he didn't want Kate involved. He feared she'd get hurt though he hadn't guessed she'd do this.

He had to prevent her following through with this terrible decision.

There was only one thing he could think to do. The one thing that had saved his life in the past. He'd vowed he'd never go back, but for Kate he'd face anything.

He sucked air past his hot throat and returned to the bars. "Got paper and pencil?"

Sally opened her handbag and pulled out both.

"Write this down." He gave the name and address of a man. "Contact him and tell him what's happening."

Sally tucked the paper away. "I'll send a telegram straight away."

Hatcher gripped the bars long after she left. Would the man still be there? Would he help? Not that Hatcher deserved help. He deserved punishment, condemnation and judgment. But Kate did not understand what she'd agreed to. Doyle would try and control her. She'd be miserable trying to make herself happy.

God, keep Kate from doing something she'll regret the rest of her life.

Two days later Johnny Styles marched into the sheriff's office. Even before the outer door closed behind him, Hatcher heard his strident ringing voice and started to grin. He'd come.

The door to the cell area opened and Johnny strode

in. He'd aged since Hatcher last saw him. His hair had turned silver, his face developed more lines. But he still carried an air of authority that made men jump to attention when he entered a room. His suit jacket looked freshly pressed, his trousers sharply creased down the center. He looked as if he'd walked out of the tailor's shop, not spent many hours traveling west.

Hatcher scratched his elbow and sniffed. Sleeping and living in the same set of clothes for days, sharing his space with assorted vermin hadn't given Hatcher a chance for much grooming. He'd been allowed to shave only twice. He could smell himself coming and going. Course in a cell this size they were the same thing. He brushed at his trousers, pulled at his shirtsleeves knowing nothing he did would improve his looks.

"Well, boy. Here we are again." Johnny stuck his hand through the bars and shook Hatcher's hand, seemingly unmindful of how soiled Hatcher was. "How do you manage to get yourself into these situations?"

Hatcher shrugged. "I had nothing to do with this one." Except he'd hung around too long. If he'd headed down the road that first day, none of this would have happened. Kate would not be in such an unthinkable position.

"I got a detailed account from the woman who contacted me. I'll start digging as soon as I leave here. We'll find the truth."

"Thank you. I didn't want to bother you but—" Hatcher told him what Kate had done. "I don't want her marrying that man."

"You interested in her yourself?"

Hatcher had learned long ago to tell this man the truth, the whole truth and nothing but the truth. "Very interested, but nothing can come of it."

"Why not?"

His gut gave an almighty and painful twist. Why not? Because he didn't deserve a woman like Kate and she didn't need or deserve someone like him. But he put a shrug in his voice as he answered Johnny. "Because of who I am. What I did. Have you forgotten?"

Johnny leaned against the wall and studied Hatcher long and steady. Hatcher returned the look.

"You're still blaming yourself for what happened? Even though it was an accident?"

Hatcher knew the truth about how he felt, the anger burning against his tormentors. "My temper was to blame."

"No more than the boys who taunted you."

"I threw the first punch."

"But not the last. And you didn't make Jerry fall and hit his head."

Hatcher scrubbed his hand over his stubbled chin. Ten years had not erased the guilt he felt. He doubted another ten years would suffice. He was guilty of a man's death, would spend the rest of his life as a vagabond, making sure it never happened again. "I am not without blame."

"You need to forgive yourself, boy, and stop running from your life. Seems God's sent you a reason to do it before it's too late."

"How do I forgive myself?" He shook himself. "Besides, I can't let myself care about anyone. I'm afraid what my anger might do. Who I might hurt."

"Have you talked to this woman—Kate? Asked her what she thinks? How she feels?"

"No. Never."

"Hatcher, God forgives. So should you."

What Hatcher wanted, or deserved didn't matter.

Freeing Kate from her promise would suffice. "Just get me out of this if you can. And please, go talk to Kate. Persuade her to give up her foolish agreement."

"I'll do my best on both counts."

Chapter Fifteen

Doyle lost no time in putting a For Sale sign on Kate's property. At least he put it up while the children were in school. They didn't see her sink to the ground as soon as Doyle drove away and wail out her pain. It was only a piece of land. But it was her home and security. She pushed away such thoughts. Doyle would provide her with a better home. The knowledge didn't ease her pain.

She clamped her jaw and stared defiantly at the sign. The only thing that mattered was Hatcher's release.

She'd accepted in her head that he didn't care to see her. Understood he would be on his way as soon as he got out of jail. If only she could be sure he wouldn't be homeless, cold, hungry and alone when he left.

Yes, he'd often enough said he wasn't alone—God was with him and nothing could take that away. She wished she could believe as strongly as he. Not that she doubted God's presence in her life, His care over her. But it never seemed like enough. She wanted so much more than a distant, all-powerful God. She wanted someone who shared her dreams, understood her fears, helped her keep her farm.

But it was not to be. Knowing God was with her

would have to be enough. His care and love would sustain her through a loveless marriage. *Oh God, my strength and my shield. My heart trusteth in you and I am helped.*

The words gave her unexpected courage. With God on her side, she had nothing to fear.

"Lord, deliver Hatcher. Give him the desire of his heart."

She would miss him always but if he couldn't be happy unless he wandered the byways of life, she would not hold him back. Not even in her mind.

She returned to the house, washed away her tears, brushed her hair and wore her tenuous peace like a cloak as she waited on the doorstep for the children to return from school. They would never know anything but the joys of living in town.

Mary raced up the driveway. Kate knew she'd seen the sign.

"Momma, you're selling the farm?"

Kate smiled. Her lips trembled only slightly. "We're going to live in town. You won't have to help with the chickens and cows again."

She'd expected Mary to be happy but Mary shook her head. "Where will we live?"

"With Doyle. I'm going to marry him."

Mary's eyes grew round.

"I don't want to live in town," Dougie yelled as he raced away to disappear inside the barn.

"We'll enjoy it," Kate whispered. How could she possibly explain all the reasons to her children?

"What's going to happen to Hatcher?" Mary asked.

Kate had tried her best to assure the children it was a misunderstanding. "I'm sure the truth will come out. Doyle is going to be his lawyer."

"You did this to help him, didn't you?"

Kate couldn't hide the truth from her perceptive daughter. "I'd do anything to see he got released."

"I've always wanted to live in town," Mary said, her voice cheerful.

But Kate heard the way it caught on the last word before Mary hurried to her room to change her clothes.

Kate looked up as a strange car drove into the yard. Then she realized the blue car belonged to Larry's Garage, but the man behind the wheel didn't look familiar.

The vehicle stopped. A dapper, silver-haired man stepped out. Someone interested in buying the farm already?

Her nose stung with sudden tears that she sniffed back. She'd get used to the idea in a few days.

She patted Shep's head, glad he remained at her side. She relaxed some when she saw the way the man kept a guarded eye on the animal and sensed he had no fondness for dogs. He remained beside the car. A good place for him in Kate's opinion.

"Mrs. Bradshaw?"

How did he know her name? "Yes, how can I help you?"

"Hatcher sent me."

Hatcher? She'd expected Doyle sent him. She tried to show no expression but guessed he'd seen her surprise.

"He wanted you to know he's hired me as his lawyer."

She rubbed a spot below her ear. "I already hired a lawyer for him."

"Hatcher didn't like the conditions."

Kate tried to mask her surprise behind a tight smile. "I see. And what would he know about any 'conditions'?"

When the man smiled he looked kind. "Seems you have a concerned friend."

Kate cast about to think whom he meant.

"A young lady by the name of Mrs. Remington."

"Sally?"

"She contacted me. Told me about the charges against Hatcher. And I came. Hatcher wants me to convince you to reconsider your agreement with that other lawyer."

Her heart leapt at the thought that Hatcher cared who she married. Could it be he hoped to be the one to put a ring on her finger?

She closed her eyes, reminded herself Hatcher would be on the road as soon as he got out of jail. Would she ever truly accept the fact and stop hoping? "Really. Did he say why?"

"Not exactly. I hoped you'd know his reasons."

Kate shook her head. "Can't say as I do."

"I defended Hatcher ten years ago in a murder trial."

"I heard he'd been charged."

"And declared innocent. Which he was, despite the rumors that circulated."

"Can you tell me what happened? Or is it confidential? You being a lawyer and all."

"Hatcher said I was to do whatever I needed to persuade you to change your mind. I'd say telling you the whole story falls into that category."

"I'll make tea." She hauled out two chairs and parked them on the step then disappeared inside.

She leaned her forehead against the cool cupboard door. Would the man tell her something she didn't know? Help her understand why Hatcher wouldn't stay? Better yet, give her some argument she could use to persuade him to reconsider? She lifted her head, glanced out the window, saw a fist-sized white cloud sweeping across the sky. The promise of rain. She smiled and poured water over the tea leaves. One never quite stopped hoping.

A few minutes later, she returned with a tray of tea and some oatmeal cookies.

"This is nice. Thank you." Mr. Styles measured in four spoonfuls of sugar and took a handful of cookies. He chewed and drank for a few minutes than leaned back. "Hatcher was twenty-three years old. His mother died that spring. His father decided to try his hand in the stock market and lost everything, including the farm Hatcher and his older brother, Lowell, had worked hard to get into pristine condition. Lowell, in disgust, left. Hatcher and his father were forced to move into town. His father fell into a deep depression. Hatcher struggled to keep things together as best he could. I tell you all this to explain that Hatcher turned into an angry young man. He got to be known as a kid with a short fuse. Other men got a kick out of setting him off, seeing him tackle everyone and anyone."

Johnny paused to enjoy more tea and cookies.

Kate rolled her cup back and forth between her palms and waited. The hot west wind drove the impotent cloud across the sky. Part of her considered going with Hatcher. She knew how to live on the road.

She shook her head. What was she thinking? She'd never do that to her children. Far better they enjoy town life and she endure the empty loneliness of a loveless marriage.

The cookies consumed, Mr. Styles picked up the thread of his story. "Well, that fateful night, they did it again. Half a dozen of them started taunting him, calling his father insulting things, making slurs against his mother. As predicted, he started throwing his fists.

No one could really remember who hit whom though Hatcher insists he remembers punching Jerry in the nose. At some point in the fight, Jerry went down and struck his head on a rock and died. The sheriff arrested the lot of them but it was Hatcher who was charged with murder in Jerry's death. The sheriff, you see, was sick and tired of breaking up the fights. But no one could say if Hatcher even struck him and all the witnesses agreed it had been a general melee. Eventually Hatcher was declared innocent."

She saw a young man dealing with too many tragedies, trapped by circumstances and pain he couldn't control, taunted by unsympathetic people. She felt a burning anger toward the people and events that made Hatcher's life so miserable he could find no way to deal with it except striking out. She wanted to scream a protest that a man had died and Hatcher unnecessarily blamed himself.

She sighed. "Didn't need to hear the story to know he was innocent. Knew it all along."

"Trouble is, he doesn't believe it."

This was not news to her, either, but perhaps the lawyer friend from his past could explain it. She shifted and looked at him. "Why not?"

"You'd have to ask him to know for sure, of course, but he told me his anger was out of control. He said he had murder in his heart. That made him guilty in his mind."

"But why should it?" She wanted to understand but she couldn't. Everybody made mistakes, did things they wished they could undo. It didn't drive them to shut themselves off from other people.

"He left home right after the trial. I tried to stop him but he said he needed to get away from people before someone else got hurt." He grew quiet. "He's still trying to get away from people. Seems to me he figures if he keeps on the move, he can outrun his past. Maybe his anger."

"But he isn't an angry man. In fact, I've never seen such a patient man."

Mr. Styles nodded.

They sat in contemplative silence for several minutes before the lawyer shook his head and returned to the reason for his visit. "Are you going to tell that other lawyer his services are no longer needed?"

This man would defend Hatcher in a way Doyle wouldn't. He cared about Hatcher, had history with him. The sort of man she could trust to keep Hatcher's best interests at the forefront.

She no longer needed Doyle. She could break her agreement with him. A snort escaped and built into a laugh.

The lawyer grinned. "Do I take that as yes?"

"Most definitely. And tell Hatcher thanks."

"I suggest you tell him yourself."

"He refuses to see me."

The lawyer gave her a considering look. "You don't seem to me to be the sort of woman who gives up readily."

She returned his steady look. Suddenly she grinned. "I'm not."

Kate stared across her fields. She didn't need to sell her farm, give up her life in order to get Doyle to defend Hatcher. God had heard her prayer. Despite her doubts, God provided a way for her. She didn't deserve such blessing yet knowing God didn't distribute his gifts according to one's merit gave her heart a golden glow.

The wheat would soon be poking through the soil

if it found moisture below the surface. She'd be here
to see it grow and mature if God sent rain. Otherwise,
she'd be here to cling to the land believing in its possi-
bilities even when it seemed hopeless. She'd trust God
to take care of her no matter what the future brought.

The lawyer man had set her free. Or rather, Hatcher
had.

She always knew Hatcher was innocent. And now
she knew why he was a hobo. Running from his past,
as Mr. Styles said. When would he stop running? When
would he realize he was not a danger to society? "He
didn't rob the store or do all that damage."

The lawyer nodded. "He told me the facts. Now I
have to prove them."

"It just puzzles me how the money got in his things."

"Someone must have planted it. Did you see anyone there?"

"I wasn't watching but I didn't see anyone and I think
I'd notice someone hiking across my field. It's not like
it's possible to hide anywhere." She waved her hand
to indicate the flat, treeless stretch of prairie. "Doyle,
the sheriff and I all went over there when they came
for him."

"You all went in together?"

Kate tried to remember. "I was so upset, trying to
get Hatcher to tell them the truth. No one would listen
to me. Let's see. The sheriff held Hatcher's hands. I was
at his side talking to him."

"And Doyle?"

Kate screwed up her face trying to picture the event.
"He was ahead of us. I remember that now."

"I'll sort things out, trust me."

He left a few minutes later.

Kate, filled with raw energy, tromped over to the

nearest field, dug down to reveal a tiny kernel of wheat, saw it had sprouted but lay in dry soil. They needed rain. Yet the idea didn't worry her. God had proved Himself the giver of good gifts again and again. He would provide for her. She stood tall, raised her arms over her head and laughed.

The next morning Kate left for town as soon as she'd done the chores. She'd moved with boundless energy all morning, anxious to attend to her tasks. She changed into a new cotton dress, pale green with sprays of darker green leaves. She'd been saving it for a special occasion and this would certainly qualify. She'd worn it only once before when she and Doyle had gone to a box social, leaving the children with Sally. Doyle's comment that she looked like a tree in bloom had ruined the enjoyment of the dress but as she twisted in front of the mirror to admire the way the bias cut skirt swirled around her legs, she admitted she still liked it just fine. And the color highlighted the darkness of her eyes. She smiled at her reflection. No hiding the eager sparkle livening her face.

She hurried out to the truck and made the trip to town in less time than normal.

First stop, Doyle's office.

She marched right in, not giving her nerves a chance to protest.

"Go right in." The secretary waved her toward the door and smiled in a way that made Kate's cheeks warm.

Did the woman know the reasons behind her sudden engagement to Doyle? Did she think Kate had sold herself? Well, she might have but no more. She filled her lungs and prayed for courage before she stepped into Doyle's domain.

He glanced up, saw her, scrambled to his feet and came around the desk to reach for her hands. "My dear, I was thinking about you. We need to select rings. Or do you want me to take care of it."

She stepped back, twisted her hands together in front of her. "I have news."

Doyle lowered his fists to his side. His expression hardened, welcome replaced with warning. "Sounds like bad news."

She swallowed hard. While he might consider it bad news, she thought otherwise. Only her nervous concern about his reaction kept her from smiling. "Hatcher has hired his own lawyer. So I no longer need your services."

Doyle's eyes grew thunderous. He drew his mouth down. "Who did he hire?"

"Johnny Styles."

"Never heard of him."

"He defended Hatcher when he was falsely accused of murder." She ignored the deepening frown marring Doyle's handsome features.

"What about our marriage?"

Kate drew off her gloves then pulled them on again and smoothed them, kept her eyes on her movements then slowly lifted her gaze to his. "Doyle, I would be doing you a disservice if I agreed to go ahead with our wedding. I am fond of you but I don't love you. And I'm not prepared to give up my farm."

"You readily agreed to sell it when you thought it would get that Hatcher guy off the hook. But not for me. How am I supposed to take that?"

Anyway you want. But to a lawyer, the implications should be obvious. "I was concerned with justice."

Doyle slapped the top of his desk. "Nonsense. You've been foolish enough to fall in love with a murderer and a thief. Have you no sense of decency?"

She felt her eyes grow glassy hard. "He is not a murderer nor do I believe he is a thief."

"And you're prepared to stand by him? Just like that?"

Kate smoothed her gloves again. "I'm prepared to stand for justice, fairness and acceptance. Seems to me Hatcher deserves that. As does everyone."

Doyle snorted. "He'll be convicted of theft in this case."

"Not if Johnny Styles has anything to say about it. He's after discovering the truth."

"Hard to argue against eye witnesses and evidence such as the money in his possession."

Kate looked steadily at Doyle remembering how he'd rushed ahead of them into Hatcher's quarters. Mr. Styles had placed suspicion in her mind. But no, Doyle wouldn't stoop to such things. After all, he was a lawyer, defender of justice.

"You came begging to me once. You'll do it again. But don't depend on me being so forgiving next time."

A shiver raced down her spine at the menacing look on his face. And then it was gone, replaced with bland indifference. "I'm sorry you're making such a big mistake but you deserve all the bad luck coming your way."

She backed out of the office and fled to the street. She hadn't expected him to be happy for her to reject him twice in quick succession. But neither had she thought he'd be glad to see her suffer. She pressed her hand to her throat. She'd always thought him a good, kind person. This glimpse at a darker side startled her.

At least she wasn't going to discover it after they married.

Relieved to have that chore done, she glanced across the street. Next stop, the jail.

She marched across the dusty street and threw back the door to face the sheriff. She would not be turned away this time. But she faced the overweight deputy rather than the sheriff. "I've come to see Hatcher."

The man huffed and puffed. "Sheriff said not to let you in," he whined.

"I'm sure he gave you a very good reason." She pushed past him to the door. Tried the knob and found it locked.

"Well, not really."

"Then I guess you have no cause to keep me out." She planted her hands on her hips and gave the man a look that she used when Dougie disobeyed. It had the same affect on the deputy. He shuffled from foot to foot, looked helter-skelter around the room.

Kate suppressed a desire to laugh. "Open the door."

The man muttered under his breath but pulled the key from his belt and stuck it in the door.

As soon as he'd turned the lock, Kate pushed past him and strode boldly into the cell area.

Hatcher leaned against the far wall, watching her, his expression as tightly closed as the door she'd just stepped through. She'd persuaded the lawman to open the door; she intended to likewise break down the locks Hatcher kept around his feelings.

She took in his soiled, rumpled clothes, his lengthening beard. Wasn't he allowed basic necessities such as hot water with which to wash and shave?

She faltered, stifled a cry and pushed steel into her

spine then jerked off the gloves and leaned close to the bars. "I met your lawyer."

"He's a good man."

"He believes in you."

"Don't you mean he believes in my innocence?"

"No, he believes in your decency and goodness."

They considered each other. Kate looked for clues as to what Hatcher thought. About her. About not running any more. "He told me the story about the accident."

"A man died."

She nodded. Hatcher might keep his expression rigidly bland, but she heard the note of despair in his voice that he would surely deny if she mentioned it. She didn't bother. "It's a shame he died. But you didn't murder him. You have nothing to feel guilty about."

Hatcher turned to stare at the cot. "Kate, what do you want?"

"I want a whole lot of things. To keep my farm. To have time to enjoy my children. To see your innocence proved."

"Did you decide against selling your farm?" he asked.

She grinned. "And against marrying Doyle."

"You'll find someone else. Someone who is strong enough to allow you to be you."

"I think I already have." She waited for him to realize what she meant.

"Good."

"Aren't you going to ask who?"

"None of my business."

His answer angered her. He avoided looking at her. Suddenly she knew he didn't ask because he understood she meant him. "Hatcher, what do *you* want?" He didn't reply. "Do you want to keep running? Do you want to be a hobo the rest of your life? Do you want to grow old alone and cold?"

He twitched. Jerked around to face her. "I have to be alone. That way my anger can never again harm anyone."

"What anger? You are the most gentle, patient man I've ever met." She lowered her voice. "You're a praying man, a Bible-reading man. Have you ever considered that you are a changed man, thanks to God's work in your life?"

He kept his eyes averted. "Do you think it's a chance I'm prepared to take?"

She stared at him. "You're going to lie down and give up? You're going to walk away and pretend you never met me?" Her voice fell to a strangled whisper. "Aren't some things worth fighting for?"

He finally faced her, his eyes revealing his torture. "Kate, it has nothing to do with worth. It has everything to do with acknowledging what I know lies within."

She gulped in air, smelled the odor of a hundred unwashed bodies of men who had stayed in the jail. Her eyes stung with anger and sorrow and defeat. "Hatcher Jones, you need to take a good look into your heart and be willing to admit what really lies there." She hurried from the room before her sobs escaped.

Kate sat in the crowded courtroom. The room filled with curiosity as sharp and annoying as the buzz of the flies on the window ledges.

Mr. Zacharius, on her right, jostled against her as he shifted. "Hot, ain't it?" he said to no one in particular but Kate felt compelled to murmur distracted agreement.

She hadn't seen Hatcher since they'd spoken in the

jail two days ago. Not that she hadn't tried. She'd gained entrance the next day but Hatcher had more than one way of refusing to see her. He'd remained on the cot, his back to her and gave an occasional snore to let her know his indifference.

She knew better. Understood he thought he protected her by refusing to acknowledge her or admit he might care. So she left him, willing to bide her time.

But she leaned forward, her fingers gripping the edge of the wooden bench as she waited for the sheriff to lead him in.

And then he stepped into view and her world narrowed to the sight of him. His hair had been cut. It shone like ebony. His scraggly beard was gone, leaving a slightly faded look on his cheeks.

She'd given Johnny one of Jeremiah's suits and shirts for Hatcher to wear. The suit tightened across his shoulders. She'd never noticed how broad he was, had seen only his leanness. The white shirt pulled the blackness from his eyes, filled them with a bright sheen as his gaze found her across the crowd. For all she knew and cared they were the only people present. She thought him the most handsome man in the room. No one would think him a hobo now. She smiled, sending him silent messages of love. He tipped his chin, whether in acknowledgement of her feelings or only a simple greeting, she didn't know. Or care. It was enough to see him. Fill her Hatcher-shaped hunger with his details.

He shifted, turned away as the sheriff led him to his place beside Johnny Styles.

Kate continued to drink her fill knowing it would never be enough. She could see him every morning as she woke, frequently throughout the day and last thing before she fell asleep at night and she'd never be satiated.

She jumped as the judge rapped his gavel, tore her gaze from Hatcher to concentrate on the proceedings of the courtroom. Mr. Jacobs was the banker when he wasn't the judge. He looked austere in a black robe.

The sheriff presented the evidence then turned to Johnny Styles with an expression that let everyone know the man was wasting his time.

But Johnny had done his homework. Under cross-examination, Mr. Anderson admitted he couldn't positively identify Hatcher as the hobo he'd chased away several times.

"Never look at their faces anymore," he confessed.

Then Johnny asked Mr. Anderson to itemize the money he'd kept in his cash drawer.

"Wasn't much. Most of my customers charge until they get some money or provide eggs and butter in exchange for what they buy. There might have been a handful of coins, several one-dollar bills. I particularly remember I had a ten-dollar bill that day. Don't often see one anymore. Had a hard time making change."

"Do you remember who gave you the bill?"

"Not likely to forget something like that, am I? It was Doyle Grey."

Kate's quick gasp was echoed by others in the courtroom, though she sensed their reaction was more admiring than hers. The judge banged his gavel and indicated Mr. Anderson should continue.

"Strange thing was he only bought a handful of candy. Annabel, his housekeeper, normally buys his supplies."

Johnny held out some coins and paper money. "This is the cash found in Hatcher's possessions. Can you look at it and tell us if you think it came from your store?"

Mr. Anderson barely glanced at it. "It didn't."

"Go ahead. Have a good look. Be certain."

"I am."

"How can you be so certain?"

"I told you I had one ten. But I didn't have any fives. There are two there. It's not my money."

Johnny turned to study the sheriff. Kate knew everyone in the room thought the same as she—why hadn't the sheriff asked these questions before he arrested a man and charged him?

Johnny turned back to the storekeeper. "Let me get this straight. You can't say for certain that my client is the man you saw around your store on several occasions."

Mr. Anderson nodded. "Guess that's right."

"And the money found in Mr. Jones's possession is not from your store?"

"That's right."

Kate knew, as did everyone in the courtroom, that Hatcher had not committed the crime.

Kate watched the back of his head wishing she could see his expression, see how he reacted to hearing his name cleared.

It took Judge Jacobs about three seconds to declare Hatcher innocent. He took more time admonishing the sheriff to make sure of the facts in the future and suggested he should get busy and find the person who had robbed and trashed Mr. Anderson's store. And perhaps, while he was at it, he could find out who'd planted the money in Mr. Jones's possession. Kate knew it was Doyle. No one else had the opportunity. Had she been so hungry for male companionship she'd been purposely blind to his faults? Because there must have been some hint of this side of him that she missed, overlooked. How had she ever thought she could marry him?

"You're free to go," the judge told Hatcher.

The murmur of shock and mounting curiosity rose like a heat wave. Mr. Zacharius turned to Kate. "Now ain't that a surprise?"

"Not to me." The wide smile she gave him made him shift back.

She stifled a giggle. She didn't mean to act inappropriately and frighten the poor man but life suddenly seemed as good and right as a soaking rain.

She pushed against the tide of people leaving the courtroom, making her way to the front of the room where Hatcher stood talking to Johnny. She grabbed Hatcher's elbow, felt him stiffen. "You're a free man." She couldn't stop smiling. All that mattered for this solitary minute was the fact Hatcher would not spend any more time in that dreary jail cell.

As to what happened next, she would deal with that shortly.

Johnny turned to gather up papers on the desk.

"Hatcher, I'm so glad." Her heart overflowed with gratitude and joy. She wrapped her arms around his waist and hugged him tight.

He stiffened, groaned, kept his arms at his sides.

Kate held him for fifteen seconds then slowly forced her arms to relax. Stepped back so she could look into his face.

He could have been wearing a mask for all the emotion he revealed.

She understood his surprise. "It's good news, isn't it? To have everyone see you're innocent. There can't be any doubt after what Mr. Anderson said."

He kept his gaze on a distant spot.

She wondered what he saw. What he felt. Or did he let himself feel anything? She wanted to shake him into reacting, revealing just a glimpse of all the emotions he bottled up inside, probably pretending they didn't exist. She'd guess he was this minute reciting scripture to block any acknowledgement of relief that he was a free man.

"Hatcher, you're free. Truly free. You can choose to stay here, become part of the community." Our family. "You belong here. I'd be pleased if you'd come back to the farm."

Slowly, like a man wakened from a long sleep, he brought his gaze round to hers. His pupils were wide, unfocused. He blinked. Narrowed his gaze. Seemed to see her; seemed to realize she stood at his side, begging for him to stay. A shudder raced up his spine and down his arm. She shivered as his paleness, the desperate hopelessness in his expression.

"Hatcher, you're a free man," she whispered, aching for the loneliness and despair she saw in his face. She shook him a little, relieved when he sucked in air. "Hatcher, please come home." She felt a queer mingling of sorrow at the ordeal he'd endured and her love that swelled and grew like bread dough left untended. Surely he saw how she felt. It must stick out all over her. She smiled tenderly. "I love you. Come home."

Chapter Sixteen

Hatcher had walked into the courtroom, determined to feel nothing, reveal nothing. Faltered for a heartbeat when he saw Kate's tender smile. Despite the sweltering heat of the room filled with the curious and vengeful, she looked fresh and cool in the same green dress she'd worn to visit him in jail. She looked like a fresh spring day. When God created that woman he put her together as nicely as any woman on the earth.

Although the only sounds were the rising murmur of interest as he followed the sheriff to Johnny's side, he heard the sound of Kate singing. Smiled inwardly as he remembered her choice of song: "Bringing in the Sheaves."

His hoped his face revealed nothing of what he felt. He'd spent ten years denying his feelings. Shutting them away, blocking them by reciting scriptures. He'd slipped up for a few days and caused Kate's hurt. He regretted that as much as anything he'd done before.

He turned from her sunlit face, realizing the sun didn't touch her, the light came from within, and pushed aside all feeling.

He heard the words spoken by the sheriff with the

same interest he would have given the scratching of a mouse in a straw stack. Knew the lies without hearing them.

Stirred himself when Johnny got up. The man had promised he'd prove his innocence. Surely would be nice to be out in the open again, breathing fresh clean air, able to wash and shave when he wanted. Maybe he'd go back to the coast. The pounding of the surf would help cleanse his mind of disturbing, distracting thoughts. Like Kate.

He smiled secretly at the picture that came to mind— Kate trying to chase down a chicken and get it in the pen. Her legs churning, her arms waving madly like a crazy windmill. At least he'd greased the windmill that last day. She wouldn't have to tackle it again for a while.

Every man's work shall be made manifest: for the day shall declare it, because it shall be revealed by fire; and the fire shall try every man's work of what sort it is. One Corinthians three, verse thirteen.

He jerked his thoughts back to the proceedings. Realized the shopkeeper said he couldn't identify Hatcher, nor was the money his. Heard the judge declare Hatcher innocent. Say he was a free man.

Johnny said it would go this way. Hatcher believed him. Or thought he did but at the verdict, he felt as if the world tipped sideways. He needed to hold on tight to something solid.

He fell back on his ten-year habit. *The Lord, which maketh a way in the sea, and a path in the mighty waters.* Isaiah forty-three, verse sixteen.

Then suddenly, as if from across a wide field, he saw Kate at his side, knew she touched his arm. Felt an abyss of emotion before him, continued to recite, didn't dare relax his restraint.

He heard her soft pleading voice. Tried to block her words. Half succeeded until she whispered, "I love you."

His stomach lurched to his throat, clawed for a handhold. His limbs had a weightless feeling. He knew he'd dropped into the void. He fought to regain control.

A hoarse sound escaped his tight throat.

"Hatcher?"

God help him, he wouldn't repeat his error. Wouldn't hang around to cause Kate any more problems.

The Lord upholdeth all that fall, and raiseth up all those that be bowed down. Psalms one forty-five, verse fourteen.

He found solid ground, sucked in reviving air. "Best if I move on."

He felt the scorching heat of her gaze, saw Johnny straightening to give him a startled look.

"Best for who?" Kate demanded.

He'd heard that stubborn note in her voice before, knew she would argue till the cows came home. "You might as well save your breath. I've made up my mind."

She grabbed his arm with a viselike grip.

Heat raced up his arm from her touch, burned into his heart like a branding iron. The muscles in his arm twitched, knotted at the base of his neck. He hunched his shoulders, ignoring the pain, ignoring the way his heart lurched toward her. Not that he expected her to give up easily. But all the begging in the world wouldn't make him change his mind. He forced his gaze to the doors, now closed behind the departed crowd.

"Hatcher, why won't you believe you aren't the man you were ten years ago? Forget the past. Forgive the past."

He didn't move, didn't answer. She'd just have to accept he couldn't stay. Couldn't ruin their lives.

"Hatcher." Her voice caught and when she continued, her words were so low he wondered if he'd heard correctly. "Hatcher Jones, I love you. I want you to stay."

He pushed past her, headed for escape.

She called after him, a desperate pleading note in her voice. "Not all prisons are made of iron bars."

Johnny caught up. "Don't be so foolish, boy. Take what Kate's offering you. Settle down and enjoy the rest of your life."

Hatcher pushed out into the sunshine, saw the stark shape of the half-dead poplar tree next to the wooden sidewalk. The drought was killing it branch by branch. He swung his gaze to take in the weathered fronts of the row of stores across the street. Mr. Anderson's store— Anderson's Mercantile. Wong's Public Laundry. Larry's Garage with the *e* broken from the end.

He sucked in air, grateful he didn't have to return to the stinking jail cell.

The world was his to enjoy.

The world would never be big enough for him to escape memories of this place. This time.

He faced the older man. "I appreciate your help. I'll find a way to pay you."

"I ask only one thing in the way of payment."

"I can't stay here. I won't do that to Kate and the children."

"I wasn't going to ask you to. That's something you have to decide on your own."

He'd expected Johnny to argue, to try and persuade him to stay. His disappointment grabbed at his throat and he coughed before he could speak. "What do you want?"

"Boy, I want you to go home and see your father."

Hatcher's thoughts stalled, his jaw went slack. Of all

the things Johnny might ask… Why not ask him to fly to the highest hill? Jump over the row of buildings? It would have been as impossible. "I don't imagine I'd be all that welcome."

"You might be surprised."

"I've spent ten years avoiding situations that would trigger my anger and you ask me to go back to where it all started?"

"Your father shouldn't die without seeing you again."

Hatcher wanted to refuse. But this man had rescued him not once, but twice. He owed him. Even if the payment he asked was far too great. "How is my father?"

"Find out for yourself if you really care."

For ten years, Hatcher had successfully blocked homesickness from his mind and now with a few words, Johnny had undone all those years. He ached to see his father, visit his mother's grave, find out where Lowell had gone. Perhaps he could make a quick visit without the townspeople discovering he was in their midst.

Johnny waited.

"Very well. I'll visit my father."

The deputy strode toward them. "Here's your things." He handed Hatcher a bundle.

"Are you catching the next train?" he asked Johnny.

"Yes. Want to go with me?"

The sooner he turned his back on this place, the sooner he'd be able to forget it. "Yeah. No reason to hang about here."

Kate stood beside her truck, watching him. He pretended he didn't see her. Ignored the ache in his bones at denying himself one last glimpse. Concentrated on the hot wind brushing his cheek, tugging at his shirt. Wished for rain so Kate's crop would grow.

He sendeth rain on the just and unjust. Matthew five, verse forty-five.

God would provide all her needs without assistance from the a man like Hatcher.

He and Johnny fell in step and turned toward the train station. Their path took them by the school. A ring of big boys stood in the far corner of the yard, chanting, "Crybaby, cry. Stick your finger in your eye. Crybaby, cry!"

Hatcher slowed his steps. He hated bullying. *Don't get involved. Walk away. Remember your anger.* He hurried on.

He heard a small, thin voice. "Go away." And ground to a halt. "That's Mary." Anger, hot and furious, filled him like a rush of boiling water. He turned off the street, strode across the dusty yard and pushed his way through the circle to Mary's side. His breath burned up his throat, scorched his tongue. Anger, denied so many years, raged like a forest fire. He took a deep breath. This is what he feared about letting himself care about anyone. Once unleashed, what would his anger turn into? Violence? Murder? He remembered the feeling when he was young. How it made him want to grab someone, something and squeeze hard. Made him want to hurt someone as if it would ease the burning of his gut.

He faced Mary's tormentors. Felt no desire to hurt them, only sadness at whatever drove them to taunt someone younger and weaker. "Boys, bullying makes even the strongest man look weak. Is that what you want?" One by one they slunk away.

Hatcher knelt in front of Mary, dried her eyes, smoothed her hair back, ignored the sharp rock beneath his right knee. "Are you hurt?"

"No, but why am I such a crybaby?"

This little girl needed a champion. Someone strong and good and understanding. He'd pray such a man would come into her life before long. Pain shafted through him. He blamed the rock digging into his knee.

"You're not a crybaby. You're a sensitive girl. You feel things strongly. That's good."

She looked doubtful. "You're out of jail." She laughed and hugged him. "Momma said you'd be free today. Are you coming home?"

He pushed against the rock, welcoming the agony as he hugged the child. "Not with you."

She squeezed her arms around his neck. "Why not? Don't you like us?"

He laughed around the constriction threatening to choke him. "I like you very much. But I'm going to see my father."

She looked into his face. "Then you'll come back to us?"

"No, Mary. I don't belong here."

She stuck out her bottom lip. "Yes, you do. Momma's been so much happier since you came. We all have." Her lip started to tremble. "Why can't you come back?"

"Mary, your momma will need you to be strong and brave. She'll need your help. Will you be sure and take care of her for me?"

Mary considered his words, looked doubtful then took a deep breath and nodded.

Hatcher pushed to his feet and hurried away without glancing back. A little girl's tears were a mighty powerful weapon.

"You handled that well," Johnny said. "I was tempted to knock a few heads together."

"They just don't realize what they're doing."

"They aren't the only ones."

Hatcher heard the none-too-subtle hint in Johnny's words but he wasn't about to waste any more time arguing about why he couldn't stay.

They purchased tickets for the trip back to Loggieville. Conscious of the curious glances from others in the waiting room, Hatcher suggested they wait outside on the worn wooden platform.

Hatcher hooked his fingers in the front pockets of his trousers and tapped his thumbs against the worn hem. When the train whistle warned of its approach he jumped just as if he hadn't been waiting for the last ten minutes.

He grabbed his knapsack, headed for the step then stopped and allowed Johnny to enter the car first.

As they settled on stiff leather seats facing each other, Hatcher allowed himself one last look at the huddled little town, lifted his gaze to the road leading toward—it didn't matter where it went.

He settled back, closed his eyes, feigning sleep. Johnny soon snored softly and Hatcher sat up. Even in sleep the man looked as neat and tidy as if someone had ironed him where he sat.

Darkness descended and Johnny slept on.

For Hatcher, narcotic sleep did not come.

With each clackety-clack of the wheels the one place he vowed to never again see grew closer.

The only place he wished to be got steadily farther away.

Chapter Seventeen

Kate watched Hatcher walk away. He'd remain a man of the road, just like her father, unless he stopped running from his past.

She climbed behind the wheel of her truck.

She should be happy he'd earned his freedom. Of course she was. Seeing him in jail had been more difficult than she could have imagined. But her happiness was laced through and through with so many other things—regret, sadness, emptiness and anger.

She grabbed hold of the anger and focused on it, let it burn down her throat and churn up the inside of her stomach like a drink of boiling acid. Stupid man. Senseless. Blind. A person could promise him the earth, fill it up with gold and silver and precious stones and he'd walk away muttering about past deeds and all sorts of nonsense.

The truck kindly started for her and she drove blindly out of town, ignoring a wave from Mrs. MacDuff. She didn't feel like being neighborly or polite or even nice. She wanted to…

She sighed so deeply her toes curled up.

She had no idea how to handle this churn of emotions, was no closer to knowing what to do when she pulled to a stop in front of her house and stared at the beast of a tractor stranded in the middle of the field with half a dozen rounds left to seed. She was in a bad mood anyways, she might as well see if the tractor would run for her.

After she'd changed into her baggy overalls, she marched across the field every determined step raising a cloud like a ball of grey cheesecloth.

She reached the tractor, stood in front of it. "You better run for me." She grabbed the crank and gave it a heave. A reluctant sputter then nothing. She cranked again. The engine caught, coughed, huffed and puffed but at least kept running.

For days the beast had run hour after hour for Hatcher but it stalled when she tried to convince it to move ahead.

Down to crank it. More coughing and sputtering. Back to the seat. Cautious, so very carefully, she edged forward. Made fifty feet before the engine conked out as if exhausted.

Down to crank. Reluctant cooperation from the beast. Back to the seat. Another fifty feet.

Two hours later she'd half finished the work that should have taken an hour at the most. She wore a coat of gritty dust. The back of her hands were streaked with mud from wiping away tears.

The beast stalled again.

Kate slouched over the seat.

Why had Hatcher left her? She'd told him she loved him. Begged him to return. Offered her home and her heart. Wasn't it enough for him? What else did he want? If he would tell her, she'd do her best to give it. If only he would stay. Or—she'd seen him head for the train station—come back.

"Lord," she wailed. "Why did You send him here and then take him away? I was happy enough before he came. But now I don't know if I can live without him." She sat motionless, breathed in the heated dust, heard the chirping of the sparrows, smelled the hot oily smell of the tractor.

She still had the farm.

Sending steel into her spine, she vowed she would finish this seeding if it took her the rest of the day and all night. She cranked the tractor again, broke her record and completed one round before it stalled.

She saw the children returning from school, climbed down and abandoned the whole business. Tomorrow she'd finish if she had to plant the rest with a hoe.

Realizing how she must look, she veered off toward the trough. "I'll be right there," she called. She washed off the evidence of her frustration and prepared to face her children.

They both raced toward her as she dried her face on the bib of her overalls. Dougie shouted before they had half crossed the yard.

"Where's Hatcher? Mary said he's gone. She's fibbing, isn't she?"

She grabbed him, held him close. "Mary doesn't fib."

Dougie jerked away from her, his expression fierce. "Why didn't he come back?"

Mary said nothing, simply wrapped her arms around Kate's waist and hung on tightly.

Kate patted her daughter's back as she tried to explain to Dougie. But how could she explain something she didn't understand herself? "He had to leave."

"Why?" Dougie shouted. "Why couldn't he stay here?"

"I don't know but he must have his reasons."

She reached for her son, wanting to hold him close, as much for her sake as his. She needed the comfort of her children's small bodies. The remembrance of their tiny fists as she held them as babies.

But Dougie jerked away. "He didn't even say good-bye."

"No, he didn't." She shared her son's pain over that neglect.

Screaming, Dougie raced to the barn.

Kate let him go knowing he would crawl into the warm manger where he often played and cry until he was cried out.

"He said goodbye to me," Mary whispered.

Kate turned her daughter's face upward. "When?"

Mary told how Hatcher had stopped at the school-yard.

Kate imagined the scene and felt a tightening in her stomach at her daughter's plight—being teased by the big boys.

"He was angry," Mary said.

His anger—the problem that drove him away from others. "What did he do?"

"Nothing. Just told the boys they shouldn't be bullies."

Kate looked toward town. Hatcher, admittedly angry had responded in a calm, patient manner. Just as always, but did Hatcher even pause to admit the evidence? She prayed he would realize how he'd changed.

"He said he was going to visit his father."

"I'm glad. Maybe he'll find what he needs there." And then return to them. "What else did he say?"

Mary smiled, blue eyes like a fine summer sky. "He said you'd need my help. Momma, I'll help you lots."

Kate hugged the child. "You are a great help." She smiled, feeling as if Hatcher had sent her a message, had indeed said goodbye in his own way.

Mary changed her clothes and went to gather eggs without being asked then went to the barn. A few minutes later both children emerged. Kate wondered what her little daughter had said to Dougie. Whatever it was, he seemed reconciled to Hatcher's departure.

Kate finished seeding the field the next day. Grateful to be done with the uncooperative beast, she limped it into the shed and dusted her hands as she walked away.

She sauntered over to the hay field, decided there might be enough to cut for winter feed if it didn't burn up before she got to it. She tried not to think of how much work lay ahead—the endless cycle of haying, harvesting, animals to care for. She couldn't manage on her own. She alternated between anger at Hatcher for abandoning her and sadness at missing him.

But she was more determined than ever to keep her farm. So what if part of her reason was so Hatcher could find them if he ever felt the need to return?

However, she needed help and swallowing her pride and fear, she posted a notice in the store, arranging to interview the applicants in the back of Mr. Anderson's store.

Lots of men arranged to meet her. But after two days she wondered if anyone would suit her. None of the men she interviewed measured up to Hatcher. Not that she hoped to replace him, knew she couldn't. She would carry him in her heart the rest of her life.

She'd look in the faces of every hobo she saw hoping for his familiar features.

At one point the farm had been what mattered most but no longer. She still wanted it. That hadn't changed but her attitude had. She needed less work, more sharing. She didn't expect the latter because there was only one person she wanted to share with, but she needed the former and so continued to talk to men about working for her.

After several more disappointing interviews, she decided her hay didn't need cutting for a few more days.

One fine Saturday, she turned to the children. "Let's do the chores as quickly as we can and then do something fun this afternoon."

They both begged to go back to the coulee.

"We never got to pick any violets," Mary reminded her.

Kate didn't want to go back to a place full of happy memories shared with Hatcher but she couldn't disappoint her children.

They hiked across the dry, dusty prairie so badly needing rain.

Dougie raced for the coulee again to check out the nest. "Look, two baby hawks."

"Stay back from the edge. Remember what Hatcher said—"

"I remember. 'A man always keeps his eye on what's ahead making sure he won't step into something dangerous.'"

"Very good." If only Hatcher didn't apply the same caution to his emotions. Would he ever let the past go?

While the children ran about, turning over rocks to watch bugs scurry away, chasing along the edge of the coulee, squatting to watch a deer tiptoe through the brush far below them, Kate sat and stared out at the landscape. And she prayed. *God, help me find someone*

to help on the farm. Help me be a good mother and sub-
stitute father to my children. And most of all wherever
Hatcher goes, let him have a roof over his head, a warm
place to escape the elements. And please, God, help him
see he is not the man he once was and fears he still is.

She laughed with her children and played tag again, though she had to make an effort not to let tears flow at how much she missed Hatcher.

As they returned home, Mary took her hand. "Momma, you're different."

Kate wondered what she meant. Perhaps her sadness showed, though she'd done her best to hide it from the children and remain positive and patient. "How so?"

"You don't yell so much. And you help us do our chores instead of just telling us to do them. I like it when you do that."

Kate hugged the child. "Mary, what a nice thing to say." She couldn't have asked for a better way to end the day.

The sun grew hotter with each day. Her crops struggled to survive. They endured several dust storms. Afterward, she tried to shovel the dirt away from her fences. And when she straightened to rest her back, she stared down the road.

"What are you looking for, Momma?" Mary asked.

"Nobody." Her head knew it was futile to hope. Her heart accepted no such verdict. *Please, bring him back to me,* she prayed, knowing Hatcher had much to learn about himself before he would even think about returning.

She could not put off cutting the hay any longer. She couldn't do it without help so she returned to Mr. Anderson's store and interviewed three more men. The first two she hoped to never see again. One was so dirty she wanted to take a bath by the time she ended the short interview. The second leered at her. It was all she could do not to rub his presence off her skin. The third man was older. Probably in his fifties. Although he could use a shave and haircut, he didn't smell and had a neat appearance. He told her he'd been a school-teacher at one time but had worked on any number of farms over the years.

"Why aren't you teaching? Seems to be a need for teachers."

"My wife died…" He shrugged. "After that I couldn't see the point in having a home."

"I'm sorry." Like Hatcher said, every man had his own reasons for being on the move.

She asked a few questions about his farming experience. "I have some hay to cut."

He nodded. "I've done that many times before. I can help you."

"Mr. Cyrus, can you come tomorrow morning?" When he agreed, she gave him directions.

He showed up bright and early, worked without break until she stopped for supper. He insisted he preferred to stay with men like himself and returned to town.

He didn't work quite so diligently the second day. She guessed he'd worked off the initial enthusiasm.

The third day she worked two hours before he showed up. She stopped to talk to him, smelled the alcohol on his breath and wondered where he found the stuff. He mumbled an excuse for being late and she let it go.

Haying meant mowing the grass, waiting for it to dry then raking it into bunches so it could be forked it into a wagon and taken to the barn to be hoisted into the loft. When the loft was full, she would stack it behind the barn. It was important to get the dry hay up before the wind tossed it around and much of it was lost.

She was mowing. The tractor thankfully cooperating for a change. She was doing three times the work he was and grew tired, hot, discouraged and cranky but she decided it would be wise to keep her frustration to herself. Mr. Cyrus had to finish the job. She couldn't do it on her own.

His job was to load the wagon and take the hay to the barn. She circled the field, passed the wagon. But she didn't see the man working. She stopped the tractor and headed across the field. Nothing smelled as good as freshly cut hay.

She found Mr. Cyrus asleep in the shade of the wagon. Nudged his boots. "Wake up."

The man struggled to a sitting position, holding his head with both hands. "Mr. Cyrus, the hay won't get from the ground to the wagon this way."

"Sorry, miss." He staggered to his feet and slouched back to work.

Before noon she had to waken him twice more. She'd let him go but then what would she do for help? She needed someone stronger than she to fork the hay into the wagon.

They worked until suppertime. Kate drooped when Mr. Cyrus left. She'd spent most of her time trying to keep him from napping. She wondered if he'd return in the morning. She almost wished he wouldn't but his help was slightly better than nothing.

But he did not return.

With no help she alternated between raking and forking the hay into the wagon. By evening, she'd made little headway and she ached so bad she could hardly move.

At this rate the cows would have to be sold. How would she feed her children?

She prepared a simple supper then dragged herself out to the barn to milk the cows. Stifling her moans, she separated and cleaned up. She forced a smile as she helped the children with their chores and homework. As soon as they were tucked in she fell into bed.

She couldn't run the farm without help.

And she couldn't find decent help.

Perhaps she'd been foolish in not accepting Doyle's offer. He would have taken care of her in relative ease. The lap of luxury as Sally often said.

But even as her muscles and body protested she knew she couldn't marry Doyle. Not even to escape this back-breaking labor.

There had to be another way to keep the farm and manage on her own.

"God, show me what to do." She fell into an exhausted sleep.

Mary shook her awake next morning. "Momma, it's time to get up."

Kate moaned. Every inch of her body hurt.

"What's wrong, Momma?" Mary demanded.

"I'm just sore. Where's your brother?"

"Feeding Mr. Rabbit."

"I'll be right out." She waited for Mary to leave the room before she inched her way out of bed. She managed to get both feet to the floor but when she tried to stand, her back knotted and a sharp pain grabbed her. She gingerly pulled on her clothes and shuffled from the room, bent over like an old woman.

"Momma." Mary rushed to her, jittered from foot to foot. "Are you okay?"

"My back is sore. I'll be better as soon as I get moving."

She bit her lip and eased a breath in. Even breathing hurt.

"I'll be fine in a few minutes," she assured both children as she waved them away to school. Dougie had eagerly volunteered to stay home and help.

But she wasn't fine. The pain did not ease up. By the time she suffered through the agony of milking the cows, she was in tears. She looked out at the hay field knowing she would not be moving a single blade today.

"God. Help me. How am I going to manage?"

Chapter Eighteen

Loggieville had changed in ten years. Two more rows of houses backed Main Street, which was a block longer in either direction. A new church with a tall steeple stood to the right of the rail station. Some things remained familiar—the schoolhouse still had the big old tree where he had played as a child. Some of the store names were familiar.

Hatcher's gaze went unbidden toward the river. From the station he could see only the line of trees. But his mind filled in the details. The level bank that provided a perfect spot for restless young men to congregate, far enough from town so they could be rowdy without bringing down the wrath of the older, quieter townspeople and where they could challenge each other in jest. Or in anger. Tree roots knotted the ground, making it difficult to stay upright as they jostled each other. Rocks of various sizes lay scattered along the shoreline. A deadly combination, as he'd learned.

He shook himself and pushed the thought deep into forgetfulness.

Johnny grasped his hand in a bone-crushing grip and shook it hard. "Good traveling with you."

Hatcher grinned. "You slept the entire trip."

Johnny nodded, his eyes twinkling. "Didn't have to worry about having my pockets lightened with you wide-awake, now, did I? You'll find your father back at the farm."

Hatcher jerked his chin in, startled at the announcement. He'd thought, assumed, his father would still be in town, working just enough to provide his needs, finding a bottle somewhere so he could try and drown his sorrows. "What's he doing there?"

"Working. Has been for three years now. You'll find many things changed."

"'Spect so." It was the unchanged things that concerned him. Like himself. The way people looked at him. His father.

"Allow yourself to be a little open-minded," the lawyer counseled. "You might be surprised what you'll discover."

With a final goodbye, Hatcher, used to long treks, headed down the road toward the farm he'd once known and loved. Who were the current owners? What changes had been made? It no longer represented home, yet he searched the horizon for his first glimpse of it. Finally he saw it in the distance and pulled to a halt to stare at his past.

Emotions he wouldn't acknowledge pinpricked the surface of his thoughts. Not old. Not new. Yet deeply familiar. Or perhaps the familiarity came from his constant denial.

He shouldn't have come back. His return could only serve to stir up trouble again. Best thing he could do was head on down the road. Continue the journey he'd started ten years ago. The journey to nowhere. He half turned.

He'd promised Johnny. He owed the lawyer a huge debt. And something stronger than fear and caution tugged at him. He wanted to see his father. He wanted to see the farm.

His chest felt too full of air as he resumed his homeward journey. He came to the last little rise in the road and detoured off the road, found a grassy knoll, sat down and pulled his Bible out. He opened to Luke fifteen and read the story of the prodigal son. He'd read it many times in the past. Knew it by heart. Knew also, it didn't apply to him. He'd never be welcomed like that. Didn't expect to. It was a spiritual lesson about what it would be like to arrive in heaven. Yet he lingered over each word.

He looked up from the page, watched a tractor dusting along a field. The new owner, Johnny said, took over three years ago and had been generous enough to let Hatcher's father return to his old home.

Hatcher lurched to his feet and returned to the dusty road. His steps lagged as he drew closer to the farm.

Memories roared into him like a flash flood swirling through a gully, washing rocks, tearing things up by their roots.

All summer his mother sat outside the back door he could now see, shelling peas or stringing beans, peeling potatoes or mending. She loved to be where she could hear and see her boys. She included Hatcher's father in that description.

He shifted his gaze to the newly painted barn, the raw, new fences angling out, the two fawn-colored cows in a pen similar to one where he and Lowell played cowboy, riding steers, being tossed to the ground more than once. One time Lowell thought he'd broken his arm and made Hatcher promise not to tell. "Mother will make us stop if she thinks we're getting hurt." Hatcher insisted on a similar promise the time he cut his hand carving a tiny propeller.

He chuckled, the sound making him blink.

It took him a long time to figure out how to balance the blades on a propeller so it turned smoothly. He laughed. The experience had been invaluable when he and Lowell decided to build a propeller-driven snow machine. What fun they'd had going to town that winter.

Hatcher stopped where the laneway intersected the road and stared toward the only home he'd ever known. He ached to visit but would the new owners welcome him or had they heard of what he'd done? Would they chase him off with a long gun?

Something tickled his nose. He brushed at it. Saw moisture on his fingertips. Stared at it in startled wonder. He touched his cheek again. Tears? He didn't cry, didn't even know how.

He scrubbed at his cheeks with the heels of his hands. Didn't intend to learn in the middle of the road.

He blinked to clear his vision. Where would he find his father? Didn't expect he'd be living in the big house with the new owners. Last time he'd seen the older man he'd been as dirty and ragged as any hobo Hatcher had encountered. Sure, he'd lost everything due to his own greed and carelessness. That didn't excuse letting himself go. He could at least have tried to pull things together instead of just giving up.

The tractor circled the field and stopped at a corner. The driver jumped off and trotted toward the house. Sure ran like Lowell. His mind was playing tricks, mixing his memories with reality.

The man glanced toward the road, saw Hatcher there

and veered toward him. Hatcher's shoulders sucked up as he prepared for the usual curt dismissal.

The man truly reminded him of Lowell. His loose gait, the way he swung his long arms, the right one always pumping harder than the left. Even the way he wore his hat tipped to one side.

The man slowed his steps, stared at Hatcher, pulled off his hat and shook his head, revealing hair as black as Hatcher's own.

"Lowell?" Could it be possible?

"Hatcher? Hatcher. Where have you been?" Lowell closed the distance in five leaps and crushed Hatcher to his chest. "My brother, I have waited and prayed for this moment."

Even if his arms weren't pinned to his side by Lowell's embrace Hatcher couldn't have moved. His feet gripped the dirt, curling the soles of his boots. It was all that anchored him. The rest of him felt like bits of wood randomly tossed together so they formed no definable shape. Nothing in his mind formed any better shape.

He felt moisture on his cheeks. His tears or Lowell's?

"Is it really you?" He hardly recognized the hoarse whisper as his own voice. It sounded as though it came from some distant spot above his head.

There is a friend that sticketh closer than a brother. Proverbs eighteen, verse twenty-four.

"Hey, brother. It's good to see you." Lowell's voice was muffled as he continued to press his cheek to Hatcher's.

Finally, with a little laugh, Lowell pulled away, his hands gripping Hatcher's shoulders as if he couldn't or wouldn't let him go. "Thank God you've returned."

Hatcher stared at his brother. "You're crying?"

"I'm that glad to see you."

"I heard Father was here. I came to see him. Didn't think I'd see you, too."

"Father lives with us."

Hatcher shook his head. None of this made any sense.

Lowell draped his arm across Hatcher's shoulders. "Come on and I'll tell you all about it." He led him up the lane toward the house.

Hatcher'd heard of dreams so real you couldn't be sure they weren't. In fact, he'd had a few of them himself. But usually he jerked awake about the time he walked toward home. He kept expecting that sudden jarring, breathless, disappointed feeling when wakefulness dropped him back into reality. But one step followed the next until they stood in front of the door.

"Marie, come see who I found. Father, you, too."

Now. It would end now. Just as the door opened.

But the door flew back, a very blond, petite woman rushed out, a towel in her hands.

"Marie, this is my brother, Hatcher."

The young woman launched herself off the step into Hatcher's arms. He had no choice but to hold her as she kissed and patted his cheek.

Hatcher set Marie on her feet, let his fingers linger a moment on her arm, waiting for the flesh to disappear when the dream ended. She continued to smile magnificiently.

He blinked. It must truly be reality. "Your wife?" he drawled.

Lowell laughed. "I told you he was droll."

Hatcher grinned at the teasing familiarity and felt the need to say something in kind. "And you have no doubt discovered Lowell is deadly serious at all times."

Marie giggled. "Oh, indeed, that's exactly what he is."

"Lowell, what is it?" A familiar voice called from

the small outbuilding that had always been their Father's workshop.

"Father, come see what the dog drug home," Lowell called.

"Lowell, what an awful way to talk about the brother you've worried about for years," Marie scolded.

Hatcher grinned at his brother. "You have?" He thought they'd be relieved to never see him again, supposed his name was never mentioned. Then his attention focused on the man who hurried toward them.

The older man stopped ten feet away. His mouth worked soundlessly at first. "Hatcher. You've finally come home."

"Yes, Father." He waited for the rejection he feared.

Tears poured down his father's face. He sobbed once, choked a bit and said, "You are as welcome as rain, my boy."

Hatcher closed the distance between them and hugged his father with a hunger bridging ten years. "Father, I am sorry. I hurt you. I sinned. Can you ever forgive me?"

The older man repeatedly patted Hatcher's back. Hatcher found the rhythm strangely comforting.

"Son, you have no need to ask my forgiveness. It is I who did wrong. I lost the farm and with it, I quit caring. You didn't deserve that. Either of you."

Hatcher's shoulders relaxed as if he'd shed a ten-year-old, rock-laden knapsack.

"Come in, all of you. Dinner's ready and waiting." Marie shepherded them inside the kitchen, rich with the scent of savory meat. She quickly added a plate to the table and the four of them sat down together as a family for the first time.

"Just like—" Hatcher broke off before he could finish.

"Just like when Mom was alive except now it's Marie." Lowell took his wife's hand and squeezed. Then he bowed and prayed. "God, our hearts are full of gratitude this day. Thank You for Your many mercies, for today restoring my long-lost brother to us." His voice thickened and he paused. "Thanks for the food, too," he finished hurriedly, as if tacking it on as an afterthought.

Hatcher, finally believing it was more than a dream, had a mind full of questions. "Johnny Styles said someone had purchased the farm."

Lowell stuck his chest out. "I did. And Father helped. He'd been saving his money."

Their father chuckled. "At the rate I was going it would be a hundred years before I had enough to make an offer."

Lowell playfully punched Hatcher's shoulders. "I made some money out in California. My aim was always to get the farm back. Brother, we put in too much sweat equity to let some stranger reap the benefits." He sobered and studied Hatcher's face. "I always intended both of us would be here but you plumb disappeared off the face of the earth. Where have you been?"

Hatcher felt their expectant waiting. "Nowhere. Everywhere. Mostly trying not to remember who I was, what I'd done."

Father leaned forward. "You are my son. You are a Jones. And you've done nothing to run from. What happened was an accident. Everyone knows that."

"I've been into trouble again. Called on Johnny to help me again."

"Another accident?" Lowell asked.

"Nobody died this time if that's what you're asking."

"I wasn't." Lowell gripped his shoulder. "I meant whatever happened, I know it wasn't your fault."

"Sorry. I guess I'm still defensive."

Lowell snorted. "So what happened?"

Hatcher told them the story. He should have known the one thing they'd hook on to was the mention of Kate.

"Tell us more about this Kate," Marie said, passing him a serving of rhubarb crisp.

"She's hardworking, determined and a good mother."

"Is she pretty?" Marie asked.

"She's not ugly."

Lowell chuckled. "Hatcher—the master of understatement."

Father leaned forward. "Hatcher, why didn't you come back sooner? It's been ten years. I thought I'd die without seeing you again."

Hatcher glanced from one to the other around the table. A great gulf existed, an expansion as wide as the Dakota sky, between the last time he'd seen his father and brother and now. "How can I expect any of you to understand what it's like to have a temper you can't control?"

His father laughed, a sound as full of sadness as mirth. "You were a boy. A boy who had been through a lot." He sobered. "Some of it my fault. Boys, I am sorry about losing the farm."

"Father," Lowell said. "It's water under the bridge."

Father thanked Lowell than turned back to Hatcher. "You might find this hard to believe but I, too, was known as a firebrand when I was young."

Lowell and Hatcher both stared. Lowell voiced Hatcher's disbelief. "You? I've never known you to lose your temper. Although—" he grinned at Hatcher

"—you were a slave driver and didn't tolerate any nonsense from us."

Father nodded. "A man outgrows some of his youthful exuberance and learns how ineffective anger is. Course I have to give your mother credit for her influence, as well. Nothing like the love of a good woman to settle a man."

Lowell took Marie's hand and they smiled as if they were alone at the table. Hatcher's thoughts turned to Kate. Sweet, beautiful Kate, who'd taken a chance on him, then begged him to stay. How was she doing now? Had she found someone to take Hatcher's place? His lungs caught with missing her.

Father cleared his throat. "All young bucks are rash."

Hatcher studied the fork in his hand. How many young bucks did his father know who flew into uncontrollable rages? *For from within, out of the heart of men, proceedeth evil thoughts…murders…all these evil things come from within, and defile the man.* Mark seven, verse twenty-one and twenty-three.

Only it wasn't evil, angry thoughts he had at that moment. He pictured Kate playing tag out by the coulee, her laughter—

Lowell tapped him on the shoulder. "Hey, little brother, what are you smiling about?"

Hatcher hadn't realized he was. "Just thinking."

When Lowell saw Hatcher didn't intend to say more, he pushed his chair back. "I found me a great cook, wouldn't you say?"

Hatcher smiled at Marie. "It was a lovely meal. Thank you."

"We've saved your old bedroom for you," she said in her soft, gentle voice.

Hatcher's eyes stung. "I hadn't planned to stay."

Lowell grinned. "Got someplace to be? Maybe back with a little gal named Kate?"

If only he could go back. He shook his head.

Lowell's expression grew serious. "Hatcher, you're not going to keep running."

Hatcher felt three pairs of eyes studying him but he stared at the tabletop.

"I don't understand," Lowell persisted.

"I don't expect you to."

"Explain what you're afraid of."

Hatcher stared at his brother. "Are you really so thick? I'm not going to take the chance I might again hurt someone when I lose my temper."

Lowell leaned forward until they were nose to nose. "Tell me something, little brother. When was the last time you were angry?"

Hatcher refused to answer but he knew. When he found Mary being bullied.

"I see you remember. And tell me. What did you do? Did you throw your fists? Pick up something to attack with? Did you feel like inflicting bodily harm?" Lowell leaned back. "I can see by your eyes that you didn't."

"Your point?"

"When I last saw you, you couldn't sit at a table without clenching your fists. You wore a scowl day and night. You didn't sit in a chair like you intended to relax. You were like an overwound spring." He sat back triumphantly. "You've changed but seems you don't re-alize it. It's time you let go of the past."

Father watched them keenly. "Hatcher, this is your home."

Hatcher looked from one to the other and slowly nod-ded. "I'll stay for a few days."

Lowell clapped him on the back. "You can help me with the haying."

Hatcher laughed. "So you're just looking for a cheap hired man."

Lowell grinned. "Come on. I'll show you what we've been doing." Father joined them as they walked along the fields and discussed crops and weather and cows. Some things had changed. More land had been broken, one field seeded with tame grass. And the rock piles had grown bigger. He nudged Lowell. "Glad I wasn't here for that."

Over the next few days, Hatcher worked alongside Lowell and Father. The work had a calming familiarity to it. To look up from his work and see the same hills, the same buildings, the same father and brother crossing the yard did something to his soul. He didn't want to call it healing or cleansing. He'd rather call it something more practical. Like familiarity.

Sunday rolled around. The family had always gone to church. No questions asked. When Hatcher lounged at the table in his work clothes, the three of them stared at him.

"You going to church in that?"

He had more clothes now. Marie had seen to that. And he had the suit Kate gave him for the trial so he couldn't plead it was the best he had. They all knew better. "Not going to church."

Three pairs of eyes blinked as if they'd never heard of someone not attending.

Father grunted but Lowell got in the first word. "I know what's going on. You're afraid to face the people. Well, little brother, I hate to burst your self-important bubble but you're the only one who is still thinking about the accident. Everyone else has moved on. Lived lives. Got married. Had babies. Lost parents. For us, for the community, what happened ten years ago is a long time in the past."

Hatcher grunted. "Easy for you to decide that."

"Find out for yourself," Lowell challenged. "Or do you prefer to keep living the way you have been? Shutting out family, always on the move? Come on, Hatch, it's time to move on." He crossed his arms over his chest and leaned back. "Unless you're afraid of the truth."

Chapter Nineteen

Kate struggled with her decision but finally asked Mr. Sandstrum to help with the hay in return for a share of it.

It created a problem for her. The hay crop was thin as the hair on Old Sam Jensen's head. She scratched around for every blade, knowing it would be precious as gold before the winter ended. Giving some of it away in exchange for help left her with the knowledge she'd run short but it came down to some of the hay was better than leaving it to dry up in the field.

She had the few loads Mr. Cyrus had managed to haul in between naps.

With the last load of hay done, hauled away in Mr. Sandstrum's wagon, there was a lull in the farmwork and slowly her back began to heal.

The garden needed constant attention. She still couldn't lift a bucket of water without pain so the children helped her haul water to the struggling plants. They helped hoe out weeds, too, but still there was much they couldn't do.

Day after day, Kate wondered if she'd made a mistake insisting on keeping the farm. Not that she would marry Doyle. She paused, smiling as she leaned over the hoe handle. Seems Doyle would be moving on anyway. The sheriff had charged him with obstruction of justice for planting the money in Hatcher's belongings. They still hadn't discovered the culprit responsible for the robbery. A hobo, long gone, seemed the most likely explanation.

She returned to hilling the potatoes and thinking about the farm. It represented home and security for herself and the children but unless she found help...

If only Hatcher would come back. She missed him so much. She glanced toward the shanty, remembering his loose gait as he came for breakfast.

She did what she did every time she thought about Hatcher many, many times throughout the day. She prayed. *Lord, keep him safe. Provide a warm dry place for him. Help him realize he's loved. And help me know what to do about the farm.*

The pain in her back grew too much to bear and she leaned the hoe against a post and returned to the house. The children were at school. Only a few more days before they'd be home for the summer.

How would she manage? She'd promised herself she'd give them more attention than she had in the past. Yet she had the farmwork to attend to as well as her regular household chores.

For the first time ever, the farm seemed burdensome, and instead of security, it felt like a ball and chain. She made herself a cup of tea and sat on the chair she'd left against the side of the house in the shade. She closed her eyes. But the sunlight drummed against her eyelids.

She sighed and fanned the hem of her skirt to cool herself. At least she had the relative relief of shade from her house and cool water from the well to quench her thirst.

Not like the many summers she'd spent with no protection but a scraggly bush and the tarp her father stretched out above them to provide protection. The sun didn't beat directly on them but still the heat built unmercifully underneath the patch of canvas.

"Momma, did you ever live in a house?"

"Katie, what a question? We lived in a house all winter."

Kate flung over on her side to study her mother. "It weren't ours. And it didn't keep out the snow. I mean did you live in a real house? One belonging to you?"

Her mother's gaze drifted past Kate to something in the distance. "As a child I lived in a little yellow house with fancy gingerbread trim where the roof peaked. There was a low little attic room under the eaves. It was cold in the winter, sweltering in the summer but it was my favorite place. I would play among the castaway things and pretend I lived in a different place, a different time."

With a huge sigh, Kate lay on her back. "Why did you leave?"

"I grew up. Met your father. He was so excited about moving west. I'd always wanted to see the West so it was easy to agree to go with him. Course I loved him lots." She smiled at Kate. "Still do."

Kate thought she must love him an awful lot to follow him around the country, year after year having no place to call her own.

"If I ever had a place of my own, I'd never leave it."

"You would if you had enough reason."

"No reason would be good enough."

Kate tried to remember what her mother's reply had

been. Seems she hadn't wanted to hear. Now she knew there might be a reason strong enough to make her leave her home and security.

Hatcher. If he sent her a message asking her to join him, would she go?

If not for her children, she'd follow him on the road as her mother had but her children needed and deserved a home.

She needed more, too. Or was it less?

But what?

Security. They all needed safety and security.

Suddenly she remembered how her mother had answered. "I have an eternal home that will be better than any house ever built."

"Better than a palace?"

"Much. It will be beautiful and it will be mine to share with those I love. Best of all, my Lord and Savior will be there."

Kate remembered how she'd thrilled to her mother's assurance.

"Katie, girl, it doesn't matter what we have here on earth because wherever we go, whether we live in a house or under a tarp, God is with us. In the Psalms it says, 'Lord, thou hast been our dwelling place in all generations.... He that dwelleth in the secret place of the most High shall abide under the shadow of the Almighty. I will say of the Lord, He is my refuge and my fortress: my God: in him will I trust.... he shall cover thee with his feathers, and under his wings shalt thou trust.' Child, what could be better than that?"

The words had comforted her—until it rained and she was cold and miserable.

But now her mother's words echoed in her mind.

It never seemed to matter that they left a perfectly

good house to camp at the side of the road, or huddle cold and hungry as her father searched for a better place for them. Through it all her mother remained calm and accepting.

Kate wanted the kind of peace and assurance her mother had. She'd thought she'd find it by having a house she would never have to leave, a place of her own. Security.

An anchor for her soul.

But it wasn't a house and farm she needed. It was trust—trust in God's love and care.

Thou wilt keep him in perfect peace, whose mind is stayed on thee: because he trusteth in thee.

She rested her tea cup on her knee and stared out at the wheat field. The plants had emerged sporadically. Some had since been cut off by the driving winds. Others had withered and died under the relentless sun. A few stubbornly held their own, but showed little growth. Her crop wouldn't be worth cutting for anything but feed, unless they got a good soaking rain soon. She considered the barn, the lean-to where the old beast was parked, the garden that struggled to survive the heat and wind.

Consider the lilies how they grow: they toil not, they spin not; and yet I say unto you, that Solomon in all his glory was not arrayed like one of these. If then God so clothe the grass, which is to day in the field, and to morrow cast into the over; how much more will he clothe you, O ye of little faith?

"Oh, Lord," she groaned. "I know You will always take care of me. Help me trust You for all my needs."

She wanted to trust God. Years of stubbornly providing her own security were hard to lay aside.

Over the next few days she struggled with her feelings often crying, "Lord, help my unbelief."

Today she headed for the garden to check and see if there were any potatoes big enough to steal from under the plant.

As she knelt and searched in the dirt for the small hard lumps that would be baby potatoes, she heard the words. "Let not your heart be troubled. Neither let it be afraid."

She jerked around to see who spoke. She was alone. She sat in the dirt between rows of green potato plants.

"Let not your heart be troubled. Neither let it be afraid."

She knew the words came from her own thoughts, recognized them as scripture. But as surely as if God had sent an angel to stand in the middle of the garden and deliver the message, she knew the words came straight from God's heart to hers. With gulping sobs, she surrendered her needs to Him, trusting Him to provide the security she craved and wanted to provide her children.

Like a flash she saw and understood several things. She couldn't manage the farm on her own but there was a way she could keep the house, provide a warm safe place for herself and the children. The solution seemed so obvious it amazed her she hadn't done it in the first place.

She'd rent out the land to a neighbor on the understanding she be allowed to keep the house and barn. The only way anyone would take it under the drought conditions was if the rent were based on crop share. The more the renter got, the more Kate got. Of course, the reverse also applied—less crop, less rent. But without the costs and work of trying to farm, she could manage with the garden and by keeping a couple of cows and the chickens.

She slowed her thoughts to remind herself: Whatever they needed, God would provide.

"Lord," she prayed as she dug out enough potatoes for supper. "I give you also my love for Hatcher. I want him to come back but I leave it in Your hands."

It was probably the hardest decision she'd ever made. She would never stop loving him and hoping for his return. No doubt she'd have to remind herself over and over that what mattered most was that God would heal his heart. Until then…

She felt considerably more at peace in the following days. She would wait until after the meager harvest or even toward spring to approach her neighbors about renting her land.

Today as she waved the children off to school, she noticed a thread of smoke twisting above the trees across the road. Her heart squeezed hard. Hatcher had once camped there.

She shook away the thought. Other hobos used the spot. She returned to the house to finish separating the milk, then grabbed a hat and headed for the garden. Even knowing how futile it was to hope, she glanced toward the trees.

A man stood in the shadows.

Kate blinked. The way he stood…the way he touched the brim of his hat…

"Hatcher?" she whispered, and stared hard trying to see more clearly.

The man stepped from the shadows. The sun flashed across his face. He started across the field.

"Hatcher," she screamed, her feet racing down the lane. She didn't slow until she was within arm's reach then she skidded to a stop, restrained herself from fleeing into his embrace. Why had he come?

"You've come back." Her words came out breathless more from the crash of emotions through her than the effort of the short run.

He didn't speak, his gaze warm and searching as he considered her chin, her mouth, her eyes.

She smiled. "I've been waiting and hoping and praying you'd come back."

"Yeah?"

"Yes. I hate to think of anyone out in the cold. I can offer you a warm place."

"I've already found one."

She ducked her head to hide her disappointment.

He tipped her chin up. "Right here." He pressed his hand over his heart. "You showed me how to feel again. How to trust. Myself, God and others. I used to fear my emotions. I thought…"

She pressed her fingers to his lips. "Shh. You were wrong. Your emotions are a gift from God. They enable to you to care. To feel. To—"

"Live and love. I want to do both right here."

"I could always use a good man." What did he mean—live and love right here?

"Could you use a husband?" His words were so soft she almost wondered if she'd imagined it.

He pulled her close. "Kate, I love you. I want to spend the rest of my life loving you and enjoying you and the children. Did you mean it when you said you loved me? Do you still feel the same?"

Her heart burst from its moors and raced wildly for her throat so her words sounded airy. "Hatcher, I love you. I will marry you and spend the rest of my life loving you and enjoying you." She snorted then laughed at his wide-eyed expression. "You are asking me to marry you?"

He bent his head and his mouth touched her lips so gently tears filled her eyes. And her heart rejoiced.

She drew him into the house. "Tell me where you've been and what made you change your mind."

"I went home."

She nodded. "Mary said you were. What did you find?"

He gave a slow, easy smile that seemed to come from somewhere deep inside. "I found my beginnings."

She sighed. "I hope you have more explanation than that."

He did. He told her about the welcome of his brother and his wife, and the open arms of his father. "And they persuaded me to go to church. There's a new, young preacher there. When I first saw him I thought he looked like a weakling. But as soon as I heard him, I knew he had a fiery spirit. His words shot straight to my heart. He talked about Jesus being the Prince of Peace. You know the verse in Isaiah fifty-three, verse five?"

Kate shook her head.

Hatcher took her hand and held it between his.

She sensed he had to tell her, needed her to understand how he'd made the journey from guilt to this quiet joy she saw in his eyes. And she ached to understand.

"It says, 'He was wounded for our transgression, he was bruised for our iniquities: the chastisement of our peace was upon him; and with his stripes we are healed.' Peace is God's gift to us. There is nothing we need to do but accept it. The preacher said, if any of us carried a burden of guilt, God's word assured us we could be free. Free indeed."

Hatcher shook his head. "It seemed too easy to me.

I sought absolution for ten years but that man stood up there and declared on the authority of God's word that peace was mine for the taking. I just couldn't get my head around it."

"You didn't want to believe maybe."

"I think I didn't know how. So I went to see Gilead, the preacher. I went with a mixture of desperation and frustration and asked him how he could say we don't need to feel guilty when we are guilty."

Hatcher chuckled. "I think I wanted to see the man cower and agree with me but he said, 'Hatcher, all of us are guilty. That's what's so amazing about God's love.'"

Kate couldn't tear her gaze from the wonder and peace she saw in Hatcher's face. He'd found healing. *Thank you, God.*

"We had a sword fight."

Kate blinked. "You dueled? What kind of preacher is he?"

"His weapon was the word of God. He quoted scriptures refuting every verse I gave to prove my belief in my guilt. God knew it was the one thing I couldn't argue against. He began with Romans five, verse eight, 'While we were yet sinners, Christ died for us.' And went on to John eight, verse thirty-six, 'If the Son therefore shall make you free, ye shall be free indeed.'

"He said Jesus was the perfect sacrifice. Did I think I could add anything to what Jesus had done? Did punishing myself serve as a better sacrifice?"

Hatcher grinned. "He left me with nothing to do but face the truth about the last ten years. I'd been refusing God's forgiveness for this one thing because I didn't think I deserved forgiveness. I believe Jesus died for my sins. Just not my anger."

Kate waited as he found the words to explain.

"I thought because it was something I used to hurt people, God couldn't forgive it. Gilead made me see the truth. My reason said he was right. My heart wasn't so easily convinced."

Kate's heart tightened as she thought of his struggle to accept forgiveness. "But you're here. I can tell by looking at you that you found a way to prove it to your heart. What happened?"

"I remembered a time I had displeased my mother. I ran off to play with Lowell without watering the baby chicks and several of them died. She scolded me. I knew I deserved it but I felt as if I'd lost her love. She came to me after I'd gone to bed and told me how much she loved me and how she knew I'd grow into a good and honorable man. I realized that her love forgave my disobedience. Just as God's love does. I knew God's love was more perfect than even a mother's love. I finally believed and accepted it."

Kate laughed from pure joy. "God is so good."

"Amen." He trailed his fingers along her cheek. "I look forward to spending the rest of my life enjoying God's goodness with you at my side."

Kate knew joy as she'd never before known as she leaned forward and received his gentle, promising kiss.

Kate wanted no fuss. She and Hatcher planned to go to the preacher and be pronounced man and wife. That's all they needed.

But Sally would have none of it. "At least let me serve tea. After all, it's a special occasion. How often do you plan to get married?"

"This will be twice but God willing, the last time." She knew if Jeremiah watched from somewhere above, he'd be cheering her on.

"Then let me show my joy. Let me do this."

Kate reluctantly agreed. "Just you and Frank and Tommy."

"The preacher and his wife, too, of course."

"Of course." Sally and her husband were standing up with them, so Kate knew her friend would be forced to keep things simple.

The children also stood up with them. It had been Hatcher's idea. "I'm declaring my love for them, too," he explained.

Kate helped Mary adjust the new pink dress. Hatcher insisted he would look after Dougie. He said he'd meet her at the church. Kate was pleased and surprised to discover he was a romantic traditionalist.

She smoothed her own dress, a soft dove-gray with gentle lines. Sally said it made her look serene. She hugged her secret. She felt serene. More settled than ever before in her life.

Kate studied her reflection in the mirror and admitted she looked extremely happy. *Thank you, God.*

"Come on, Mary. Hatcher and Dougie will be waiting."

They got into the old truck and Kate covered their dresses with a sheet to keep them spotless.

Mary couldn't stop wriggling with excitement. Kate smiled, barely able to restrain her own body.

"Momma, can I call him Daddy?"

Kate pressed her lips together and held back tears. It wouldn't do to show up at her own wedding with her face streaked.

"I know he'd be pleased."

Mary nodded. "Poppa won't mind, will he?"

Kate realized Mary had the same feeling of Jeremiah's closeness as she. "I think he'd like it. All he would want is for you to be happy."

Mary bounced then clasped her hands in her lap. "I'm very happy. I love Hatcher."

"Me, too."

Mary giggled. "Suppose that's why you're marrying him."

Kate chuckled. "You're beginning to sound like Hatcher—Daddy."

"That's good, isn't it?"

"It's very very good."

They pulled into the church parking area. Sally rushed toward them. "Hurry, everyone's waiting."

"We're ready." Kate took Mary's hand and squeezed it. Mary squeezed back.

At the church door, Sally stopped. "Mary and I will go first and then you follow. We're going to do this right."

She and Sally hugged.

Sally had wanted so much for Kate to have a big wedding with the whole community in attendance. Kate explained Hatcher wasn't comfortable with meeting the whole community yet. He'd attended church with her, gone to the store, but he'd spent ten years avoiding people. It would take time.

She pushed open the door and gasped.

Every pew was filled. The church was decorated with wildflowers and greenery. The organist played the wedding march as Kate stared. Someone stuck a bouquet in her hands. Hatcher stood at the front waiting for her.

Their eyes locked and suddenly she didn't care if the President attended. She saw no one but Hatcher and slowly followed Sally and Mary down the aisle.

She reached his side, drank in his look of love and took his arm as they faced the preacher.

A few minutes later they were pronounced man and wife. "You may kiss your bride."

Hatcher's smile sent fire into his eyes before he lowered his head and kissed her.

The congregation clapped. People reached for them, shaking hands and brushing their cheeks with quick kisses, as they marched down the aisle.

"I'm sorry," Kate said as they rushed through the door. "Sally must have done this."

"I'm not sorry. It's just what I needed. To see everyone glad for us."

"Then I'm glad she did it."

Sally leaned over Kate's shoulder and whispered. "It's just the beginning."

"What do you mean?"

"The community decided they wanted to do it right. See for yourself."

Kate turned to see men setting up tables, women putting out food. To one side stood a smaller table piled with gifts.

"I can't believe it. I said small," she scolded Sally.

But already people were filing by shaking hands, congratulating them. Many offered advise to Hatcher. "She's stubborn, best be careful." "Don't let her rule the roost." "We admire this little woman. She's had a hard time these past three years. Glad to see she has someone to share her load." And all of them welcomed him to the community.

They were led to the place of honor, at the head of a small table and the women served them. The others grabbed chairs and gathered in a circle around them.

Kate turned to study her new husband. He smiled

widely. How she loved that smile. He winked at her. "What is my wife thinking?"

"I'm hoping you're not finding this overwhelming."

"I'm enjoying every minute of it. I intend to enjoy every minute of my life from now on. And make up for ten years I wasted. Are you ready for the fun?"

"I love you," she whispered.

"And I love you."

The children giggled. Hatcher laughed. The crowd cheered and clapped until he pulled Kate to her feet and kissed her soundly.

"To God be the glory," he whispered for her ears alone.

"Great things He hath done," she whispered back.

* * * * *

Ruth Axtell Morren wrote her first story—a spy thriller—when she was twelve, and knew she wanted to be a writer. There were many detours along the way. She studied comparative literature at Smith College, taught English in the Canary Islands and worked in international development in Miami, Florida, where she met her future husband.

She has divided the intervening years between the Netherlands and the down east coast of Maine.

She gained her first recognition as a writer when her second manuscript was a finalist for the Romance Writers of America Golden Heart® Award in 1994. Ruth's second novel, *Wild Rose* (2004), was selected as a Booklist Top 10 Christian Novel in 2005.

Ruth loves hearing from readers. You can contact her through her website at ruthaxtell.com.

Books by Ruth Axtell Morren

Love Inspired Historical

Hearts in the Highlands
A Man Most Worthy
To Be a Mother
A Gentleman's Homecoming
Hometown Cinderella

Visit the Author Profile page
at Harlequin.com for more titles.

HEARTS IN THE
HIGHLANDS

Ruth Axtell Morren

And let us not be weary in well doing,
for in due season we shall reap, if we faint not.
—*Galatians* 6:9

Wherever I wander, wherever I rove,
The hills of the Highlands for ever I love.
—Robert Burns, "Farewell to the Highlands"

For Susan.

Remember, it's never too late.

Chapter One

London, 1890

"Imagine waking up, a knife at your throat—"

Since Reid Gallagher stepped into his great-aunt's parlor, Maddie had been transported to another time and place.

He leaned forward in the velvet upholstered armchair, rumpling the lace covers on each arm with his strong hands.

"It was touch and go for a while there." Humor underscored the quiet rumble of his words. "They stormed us on horseback, surrounding our camp in the dead of night, brandishing their knives and cudgels. All we could do was fumble for our weapons in the dark—"

Maddie sat riveted, listening to the rugged man with the lean, deeply tanned face, sun-bleached sandy hair and thick mustache a shade darker. His words evoked a kaleidoscope of images—a British surveying party in the midst of the lonely desert, the night air cool, the stillness broken by a band of rebels, the neigh of horses and bray of camels....

"Oh, dear heavens!" Lady Haversham left off stroking her Yorkshire terrier. "Was anyone killed?"

He looked down, his tone grim. "Two, including Colonel Parker, the head of our expedition. Our men rallied immediately, of course. We sleep with our weapons near at hand, so we were able to rout the group in no time—"

"My smelling salts!" Lady Haversham fanned her face. "I feel about to faint. Madeleine!" The terrier, Lilah, jumped up with a sharp bark.

Maddie hurried to her employer's side. "Hush, Lilah!"

"Do please hurry." Lady Haversham sat with her head against the antimacassar, her eyes closed, her breathing shallow.

Maddie reached for the tapestry bag that kept a host of things Lady Haversham might need at any given moment. In a second, she located the small vial and waved it under the elderly lady's nostrils.

She started at the whiff. "Oh!"

Maddie immediately withdrew the vial and fetched a small cross-stitched cushion to place behind her. At the terrier's continued barking, she took the tiny dog in her arms. "See, your mistress is perfectly fine," she crooned, petting Lilah's long, silky hair until the dog was quiet.

"That's better," Lady Haversham said. "I felt so light-headed for a moment." She reached for her pet. "Come, my darling, Mama's right here."

The russet-colored terrier settled back down on her mistress's lap. Mr. Gallagher stood beside his great-aunt's chair, anxiety etching his brow. Lady Haversham reached out a hand, which trembled slightly. His sun-browned one grasped her pale, age-spotted one like a great bird enfolding a baby bird under its wing.

"You see, my boy, how I am. I'm so glad you've come home at last." Her voice quavered while her watery blue eyes gazed up into his with relief.

Mr. Gallagher's glance shifted to Maddie, and she was struck by their light hue against his dark, weathered features, like finding a bright blue marble amidst rough burlap. She gave a hesitant smile, wishing to reassure him. If only she could tell him a week didn't go by that Lady Haversham wouldn't come near to dying in one form or another.

But Mr. Gallagher had turned his attention back to his great-aunt. "Maybe I should call your physician?"

"No, don't trouble yourself. I'll be well if I just sit quietly." She closed her eyes again, but kept her hold on her nephew's hand, her gnarled fingers clutching it as if to a lifeline.

"I worry about you, living so far away in a heathen land. I don't know what I'd do if anything happened to you. You and Vera are my only relations."

Something flickered in the tall man's eyes, as if he weren't used to having any emotional ties. "You needn't have worried. You see me here fit as always. Don't upset yourself anymore thinking of it."

Lady Haversham reopened her eyes. "I can't help it. Thank God you're back on British soil. At least this incident caused your return, for which I am grateful. I hope you are home in England for good."

"I'm back for a few weeks, at any rate." His tone betrayed no joy at the fact. "Until the two governments satisfy themselves that it's safe to continue our work."

When it appeared his aunt had recovered, Mr. Gallagher slowly disengaged his hand from hers. "The situation as it stands now is that two bands of Bedouin presently think they own the Sinai. There are continual skirmishes between the two tribes. Our British party happened to be caught in the middle of this one. The Tuara who attacked our camp wanted to make sure we were hiding no Tiyaha among us."

Lady Haversham waved away his description. "Oh, it's too confusing for me. All I know is my heart can't take the thought of you among those savages."

"Well, you needn't fear for now. The attack on our camp stopped all work while both the Egyptian and British authorities investigate things." He moved back a pace and ran a hand through his hair, leaving the thick blond strands disheveled. Maddie could hear the frustration underlying the words, and she sensed he was a man who wouldn't willingly endure enforced idleness.

Lady Haversham continued to stroke Lilah's long hair. "Well, I am thankful for that at least. Please ring for some tea, Madeleine. I'm sure we could all use some. This news has been most upsetting...." The old lady brought her lace-edged handkerchief up to her mouth and shook her head.

"Of course." Maddie headed for the bellpull.

With a last look at his aunt, Mr. Gallagher returned to his chair. "I'm sorry, Aunt Millicent. I shouldn't have been so blunt."

"It's not your fault. You haven't been back in a few years. It's understandable you didn't realize my frail condition. The least thing upsets me. It's my heart, you see. Dr. Aldwin says I mustn't have anything upset me."

"I didn't realize how...delicate you'd become since I last saw you." He gave an awkward laugh. "I've been so far from British society during that time, in the company of men, I've forgotten how to put things more gently for a lady's ears."

"Good heavens, you mustn't let yourself become uncivilized." Lady Haversham sat straighter, letting the cushion fall to the floor and causing Lilah to let out a bark. "We shall have to remedy that now you're back in London. Of course, I no longer entertain. My nerves can't take crowds. But your sister and her husband can organize things."

He leaned forward, alarm in his blue eyes. "Aunt Millicent, you know I'm not interested in attending parties—"

"Nonsense. Your friends and acquaintances want to know you're back in town. It would be a disservice to deprive them of your company."

He scrubbed a large hand across his jaw, as if wanting to argue the point but afraid of upsetting his aunt further.

Maddie resumed her own seat and took up her needlepoint.

His aunt settled Lilah back down. "As I was saying, Vera will hold a few teas for you, perhaps a musicale one evening."

"I'm here only to cool my heels until the ambassador finds out what kind of trick the sultan is playing—"

"I know you don't like to socialize. But your friends will be hurt if you come stealing into town like a thief in the night, no one the wiser."

"I only came back because I was forced to...."

Maddie wrenched her attention away from this interesting exchange when a black-clad maid with frilly white apron entered the room. Knowing exactly how Lady Haversham preferred her tea, Maddie set about pouring the older lady's cup first. But her heart couldn't help being moved by the man who so clearly felt out of his element in London. She remembered her own difficulty readjusting to England when she and her family had first returned from the Middle East.

Maddie placed the cup and saucer beside Lady Haversham and took Lilah from her. "Give her a little platter of cake."

"Yes, my lady." Maddie set the miniature dog on the carpet, knowing she'd probably have to clean up after her within the hour. As she approached Mr. Gallagher's chair, the dog following at her heels, Maddie felt a tremor of nervousness at addressing him directly. "How do you take your tea?" she inquired above Lilah's barking.

"Just one lump and a wedge of lemon, thank you." He spared Maddie only a glance then sat back, an elbow against the chair's arm, his fingers idly smoothing his mustache, his thoughts clearly elsewhere.

"Very good," she said, stifling the desire to be noticed by this man. By now she should be used to being overlooked by Lady Haversham's visitors like another piece of furniture in the room. Taking herself to task, she walked back to the tea cart. The terrier jumped onto the settee and leaned eagerly toward the loaded cart, barking her interest in its delicacies. With a grim sigh, Maddie cut her a sliver of cake and placed it on the flower-edged Limoges dessert plate. Lilah was ahead of her, already back on the ground and barking her impatience. Maddie set the treat down on the floor, where Lilah immediately began to devour it, her little body twitching in eagerness.

Maddie proceeded to pour Mr. Gallagher his cup, hoping Lilah would hold down the cake at least until their guest had departed. When she returned to him, he reached for the cup before she had a chance to set it down.

"Thank you. Perfect," he added with a smile of approval at the wedge of lemon she had set beside the cup on its saucer.

The sudden smile relieved the harshness of his features. Maddie felt a warmth steal over her. Dismayed by her own reaction, she stepped away from him. "Would you care for a slice of cake?"

"That would be fine." Again he gave her a smile, which affected her more than it should for such a brief, superficial exchange. A part of her yearned to prolong the conversation. Instead, she bowed her head and hurried back to the tea table.

She scolded herself for the pleasure it gave her to fill his request. Knowing how good her employer's appetite was, Maddie cut Lady Haversham a large slice.

"I've brought back some pieces collected last year at a dig in Hawara," Mr. Gallagher said to his aunt. "The British Museum was quite pleased with them. I'll be doing a series of lectures while I'm here."

"Your Uncle George had quite a collection of artifacts himself from all his travels in the Orient."

He smiled, looking more relaxed than he had since he'd entered the overstuffed room. "Yes, I recall. He used to show me things every time I visited."

"He had countless items. I've kept everything carefully stored in boxes over the years." She sighed. "If anything should happen to me, what is to become of all of it?"

He cleared his throat, as if uncomfortable with the drift of the conversation.

"There was a pyramid at the site of our dig."

She brightened. "How fascinating."

When Maddie had poured her own cup, she set it down to cool and took up her needlepoint. Under the guise of rethreading her needle, she observed Mr. Gallagher, unconcerned that he would notice. His focus was on his great-aunt, as he described the project. Thankfully, Lilah had settled at Maddie's feet for another nap.

Although he wore a well-tailored sack coat, vest and trousers, the light khaki material of the trousers and the lightweight tweed of his jacket gave Mr. Gallagher a much less formal look than the average man about London. The few gentlemen to visit Lady Haversham—her solicitor, physician and old Reverend Steele—all wore long dark frock coats with matching vests and trousers, their somber colors seeming to underscore their lofty positions.

This man's lighter-colored garments, like the desert sand, brought a foreign element into the parlor, making the room with its heavy dark furniture and surfaces covered with bric-a-brac suddenly appear more confined and overcrowded than usual.

Maddie drank in Mr. Gallagher's words as he described the relatively new study of how long-ago civilizations had lived their daily lives. Maddie could picture it all so clearly because she'd spent a good portion of her girlhood in the Holy Land with her missionary parents. Egypt was very close to Palestine, and Mr. Gallagher's narrative brought back memories of desert sands, swarthy people riding their camels or donkeys and bleached huts at the foothills of scrubby mountains.

As he described the harsh conditions of the dig, Maddie pictured him in wrinkled khakis and tall scuffed boots, a battered hat shading his piercing blue eyes from the sun. She'd noticed their color as soon as she'd been introduced to him, the moment he'd taken her hand in his in a strong, though brief, handshake. She judged him to be in his late thirties or early forties.

Mr. Gallagher would probably be startled at how much she already knew about him. When Lady Haversham wasn't discussing her various ailments, she boasted of her great-nephew, who had followed in his great-uncle's footsteps to become an Egyptologist and surveyor to the Crown in the lands between Africa and India.

Maddie's attention quickened when she heard Mr. Gallagher tell his great-aunt, "The Royal Egypt Fund is sponsoring the lectures. It's in their interest to promote Egyptology with the general public."

"Yes, your uncle was on the forefront of getting the government interested in the artifacts over there. You must tell me when you're to lecture, although I hardly get out anymore, you know. It was a dreadful winter. I didn't think I'd survive that attack of pleurisy. Then with my usual neuralgia, I don't know how I manage."

"My first lecture is at the end of the week."

"Oh, goodness. Well, this April weather is still much too changeable for me to venture forth."

"Of course. I wouldn't expect you to take any risks with your health."

Maddie hoped he'd say more about when and where the lecture would be.

There was a lull in the conversation, then Mr. Gallagher said, "I've brought back a mummified head."

"You haven't!" His aunt's eyes widened. "How ever did you find one?"

His fingers stroked his chin as he mused, "Sometimes it's when you stop searching for something that you find it." His glance crossed Maddie's at that moment, and she realized she'd been staring at him.

To cover her embarrassment, she blurted out, "Would you like some more tea?"

"Oh, my yes, how remiss of us," his aunt said immediately.

He looked down at his cup as if he'd forgotten he'd been holding it. "Yes, that would be just the thing."

Before Maddie could rise, Mr. Gallagher stood and ambled over to the tea cart. Lilah stirred, but she only twitched her nose at the toes of his boots and didn't bark.

Maddie felt dwarfed by the man's above-average height as he paused in front of the cart. He continued his line of conversation as he held out his cup and saucer to Maddie with a smile.

"We discovered several mummy portraits dating to the Roman period. The site around the pyramid appears to be a royal burial ground."

"Your Uncle George always wanted to find some proof of this procedure, but alas, was unsuccessful."

Maddie poured the tea, hoping her hand didn't shake. Then she lifted one lump of sugar with the silver tongs and set it into the cup with a small plop, fearful the tea would splatter. All the while, she was aware of his hand holding the saucer. Strong looking, tanned, like his face, to a deep hue. Then she noticed the gold wedding band on his ring finger. Lady Haversham had told her he was a widower of many years. Maddie's heart went out to him in sympathy, thinking how he must continue to mourn his late wife, if he still wore the ring.

She discarded the used lemon slice and took a fresh one with another pair of tongs, then placed it on the edge of the saucer. There it slipped off, and as her hand flinched, trying to retrieve the lemon, he covered it for an instant with his free one.

"Steady there." A trace of humor laced his husky voice.

She met his blue gaze and whispered a thank-you. "Anytime," he murmured, before moving away from her.

She sat for the rest of his visit remembering the feel of his warm palm against her skin. Warm like the Egyptian sun.

Her mother used to say, "Your hands are always like ice." Her father would immediately reply, "Cold hands, warm heart."

Was it true? Did she have a warm heart? Sometimes, lately, she felt it squeezed dry by her employer. She shook aside the thought, reminding herself of her Christian duty to serve.

Mr. Gallagher sat back down. "I'll be featuring the mummy's head at my first lecture. It should draw a crowd."

His aunt cut into her piece of cake. "When is the lecture precisely?"

Maddie's hand stilled on her cup as she listened to his answer.

"The first one will be Thursday morning at ten. Another will be held on Friday afternoon. We'll judge which times draw the most attendance before scheduling the others."

Thursday at ten. That would be perfect. Lady Haversham generally didn't stir until noon. Maddie would have plenty of time to get to the museum and back before she was even missed.

Thursday at ten. She committed the time to memory and determined to read everything she could lay her hands on about Egyptology in the meantime.

A new fear cropped up. Would Mr. Gallagher see her at the lecture? If so, what would he think? She didn't want to appear forward in any way. After all she was only his great-aunt's paid companion.

Paid companion. The ugly words reminded her who and what she had been for the last decade of her life.

From a young woman who'd dreamed of serving the Lord on the mission field, to a poorly paid employee at the beck and call of a spoiled society lady, the only difference between Maddie's position and that of the other servants was the dubious distinction of sitting at her employer's table. In everything else, she was repeatedly demeaned by word and gesture countless times a day.

Maddie sat back with a sigh, telling herself, as she'd been telling herself each day since she'd begun her job under Lady Haversham, that she should take joy in her service. She'd almost convinced herself until this afternoon, when Reid Gallagher had entered this airless parlor and reminded her of that other world out there that once had been her world, too.

Chapter Two

"These gilded mummy masks are particularly nice specimens." Reid held up a pair of shiny gold heads for the audience to view. His eyes scanned the packed hall of the British Museum. The Egyptian Fund would be pleased with the sold-out crowd. There were even people standing in the back.

"We also have coverings for the upper parts of the body and the feet." As he spoke, he set down the masks and took up the carved forms, the former showing crossed arms, and the latter, bare feet molded in gold.

"These were discovered in what we presume is a burial ground in Hawara, a few miles west of the Nile. The pyramid in the midst of this area was the burial tomb of King Amenemhat III.

"We were fortunate to uncover so many undisturbed items. Because they were buried so well, looters hadn't yet discovered them."

Reid kept looking from the objects he described to the people in the audience, trying to gauge if they were following what he was saying. He knew from previous presentations that his audience was composed of people from all walks of life. Few would have any in-depth archaeological knowledge.

His eyes swung back from the rear of the hall toward the front. Suddenly, his gaze backtracked, thinking he'd recognized a face. He had to peer behind a lady's wide straw hat, flanked on either side by two large bird's wings. A young woman sat behind and to one side of it. She appeared to be listening intently to his talk. A pity that from where she sat, there was little detail she'd be able to discern of the artifacts.

"This king lived in what is known as the Middle Kingdom." He held up a large sculpted head of the pharaoh, all the while trying to place the face of the young woman. Reid had few acquaintances in London anymore, much less female ones.

Then it came to him. Aunt Millie's latest companion. Reid glanced once again at the woman in the back as he explained how excavations were carried out. "We use a system called stratification, where a series of layers are carefully dug."

He walked over to the tables covered with dozens of pots and numerous pottery fragments. "These pieces of sculpture and glazed faience were obtained in this manner. Although it's more dramatic to come across a large monument like a pyramid, as my acclaimed colleague William Petrie says, to uncover the secrets of the past, it's much more significant to study the everyday utensils of these buried sites. Hence, our emphasis on pottery shards."

Although the young woman sat at the very rear of the large hall, Reid was almost sure she was the young lady he'd met in his great-aunt's parlor the other day. She'd participated little in their conversation, but he'd been impressed with her quiet, competent manner toward

Aunt Millie. What a contrast to her previous companions, women of indeterminate age with their nervous titters who fluttered around Aunt Millie every time she had an attack of the vapors.

Reid himself hardly knew how to deal with Aunt Millicent's nerves. As a boy he'd always been slightly afraid of her exacting ways. He'd been relieved the other afternoon, when he'd thought Aunt Millie about to faint, and the steady Miss Norton had given him a reassuring look. Her light brown eyes had been sympathetic, as if telling him not to worry, she'd been through enough of these spells to manage.

Reid wrapped up the lecture with a brief description of the ancient Egyptian symbols called hieroglyphics that covered several wall painting fragments on display.

As the audience poured out of the lecture hall, Reid was immediately besieged by people asking him questions. He listened patiently and replied as briefly as possible knowing from experience that he could be kept hours after a lecture if he wasn't careful.

The hall had cleared of most people when he spotted Miss Norton again, this time making her way to the front tables. He was in midsentence with a gentleman.

"Excuse me a moment, would you?"

"Oh—what? Certainly, Mr. Gallagher, certainly."

Reid headed toward Miss Norton, glad he'd have a chance to repay the woman's kindness to his aunt. He stood in front of her with a smile. "Miss Norton?"

"Yes?" she said, her eyes widening in surprise. They were the same shade as her hair, a light tawny brown.

"Did Aunt Millicent decide to brave the weather and come to the lecture?"

"Oh, no—that is, she would have liked to but she didn't feel quite up to it—"

Of course his aunt wouldn't have come to this crowded lecture hall. Too great a chance of catching some infectious disease. "I understand completely. I hadn't expected her to show. You came on your own, then?"

Her cheeks deepened with color, creating an attractive effect. "Yes…"

"You're interested in Egyptology?"

"Yes. It's a fascinating subject. I—I heard you mention the lecture to Lady Haversham. I thought it would be educational. I used to live in Palestine, you see," she said quickly, her voice sounding breathless.

He raised an eyebrow, his interest deepening. "Really? When was that?"

She looked away as if embarrassed. "It was years ago, when I was a girl. My parents were missionaries there for some years."

He sensed more to the story. When she remained silent, he cleared his throat. "I hope you enjoyed the lecture." Too late he realized it sounded as if he was hunting for a compliment.

"Oh, yes, very much so!"

Her enthusiasm encouraged him. "I'm glad. With a general audience, it's hard to know whether one is hitting the right note. I don't like to simplify things too much, but neither do I want to make things so technical I lose people's understanding."

"Oh, you adopted just the right tone, I believe. When I looked around me, everyone seemed most attentive to everything you were saying."

His lips curled up. "No one dozing off or fidgeting?"

She returned the smile. Her mouth was wide and generous, creating the impression that when she enjoyed something, she wouldn't stint with her feelings.

He was struck once again by the color of her eyes, a warm caramel hue. His mother, a painter, had instilled in him a sense of color, line and dimension, especially for the human face.

"I don't believe so, though the hall was so crowded, I wasn't able to observe everyone."

"I usually make eye contact with my audience. That's how I saw you, although I'm surprised I spotted you, you were so far back."

She laughed. "I was behind someone with quite a prominent hat."

He chuckled. "Yes, I noticed the bird hat. It's a wonder you were able to see any of the artifacts at all. I wished I'd known you were here this morning. I would have had you seated up front."

"That's quite all right. I was fine where I was…although it *was* difficult seeing any of the detail of the objects."

"Would you like to see them now?"

She moistened her lips, her glance straying to the artifacts. "That's actually where I was headed when you saw me. I didn't mean to interrupt you." She indicated the group of people waiting to speak to him.

"If you're worried about them, don't be. Come along." Giving her no time for further consideration, nor to ask himself why he was taking the trouble with her, he took her gently by the elbow and directed her toward the front.

"Oh, Mr. Gallagher—" Reid turned to see the museum's assistant curator approaching him. The slim young man cleared his throat and lowered his voice. "There are some gentlemen, museum patrons, you understand, who wish to have a word—"

"Yes, in a moment." Before he knew what he was

doing, he lowered his own voice, and indicated Miss Norton at his side. "A donor." He mouthed the words, "Major donor."

The man's lips rounded in a silent O. Then he quickly backed away, bowing and smiling to Miss Norton.

Reid led her to the nearest table. When they reached the artifacts, Miss Norton turned to him. "You needn't stay with me. I don't want to take you away from those waiting to speak with you—"

For some reason, her very reluctance to keep him at her side strengthened his own resolve to remain there. "I told them you were a possible donor."

She stared at him. "A what?"

He grinned, and suddenly he felt like a mischievousness boy despite his almost forty years. "If they think you're a wealthy patroness of the museum, you're sure to be escorted to the front at the next lecture."

Her large eyes lit up with amusement. The next second she frowned. "I don't like being dishonest with people."

"You weren't. I was. Being put on the lecture circuit is both a blessing and a curse. Apart from being an archaeologist for the Egyptian Fund, I'm also expected to raise money for future digs."

"I should think that wouldn't be so difficult. The place was packed today."

His eyes scanned the lingering groups of people. "The fund will be pleased. The more we can generate interest in all things Egyptian, the more easily we can seek donations."

She nodded. "It sounds a little like missionary work. They both depend on funding from home."

"Yes, indeed."

He indicated the first display. Miss Norton looked

over each artifact, marveling at things that had been preserved for so many centuries beneath the earth. She bent over the gold masks. He was pleased to note she didn't touch them, but looked at the brilliant surface painted with dark strokes to signal eyes and eyebrows, mouth and nose.

"What did you think of the talk?" Mr. Gallagher stood close to her, keeping his back to the lingering crowd, hoping that would keep them from being interrupted.

"It was wonderful. I never realized there was so much to know about the ancient cultures. When I lived in Palestine, it seemed we were living in Biblical times."

She continued studying the artifacts, as he explained each one in more detail.

When they headed back to the lobby, a few people immediately came toward him. "Mr. Gallagher—" several voices began at once.

Ignoring them, he turned to Miss Norton, reluctant to end their time together so soon. "The lecture has left me quite thirsty. What about joining me for a cup of tea?"

She swallowed, and he was afraid for a moment she would refuse. "I'd love to," she finally said, before adding, "but I really need to get back to your aunt."

He nodded, surprised at the disappointment he felt. "That reminds me…you were very good with her the other day. I wanted to express my gratitude. I thought she was going to faint, and I wouldn't have known what to do."

Once again, Miss Norton's cheeks tinted pink. "By the sounds of it, you're used to much graver emergencies in the desert."

"But I'm only used to dealing with men in critical situations. I have no idea how to help an elderly female."

"Well, thankfully, it was no more than a passing moment and your aunt was perfectly fine afterward."

"Yes." His first impression hadn't been wrong. Miss Norton did understand his aunt.

She moistened her lips and glanced past his shoulder.

Before she'd think of another excuse for turning down his invitation, he held up his hand. "Now, what about that tea? It'll only take a few minutes. There's a place right around the corner."

Instead of replying, she took out her watch. "I have a few minutes before having to return...." Her words came out slowly, as if still debating. "Lady Haversham generally expects me there for dinner at one o'clock."

He took out his own watch. "It's only half-past eleven. I'll make sure you're back in plenty of time... with time to spare." Understanding laced with humor underscored his words.

"All right."

"Good then." He felt lighthearted all of a sudden. He glanced back around him, knowing he'd have to tell the assistant curator something. "If you'll excuse me a moment, I'll be right with you. I just need to tell a few people I'm off." He marked his words with a touch to her elbow, as if afraid she'd disappear into the crowd again.

"Certainly. I'll get my things from the cloakroom."

"Good enough." With another brief smile, he headed away from her.

Maddie was left standing, wondering if she'd done the right thing accepting his invitation.

She retrieved her umbrella and coat, her mind in turmoil. Would she have enough time to swallow down a cup of tea and then walk all the way back to Belgravia? If she should be late for Lady Haversham…

Since she'd begun her employment a year ago, she'd never yet missed a day nor been late when Lady Haversham expected her by her side. Before she had time to wonder about the consequences, Mr. Gallagher returned and once again took her arm. How odd it felt to have a gentleman guiding her in such a protective manner.

Once out of the building, he turned to her. "Do you mind if we walk? I feel I've been cooped up all morning."

"Not at all. I walked to the lecture, as a matter of fact."

He stared at her. "You're joking. That's quite a hike from Belgravia to here."

Her cheeks warmed and she glanced down. "I enjoy walking. Too much of my time is spent indoors sitting, so I walk whenever I get the chance." No need to mention that she also did it to save the unnecessary expense of a cab or omnibus.

She sensed his scrutiny. "I imagine my aunt requires you at her side quite a bit."

She bit her lip, striving to answer honestly, yet not be critical of his relative. "It's the nature of my job."

"I suppose so." He didn't pursue the subject. No doubt his interest in the topic of paid companions had waned.

By the time they were seated in the tearoom and the waiter had taken their order, Maddie removed her gloves and decided to forget about Lady Haversham and enjoy herself. She couldn't remember the last time she'd been to a public eatery. She glanced around at the charming interior. Dark wood oak beams framed the low ceiling. They sat at a small, round table covered with a spotless white linen tablecloth. A small bouquet of forget-me-nots and daffodils was placed at its center.

Mr. Gallagher leaned forward. "Tell me about your time in Palestine, Miss Norton."

She folded her hands and looked down at the tablecloth. "There isn't much to tell. We lived in Jerusalem from when I was eight until I was fourteen."

"You said your parents were missionaries?"

"Yes." She was glad to be able to speak about them instead of herself. "Papa felt a call to the mission field when he was a young man—both my parents did, actually. They went to Palestine under the auspices of the Foreign Mission Society, when representatives of the society came to our church to speak one Sunday."

"I'm surprised they took a young child with them."

She couldn't help smiling. "Not only one. Three. I have two older brothers."

He shook his head. "I can't imagine being responsible for anyone but myself over there. And you all survived your time in the field?"

"Yes. I won't say it was without incident…." Her words slowed. "My parents probably wouldn't have come back when they did, but I had fallen ill with malaria."

"The Middle East can be a harsh place."

She found him observing her, his long fingers idly smoothing down the ends of his mustache. She could feel her cheeks redden under his gaze, wondering what he saw—a woman past her youth, with eyes that tended to look sad even when she wasn't, cheeks that gave away her emotions, a too-wide mouth. Her eyelids fluttered downward as the moment drew out.

"Most foreigners succumb to malaria at one time or another. I've gone through enough bouts to dread the symptoms."

She sighed. "I grew to know them quite well. It was after my third attack that my parents decided to return to England."

He continued stroking his mustache, studying her. He had such a direct way of looking at a person, she felt he could read her innermost thoughts.

"I'm still amazed that a European woman and her three young children survived the experience as long as you did."

"My two brothers were old enough that my parents would probably have braved it out longer, if they had fallen ill, but I was younger, and somewhat frail when I was a child." She gazed out the window. Her parents had had to make so many sacrifices on her behalf. She turned back to him, recovering herself with a smile. "My two brothers are now missionaries in their place."

"In Palestine?"

"No. One is in Constantinople, the other in West Africa."

He whistled softly. "Your family is spread far and wide. Are your parents still alive?"

"Yes. Papa has a small curacy in Wiltshire." She steered the conversation away from her family. "Tell me how you came to be involved in Egyptology, Mr. Gallagher."

He eased back against the small wooden chair. "The question is more, How could I help not becoming involved? I lived a good many years in Egypt when I was growing up. My father was a diplomat. When I came back to England to school, my great-uncle—Lady Haversham's husband—took up where my life abroad had left off."

He was interrupted by the waiter bringing them their tea. Maddie absorbed what he'd told her, watching him as he spoke to the waiter. Although he addressed the man casually, seemingly as at ease in this quaint tearoom as in the great lecture hall, she continued to sense a man outside his natural element. Today he was as well dressed as he had been at his aunt's, in a starched white shirt, finely patterned silk tie and sack coat of dark broadcloth, yet she couldn't help picturing him in more rugged garb, such as he must wear in the desert.

As she stirred sugar into her tea, Maddie chanced a glance at her own navy-blue dress. It was the same one she'd worn the day he'd come to visit his aunt. Well, that wasn't surprising, being one of only three gowns she owned. It was certainly appropriate for a paid companion, but not up to standards to be seen in a gentleman's company. She must look like a nursemaid or governess beside him. What would the waiter or the patrons sitting around them think of such a handsome man escorting such a dowdy female?

The waiter moved away from their table and Mr. Gallagher turned his attention back to her. "I really wanted to thank you today for how you are taking care of Aunt Millicent. You seem to have a way with her."

"You have nothing to thank me for. I'm just her companion. She has a whole legion of servants to take care of her. As well as a fine physician," she added, thinking of how often Dr. Aldwin was summoned.

"She seems to rely on *you*, however."

Maddie removed the spoon from her cup and placed

it on the saucer, uncomfortable with the compliment. "I'm only doing my job."

"How long have you been a…companion?" He hesitated over the word, as if unaccustomed to the term.

"Since I left home."

"When was that?"

"When I was eighteen." In the silence that followed she wondered if he was calculating how old she must be. On the cusp of turning thirty, she could have told him.

He only nodded, and again, she had that sense that he was evaluating her words, taking nothing at face value. He was probably cataloging her as a spinster securely on the shelf.

She shook aside the depressing thought and imagined instead that it was probably a painstaking attention to detail that made him a good archaeologist. She was still amazed he had remembered her name—or her, for that matter. He'd hardly glanced at her during the time he was at his aunt's for tea.

"How long have you been involved in archaeology?" she asked, returning to the topic she was really interested in.

Humor tugged at his lips, half-hidden by his mustache. "Oh, forever."

She smiled at his evident pleasure in the topic. "You said Lady Haversham's late husband was engaged in the field?"

"Yes. Good old Uncle George. It was he who gave me my love of archaeology."

She hadn't been with Lady Haversham long enough to know too much about her employer's late husband, although she knew he had often gone abroad. "Was he an archaeologist?"

"They didn't have them back then. He was more an adventurer and explorer. When he came to Egypt, he fell under the spell of the pyramids. He began to bring home anything he could find. It was all quite a free-for-all back then—any tourist or traveler taking what he could find, whatever the looters hadn't gotten over the previous centuries." His tone deepened to disgust.

Maddie rested her chin on her palm, glad to be taken away from her present world to one so close to that of her girlhood.

"By the time I came back to England, my father had been posted somewhere else. So, I began to spend my summers with Uncle George and Aunt Millicent. He was living in London by then. He'd show me parts of his collection. He had some incredible things—from Greek amphorae to Roman headdresses, but his real love was Egyptian artifacts. He had pottery, jewelry, bits of sculpture." He sighed. "I don't think I ever saw the whole thing. I wonder where it all is now."

"I haven't been with your aunt for very long. I know she has many things stored away. She often talks of her travels when she was younger. She was very excited when she knew you were coming home."

He looked sidelong through the window at the street. "I haven't considered Britain my home in many years."

Maddie bit her lip, afraid she'd said something wrong. But he turned back to her and began telling her about some of the digs he'd been involved in. Once again she was transported to another time and place, her present dreary existence swallowed up by that other world.

Suddenly a clock tower down the street struck the hour. She sat up and pulled out her watch. It was half-past twelve! "Oh, I really must get back. Thank you so much for the tea." She began to rise.

"Steady there." He snapped open his own watch. "You have plenty of time to get back if Aunt Millicent still dines at one. Wait, and I'll get you a cab."

Maddie sat back down, but felt the tension grow in her. She had wanted to avoid having to take the omnibus back. What would a hansom cost? Oh, dear, it couldn't be helped now. She had no time to cover the distance by walking.

Mr. Gallagher signaled the waiter and settled the bill. Maddie had to restrain herself from drumming her fingers on the tabletop. She gathered her bag and gloves.

Finally, he stood and she joined him immediately. "I can catch an omnibus a few blocks from here."

"Nonsense. You can catch a hansom right out front and it will be a lot quicker."

She bit her lip and said no more, thinking again how much the fare would cost. After they'd collected her coat and umbrella, they stood on the curb.

It didn't take Mr. Gallagher long to hail a carriage. When it arrived, she suddenly realized that their morning together was over. It seemed scarcely to have begun. She couldn't remember a time in her recent memory when she'd had such an enjoyable outing. Disappointment stabbed her.

"I—thank you again," she said, stumbling over the words in her effort to express her gratitude.

He held the door open for her. "The pleasure was mine. I really wanted to do something for all your kindness to my aunt."

Maddie held her smile in place, unable to help feeling just a bit disappointed that it hadn't been more for him than an act of kindness for an employee of his relative. It was thoughtful of him, all the same. Not many family members would take any consideration of a paid companion.

She placed her hand in his to bid farewell, and again she felt his strength and protection—which left her a little bereft when their hands separated.

She settled in the small space of the cab and placed her belongings at her side. Lastly, she took one more look out the window and gave a wave when she saw him still standing on the curb. He was a tall, lean man, his appearance that of a rugged adventurer and explorer, as he'd described his uncle, charmingly out of place on the London sidewalk.

He returned her wave with a small salute of his own, and she had another mental image of him in the desert, a camel as his mode of transportation, a host of Bedouins his companions.

As the carriage made its way from Bloomsbury across town to Belgravia, Maddie took out her purse and got her fare ready. She sighed, knowing she'd have to make up for the money in another quarter. She shook her head. There weren't many areas where she could cut back more than she already was. She couldn't *not* buy stamps for her weekly letters to her parents or brothers.

She was back at Lady Haversham's much more quickly than she was used to. A glance at her watch told her she still had time to wash up and tidy her hair.

When she descended the cab, she handed the coachman his fare.

"Oh, that's all taken care of, ma'am."

She blinked. "What do you mean?"

"The gentleman what hailed the cab for you. He took

care o' your fare." He smiled. "And a generous tip, as well, to get you here quickly."

She stepped back on the sidewalk, astonishment leaving her speechless.

He tipped his hat to her. "Good day t'ye." With a snap of the reins, he was off.

Maddie looked after him a moment. She had underestimated Mr. Gallagher's attention to detail…as well as his kindness. She blushed, as it occurred to her that it only meant he understood the reduced circumstances of a paid companion.

Remembering her duties, she turned about and headed up the walk to the front door. She'd have to thank Mr. Gallagher the next time she saw him.

If there was a next time. Then she remembered his words, *At the next lecture.* All at once her steps grew lighter as she hurried up the steps.

Chapter Three

A few mornings later, Reid sat in his great-aunt's parlor for a second visit, this time in answer to a note from her. He'd been intrigued by her words that it was "about an important matter."

Aunt Millicent sat alone in her parlor, enthroned in her high-backed armchair. Despite her diminutive size, she appeared regal in her dark brocaded gown with several gold chains down the front.

He wondered briefly where her companion was and remembered the pleasant time they'd had over tea. The young lady had been a ready and willing listener, though he'd certainly never meant to go into such detail about his work.

"Thank you, my dear, for coming so quickly." Reid leaned down to kiss his aunt's cheek, which was soft and wrinkled but still smelled of the lavender water she'd used as long as he could remember.

"I was happy to oblige." He took a seat across from her. "Where's Lilah?" he asked, noting also the absence of the terrier.

"Miss Norton took her out for her morning walk."

He glanced toward the heavily curtained window. "It's a bit drizzly for a walk."

"Oh, Lilah's walks are very short. Miss Norton will protect her with an ample umbrella."

He tried to picture the willowy Miss Norton scurrying after the tiny dog, a large black umbrella over them both. He turned his attention back to his aunt. "And how are you on this damp morning?"

She made a face. "Not well, I'm afraid."

He leaned forward, clasping his hands loosely between his knees. "What is it?"

She patted her chest. "Oh, the usual, dear boy. My heart. Some days I feel I can hardly breathe."

"I'm sorry. Is there nothing they can do for you?"

"I think I've had every pill and potion invented, but to no avail. Dr. Aldwin says I must have total rest, but you know it's impossible not to worry about things. I find myself lying in bed at night just thinking of you off in foreign parts, and Vera with her children. Little Harry, you know, is going away to school this autumn." She shook her head. "I do hope they choose the right school for him."

Reid hid his smile. As long as he could remember his aunt had been a worrier. "Well, I'm glad you sent me a note. I would have come by soon at any rate."

"I hope I didn't disturb you at your duties, but I really felt I had to see you after the other day."

"Tell me what I can do for you."

"I've been thinking about what we discussed."

He tried to remember what they'd talked about. He hoped she wasn't still dwelling on the attack on their camp.

"It's about your Uncle George's collection."

Reid was immediately interested. "Yes, I was thinking about it, too, since my visit. He must have some highly valuable pieces in it, from an archaeological standpoint."

"I'm sure everything in it is of the utmost value."

He hid another smile, remembering how protective his aunt was of Uncle George's reputation. "Yes, perhaps so."

"I would like to ensure that it is well taken care of at my demise."

He rubbed his hands over his trouser legs, uncomfortable with her behaving as if she was at death's door each time he visited. "Yes… I suppose it would be good to make some provision if…in the unlikely event…" He coughed, uncertain how to proceed.

"I'm glad you understand. Your Uncle George would have wanted the collection to be used for the advancement of science. He told me many times he wished to leave it to some museum or university, but he passed on before he could act upon his deepest desire, and has left me to dispose of his collection as I see fit."

"I see. Do you have anything in mind?"

"I'm much too ignorant of all he has to make such an important decision, which is why I wanted to consult with you." She folded her hands in her lap as if in preparation of an announcement.

"I'd be happy to advise you in any way I can."

"Your Uncle George was very fond of you. Alas, we never had any children of our own, so you were like a son to him." She smiled in recollection. "You'll never know how happy it made him when you decided to pursue his hobby."

"We spoke often of our mutual love for Egypt and its history." Reid had many pleasant memories of his uncle.

"Of course he could never pursue it full-time, what with his work in the consulate." She fingered the long chains around her neck. "Those were the days. So many parties, so much delicate negotiating with the government officials, the native sultans…" She sighed. "Once we returned to England, of course, his work with the Foreign Office again kept him so occupied, all he could do was put away most of his collection, in the hopes that someday he'd have the time to catalog it properly."

Reid nodded, remembering his many conversations with Uncle George on this very subject. But then his uncle had died suddenly in his early sixties, and Reid had gone abroad, so he'd never really bothered to think about the collection again.

"I've come to a decision." Reid waited, wondering what she was going to say. "I want you to take charge of organizing the collection and together we can then decide where to donate it. I was thinking of the University College."

Reid whistled softly. Although he'd never seen the entire collection, from what he remembered, this would be a sizable donation to the college.

"Of course, because it's such a large bequest, I want to make some stipulations."

"That is perfectly reasonable."

"Yes, I thought so. Firstly, I want you to have sole charge of it, and any decisions that are made by the institution have to be approved by you."

He sat still. "I don't know what to say." Her announcement certainly demonstrated a great degree of trust in him—an element in short supply these days among those working with ancient ruins, where so much pilfering and secrecy went on.

She smiled. "I'd hoped you'd be pleased."

Reid considered the enormity of the task. "I...am," he managed, still trying to take it in. "It will take some time. I haven't ever seen everything Uncle George amassed."

"Oh, it will take months perhaps. He left boxes and boxes of things, all labeled, of course. I've had them brought down from the attic and the stables to his study and library."

He shifted in his seat. "I don't know how much time I would have to devote to it. I need to return to Egypt at some point."

She pursed her lips, and he recognized the signs of her displeasure. "Couldn't someone take over your duties there for the time being?"

"Perhaps I should have a look at the collection first. With the help of some assistants, it's possible we could manage to catalog the items more quickly."

She shook her head. "Oh, no. I couldn't bear to have the house invaded by strangers."

"It wouldn't be anything like that. Museum workers tend to be very quiet, and perhaps with only one assistant, I could manage, at least enough to have the collection moved."

"No, no. I couldn't have it. My nerves wouldn't bear it." She clutched her gnarled hand to her mouth and turned away.

"All right, no one need come," he assured her, not wanting to have to deal with a swoon. He wondered if Miss Norton would be coming back soon. She seemed to have a gentle yet effective way of dealing with his aunt.

Before he could rise, his aunt spoke again. "I knew you would understand. Would you like to look at the collection now or come back tomorrow?"

She seemed fully recovered. Reid flipped open his watch. "I have time now to begin to look at things, get a feel for the scope of the work. You said everything has been brought here?"

"Yes. You can go right into your uncle's study and the library. I'll ring for the maid to escort you."

Reid stood, preferring to come to no decisions until he'd seen the state of the collection. Time enough then to think what this job of cataloging would entail. Time enough to think what remaining so long in England would mean...

The moment Reid entered the study, memories of his uncle surrounded him. The scent of his brand of pipe tobacco lingered in the air. It seemed nothing had been changed from when his uncle had last sat here. The glass-enclosed bookshelves were crammed with leather-bound volumes and portfolios. The gilt-edged desk blotter still had ink stains on its green surface. Reid stepped farther into the room and examined the desk's surface. Even his uncle's pipe rested against the edge of an ashtray—a glazed piece of pottery from Crete.

He turned to the black-clad maid. "Thank you. I'll just look around."

She gave a brief curtsy. "Very well, sir. Just ring if you need anything."

The door shut behind her and stillness descended once again. Reid remembered his hours sitting on the straight-backed chair facing the large walnut desk, his uncle in the swivel chair in front of it. Uncle George would light his pipe and take a few puffs, the chair squeaking as he leaned back with those first satisfied puffs. Then with a conspiratorial grin, he'd show Reid an item or two and tell him the astonishing tale of how he'd come to acquire it. Then he'd finger the side of his nose and say with mock severity, "And not a word to your Aunt Millie about it!"

Reid would promise with all the solemnity of a boy entrusted with a secret by so great a man as Uncle George.

His uncle's life had seemed one adventure after the other, and Reid had longed to grow up quickly to follow in his footsteps.

Reid smiled to himself as he picked up a brass envelope opener—a medieval knife from the early Ottoman Empire—and fingered its sharp edge. He'd had a few adventures of his own since then. It would have been nice to sit here once again and swap stories with his uncle—but sadly he'd never have the chance now.

He took a deep breath and straightened his shoulders, remembering what he'd come for. Behind him, against one wall, were stacks of boxes. He peered at the topmost one: Egypt: Saqqâra Pyramids, September 1839. He took out his pocketknife and carefully cut the string holding the box shut.

Everything inside was tissue wrapped. Reid took out a few items—vases, a female statuette, a broken piece of blue porcelain tile. The box was crammed full.

He set the things on the desktop and entered the next room. The library was also as he remembered it, but stacked in its wide center were piles of boxes. He whistled as he looked around.

This could mean months of work. He wasn't sure how many notes his uncle had taken, but he'd have to uncover them if he hoped to place and date the relics stored in the boxes.

He walked slowly around the room, reading labels

where they were available, opening some of the boxes and looking at the samples inside. When he reached a smaller box, with the word Notes scrawled across it in black ink, he slit it open quickly. Inside he found leather-bound notebooks.

He leafed through one. His uncle's travel journals. He deciphered the neat ink scrawl. Some pages were stained, many were yellowed with age, while others were still clean and very legible. Many had to do with his uncle's official functions, but others detailed his archaeological endeavors. "Eureka…" he breathed, his excitement mounting.

After skimming a few pages describing a harrowing climb into a tomb, Reid closed the worn notebook. For all his adventurous side, his uncle had been a meticulous recorder. A life's work summed up within the pages of a dozen or so notebooks. Uncle George had been a pioneer in a new branch of science. The few pages Reid had read reminded him a lot of his own work, but it also brought to the fore how primitive his uncle's foray into this new field had been.

He let his gaze roam around the room. Regardless of the enormity of the task, it had to be done. The record of the past needed to be cataloged and analyzed. The treasures needed to be brought to the light of day and shared with scholars.

With a sigh he eased himself down on the floor and positioned himself cross-legged on the soft Persian carpet. Opening the journal to the first page, he began to read.

August 12, 1840. Toured the inner chambers of pyramid. Intensely hot. Came to chamber of sarcophagi. Massive tombs. Crawled down narrow chamber, about two hundred feet lower... Air became thicker and staler the farther we went. Hoped no noxious gases lingering there. Wouldn't have wanted to join the mummies resting there, only to be found by a future explorer a century or so from now.

My dragoman almost left me. He didn't like invading a tomb... Can't be helped, I told him. Had to pretend an indifference I was far from feeling...

Reid wasn't aware how much time had passed when the sound of a throat clearing behind him brought him back to the present.

He looked up to see Miss Norton in the doorway, holding a tray. He stood, then immediately bent to rub the top of his legs, which had become stiff. "I'm sorry, I didn't hear you come in."

She smiled. "Please don't get up. I didn't want to disturb you, but when Lady Haversham told me you had been here since this morning, I thought you might like some refreshment about now."

The words made him realize he was both thirsty and hungry. He walked toward her to relieve her of the tray, appreciating her thoughtfulness.

He set the tray on a desk and flipped open his watch. It was just past noon. "I didn't realize I'd sat there so long, although my body certainly does," he added with a grimace as he rubbed the kinks out of his neck.

She poured a cup of tea, adding a sugar cube and placing a slice of lemon on the saucer. The simple task captured his attention. Perhaps it was the slim shape of her hands, or her graceful motions, or simply the fact that she'd remembered how he took his tea. She handed him the cup.

"Thank you."

"I brought a plate of sandwiches, in case you were hungry. Or if you'd rather, your aunt dines at one."

"Actually, I'd prefer just the sandwiches. That way I can work for another hour or so before leaving. I need to get back to the museum to continue with the other collection. If you could make my excuses to Aunt Millicent."

"Certainly. I'm sure she'll understand."

She offered him the plate of sandwiches and he took one. "Just seeing them makes me realize I'm famished."

She smiled, and he noted again how expressive her face was. His artist mother had dragged him through every museum in whichever country they'd been living in. Now he valued the lessons. It gave him an appreciation for the human form.

Miss Norton reminded him of paintings from the Italian Renaissance, he decided, with her pale skin and tawny hair. She had a rather thin but mobile face, her caramel-brown eyes large and her mouth generous. Botticelli. Botticelli's *Birth of Venus* with its mixture of sadness and kindliness in the shapely eyes.

He hadn't realized he'd been staring until she moved away from the desk and gazed at the opened boxes on the floor. "My, I never realized there were so many things in storage."

"Nor did I." He leaned against the desk and took a bite from a sandwich quarter.

She peered into an open box but didn't take anything out, which also pleased him. Most people would grab anything unusual with no regard to its fragility. He had noticed the same thing at the museum. Although she'd asked a lot of questions about the mummy masks, she hadn't touched anything.

She paused at the open journal on the floor.

"Notes?"

He nodded. "Travel journals, but they contain quite some detail on the artifacts. My uncle did some extensive exploration in the years he was in Egypt."

Her eyes widened with interest. "When was he there?"

He calculated. "From the midthirties to the midforties."

"We were in Palestine from 1868 to 1874."

"I didn't go over until 1880," he told her. "Ten years ago."

She nodded, her expression pensive. "I remember our boat stopping in Alexandria. It seemed such a busy place filled with so many turbaned people. I was only a young girl, so it's a jumbled memory."

"I spent a few years as a boy in Cairo in the…let's see…early sixties. When I went back out this time around, I was much older, a full-grown man of thirty." He looked down at the remains of the sandwich in his hand. "Set on leaving England and never looking back." He looked up, embarrassed at the words that had slipped out, probably as a result of having gone back in time since he'd entered his uncle's study.

She didn't seem perturbed by his reply. Instead her gaze appeared to radiate empathy, as if she knew exactly how one sometimes cannot bear memories of a place.

He set down his sandwich and brushed the crumbs from his fingers. "Egypt was just the challenge I needed at the time. I sought action and adventure."

"Did you find it?"

He squeezed the lemon into his tea. "I found my fair share."

She took a few more steps around the boxes. "Your uncle seems to have been a man of adventure, as well."

"Yes, his journals make for some interesting reading. I wish I had the time to delve into them more fully." He set his cup down, frustrated once again as he thought of the task ahead of him. "My aunt wants me to catalog all these artifacts."

She turned her attention back to him. "My goodness. Can you do it all yourself?"

"Hardly. But she insists no strangers are to come to the house."

"I understand," she said. "Her nerves."

"Tell me, just how badly off is she?"

She folded her hands in front of her. "She is under regular medical care."

"Is she—" how could he phrase it politely? "—as serious as, well, you saw her the other day?"

"It's hard to say. I've been here scarcely a year." She pressed her lips together as if debating whether to say more. "She dismissed her previous companion, I'm told," she went on more slowly, "and the one before that." She gave him a small smile. "So far, I seem to have suited her, but I'm new yet."

He remembered how particular his aunt could be. It was unfair to ask Miss Norton to make any judgments about his aunt. She was only an employee, after all, her position at the mercy of Aunt Millicent's whims. "I apologize for my questions. I realize you probably don't think it your place to form any opinions."

"I may form opinions, but as to voicing them…" She shrugged and turned away from him to study something in one of the boxes.

"All right, fair enough."

She straightened. "I had better leave you to your lunch—and work."

"Thank you for the refreshment. It was just what I needed."

"I'm glad I could be of help." She paused a moment. "I—I wanted to thank you for…taking care of my cab fare the other day. It was most generous of you."

He waved away her thanks, having already forgotten about it. "It was the least I could do for keeping you so long over tea." He had no idea how much paid companions earned, but he imagined it wasn't much. He could hardly conceive of a life at the beck and call of another. He was used to the independence of working far away from civilization and its strictures. Occasional loneliness was the main drawback, and he'd learned to deal with that.

Miss Norton nodded, her cheeks bright pink, making her look more strikingly than ever like her famous portrait counterpart. What was such an obviously bright, not unattractive, young woman doing in such a position?

He looked away, having steeled himself over the years not to notice any woman's charms. There'd only been one woman in his life.

"I thank you, all the same, for your thoughtfulness. It was most kind of you."

Uncomfortable with her gratitude, Reid cleared his throat and picked up his teacup once again.

"Well, let me or any of the servants know if you need anything while you're here."

He frowned at the way she lumped herself with the servants. She was too intelligent and refined. Probably, as most paid companions, a gentlewoman down on her luck, reduced to the semiservant position. He remembered that she said her father was a curate. She was probably helping to support her elderly parents.

She had reached the door when he had a thought. Just before she disappeared through the doorway, he said, "You wouldn't be interested in helping me catalog some of this stuff, would you?"

As soon as he uttered the words, he already regretted them. He usually considered things carefully before making a decision.

What did this young woman know about ancient artifacts? He didn't need someone who would require careful supervision. It would be difficult enough sifting through his uncle's notes, trying to match them to the heap of antiquities.

As Reid watched the surprise in her eyes turn to excitement, something tugged at him. A sense of compassion stirred within him as he thought how narrow her life within these walls must be.

She had lived in the Middle East and had some knowledge of the ancient world. More importantly, she knew how to follow instructions and how to be silent, two qualities he valued highly in any assistant.

"Do you think I could be of help?"

He nodded slowly. It just might be the perfect solution. His aunt couldn't object to her as a stranger, and she was right here, available any time he chose to come by.

"I told Aunt Millicent I'd need help. I don't think she realized the scope of it. Since she balked at any suggestion of an outsider, I don't think she'd have a problem with someone in her employ lending a hand a couple of hours a few days a week."

"I'd certainly be willing to do anything to help."

Her gaze roamed over the boxes around her. Then she drew her two eyebrows together. "I don't know if she will allow me to assist you, however."

"If you'd rather not, just say the word. It's no problem."

"Oh, no, it's not that at all. I think it would be fascinating work. It's just…well, perhaps *you'd* better broach the subject with your aunt."

He nodded. "If you're concerned about Aunt Millicent objecting, don't. I'll handle that aspect of it." If his aunt could force him to remain in Britain for a few months, she'd have to agree to some of *his* conditions, as well.

"I…" She hesitated, and he wondered again if she was having second thoughts about undertaking the work. "I—what I mean is…don't be discouraged if your aunt says no." She pressed her fine lips together and looked down, as if hesitant to say more.

He breathed a sigh of relief that that was her only qualm. "I've known her since I was a boy and learned how to get my way. Being a favorite nephew does have its advantages upon occasion."

A smile tugged at her lips, and he was heartened. She really had a most sympathetic face. There was something radiant in it when she smiled.

He rubbed his hands together, his eagerness to begin the task starting to grow. "Very well, then. I'll let you know when you're to start."

Her eyes lighted up and he felt a tingle of warmth steal into his heart, as if he'd given a child something delightful on her birthday. It occurred to him there wasn't much brightness in her life. If he could give her a little bit, then maybe his time in England would not be altogether wasted.

Chapter Four

Maddie's gaze went from the small limestone fragment on her left to the battered notebook on the table in front of her. She compared the description:

> Profile of king? Young prince? Standing on left. Sun God Ra with bird's head on right. Offering of bull, chickens. Seated monkey. Found at KV 2.

If this artifact matched the description in Sir Haversham's notebook, then it meant that everything in the box may have been found at the same location.

Maddie blew away the strands of hair tickling her forehead, sensing the excitement in her begin to grow. She scanned the fragments of pottery laid out on the long table before her. The last fortnight had involved painstaking work, first, unpacking a portion of the boxes and trunks and piling the remainder against one wall of the library. Then began the detective phase of deciphering the spidery handwriting in the stack of notebooks and various loose sheets of paper and matching descriptions to contents of boxes.

She glanced at Mr. Gallagher bent over a black stele

covered in hieroglyphics. Her hunch that his attention to detail made for a good Egyptologist had been confirmed for her over the time they'd been working together. He had been uncompromising in his process of carefully unpacking each box and laying out the contents in a separate area, labeling what could be readily identified.

He'd given Maddie a quick training in some of the common artifacts from steles, sarcophagi fragments, plaster casts of wall reliefs covered in pictures, amulets, potsherds, faience vessels, wood carvings and basalt statue pieces. Mr. Gallagher had also given her a crash course in ancient Egypt, charting out for her the Old, Middle and New Kingdoms when the pharaohs had ruled. She'd gazed in fascination at the drawings he showed her of the massive tombs they'd built for themselves, some reaching skyward in the form of pyramids, others stone chambers underground, only recently rediscovered by the explorers and archaeologists traveling the length of the Nile River.

She realized how well he'd laid the groundwork before he'd ever set her to work to assist him with identifying the artifacts. It was only in the past few days he'd allowed Maddie to begin reading his uncle's notes.

She hesitated to interrupt him now with her discovery. She'd learned in the last two weeks how single-minded his concentration was once he began to work. It only took one instance, when she'd read the barely disguised impatience in his eyes, to keep her from disturbing him unnecessarily.

Her times of unhindered concentration were another story as she remained at the beck and call of her employer. She turned now as a parlor maid entered the room and motioned to her.

Maddie rose and removed the white apron she'd worn when working among the artifacts. After folding it and placing it on the back of her chair, she left the room.

"Lady Haversham wants you, miss," the maid said.

Maddie no longer bothered to ask what the trouble was about or if it couldn't be taken care of by one of the staff of servants. Lady Haversham had made it clear when she called for Maddie, only Maddie would do, whether it was to pick up a fallen handkerchief or take Lilah out for a walk in the backyard.

"Thank you, I shall go to her at once."

As soon as Miss Norton left the library, Reid tossed aside his pencil and straightened on the tall stool.

In the scant hours he had Miss Norton's able assistance each day, it seemed his aunt couldn't do without her for more than half an hour at a stretch. He drummed his fingers on the tabletop, debating how to resolve the issue.

His concentration shot for the moment, he pushed back from the table and stood. Clearly, his aunt had no idea how much work was involved in what she'd set him to do. He gazed at the multitude of artifacts neatly laid out on every available surface in the large room. It wasn't even half the stuff. His eyes lingered on the gilded bust of a young Egyptian prince—one of the prizes of the collection so far.

He still didn't know where Uncle George had picked it up. He'd have remembered seeing it as a boy. It was most likely from the Valley of the Kings area. His uncle had spent several months in Thebes exploring the temples and tombs in and around Karnak and Luxor.

He wandered over to the space where Miss Norton had left her work. Taking up a pencil, he tapped it lightly back and forth against the tabletop between his fingers, his mind returning to his first thought. He hated the time wasted. He knew Miss Norton's first duties were to his aunt, but he didn't think he was being unreasonable in requiring her services in the midafternoon hours when his aunt had her accustomed nap.

The sound of the door reopening interrupted his thoughts. He turned with relief to see Miss Norton. His relief was short-lived as her first words were, "Excuse me, I need to run to the post for a moment."

He merely nodded, realizing it would do no good to express his displeasure to her. She had no control over his aunt's whims.

She approached the table where he stood. "I—I'm glad you're up from your work. I didn't want to interrupt you earlier, but I think I found something." She pushed the notebook toward him.

He was immediately attentive, following her words as she read the journal's entry and showed him the fragment. "And look here, the entry before this one describes a wooden crocodile figurine." She held up a broken carving, her arm grazing his. She immediately moved away. "Well, this one was in the same box." Her voice rose, its lilting tone conveying her enthusiasm. Reid focused his attention back to what she was saying, his arm still feeling her light touch.

"I was just going to read the next entry when I was called out."

He took the notebook from her.

We found a cache of faience and terra-cotta cooking vessels, ornamental vases near the Theban necropolis.

Reid surveyed the articles before him, idly smoothing down his mustache with thumb and forefinger. His excitement grew the more he compared the journal entry descriptions with the objects ranged on the table. "I think a good many of these would qualify...yes," he murmured, examining a terra-cotta pot on legs. "And it would confirm my feeling that he found these near Karnak." He turned to her with a smile, his earlier displeasure dispelled. "Well done, Miss Norton, your first breakthrough."

She returned the smile, her face blushing. He thought once again of Botticelli's *Venus*.

Reid snapped his fingers, remembering something he had intended to do that day. Now was as good a time as any since Miss Norton would have little chance to do any more work that day. Her discovery made up for any lost time, however, and he could easily continue where she'd left off and gain a few hours' progress.

"Before you head out, I have something for you."

Her brows rose. "Something for me?"

He went to his portfolio and pulled out an envelope. "Your first fortnight's wages."

Her wide eyes grew rounder. "Wages?"

"Yes, I realize we never went over them. I thought what I usually pay a part-time assistant would be satisfactory."

Since she didn't reach out her hand to take the envelope, he held it out to her.

She took a step back. "Oh, Mr. Gallagher, I think you misunderstood. I never expected wages."

He laid the envelope beside the notebook. "I think it's *you* who misunderstood. I never would have requested your help in any capacity but a straightforward business transaction."

She moistened her lips, deepening their rosy hue, and turned her face away from the table. "Of course, I understand that, but I never expected you to pay me in addition to what I'm earning from Lady Haversham. I—I feel d-dishonest collecting what amounts to two salaries at the same time."

"No need to. They are wholly separate services you're rendering. I made it clear to my aunt I needed an assistant and you've proved an able one. She agreed to share your services." Before she could protest further, he ended the discussion. "I don't expect to argue about this. It's a paltry enough sum and you deserve every penny. Much of this work is tedious but it's got to be done, and my time is limited. If you don't accept it, I'll have to find another who will." He folded his arms across his chest.

Still she hesitated. Finally, she picked up the envelope and held it by the corners. "Very well. I shall only accept it on behalf of my brothers' work in the mission field." There was something, while not defiant, yet firm, in her quiet words.

He shrugged, rocking back on his heels. "You can do whatever you please with the funds. They're yours."

She bowed her head. "Thank you." Without another word, she left the library.

After she'd gone, Reid sat at her place and continued with the notebook she'd worked on, glad that he'd hired Miss Norton. Aside from the interruptions, she was a most helpful assistant—quick to learn, interested in the subject matter, quiet and steadfast in her work habits. He couldn't think of a better work partner. He remembered her pleasure when he'd complimented her on her discovery. Her tawny eyes had lit up, color suffusing her cheeks, and her rosy lips had widened into a generous smile.

Reid shook aside the image. He had no business noticing Miss Norton's attributes other than those directly related to the work involved. He turned his attention back to his uncle's notes.

Little by little he matched more objects with those described in the journal. Several times, Reid stood and went to another part of the room, thinking he'd seen an object like the one described by his uncle. Little by little, piece by piece, he began to amass a picture of an excavation site. The thought flitted again through his mind of what an able assistant Miss Norton was.

Maddie paused at the top of the stairs, her hand on the newel. After a trying afternoon of waiting on Lady Haversham, the evening was finally her own. It mattered little that it was almost nine o'clock. She was grateful for at least one hour of peace and quiet before retiring.

She gazed down the length of the grand staircase, feeling the pull of the library. She could hardly wait until tomorrow to take up the thread she'd discovered in the late Sir George's notebook. She loved finding herself in the world of adventure Mr. Gallagher had opened up to her.

She debated a second longer. She didn't like going into the library outside of the daylight hours, feeling like an intruder, but her curiosity was too strong. Finally, she took a step down. Just another peek at the notebook, she decided, to reread the entry she'd stopped at.

As she approached the door, she perceived a crack of light under it through the gloom of the corridor. She turned the knob slowly, but as the door opened, she breathed a sigh of relief, seeing Mr. Gallagher.

Then she frowned. Had he been here all afternoon and evening…and everyone unaware of it? She cleared her throat softly. He looked up immediately. "Oh, you're back, Miss Norton."

"I didn't know you were still here. Or did you leave and return?"

Only then did he seem aware that night had fallen. He glanced at the darkened windows before rising. With a loud yawn, he took a leisurely stretch, making Maddie aware of the lean, taut length of him. She shifted her gaze to his rugged face. "No, I've been here all afternoon. I didn't realize it had gotten so late."

She gave a surprised laugh. "It's past nine o'clock."

"Is it?" He didn't seem unduly concerned. "Come, look what your discovery has led to."

She hurried to his side. Her wonder grew as he showed her all the artifacts that he'd labeled in the time she'd left him. He'd even pinpointed the area on a map tacked up to the wall.

"I was able to locate pieces from two other cartons of artifacts." He stood, rubbing the back of his neck. "Your careful observation this afternoon certainly helped me put a dent in this project."

She warmed at the brief words of praise then sobered, remembering the generous sum of money he'd paid her that very afternoon. "I'm sorry I had to leave so abruptly. I wasn't much help to you. My goodness, this represents hours of work." She shook her head at the array of meticulously labeled objects ranging from broken bits of pottery to carved masks.

"Don't worry about it." His low voice soothed her.

"I'm just grateful you noticed the connection. It took some astute observation."

She said nothing. Suddenly she frowned. "Have you eaten? Did you ring for the maid for any refreshment?"

He shook his head, looking a bit sheepish. "To tell you the truth, I cleanly forgot all about the time of day—or night," he added with another glance at the dark windowpanes visible through the long, parted velvet drapes. "I could use something now. With your permission, I'll rummage through my aunt's pantry." A sly grin tugged at his lips. "I used to sneak down in the middle of the night as a boy. Let's see if I can remember where everything is."

"Come along," she said with a laugh. "You don't have to do any sneaking. I'm sure Lady Haversham would be upset if she knew you'd sat here so many hours without having something sent up." As they extinguished the lamp and exited the library, she said, "What were you doing up at midnight in those days?"

"Oh, I'd get to reading some adventure story and wouldn't be able to put it down even after I'd been told to put out my light. By the time I'd finished the book, I'd be famished."

She smiled in understanding. "That reminds me of how I felt this afternoon when I had to leave off reading your uncle's notebook, as if a good story had been snatched out of my hands at the most exciting spot."

He chuckled. "I would have left it for you, but I felt the same, like I had to pursue that lead. My own trail had grown frustratingly cold and I wasn't making any headway."

She pushed open the kitchen door. "Well, I'm glad I gave you some kind of start today." She turned up the gas lamps and headed toward the pantry. "What would you like? There's some cold roast from dinner."

"Nothing too much. If you have an apple, maybe a piece of cheese."

"Are you sure that's all you need?"

"Yes, I really should head back to my rooms. I need to get an early start tomorrow at the museum."

She nodded and ducked into the pantry. A few minutes later, she set a plate of thick slices of bread and cheese and quartered apples before him.

"Thank you," he said, from where he sat on a stool at the worktable. "This is more than adequate."

She offered him a glass of buttermilk.

"Won't you join me?" he asked with a gesture at the plate.

Her heart skipped a beat at the invitation. Suddenly the cavernous kitchen took on intimate proportions. "No, thank you. I'll just have a glass of buttermilk."

"I hope I'm not keeping you up."

"Not at all. I had just read to your aunt and was going to head up to my own room. I couldn't help coming down to look at the notebook again. Just to be sure I hadn't fooled myself this afternoon." She smiled.

"I can understand perfectly. It's the reason I couldn't leave this afternoon."

"Your uncle must have been an interesting man."

He nodded, munching on an apple slice. "He was. You must have gotten a sense of the risks he took on his travels."

"I'm amazed at the number of times he barely escaped with his life." Maddie rested her chin on her hand, finding the same level of companionability with Mr. Gallagher that she'd experienced in the tearoom.

They continued speaking about Egypt and the discoveries made there over the last decades. Mr. Gallagher tore off a piece of bread. "Unfortunately, there has always been a spirit of competition amongst the different national expeditions—the Brits trying to beat the French, who are trying to beat the Germans—with who can unearth the most artifacts." He shook his head. "We'd have probably made more headway and prevented some of the needless destruction if we'd worked together."

When he'd finished the light snack, she offered him some more, but he declined. "I really must be going. Thanks for the fare. It should hold me till morning." He gave her another grin, and she realized for the countless time in the last fortnight how ruggedly handsome he was.

"A-are you staying far from here?" she asked, hoping the question wasn't too personal.

"Not too far. I'm at the Travellers Club in Mayfair. It's an easy walk."

She wondered at his staying at a club instead of with family or in a flat of his own. As if reading the question in her mind he said, "It didn't seem worthwhile getting my own rooms. When I come to London, it's usually for a short stay. It's more convenient just to put up at my club."

"Yes, I suppose so." She well knew how dismal a rented room could be. Did he have a place to call home in Egypt or did he live as a nomad in the desert? She wished she could ask but knew she'd never dare. He held the door open for her as they exited the kitchen together.

She escorted him to the front door where he'd left his jacket, thinking all the while that it was a pity such a man was so alone. She knew he had a sister in London in addition to his aunt, but he didn't appear terribly close to them.

The night was fresh but not cold when they stood on the stoop.

He took a deep breath, a look of disgust clouding his chiseled features. "I don't know how people live in this city. The air smells of sulfur and you can never see the stars."

She glanced up at yellow-gray aureoles of the gas lamps against the dark sky. "I guess we forget what clean air and a night sky are like."

"On the Egyptian desert you can begin to comprehend what a 'blanket of stars' really means. Between the cold dank winters and soot-filled air, I don't know why anyone would want to inhabit London."

She didn't know what to say. That not everyone had a choice? That not everyone had the freedom he seemed to have?

He grinned. "Don't pay any attention to me. I've never liked this city and feel like a mule with a bit in his teeth every time I'm forced to step back in it."

"I—I hope for your sake then that your time here will be short." She said the words while fighting the wish that his stay would be lengthy.

"Thanks...though it looks like I'll be here for a while."

"May the Lord grant you the grace then to support it."

"I am grateful for the guidance He gave you today in making the connection in that journal." He took a step away from her. "I'd better let you get some sleep. Thanks for the snack. Thanks even more for your help in the library." He stood a few seconds longer, and she wondered if he was as reluctant to leave as she was to have him leave.

"Well, good night," he said at last, taking another step away.

"Good night, Mr. Gallagher."

With a wave, he turned and began walking briskly down the gaslit street. Maddie stood watching him until he'd disappeared into the evening mists. With a sigh she stepped back inside and closed the door behind her. Why did it seem she was enclosing herself inside a tomb like those of the pharaohs while Mr. Gallagher had fled to the only freedom available?

Had the last decade of her life been nothing but a futile servitude? She'd believed she was following the Lord's will for her life, but seeing it now through Mr. Gallagher's eyes awakened all the long-ago dreams of the call of the mission field in a faraway land. Had she missed her true calling?

Chapter Five

The next afternoon Maddie sat in the parlor, once again overseeing the tea service. This time not only did Mr. Gallagher sit with Lady Haversham, but also his sister and her three children.

Over the din of the two rowdy boys, Lady Haversham said to her great-niece, "Reid must get out in society a bit while he's home. You know I can't do as much as I'd like. I was counting on you and Theo to organize a few things."

"Of course, Aunt Millicent. You know we'd love to." Vera Walker adjusted the lace fichu at her neck. "What about a musical soiree here Friday a week?" She turned to her brother, her tone gaining enthusiasm. "I could invite your old school chums Harold Stricklan and Steven Everly. Did you know Steven was just made vice president of Coutts Bank? Theo just ran into—"

Before she could finish the sentence, her oldest son rushed by her and bumped into her knee, sending tea sloshing from her cup into her saucer and onto her silk dress.

"Harry! See what you've done to Mama's frock! You naughty boy!"

"I'm sorry, Mama." He didn't stop but whipped around the settee, closely followed by his brother.

"Timmy!"

At the same time his sister, who was sitting on the floor beside the sleeping Lilah, petted the dog too briskly and Lilah sat up and began to growl.

Lady Haversham leaned forward in her chair to see what was being done to her pet. "Careful, child! Madeleine, take the children to the garden, please."

"Yes, my lady." She rose immediately, knowing the command had been coming. Stifling a sigh, she rounded up the children, who jumped at the chance to be free of the confines of the parlor, and herded them downstairs.

"I had to let go their nursemaid. The woman was unreliable—" were the last words Maddie heard as she closed the parlor door behind her.

Harry, the oldest boy said to his younger brother, Timmy, "I bet I can beat you at jacks."

"No, you can't!"

The two continued arguing.

"Hush, children, until we're outside." Maddie took the two youngest firmly by the hand and began walking toward the staircase.

She herself wouldn't have minded a brief respite in the garden if it weren't for the fact she would have no peace for the next half hour.

Once in the backyard, the boys forgot their game of jacks and started running around the bushes.

Maddie clapped her hands, trying to get their attention, knowing Lady Haversham would be upset if any flower beds were trampled. "All right, children, what would you like to play? What about graces?"

"That's a girl's game!" The two boys made faces, their shouts drowning out their sister's assenting voice.

"What about hoops and sticks?"

"Blindman's bluff!" The boys jumped up and down until Maddie complied. It was no use arguing with them, she'd learned. She procured a large silk handkerchief from her pocket. "Who's to go first?"

"You! You! You!"

"Very well." She tied the scarf around her eyes. Before she could prepare herself, the older boy, an oversize ten-year-old, grabbed her from behind by the elbows and twirled her around. She groped the air in front of her to keep from losing her balance.

"You can't catch me!" Harry's voice came from a few feet away. Immediately they all copied him. Maddie swung around as each voice neared her but she was never close enough, and she didn't want to take the easy way out and catch Lisbeth, the youngest. She knew she was moving farther down the garden, as their voices rang out from that end.

From past experience, she knew the boys would have her at their mercy until they tired of the game and needed her attention for a new amusement. In the meantime, she needed to grit her teeth and play along, hoping not to trip along the uneven brick walk, and praying she wouldn't damage one of Lady Haversham's prized bushes.

Tired of the women's chatter around him, Reid wandered to the window, teacup in hand. He'd been sorely tempted to follow his niece and nephews out but Vera had insisted on his participation at that moment in planning her soiree. As the two women worked out the details of an afternoon musicale, he took a sip of tea and peered down into the garden, wondering what his unruly nephews were up to.

He spotted Miss Norton first, barely visible under an apple tree's bower of blossoms. Her hands were upraised and she appeared to be calling out to the children. He didn't see any of them at first, then one by one he saw them all up in the tree. His lips twitched in a smile until he discerned that Miss Norton was trying to get them to come down and not having an easy time of it.

Remembering the unmannerly behavior of the children the short time they'd been in the parlor, he set his teacup down on the tea tray and headed toward the door.

Vera broke off in midsentence. "Where are you going, Reid? We haven't decided on the guest list for the musicale."

He was already halfway across the room. "You and Aunt Millicent take care of it. Just let me know the date and time, and I'll show up. Now, if you'll excuse me, I'll only be a moment."

Before Vera could ask him anything more, he shut the door behind him.

When he reached the garden, he heard the children's shouts and laughter.

"You can't get us unless you climb up."

"You must get down immediately, Harry, and you, too, Timmy. Your sister might hurt herself. Where are you, Lisbeth?"

The six-year-old girl only giggled in glee.

"You know your aunt won't like it that you're in her apple tree. It's her best orange pippin."

"We won't come down till you come up!"

"You aren't playing by the rules. Now come down, Timmy."

In reply, the boy shook the tree branch at her and a shower of blossoms littered the ground. "It looks like it's snowing!"

"Oh, you mustn't do that. Your aunt won't have any fruit in the autumn if you knock the blossoms off now."

Reid reached the tree and spied Lisbeth first on a lower branch. "Whoever thinks he can beat me in a race around the square gets a half crown." He turned away from the tree, calling out over his shoulder, "Last one down's a rotten egg."

As he walked toward the garden gate, he heard scrambling and shouts as three small bodies shimmied down the tree.

"Lisbeth's a rotten egg!" The boys called over their shoulders as they caught up to Reid. Lisbeth began to cry.

Miss Norton removed her blindfold and smoothed her hair before going to crouch by the weeping child.

"There, Lisbeth, why don't you come along with me, and we'll show those boys you can beat them in the race?"

Reid's niece sniffed.

"Where's your handkerchief, honey?"

Leaving the child with Miss Norton, Reid herded the boys into the mews. They ran down the alley until they reached Belgrave Square. Reid took them to the nearest tree and marked out the starting place. "You'll run inside the square, all around and end back here."

Harry's chest puffed out. "That's easy."

"We'll see. Now, let's wait for your sister and then when I say 'go,' run with all your speed. Watch that you don't cheat by cutting the corners or you'll be disqualified."

As Miss Norton crossed the street and approached them, holding his niece by the hand, he smiled. "I thought you could use some reinforcements."

"Indeed, thank you." She shaded her eyes and looked across the large, tree-studded square. "Are you sure it's not too far for the children?"

"They needn't complete the course. I'm only hoping to rid them of some of their excess energy."

"Yes, I see." Her eyes twinkled, and he noticed again how exactly her eye and hair color matched, a rich, caramel color like the toffees he used to enjoy as a boy.

He cleared his throat and turned his attention back to the boys. "All right, on your mark." They lined up at the spot he indicated. "Go!"

He jogged alongside them, making sure not to overtake them. Lisbeth soon trailed behind and began to cry. By the second corner of the square, he glimpsed Miss Norton, who'd once again taken the girl by the hand and walked along beside her, encouraging her. Harry ran ahead of Timmy by a good lead, but as the older brother rounded the third corner, his foot tripped on a tree root, and he went flying headlong.

Reid ran up to him, the boy's sobs reaching across the large square. The fall hadn't looked serious enough to merit the boy's wails. Reid knelt by him.

His nephew clutched one knee in both hands. "I... th-think it's br-broken...!"

The trouser leg was torn and the knee scraped. Reid probed the area around it gently, but determined that no further damage had been done. Timmy leaned over his brother, panting heavily. "Does this mean I won the race, Uncle Reid?"

This only made Harry sob the louder. "You didn't win! That's not fair! Tell him he didn't win, Uncle Reid! I was ahead. You saw me!"

Reid smiled at Timmy. "I think it means there'll be a rematch once your brother's fully recovered. What do you think, Harry? Does that sound fair?"

He swiped a sleeve across his runny nose. "I would've won fair and square if that tree root hadn't been in my way." He glared at his younger brother. "I would've beat you today, just like I'll beat you by a furlong anytime we race!"

"I wasn't the one who fell on my face and then cried like a girl!" Timmy began hopping on one foot and then the other. "Waaa!" he bawled in imitation.

Miss Norton and Lisbeth reached them. Miss Norton knelt on Harry's other side. "Is he badly hurt?"

"Nothing more than you see. Come on, champ, let's see if you can stand." He held out a hand to his nephew. "'Attaboy."

Harry wiped his nose again. "It hurts something awful, Uncle Reid."

"Skinned knees always hurt. The trick is not to let on to the ladies." He winked in their direction. "Come on, let's show the others what a brave fellow you are." Draping an arm around the boy's shoulders, Reid urged his nephew forward. He turned to Miss Norton. "I'll take him to the kitchen and get him cleaned up if you take charge of the other two."

"Of course, thank you. Come along, Timmy, Lisbeth." She took them each by the hand and directed them back to the house.

Timmy resisted. "I don't want to go back yet."

She pulled him gently forward. "Your mother might be getting ready to leave."

Lisbeth tugged on her other hand. "I want to stay outside, too." Timmy took advantage of Miss Norton's inattention to break away from her and dart toward the middle of the square.

"Timmy!" The single word stopped the boy in his tracks. Timmy stared round eyed at Reid's sharp tone. "Take hold of Miss Norton's hand if you don't want to feel the palm of mine on your backside."

Timmy debated for only an instant. He dragged his toes in the dusty path but he didn't disobey. As soon as he was at Miss Norton's side, he gave her his hand and put the thumb of the other in his mouth, staring at his uncle as if he'd suddenly sprouted horns.

As they walked toward the house, Reid said to Miss Norton, "Don't let them forget who's in charge."

She gave him a quick look. But she said nothing, only pressed her lips together and looked down at the ground. "Yes, sir."

Wondering if he'd said something wrong, he walked alongside her and the children in silence to his aunt's house. He'd been only trying to help. Had he offended Miss Norton in some way?

Maddie reentered the parlor, clutching Timmy and Lisbeth, Mr. Gallagher's words still stinging. Although spoken softly, they'd made her feel incompetent and inadequate—the way she always did when put in charge of Mrs. Walker's children.

As soon as she entered the parlor, Mrs. Walker's glance went from one child to another. "Where is Master Harry?"

"He's with his uncle." Maddie hesitated to say anything about the scraped knee. Cowardice won and she kept silent. She immediately regretted her decision.

Lisbeth ran to her mother's lap. "Mama, Harry fell and cut his knee! He was crying and bleeding!"

Mrs. Walker's gaze flew to Maddie. "What has happened to my son? Tell me at once."

"He tripped over a tree root while running."

Lady Haversham leaned forward. "Whatever did you have him running for?"

"The boys were running a race."

Timmy pulled at his mother's arm. "You should have seen me, Mama."

Lisbeth reached up to get her mother's attention. "I was running, too."

Timmy thrust his chin out. "I would've beat Harry if he hadn't gone and fallen."

Mrs. Walker put her hands over her ears. "Please, children, don't interrupt your Mama when she is talking. Now, Miss—Miss—"

"Norton," Maddie supplied for her.

"Yes, will you please tell me why my children were involved in running a race?" Her glance swept over her daughter. "And why are they so disheveled?"

"It was Uncle Reid's idea." Timmy's voice wobbled. "He shouted at me, Mama."

"Shouted at you? Oh, goodness. Now, where is Harry?"

"He's perfectly fine, madam. Mr. Gallagher is looking after him."

"What is this about Master Harry?" Lady Haversham thumped her cane on the carpet. "Maddie, I demand to know what has happened to him!"

Sensing her mistress's agitation, Lilah jumped down from the old lady's lap and began dancing around her feet, barking in staccato bursts.

Mrs. Walker's voice rose over the din. "I placed the

children in your care, Miss Norton, with full confidence that you would manage."

"Yes, ma'am." Maddie prayed for patience and hoped Mr. Gallagher would soon return to calm his sister down.

Mrs. Walker covered her ears again. "Can you please shush that dog, Miss Norton?"

Maddie fished out a treat from Lady Haversham's bag and gave it to the dog. Lilah gobbled it up quickly, leaving Maddie's palm wet, and immediately barked for another.

"Aunt Millicent, can something not be done to calm your pet?"

Lady Haversham fanned herself. "It's because she senses something is wrong. She's a very sensitive animal. There, Lilah, dear, you mustn't worry. Now, Madeleine, please tell us what has happened to Master Harry."

"He's fine now."

Maddie whirled around in relief as Mr. Gallagher walked in with Harry.

"Look, Mama." Harry pointed to a plaster across his knee.

Mrs. Walker ran to her son. "Harry, whatever happened to your trousers?" Not waiting for his reply, she turned again to Maddie. "What is the meaning of this, Miss Norton? My son is not only hurt, but his best pair of trousers is ruined. Whatever have you done with the children?"

Mr. Gallagher went to pour himself a cup of tea. "Calm down, Vera. If you need to vent your spleen at someone, do it to me. Your darling boys were doing their best to disobey Miss Norton, so I took them to the square for a footrace."

Mrs. Walker let her son's arm go and turned to Reid. "To the square? In the midst of traffic? Reid, whatever were you thinking?"

"Attempting to wear out your unruly offspring."

"How can you say such a thing of your own flesh and blood!"

"That may be, but they need to learn to obey their elders."

Mrs. Walker knelt beside Harry. "Does it hurt very badly, darling?"

"It hurt awfully when I fell, and Uncle Reid put something on it that stung like the dickens, but now it's better. Uncle Reid told me how all the men in the desert buck up. They bite a bullet, isn't that right, Uncle Reid?"

"That's right, sport."

"We didn't have any bullets, so Uncle Reid gave me a wooden spoon to bite on."

"I should hope we don't have any bullets!" She shook her head at her brother. "Teaching him such vulgar things. Wait until your father hears about this." She fixed her gaze once more on Maddie. "In future, please be more careful with the children. Lisbeth is delicate and the boys need careful supervision. I don't expect them to be removed from the garden—"

"Vera, didn't you hear what I said? I took the boys from Miss Norton because they were acting like little dervishes."

She sniffed and resumed her seat. "Well, I never! I didn't expect you to insult my children. I'm their mother and ought to know them better than anyone!"

Mr. Gallagher poured another cup of tea and brought it to his sister. "Why don't you drink this and let it settle your nerves? As you can see, Harry has survived his ordeal." He turned to Maddie. "How about you, Miss Norton, could you use a cup of tea?"

Before she could reply, he frowned. "You look ready to collapse." He took her by the elbow and led her to her accustomed seat, then returned to the tea cart.

"Now, did you two ladies decide on an afternoon of torture—excuse me, musical delights—for me?"

His aunt gave him a reproving look. "Reid, you are incorrigible. Now, give me Lilah. She's had too much excitement."

He scooped the dog up in one hand and held a tea-cup and saucer in the other. "Here's your mutt, Aunt Millie."

She took Lilah onto her lap, still looking at her nephew in disapproval. "Your sister is putting herself out for your sake. You should be more appreciative of her efforts."

He approached Maddie and handed her the cup. "You'd best buck up, as I told Harry," he said with a wink.

"Now, Reid, pay attention," his aunt continued. "We've drawn up a list of twenty guests to invite, most of whom you are acquainted with. By the way, did you know Cecily Mason is widowed? Such a beauti-ful woman and still so young."

Maddie had met Mrs. Mason once at a similar tea in this parlor and remembered her as a very attractive, poised woman. Was Lady Haversham hoping to play matchmaker for her nephew? Maddie looked down at her teacup, realizing the thought filled her with dismay.

The conversation continued in a buzz around Mad-die as the women discussed the guest list. Thankfully, everyone, including the children and Lilah, ignored her for the moment.

She thought of how Mr. Gallagher had so staunchly defended her and felt cocooned in a cloud of wonder at how one man—whom she hadn't even known a fortnight ago—could become her champion.

Finally, she lifted her teacup to her lips though her hand still trembled. Taking a small sip of her tea, she found he had sweetened it.

He'd remembered from their times of taking tea in the library how she took her tea...a lump of sugar, no lemon, no milk.

She glanced at Mr. Gallagher. He sat to her left, close to his sister. He was as handsome in profile as he was facing forward. He was still very much a mystery to her, a man who kept the few words he spoke to her during their times in the library strictly on the work at hand. She had learned so much on the subject of Egyptology from him, yet she had gleaned almost nothing about the man himself. His actions, on the other hand, spoke volumes. He was always patient in explaining the work to her. This afternoon, she'd witnessed compassion, camaraderie, a way with children, authority, a sense of humor.

What had compelled him to leave England and stay in the desert for so many years?

Maddie took another careful sip of tea. Mr. Gallagher's personal life was no business of hers, she reminded herself. Like Lady Haversham, he was her employer, and her only obligation, besides fulfilling her duties satisfactorily, was to shine Christ's light into their lives, as was the duty of any man or woman of faith. She didn't know anything of Mr. Gallagher's faith, but she did sense a reserve that perhaps spoke of a wound not fully healed.

How she longed to offer a healing balm to that wound.

* * *

Maddie wrote to one of her brothers that evening at her desk.

> Dearest Todd, I have the most wonderful news. The missionary society shall be receiving an additional bank draft this fortnight for your labors in West Africa.
> You ask how I am able to manage this on my meager salary. Well, the Lord has blessed me with a bit of additional work.
> You know Lady Haversham has a nephew? I think I wrote you about him, Mr. Reid Gallagher. He is an Egyptologist…

Maddie went on to describe how she had come to be his assistant. As she reached midway down the other side of the paper, she held her pen in the air a moment before continuing.

> He is a most considerate and generous man. I had told him that any additional payment was not necessary beyond what Lady Haversham pays me. But he insisted. I told him the money would go to missions work. This didn't seem to bother him at all. I know you'd like him.

Maddie stopped and turned the sheet over to reread what she'd written already. It occurred to her halfway through that she had written almost exclusively about Mr. Gallagher.

She picked up her pen again. "He is an older man," she continued, then paused again. Her brother would

probably form a picture of a sixtyish gentleman put-
tering about in a museum, when the reverse was true.
Mr. Gallagher was a man in his prime, vitally alive,
virile and the very opposite of a doddering professor.

Maddie chewed on the end of her pen. Was she mis-
leading her brother? She hadn't said Mr. Gallagher was
Lady Haversham's *great*-nephew, just her nephew. With
that last sentence, she was deliberately implying he was
much older than her almost thirty years.

Her glance strayed away from the page, picturing
Mr. Gallagher's handsome features. She didn't know
how old he was but didn't think he could be above forty.
What would her brother think if he knew this and read
her letters full of her activities at Mr. Gallager's side?
Would he begin to suspect anything of her growing
feelings for the man?

She swallowed, looking back down at her words.
She hated deception and considered starting the letter
over or crossing out the last sentence and inserting the
word *great* to the reference to nephew, but finally she
shook her head. That would look much too obvious.
And as far as starting afresh, she really didn't want to
waste a whole sheet of paper.

With a sigh, she continued writing, but this time
made a deliberate effort to talk about Lady Haversham,
her niece's visit and then went on to talk of last Sunday's sermon. She didn't close the letter until she was
satisfied that other items filled as much space as all
she'd written of Mr. Gallagher and her work with him.

The exercise was for her own good. She must put
things back into perspective. She was only an employee
of Mr. Gallagher's. In a few weeks, he'd be back in his
beloved Egypt, and she…

She looked down at the envelope, which would soon be on a ship on its way to West Africa, while she remained behind, doing her small part to help those who were bravely carrying out the Lord's great commission.

Chapter Six

Reid paced the library, his steps muted by the thick pile of the carpet, as he dictated to Miss Norton.

"The faience vessels and fragments are likely from the area surrounding the small temple at Karnak. They are painted blue and have black lines and other markings. By their similar shape and color to those found at Gournah by Champollion on his Franco-Tuscan Expedition, I would place them in the Middle Kingdom—"

He broke off at the sound of a pen falling. He turned quickly to see Miss Norton fumbling for it. He noticed her other hand was rubbing her temple.

"Are you all right?" She looked pale, but only nodded and attempted to continue writing.

"Are you sure?"

"Just a bit of a headache is all. I'll be all right. Pray continue. You ended with 'Middle Kingdom'?"

"Never mind that. How long have you had a headache?"

"It's nothing, really."

In a few strides, he was at her side. "Look at me."

Slowly, she turned her face up to his and he was

struck by the shadows under her eyes. "Have you been getting enough sleep?"

Her gaze slid away from his. "I... I was a little restless last night."

He frowned, thinking how often she was summoned by his aunt. Did she ever have any time to herself? "How long has it been since you've been outside, getting some exercise?"

"I... I don't remember." Her voice was barely above a whisper now.

He stepped away from her and stroked his jaw. "Is this job too much? I know my aunt has you at her beck and call every moment of the day. If this job is taking away from your only time to get outside and get some fresh air—"

Her large eyes shot to his. "Oh, no, Mr. Gallagher. I'll be fine—"

He didn't let her finish but wheeled around and headed toward the door. "Come on."

"Where are you going?"

"Get your hat and shawl or whatever you need and come along. I'll meet you in the front hall."

She stood and began to follow him. "But your dictation—"

"It can wait. Now, I'm taking you for a walk before you become seriously ill."

"That's not necessary, Mr. Gallagher. I'm perfectly fine, I assure you. I can take a powder—"

He stood by the doorway, his hand on the knob. "I don't need my assistant to fall ill on me. Now, we do this my way, or I'll have to get myself another assistant."

She shut her mouth and preceded him out.

Once outside, Reid led her across the square at a

brisk pace. "I'm not going too fast for you?" He slowed his pace as he realized her skirts might be hobbling her.

"Not at all," she said, keeping up with him. At least she didn't wear that ridiculous high bustle women favored these days. That contraption always reminded him of a one-humped camel. He glanced at her. She wore a nondescript brown skirt and tailored jacket. The colors offset the lighter shade of her hair. The outfit was similar in its simple lines to a riding outfit, although the narrow skirt looked hard to take long strides in. He slowed his steps some more.

He hoped he hadn't spoken too roughly to her. He really didn't know how to deal in the pleasantries women expected. With men, he was used to saying things straight-out, not wasting precious words. It had been too many years since he'd made time in his life for women.

There was something about Miss Norton, however, that brought out his protective instincts. Was it that his aunt seemed to take such advantage of her and she seemed so incapable of resisting the abuse? His aunt had always had some companion working for her whenever Reid had visited her in latter years, but he'd never paid much attention. They usually seemed faded women long past their prime and Reid hadn't given them a second look.

Why had Miss Norton warranted not only a second look, but a place in his work? Was it because she seemed much too young and attractive and lively? The words came to his mind thinking of her enthusiasm whenever they came upon a particularly choice artifact, or her willingness to play along with the children's games....

In short, Miss Norton seemed the least "companion" type he'd ever seen. He kicked at a pebble in the pathway cutting through the square. What did he know of companions?

"How—how—" Now he was being as hesitant as Miss Norton. He cleared his throat and began again. "How did you end up working for my aunt?" he asked her, fixing his gaze straight ahead.

"An old friend of hers lives in the same village as my parents. She happened to mention your great-aunt to my parents, and as I was looking for a situation at the time, I wrote to her."

He glanced sidelong at her. "Have you always been a companion? Why not teach?"

She seemed to swallow a laugh. "You saw me with your sister's children and you can ask that?"

"Not all children are as spoiled as my niece and nephews."

"They are not bad children," she said immediately. "I didn't mean to imply that. I merely lack the authority to keep them in control. It's not to say I don't enjoy children or teaching them. But somehow, the first situation that came to me when I was much younger was that of a companion." She smiled a faraway smile. "That was a good situation. The lady was a bit of an adventurer like yourself, except she confined her travels to Europe. When she wasn't in England, she would spend several months in France or Italy. I enjoyed traveling with her. She put me in charge of making all the arrangements. She had a wide circle of friends and acquaintances. She was a kind and generous person."

Reid wondered that someone in that circle hadn't latched on to Miss Norton...a gentleman, he admitted reluctantly. As he observed her under the dappled light of the tender green foliage overhead, he noticed her hair, pulled into a heavy knot at her nape, was definitely worthy of Titian. Her skin was porcelain—flawless, delicately tinted at the cheeks. And her eyes—a man could get lost in those soulful eyes.

He coughed, shifting his gaze back onto the street. "You must have met a lot of people."

"She—Mrs. Worthington, that is—enjoyed entertaining artists and writers."

"You never—uh—met anyone?" He felt annoyed at himself for fishing, but couldn't help it.

"I met many people through her."

He took her arm lightly as they crossed the street and made their way down Upper Belgrave.

"I mean…no one in particular…?" He stopped, embarrassed at his own ineptness at framing the question.

She looked at him. "You mean a gentleman?" She shook her head. "Oh, no, no one like that."

Subject closed. Served him right for prying. He certainly wouldn't appreciate anyone probing into his personal affairs. His family had long respected his silence on Octavia. "What happened to your employer?"

"She had such a youthful spirit that I often forgot how old she was becoming. She died peacefully in her sleep a little over a year ago. We'd been together for several years."

"I'm sorry. You must have been close."

She smiled gently. "Yes."

When she offered no more, he risked another question. "So then you went in search of a new position."

"Not immediately. I spent a fortnight with my parents. But then, yes, I wanted to seek employment. I… I didn't want to stop sending my brothers my support."

He narrowed his eyes at her, remembering her earlier reference to their missionary work. "Is that where all your income goes?" He immediately realized the impertinence of the question. "Forgive me, Miss Norton, I didn't mean to pry."

"That's all right. I help support my parents, of course. But as you see, I have no dependents, so yes, most of my income goes to the Lord's work in the mission field. There's so much need there. My brothers write to me about the work, and I only wish I could do more. My brothers are the ones giving their lives for the Lord's work. I'm just doing a very small part to help them carry it out."

Taking abuse from his aunt and scrimping and saving every penny didn't seem such a small thing from his point of view, but he said nothing.

"It's a lovely day, is it not?" she asked.

Sensing her wish to change the topic, he complied. "London does have its moments, though they are few and far between." He spoke the words, but his mind was dwelling on what she'd told him. "There are days, as today, when the wind is blowing in the right direction, houses aren't having to be heated so much, that one can almost see blue sky." He looked up, observing the sky through the trees. "The air has almost regained a sense of freshness...the stench of the summer heat hasn't yet begun."

She laughed. "I confess, I did enjoy the months with my first employer that we spent outside of England. The Italian countryside is particularly beautiful."

"Yes. I spent many summers when I was a lad near Florence. My mother fancied herself a painter."

She looked at him with interest. "Really?"

"Yes. She achieved some success, actually, as an illustrator of botanical books."

"What was her name?"

"Andrea Farringdale."

"Not Gallagher?"

He shook her head. "She kept her maiden name professionally."

"Is that unusual?"

"Yes." He smiled. "My mother was an unusual lady. A pioneer in many ways. She believed women should receive the same education as men and never let the fact that she was married and the mother of children stop her from pursuing her own career."

A light came into Miss Norton's tawny eyes. "Your mother sounds very special."

"Yes. She gave me an appreciation for art."

"Perhaps she influenced you in the direction your interest took toward ancient art."

"Undoubtedly to a degree."

They walked along in silence for several minutes until they reached another green spot at Eaton Square. He glanced over at her and was glad to see color in her cheeks. "Are you tired?"

"Not at all."

"How's your head?"

She smiled, surprise in her eyes. "The headache's gone."

"You've just been spending too much time indoors."

"I suppose so. I do get out a little, for Lilah's walks and a few errands for Lady Haversham, but those are short walks. It's difficult to find time for a long walk like I used to. But I'd hate to give up my work on the artifacts," she said quickly.

"I understand." Of course he did. Aunt Millicent was getting more and more difficult to please. She had always been a demanding woman, but it had not been so apparent when she had had a busy social life. It must be hard for her now to be so limited in her activities. It probably made it inevitable that she took her frustrations out on an easy victim.

"Please don't feel obliged to find another assistant, Mr. Gallagher. I usually don't suffer from headaches."

"You have to promise me you'll make the time to get out for a walk, even if it means shorter hours in the library." He held her gaze, not satisfied until he had her assent.

She nodded, her expression serious. "I promise to do my best."

A smile tugged at his lips. The words didn't mean total acquiescence. "If that's all you can do, I'll have to accept it for now." In the meantime, he'd have a talk with his aunt. There must be something that could be done. Miss Norton looked far too frail to continue under the strain of two demanding employers.

"All right," he said, taking her arm in his once again, "let's get back to work."

Reid spent the following days pondering the situation with Miss Norton, and believed he'd come up with a good solution. It only remained to convince his aunt.

A few afternoons later, returning with his aunt from a visit to old friends, he glanced at her in the carriage. The visit had gone well. She was in a good mood.

"Not too tired?" he said.

"A bit. I do want to thank you, Reid, for accompanying me. It has been a good while since I'd been to see Sally Thornton."

"I'm glad to have been of service."

"Cecily Mason is still quite attractive, is she not?"

"Mmm, hmm," he said, thinking of the beribboned lady who had sat too close to him, claiming an acquaintance from more than a decade ago, insisting he call her Cecily, as she kept referring to him as Reid.

"Cecily moved back with her parents when she lost her husband last autumn." His aunt clucked her tongue. "She was desolate with grief. Such a loving wife… I was glad to see her looking so well today."

"Yes." She didn't strike him as the grieving widow at all. Her cloying eau de toilette still lingered in his nostrils. He pushed back the window shade, deciding to bring up the topic uppermost in his mind. "With the weather so warm, I was wondering if you wouldn't like a little trip to the country. It might do you a world of good."

"A trip? Me? Oh, gracious, I couldn't possibly travel."

He looked across at the horrified expression on his aunt's face. "Pity."

"Where were you thinking of traveling?" she asked when he said nothing more.

"I have a friend at the club who has a house in Scotland. He's told me to make use of it for as long as I wish."

"Scotland! Goodness, as far as that? The trip alone would do me in."

"I don't know about that…with the train, it's not such a grueling trip. You'd wake up and be there. And once you're there, it would be to relax and enjoy the fresh air. It's a wonder you can even breathe in the city."

"You're right about that. I find myself gasping for air at times, it's become so noxious." She shook her head. "And growing worse each day."

"Why don't you think about it? Miss Norton and your maid would accompany you to see that you're comfortable."

She looked out the window and broke open her black lace fan. "Oh, I couldn't possibly consider it. Scotland is much too far."

Well, he'd tried. He'd just have to come up with another solution, his resolve stronger than ever to get Miss Norton out of the city for a while. When was the last time she had had a real holiday?

The quartet of musicians began the first strains of a Brahms violin concerto. After an hour of hustling about overseeing the serving of tea and cakes to the numerous guests at Lady Haversham's afternoon musicale, Maddie welcomed the chance to sit down. She glanced at her employer then at Lilah in a corner not far away from her mistress. For the moment, everyone seemed settled.

The music soon soothed her frayed nerves. After a few minutes her gaze strayed to Mr. Gallagher. He sat on the settee between two fashionably dressed, attractive ladies. Maddie judged them to be around her own age. Both were widows with a secure position in society and independent means. The fact alone of having been married gave them a cachet far superior to Maddie's, as if having procured one husband vindicated them for all time. Even if they never married again, the term *spinster* could never be applied to them.

Cecily Mason leaned over to whisper something to Mr. Gallagher and he smiled and gave a slight nod. At that moment his glance met Maddie's. She quickly looked away, feeling her face heat at having been caught staring at him. She clenched her hands together in her lap and tried to appear as if she were merely interested in the music.

When the musicians took a break halfway through,

Maddie went to see if Lady Haversham needed anything, but she found the old lady engaged in a conversation. "You'll never believe what my nephew has convinced me to do!"

Her acquaintance, another elderly lady, leaned forward, her lace cap trembling. "I couldn't possibly imagine. Do tell me."

"He has prevailed upon me to accompany him to the Scottish Highlands!"

Maddie stared at her. Lady Haversham traveling to the Scottish Highlands?

"Never!"

Lady Haversham tapped her fan against the lady's arm. "I told him my constitution was much too delicate, but he insisted the outing would do me good. Imagine a month of that bracing air."

"Oh, goodness, I don't think I'd be up to the journey."

Lady Haversham glanced at Maddie. "Well, I have Madeleine. And my maid, of course. And Dr. Aldwin has given me his blessing. He even recommended a colleague of his in Edinburgh."

"Does this mean you've reconsidered my suggestion, Aunt Millicent?" Maddie started to hear Mr. Gallagher's low voice behind her.

Lady Haversham looked up at him with a mischievous smile. "I hope I don't regret this. But Dr. Aldwin thought it an excellent suggestion when I mentioned it to him."

"Well, I'm glad to have an ally in him." Mr. Gallagher took a cup of tea a maid offered him. He turned to Maddie with a smile. "Ever been to the Scottish Highlands?"

She wasn't used to seeing him in a dark frock coat.

It set his tanned face off to further advantage. "No. I'm told they are breathtaking."

He stirred his tea. "They are. I haven't been up that way in years, but I have a friend who's offered me use of a place. Did Aunt Millicent tell you?"

"No." Her glance strayed to her employer, but her attention was on her old friend. "I'm surprised—but glad that she's agreed to go. The outing should do her good."

"That's what I'm thinking." He continued looking at Maddie, who felt herself blushing under his scrutiny.

"What about your work?" She frowned, remembering the reason he came by almost every day. What if she shouldn't see him anymore…? The thought brought her up short.

He shrugged. "A week more or less won't make much difference either way. Since the work is held up in Egypt indefinitely, there's no undue rush to finish things here. I don't mind the chance to get out of London for a fortnight or so, I can tell you that. You should enjoy it."

He would be accompanying them. On the heels of that thought came his last words. She would be going, as well. It finally began to sink in. A holiday away from London, with Mr. Gallagher…

It seemed almost too good to be true. Her heart began to sing with a lightheartedness she hadn't felt in a long, long time.

When the concert resumed, Reid found himself once again sandwiched between Mrs. Cecily Mason and Mrs. Augustina Drake, both of whom he'd known only slightly in his youth. He shifted on the hard horsehair settee, moving his thigh away from the one lady's, only to find his other brushing Cecily's. He hid a grimace when she immediately turned to him with a smile.

"How long do you plan to be in London this time, Reid?"

He smoothed down one end of his mustache with his thumb. "Not long," he whispered back. An older lady on a straight-backed chair in front of him turned to glare at them, and Reid wished he could offer to exchange seats with her.

"I'll be sure to invite you to a few functions. There's so much going on in London now. You must be famished for society."

He turned his attention back to the music, wondering how many more movements to the piece there would be. He folded his hands on his knees and felt like an accordion. The least movement to ease his muscles would bring him in unwanted contact with two females whose puffy sleeves, ruffled skirts and dangling jewels seemed to be everywhere he moved.

A soft sound in the corner drew his attention. He craned his neck to the back and saw Lilah vomiting on the carpet beside Lady Haversham's chair.

His aunt motioned to Miss Norton, who had already risen from her place.

Grateful for any excuse to move, Reid stood and headed their way. Before Miss Norton had a chance to bend over the dog, Reid scooped up Lilah, thinking she barely weighed over a pound.

Once outside the drawing room, Miss Norton closed the door softly behind them. "Mr. Gallagher, you needn't have troubled yourself. I can take care of Lilah."

"Where should I take her?"

Without another word, she led him to his aunt's private sitting room and indicated the cushioned basket on the floor. Miss Norton knelt down and smoothed the dog's silky head, careful of her pink bow. "There, sweetie, that feels much better, doesn't it?" The terrier curled up and went to sleep under Miss Norton's soft strokes.

She met Reid's gaze across the small basket. "Lady Haversham feeds her too many rich treats and Lilah invariably gets sick."

He pictured the gaunt stray dogs roaming the streets of Cairo, their ribs prominent through their thin fur. "Spoiled mutt."

She smiled. "She does keep your aunt company."

He wanted to say, *So do you without being treated half so well,* but kept silent.

"You didn't have to interrupt your enjoyment of the music. Lilah will be all right now."

"If you call being jammed between two practical strangers enjoyment. I should thank Lilah for giving me a reason to stretch my legs." He did so now, easing his long legs in front of him.

With a glance in that direction, she resumed stroking the dog. Reid found his gaze lingering on her face. "Botticelli," he murmured, noting the tint of her cheeks, the downward sweep of her dark golden lashes—

"I beg your pardon?" Her lashes fluttered upward again.

Reid was held by those large tawny eyes, their expression tender, inquiring. He broke the connection and coughed. "Nothing…just a stray thought…"

He forced his attention on the small dog. What was getting into him? This was his assistant, not a painting in a museum…and *not* a single, attractive woman.

Before he could go any further with his train of thought, Miss Norton stood. "I suppose we'd better get back. Mr. and Mrs. Walker went to a lot of trouble to arrange this afternoon's entertainment."

"My sister loves nothing better than organizing entertainments, and as you've no doubt observed, my brother-in-law loves nothing better than snoozing through them." He rose to his feet more slowly and followed her to the door. "Although if I had the choice of facing down a hostile tribe of Bedouins or returning to the drawing room, I'd prefer the former."

She smiled in understanding and again he was struck by the soft expression on her face. "Definitely a Botticelli," he said to himself before turning away and holding the door open for her.

Reid endured another hour of music followed by polite small talk with a bunch of people he scarcely remembered and with whom he had little in common. It was early evening by the time he headed back to his club, walking through the Green Park and St. James's until he reached Pall Mall.

"Good evening, Mr. Gallagher." The porter took his hat and umbrella from him. "Fair weather, isn't it?"

"Yes, it's a fine evening, John."

Reid walked across the spacious lobby, nodding to the few gentlemen present. Most were still in the dining room. He decided to skip supper, having eaten more than he was accustomed to at his aunt's. He was getting tired of roast beef and Yorkshire pudding and similar heavy meals almost every evening. He missed the lighter fare of rice or couscous with a sparse serving of goat or lamb, and dates and almonds to finish with, usually eaten around a campfire in the dark desert night.

"Reid!" A tall gentleman with a beard headed across the carpeted floor. "By golly, man, is that you?"

Reid stared a moment trying to place the voice and face. "Cyril? Cyril Melshore?"

"The very one. How are you, Reid? Where the blazes have you been all these years?" The two clasped hands, Reid heartened to see an old friend, one with whom he knew he shared a lot.

"Mainly in Egypt. What about you? The last I heard you'd gone to the Far East."

"Been there and a whole host of other places. Now I'm an old married man, settled in the suburbs." Cyril laughed, a vigorous sound in the hushed lobby. The man looked the picture of health and well-being, his thick reddish hair waving back from a broad forehead, a neatly trimmed beard covering the lower part of his face. "I've become a family man."

"I see." Reid blinked, taken aback for an instant, remembering his friend's penchant for adventure. He shook away the surprise and held out his hand again. "Congratulations."

"Thanks. Listen, have you eaten?"

"No—yes, actually. I've just come from a relative's. I feel I've been fed the whole afternoon."

"Where're you headed then?"

"I was going up to the library."

"Mind if I come along? We have a lot of years to catch up on."

"Of course not." It would be good to talk with Cyril.

The two settled into leather armchairs by an unlit fireplace. A few other gentlemen sat reading newspapers in various corners of the large room.

"I always loved this place. A home away from home."

Reid looked around the book-lined room. "Yes, a fine haven from the rest of London."

Cyril grinned at him. "It does take getting used to once you've lived in the East."

Reid steepled his fingers under his chin. "Let's see… the last time we saw each other, you were heading over to China to clerk in some counting house. As I recall, you were quite anxious to leave Europe."

He chuckled. "Yes, I wanted nothing more than to explore far-off lands. Well, I ended up in Bangkok. I managed a trading house for several years."

A footman walked silently by, turning on the lamps.

"So, I'm here in London cooling my heels for a few weeks at least," Reid summed up after the two had spent a good hour bringing each other up-to-date. "My time isn't completely lost since I'm cataloging this collection left by my great-uncle."

"Sounds like a veritable treasure trove."

"It is an amazing collection."

"I must get over to the British Museum and see what their latest acquisitions are." Cyril's brown eyes twinkled. "You know I live a very staid life now, to work in the City every morning, home every evening."

Reid shook his head, still amazed at the change. "Well, I'd say you led a pretty adventurous life when I knew you. I guess you deserve to enjoy the fruits of your labors."

"Yes, I'm grateful I came back from my travels alive and in one piece—and with a sizable fortune," Cyril added with a gleam in his eyes. "I had known Sarah growing up. When I saw her again, suddenly I was lost. Didn't stand a chance. I decided then and there it was time to settle down." He gave a satisfied sigh. "A man reaches a certain stage when life is no longer enjoyable if there's no one there to share the journey with." As if realizing how his words sounded, he looked away. "Sorry, old chap. I guess there's been no one since…"

"No, no one," Reid said quietly.

Cyril nodded. "Hey, did I tell you about the time I was chased down by a tiger in the jungles of Siam? Caught without my rifle!"

Reid listened as Cyril went on with another story. This time he found his mind wandering, feeling as if the two were a couple of schoolboys trading exploits just to feel good about themselves.

"You say you're living in the suburbs now?" Reid asked more out of politeness than any real desire to know. Suddenly he felt the full fatigue of a day spent making small talk.

"Yes, in Ealing. It's a pretty area. I take the train into Paddington every day. You should come out and visit us. We have a small villa, very comfortable."

"I'm not in London for very long. I'll be heading up to Scotland next week."

Cyril showed interest in that, and the two began talking about trout fishing.

After his friend left for the train station, Reid sat awhile longer in the library. He tried reading the paper, but found himself going over his conversation with Cyril. He shook his head, still amazed at the idea of his old friend a satisfied husband living in the suburbs.

In less than a month Reid would turn forty. He thought of the acquaintances he'd already lost. The rest seemed to be enjoying a comfortable middle age surrounded by family. He stretched out his legs before him, his gaze unseeing on the dark empty grate of the elegant carved-oak fireplace. He stroked his mustache absently. How much longer would he have? Would he, too, catch some fever on his return to Egypt or the Sinai and disappear into the tapestry of his generation?

He rose and stretched, shaking off the gloomy thoughts. He'd get an early night and hopefully be in better shape to accomplish some work in the morning. He remembered his aunt's surprising announcement this afternoon and wondered why she'd changed her mind about Scotland. He shook his head and smiled. Who could fathom the mind of a woman?

He went up to his room and turned up the gaslight. Everything looked neat, the bed made, his pile of books stacked on the bedside table. Oil portraits of past club members stared down at him from their shadowy positions along the damask walls.

He took off his jacket and hung it on the back of a chair then loosened his tie. He poured himself a glass of soda water, brought up earlier by a waiter who knew his habits. He riffled through the envelopes left for him on a silver tray. An invitation from Cecily Mason for a garden party in Chelsea. His aunt seemed determined to throw him in the company of women she deemed suitable for a lonely bachelor.

Reid donned the light cotton pajama pants favored in the Orient for daytime wear. He had grown to prefer the loose cotton trousers with their drawstring waist for sleeping to a nightshirt. He wound his clock and set it. Then he picked up his wife's photograph.

He kissed the framed photo as he did each night. "Good night, my dear." Octavia had been a beautiful woman. It was his favorite picture of her. It had been taken when she was twenty-eight, a year before she died. They had been at a party in London and a renowned photographer had been in attendance. So taken with her beauty, he'd asked her to sit for him and hadn't even wanted to charge a fee.

Octavia had agreed to the picture, saying she wanted Reid to remember her just like that. Her rich dark hair was worn high on her head. Her deep-set dark eyes looked back at him in that understanding way she had. How little the two of them realized her words would prove so prophetic. He rubbed the polished ebony frame.

She'd been his faithful companion for the past decade. Wherever he'd traveled, from India to Egypt, she'd been there every night to bid him good-night at day's end. "Good night, my love," he repeated, setting down the picture. She was his first and last love. And if he could offer her nothing more, he offered her his undying fidelity. It was the least he could do.

Chapter Seven

Maddie stood beside Reid in the library surveying their work of the past few weeks. Every surface was covered in bits of pottery, statuettes and bas-relief fragments. Sheets were spread on the floor and artifacts placed in neat arrangements on them.

Reid had managed to translate several fragments of hieroglyphics. She still marveled at the ease with which he uncovered the meaning of those strange figures on so many surfaces.

He was pointing to a piece of frieze now, his handsome features tilted in concentration.

"This shows Seti I paying homage to the god Ra. He's bringing him offerings of fruit and cattle after a victory in battle. Here he is seated on his throne, receiving homage from his own people."

Maddie studied the stylized figures, stiff and primitive. Reid had taught her to appreciate the beauty in the simple lines.

"So much idolatry." She traced an outline of the god-king.

"They had to worship something."

"But they had the truth so near."

"Moses?"

She nodded.

"It's easy to ignore the truth when it doesn't suit."

Was he being personal or speaking in that detached manner he employed when analyzing artifacts?

"It's amazing how God sent Joseph and Mary with the infant Jesus to Egypt into hiding. I wonder where they lived along the Nile," she mused, looking at the large diagram Mr. Gallagher had drawn and she'd helped fill in each time they'd identified a location from his uncle's treasures. The long river wound its way from the delta where the Port of Alexandria was located, past Cairo and the Giza pyramids then down along several other locations of temples and pyramid ruins until it arrived at Karnak and Luxor.

"There's a small basilica in Cairo dating back to the fourth century where they allegedly came for a short period."

Maddie looked at him in wonder. "Is that so?"

"Tradition has it so. If hiding was their main intention, they'd probably stick to one of the more populated areas." He shrugged. "But we'll probably never know."

She smiled. "Don't you think an archaeologist may someday discover something?"

"It's hard to say. The humbler a person's station, the more anonymous what he leaves behind. The Egyptian pharaohs made sure their names were carved everywhere. A fragment of a poor man's clay pot could have belonged to anyone."

She nodded.

They continued working in silence several more moments. Maddie at her end of the room, copying in a fine, neat hand Mr. Gallagher's notes about each identified object.

Mr. Gallagher hunched over his end of the table, studying the hieroglyphics on a vase and jotting down notes.

When she rose, Mr. Gallagher looked up. "Is it noon already?"

"Nearly. I've gotten to the end of this section." She showed him her morning's work.

"Good." He tapped his pencil against the tabletop. "Has my aunt told you we're to leave for Scotland on Monday?"

"Yes. Her mind is quite occupied with the arrangements."

"I told Aunt Millicent she needn't worry too much. My friend's house is fully staffed."

She smiled. "I think your aunt plans to take anything including bed linens and tablecloths she feels might not meet her standards."

"I'm hoping the weather holds so I can spend most of the time out of doors. Make sure you bring warm enough clothes. It's always cooler and damper up there."

"Yes, I'll be sure to, thank you."

"I used to go up to Scotland quite frequently when I lived in England, though usually only as far as the Lowlands." He glanced toward the row of windows. "Octavia's family had a place near the border along the River Tweed."

"Octavia was your…wife?" she asked.

"Yes." He said no more, his head bent over his notes again.

Maddie couldn't help adding, "You still wear your ring."

The only sign that he'd heard her was that his pencil stopped in midmotion.

"That's because I'm still married to her." The words were matter-of-fact, yet they made Maddie feel like a child who'd spoken out of turn.

Feeling chastened, she bowed her head and left the room, closing the door softly behind her. When she was alone, she took a deep breath, leaning against the solid door of the library. What had she been thinking to ask such a personal question of her employer? It had been the first time he'd talked about his late wife. But his closed expression and his clipped words showed her he did not welcome any conversation about her.

As she walked down the corridor, she remembered his tone of voice. *That's because I'm still married to her.* He spoke in the present tense. Hadn't he been widowed at least a decade?

What devotion. She'd rarely, if ever, seen it in a man. His wife must have been very special. Maddie tamped down her own feelings. Mr. Gallagher was her employer, nothing more.

As she entered the parlor, she saw Mr. Gallagher's sister sitting there conversing with Lady Haversham. Mrs. Walker leaned forward. "You saw him yourself. Poor Cecily was doing everything she knew to be entertaining, but it was as if she was talking to one of those stone tables Reid spends hours poring over. I was distressed for her."

Maddie moved as quietly as possible to take her usual place, trying not to listen to the conversation but unable to shut it out. She picked up her needlework, focusing on the stitches before her. But the more the ladies spoke, the more she resented hearing anyone, even his closest kin, discussing Mr. Gallagher's personal life.

She pulled her silk thread through another hole, her mind conjuring up the late Mrs. Gallagher, a woman no doubt fine not only in feature but also in temperament, a woman noble of soul. She'd have been sweet tempered—

"Well, then, why don't you come along with us to Scotland?" Lady Haversham's voice broke into Maddie's thoughts, bringing them to an abrupt halt. Her glance shot to Mrs. Walker.

"Me?" Lady Haversham's niece looked taken aback. "Why, I'd never considered it.…"

Lady Haversham clasped her hands together on her lap. "Think of it now, my dear. Why, it's just the thing. The children will benefit from the good mountain air, you can organize our activities and see to it that Reid doesn't spend all his time in the library."

"Yes…" She nodded slowly, listening to her aunt's arguments.

Maddie's heart sank. She bent more closely over her needlepoint, trying to shut out her thoughts. She had no business thinking of Mr. Gallagher at all—not as anything more than her part-time employer. If he should be there during their holiday, what better than to have his sister and her children along? He got to see them so little.

"Maybe I could invite Cecily up for a few days," Mrs. Walker mused.

Maddie's mood plummeted even further.

"That's a wonderful idea. I hear from Reid it's a large estate."

"Yes, I shall talk to her about it and see if she can manage to get away from London for a few days," Mrs. Walker continued with a brisk nod, satisfied that she had hit upon a wonderful solution. "She's such a busy lady with her various charities."

Maddie tried to blot out the image of Mr. Gallagher with Mrs. Mason…visiting, hunting, riding…

She pricked herself with her needle and started. Goodness, she was going to ruin this seat cover if she wasn't careful. Taking herself sternly to task, she set another stitch, but already her excitement over the upcoming holiday was severely dampened.

Without her work on the artifacts, there would be no reason for her to be in Mr. Gallagher's company. Would she see him at all?

The trip she'd been so looking forward to now only seemed another extension of her dull days in London.

Chapter Eight

Her fears began proving true as soon as they left for Scotland. During the overnight train trip, Maddie hardly saw Mr. Gallagher. After settling them in their private compartment, he left them, presumably to sit in the smoking car in the company of men.

She could hardly blame him, as she had to endure the restlessness and noise of three young children, the chatter of the women and the yap of an excited terrier. Thankfully, with the services of a new nursemaid, Maddie was not responsible for the well-being of Mrs. Walker's offspring.

Maddie admired the sturdy young woman who seemed unfazed by the children's boisterousness. Just when the noise of the children threatened to upset Lady Haversham, Mr. Gallagher reappeared and took them off to tour the train, the nursemaid bustling along after them. Maddie tried to stifle the feeling of abandonment. She couldn't help remembering her time in the square with Mr. Gallagher and the children, when he'd been her champion.

Early the next morning, they arrived in Edinburgh's bustling station to take a local line to Stirling and from there to Aberfeldy. Amidst a bath chair for Lady Haver-sham, porters' carts piled high with their luggage, Mad-die carrying Lilah in her basket, the nursemaid herding the awestruck children, it was a miracle they all made it in one piece to their next stop. The last leg of the journey was completed in two hired coaches to the village of Kenmore.

Maddie drew in her breath at the countryside. Ken-more was situated at one end of Loch Tay. The long lake reflected the pristine blue of the clear sky. Tree-covered hills rose above it, the outline of a higher mountain ridge behind it. Their coaches crossed the bridge over the River Tay, leaving the small village, and continu-ing along a dirt track through the forest. On one side, she caught glimpses of the lake as the road climbed higher up the hillside.

Suddenly the carriage entered a clearing and Maddie couldn't help but gasp. It was like a fairy-tale setting. A large, gray stone turreted structure like a miniature castle stood half-hidden against the heavily forested hills. Far below them lay Loch Tay. Puffs of white cloud floated against the trees, offering a magical aspect to the scene, as if they were halfway to the heavens.

Maddie had little time to admire the setting. As soon as she descended from the carriage, her attention was taken up with Lilah. She secured the yapping dog to her leash. "I know you want to run about, dearie, but we mustn't lose you," she murmured to the squirming animal in soothing tones.

Lady Haversham motioned to her from the chair being pushed along by a footman. "Be careful of Lilah. I feel a distinct chill in the air. I don't want her catch-ing cold."

Maddie bent down to adjust the collar before the

dog wriggled away. "She won't. I'm sure the fresh air is good for her."

She looked around for Mr. Gallagher, but she saw he was occupied with the footmen with the cases and trunks.

"Maddie, I feel faint." Lady Haversham leaned against her chair, the back of her hand to her forehead.

Maddie pulled on the leash and hurried to her employer's side. "Just hold a moment longer, my lady. We'll soon have you settled in your room."

The next hour was filled with confusion as each one of the carriage's occupants demanded the attention of the awaiting servants. Maddie admired the housekeeper's calm manner in directing the guests to their rooms. The children and their nursemaid were dispatched to the nursery, with instructions for porridge to be sent up for their supper.

Maddie sat with Lady Haversham over her supper tray and then read to her. By the time she came downstairs, everything was once again quiet. She wandered down the wide curved stairway lined with stuffed animal heads, to the spacious flagstone foyer below. As she passed one door, she heard a murmur of voices behind it. She quickened her pace away from it.

She opened the heavy front door and shivered at the drop in temperature. The early June sky was still light...the gloaming, the Scots called it. The horizon was tinged lavender. She tightened her shawl around her shoulders and ventured onto the gravel walk.

She breathed deeply of the evening air, feeling with each breath that her very lungs were being cleansed of the polluted London air, where tiny black particles dusted every surface. She reached a stone balustrade, which fronted the house, and marveled at the view of the lake far below. She didn't know how long she stood gazing at it when she smelled cigar smoke.

"Silence is indeed golden."

She turned to see Mr. Gallagher crossing the space separating them. Her heartbeat quickened with each step. He had changed out of his traveling clothes and wore a tweed Norfolk jacket. The slight breeze ruffled his thick blond hair.

"I didn't know anyone was out here," she said, afraid of intruding on his own quiet time, while longing to draw closer to this solitary man.

"It's a large enough space and I know you are not a chatterbox." Humor laced his low voice, as he turned to tap the cigar against the stone balustrade.

She clasped her hands in front of her, falling silent, not wanting to do anything to make him wish her gone.

"I'm glad to see you survived the journey." His blue eyes swept over her.

"Survived? Oh—yes, thank you." She brushed back a tendril of hair.

He cleared his throat and looked away, as if aware he'd been staring. "I'm sorry I took the coward's way out and made myself scarce most of the time. I figured you were well looked after with the legion of servants at our disposal."

She swallowed, reminding herself she was one of those servants. "You were very good with the children."

He shrugged and looked over the landscape. "As you said, they aren't bad children, just high-spirited, as is natural, and a trifle overindulged. Vera seems to have found them a good nurse."

"Yes, she struck me as very able."

He leaned his elbows against the wide balustrade.

"She seems to know all their tricks and refuses to fall for any of them."

Maddie looked down, remembering her own ineptitude. "Yes."

He turned to her. "I didn't mean to imply you were any less capable with them."

Her glance met his. His perceptiveness was uncanny. How could he have sensed how incompetent she felt?

"You're not used to being around children, and you had the added disadvantage of having to answer to both my sister and aunt."

She blinked away the tears that threatened, realizing how long it had been since she'd experienced such thoughtfulness. "You're not used to children, either."

"No, but I can give my sister a hard time about her unruly children." His mouth tugged upward and she couldn't help smiling back.

Maddie said nothing more, too affected by the man's sensitivity. What did he care what she felt?

He flung the cigar down and crushed it out. "Excuse the smoke. I rarely indulge but it has been a trying day," he said.

She gave a look around her. "It's a beautiful spot. Thank you so much for including me in the invitation."

He shrugged. "I thought you could use a change of scenery. Tomorrow I'll show you some of the landmarks." He pointed to the west where the sun was beginning its slow descent behind the mountains beyond the loch. "See the peaks?"

"Yes."

"The highest is Ben Lawers. It's almost four thousand feet."

"It's majestic."

"I've always wanted to climb it."

She looked at him curiously. "Why?"

He turned to her. "Why not?" He smiled, a smile that began in his blue eyes and slowly reached his lips. "Think of the view from the summit. On the other side of the range lies Glen Lyon, which I'm told is one of the loveliest glens in all the Highlands."

"It sounds spectacular." She was no longer looking at the mountains but at Mr. Gallagher's profile. He was a man of action, she saw, like her brothers, and her parents before them. While she was…what? What did she have to show for her life?

"Wouldn't you like to climb it, too?" His eyes met hers once more.

She? Her gaze traveled up the mountain's fluted silhouette and over the lower peaks beside it. They were massive, dwarfing the scenery below. "Yes," she found herself breathing, hardly aware of what she was saying. "Has any woman ever climbed it?"

"I don't know. I don't imagine so, but what does that matter? You could be the first." There was a challenge in his blue eyes.

She continued looking at the mountain range. He never seemed fazed by the idea of a woman accomplishing anything. It must be the influence of his unconventional mother. She wondered what his wife had been like. Had she been just as remarkable?

She drew in a lungful of the sharp air. "The thought is appealing, I'll admit."

"Think about it, Miss Norton."

She said nothing more, hardly capable of imagining herself scaling that peak.

He yawned. "I think I'll head in and make it an early night."

"It has been a tiring day."

"Are you coming in?"

"I'll be along in a minute," she replied.

"All right, take your time. You've earned some peace and quiet." He tapped the stone balustrade with a fist before finally moving away. "Well…good night."

"Good night." She watched his silhouette until he'd disappeared through the door, feeling a pang that she couldn't have thought of something more interesting to say to hold him a moment longer. Was he disappointed in her response to climbing Ben Lawers? If he could only see how her soul had soared within her at his suggestion.

With a sigh she turned back to the mountains. The pink-and-lavender tinge along the horizon was deepening as the sun fell below the highest peaks. Down below, the loch looked a silvery lavender.

Thank you, Lord, for bringing me here. "You know my downsitting and my uprising," she quoted from the psalm *You knew this was just the place I needed to come.* Her glance strayed back to the Ben Lawers. Who knew? Maybe someday she would scale its summit. She smiled at the remarkable thought.

Maddie didn't see Mr. Gallagher at all the next day until dinnertime. He entered the great room where the rest of the family had already assembled and glanced about. As soon as he spotted her in one of the far recesses, he smiled.

He looked rested and refreshed, and she felt a twinge of envy at his freedom to be out and about enjoying the hills and dales, while she'd been cooped up most of the day. It wasn't that she'd had so much to do. Lady Haversham had spent most of her time with her niece, so Maddie felt at loose ends more than anything. Even her duty of walking Lilah had been co-opted by the children, under the watchful supervision of their nursemaid. When Lady Haversham had discovered that the young woman had grown up on a farm with dogs, she'd entrusted her precious pet to her.

Before Mr. Gallagher could make a move toward Maddie, Vera approached him with a drink. "Where have you been the whole day, while we've been sitting around trying to amuse ourselves?"

He rubbed his hands together before the massive stone fireplace, his cheeks ruddy from the outdoors.

"Exploring the region. I talked with the local gillie and found out the best salmon beats along the river and where to hire a boat to fish on the loch. I also scouted around a bit and discovered some good walking trails on the property."

Vera frowned. "I hope you discovered some local families, as well. I don't mean to spend all my time in my own company."

He took a sip of the amber liquid. "I thought I'd leave that part of the exploration in your capable hands, Vera. There's a good brougham and wonderful stables. You can ride into Kenmore or farther afield to Aberfeldy and make the rounds."

His sister's lips firmed in a distasteful line. "You are impossible. You expect me to leave my calling cards without your lifting a finger to help."

He grinned. "That's right, my dear. I'm here to enjoy the river and loch."

"I hope you don't mean to become a hermit. I expect you to accompany us on a few of those visits."

"As long as it's only a few. I don't mind talking with some of the local anglers." He turned to Maddie. "Do you fish?"

"Does she fish?" Lady Haversham spoke up for her. "What kind of a question is that for a lady's companion? Of course she doesn't fish. I hope you don't plan to spend all your time at the river."

"No, Aunt Millicent, I propose to rise early and spend the mornings there."

Once again, Maddie had to swallow her disappointment that she couldn't share a moment with Mr. Gallagher.

As they were walking into dinner, however, he approached her. His eyes narrowed as he studied her face. "You look pale. Didn't you get outside today?" His tone was stern.

"No." Was he angry with her?

His frown deepened. "Did my aunt keep you too busy?"

"Not at all. I just didn't want to stray too far in case she might need me."

"I never did hear whether you fished or not."

"I used to…with my brothers." She was taken aback by the quick switch in topic. "That was a long time ago and in a little mud hole near home, so I don't know if that qualifies."

"You'll find it a bit more challenging here. The area has the best salmon fishing of any in Britain. If you'd care to have a go, I'll be leaving at sunrise, if that's not too early for you."

She stared at him. He was inviting her to go along with him. "No, it's not too early."

"In that case, you can meet me at the front door. Don't worry about breakfast. I'll have the cook prepare us some sandwiches." He glanced toward his aunt as they entered the oak-paneled dining room. "And don't worry about Aunt Millicent. We'll most likely be back long before she's up."

She nodded her head, again grateful that he seemed to know her concerns without her having to voice them.

She found it hard to swallow at dinner and every once in a while took a surreptitious glance Mr. Gallagher's way. He had singled her out and invited her fishing. She knew from her brothers and father that fishing was not a social activity. Those passionate about the sport enjoyed the peace and quiet of it. It would be no more than working alongside Mr. Gallagher in the library. Yet, she knew from those moments the sense of companionableness she'd experienced with him.

Why had he invited her along? She couldn't fathom an answer.

Maddie woke to the shrill sound of birdsong. A second later she remembered Mr. Gallagher's invitation. Was she too late? She breathed a sigh of relief when she read the clock face. It was just past four.

The sky was still dark, although a pale tinge along one horizon signaled that daylight was not far off. Maddie closed her casement window and hurried to dress.

Hoping he hadn't left without her, Maddie walked softly down the stairs toward the front door. Mr. Gallagher was already there, looking properly like a country gentleman in his tweed jacket and trousers tucked into high leather boots.

"Good morning, I hope I haven't kept you waiting."

"No." He eyed her gown with a frown and she bit her lip, wondering what was wrong with her old black serge skirt and bodice. She pulled her knitted shawl more tightly around her shoulders.

"Let me see your shoes."

Beginning to worry, she lifted the hem of her skirt just enough to reveal her low walking boots.

"What you really need is a pair of Wellingtons." He gave her skirt another critical glance. "You won't be able to do any wading in that. Why women's dress has to be so impractical is beyond me," he muttered. "Here, this might keep you warmer." He handed her a folded woolen square.

"Oh!" She took the tartan shawl. "Thank you."

"Wrap it around yourself like the local women do. It'll keep off the morning chill."

She discarded her own smaller shawl and did as he suggested. She felt immediately cozier.

"Let's see if we can find you a pair of better footwear in here." He led her to a small room that held an assortment of cloaks, mackintoshes and umbrellas. A row of boots was ranged along a low shelf. He inspected one pair of boots, then another, glancing at her feet as he did so. He finally approached her holding a black pair in one hand. "Here, try these, they're the new rubberized Wellingtons."

She sat on a bench under a rack of coats along one wall and bent to unbutton one of her boots. Her fingers fumbled in the dark, aware of his gaze on her. He was probably regretting having to wait for her.

"Let me." Before she knew what he was about, he crouched down in front of her and gently moved her hands out of the way. "Your fingers feel like ice," he said, his own nimbly undoing the row of buttons. The next second he slipped her boot off, his fingertips gently brushing her heel. "All right, let's see how this fits." He held out the knee-length boot and she grasped it by the top edges and pulled it on.

She wiggled her toes in the space in front.

"It seems fine."

"Good. Now for the next one." This time, without asking her permission, he took her other foot in his large hand and undid the top button. In a few seconds, he had that one off, as well, and was holding out the second boot. Maddie was glad of the dark, afraid he'd see how ruffled the contact left her.

"Well, at least they should keep you from getting pneumonia," he said, looking down at her feet. "If we could do something about those long skirts, you would be in fine shape to wade. Have you ever worn a pair of those bloomers?"

Her eyes widened at the mention of the controversial female garment. Only suffragettes and sporty women wore the wide, knickerbocker-like garment, to the scandal of respectable females. "No."

"Pity. Well, come along then, the morning's advancing."

He picked up a collection of long rods and baskets he'd left by the door. She offered to carry one of the baskets.

She had no time to do more than take a deep breath of the cool morning air before he was disappearing down the drive. She hurried after his long strides, the memory of his gentle hands touching her feet lingering in her mind.

He glanced over his shoulder. "Do you mind a bit of a walk?"

"No. I'm used to walking."

"Good. We'll head toward one of the pools on the river this morning," he said, his tone clipped from his stride. "It's one of the gentler areas. It's said even a lady in long skirts might fish it without having to wade."

He waited for her to catch up and held a branch to one side to allow her passage.

The vegetation around them was wet as if it had rained in the night, although she hadn't heard anything. More likely just the mist Scotland was known for. The air smelled of earth and leaf mold and green vegetation. Swirls of white mist drifted upon the trees and over the lake below them. All around them birds lifted up a cacophony of sound as if impatient for the day to get under way.

After about a mile of walking, they reached the village of Kenmore and heard the rapids at the head of the River Tay. The sounds of rushing water drowned out the birdsong. They bypassed the village and continued along a narrow track along the river, which flattened and widened as it meandered through the forest.

A short walk along the north bank took them away from all signs of civilization. When they reached a bend in the river, Mr. Gallagher stopped.

He set everything down on the damp grass and she followed suit with her basket. "We'll try this pool today. The gillie tells me the salmon are running. There are also plenty of trout and grayling. Have you ever fly-fished?" He glanced up at her from where he squatted by an open basket.

She shook her head.

He held up a feathery object. "These lures mimic the insects the trout and salmon are accustomed to feeding on in these waters."

Maddie peered over his shoulder at a colorful array of feather-clad hooks. "How pretty."

He held one out to her and she took it. It was an intricate design of feathers tied around a hook. "Mayflies, dragonflies, stone flies, midges, take your pick," he said, turning to survey the river. He was quiet a long time and Maddie knew better than to speak. Too much commotion would scare the fish away.

He inspected the flies again. "I think…a nymph for you." He selected one of the smaller hooks and picked up one of the rods from the grass.

She crouched beside him and watched as he attached the fly to the line. "The trick is to tie one of these flies to this thin line called the leader, which then attaches to the heavier line." As he spoke, he demonstrated what he was saying, amazing her with how deftly his fingers managed to tie a knot in the thin filament. She thought once again of his fingers undoing the small buttons on her boots.

He proceeded to select a fly for his own rod and secure it to the line. As he prepared his own rod, she stood quietly, enjoying the break of day. "Bless the Lord, oh my soul, and all that is within me, bless His holy name," she recited to herself. Suddenly she felt freer than she had in a long time.

He stood and motioned for her to follow him to the edge of the bank. "The next thing is to learn how to cast." He pointed forward. "See the insects hovering on the surface?"

She nodded, seeing the dancing insects above the dark waters in the pale light.

"You want to emulate them. Watch." He set his own rod down and took hers from her. "Instead of flicking your wrist as you normally would, you need to use a longer, slower movement in order to get the line to go in a wide arc into the water. Unlike a lure, the fly won't offer any weight to aid you, only the line."

His arm arched behind him then moved forward in a long, smooth curve. Unaware she held her breath, she watched the line flow out in a smooth curve and land halfway out in the river, upstream from them. She let out her breath, scarcely making out the fly on the barely rippling river surface. Then it floated with the current downstream. A moment later, there appeared a tug on the line.

"Yes…" She glanced at Mr. Gallagher, detecting the slight smile playing beneath his mustache. "Now, to make sure he's well secured on the hook." His wrist barely moved as his other hand came up to switch hands on the rod. He used his right hand to play the line in. In a few moments he had reeled in a good-size speckled trout. Handing the rod to Miss Norton, he waded in to land it in a net.

He hefted it in his hand. "Half a stone, perhaps a bit lighter."

She beamed at him, enjoying his satisfaction. "Wonderful."

After depositing the fish in the creel, he came back to her. "All right, now it's your turn."

She gave a nervous laugh. "You make it look so easy. I'm sure it's not."

"It's not as complicated as it might seem if I try to explain it to you. It's best you just try it and then keep on practicing it." He handed her the rod and stood away from her.

She could feel herself grow nervous under his observation. Her first attempt landed the line somewhere close to the bank. She turned to him shamefaced. "It doesn't go where I want."

He approached her. "That's because there's no real weight on the end. Here, let me guide you through it." The next thing she knew, he stood just behind her, his hand covering hers. She couldn't breathe, feeling the length of his strong arm against hers. His other hand held her gently by the opposite shoulder. Before she could react, she felt him take her hand and the rod it held and move it swiftly up and behind, then forward. She watched, openmouthed, as the line made its wide arc far above the water and land.

"Not perfect, but you get the general idea." Mr. Gallagher's voice sounded somewhere above her head.

He let her go and stepped away from her. He cleared his throat. "Keep an eye on the fly. Let it drift with the current. If nothing happens in a bit, take it up and cast it once again."

She was too overwrought to hear much of what he said, much less follow his instructions. She blindly moved her wrist, but that only jerked the line.

"Easy there or you'll scare the fish." He took the rod from her and reeled in the line. Then he guided her through the casting just as before. "Let gravity do its work once you let it go."

She nodded, hardly knowing what he meant.

He stepped away from her and watched her do it on her own. "That's better. All it takes is a little practice. I'm going to move a little farther upstream but within sight. Just call me if you need any help."

She nodded, feeling half-relieved that his too-observant eyes would be away from her, and extremely sorry to lose his closeness.

Reid selected a spot about twenty-five feet away from Miss Norton. He knew he liked to master something without someone hovering over him. From where he stood, he could easily watch her if she got in trouble, but still remain far enough removed to give her a sense of solitary peace.

He tried to dismiss the sensation of holding her while guiding her through the fly casting, yet, like the mysteries the artifacts he dug up produced, it teased him, compelling him onward to discover more thoroughly the reason for its origin.

The feel of her smaller hand in his, his larger frame so close behind her had been… He searched for a word to describe what he'd felt. *Unsettling* came to mind. He still felt unsettled.

He realized he hadn't held a woman in a very long time. The rare times he'd come home he gave his great-aunt and sister a mere peck on the cheek and moved away from them.

He waded out a bit and cast his line, determined to shake off the memory. It was merely the strangeness of it. Unsettling, he repeated to himself for the third time before relegating the word and sensation to the outskirts of his mind, like an unsolvable but insignificant mystery.

He felt a tug on his line and, with relief, concentrated on the fish caught by his hook. It was hardly a challenge, but it was satisfying. The fish were biting and they were plentiful.

After landing a few more trout, he began to feel the kind of calm that he hadn't experienced since arriving in England, the kind that came only with solitude, the kind he was used to in the desert. He gazed around him. The morning was glorious. Light and shadow began to dapple the area as the sun rose above the trees.

He felt a sense of satisfaction that he had accomplished what he'd set out to do with this trip to the Highlands. He had Miss Norton away from the stuffy atmosphere that surrounded his aunt. He hadn't liked the pale look of her last evening. He wouldn't have this trip be in vain even if he had to personally escort Miss Norton on a daily fishing or hiking excursion.

The notion wasn't in any way displeasing, the more it lingered in his mind. For one so used to being in the company of men, the thought of her presence was at once peaceful and gentle.

In a short time Reid had caught half a dozen respectable trout. He removed the hook from his last trout and placed the fish in the creel when he heard Miss Norton shout. His gaze flew to her and he saw her body jerk forward.

He dropped everything and sprinted toward her. She must have hooked a good-size salmon for that kind of force on her line.

"Mr. Gallagher! I think I've caught something!"

A few seconds later he was at her side. Seeing her in danger of being dragged off the edge of the bank, he didn't think but wrapped his arms around her and grasped the rod with her.

For the next several moments the two fought the fish. "Keep a firm hold, play out some line." His voice remained calm, even as he gripped the rod.

He loosened his hold a fraction to allow her to land the fish herself, but no sooner had he slackened his grip that she jerked forward again. "Help!" she called out.

His hands tightened once more on the rod.

Even as his rational mind remained cool, using his experience and knowledge to land the fish, another part of him felt ripped apart. This time it was no slight touch, but the greater impact of Miss Norton fully in his arms.

His senses felt bombarded with light and sound and color—the feel of Miss Norton's shoulders against his chest, the splash of the fish as it surfaced and receded again, the tug of the line, the sheen of the water now that the sun's rays had hit it, awakening its dark depths just as his own senses were being forced awake.

"He's a big one," he murmured. "And strong." Miraculously his voice came out sounding steady and normal, and not as if he were being punched in the gut, knocked in the head, inundated with a sweet taste in his mouth, a roaring in his ears, light and sound exploding in him like a rocket launched in the desert night.

Miss Norton's straw hat fell off and his chin bumped into her soft hair, its feminine fragrance hitting his nostrils like a potent elixir spreading to every particle of his being.

Oof! Her body hit his and he absorbed the impact, his arms involuntary tightening around her. He felt chilled and burned wherever his body touched hers. Dear heavens, what was happening to him?

Maddie fought the sensations assailing her even as Mr. Gallagher and she fought the salmon. They pitted their strength against it for several more minutes, and then as suddenly as it had begun, it was over. The fish, spent from its valiant struggle, was reeled in and trapped in a net. Mr. Gallagher didn't look at her, his attention fixed on the salmon, his fingers deftly removing the hook.

"It's beautiful," she said, her voice coming out breathless as she leaned over him.

"Yes." He took the fish up in his hands. "I'm surprised it didn't break your line. It looks a good two stone. Congratulations."

For a second their gazes locked, hers lost in his deep blue one. "I—we both caught it," she managed.

"He was on your line. He's yours."

She chuckled, the sound nervous to her ears. "Beginner's luck?"

He looked away from her. "Whatever you want to call it, it's still your catch." He rose and placed the fish into the creel. "How about some breakfast?"

"All right." She set down the fishing rod as he fetched the hamper, and she wondered if he was as intent on finding a task as she was. Did he feel as self-conscious as she did after the moments they'd just experienced? Now, it hardly seemed real. Had she actually been held tightly in his arms?

He laid out their simple breakfast of oatcakes and a flask of tea. She watched him furtively as she spread a plain linen cloth on her lap and received the oatcake he handed her.

He began to raise the food to his mouth, but froze in midmovement when she bowed her head. "Dear Lord," she said, "We thank you for this beautiful morning, the bountiful fishing and for this meal we are about to partake of. Please bless it, in Jesus's name."

"Amen," he repeated with her.

She bit into the cold oatcake, its hearty texture satisfying. As the two sat silently eating their breakfast, she replayed in her mind the feel of his strong arms around her. It had been more than the physical wonder of the contact. As she remembered the moments, she thought how wonderfully protected and how bound to this man she'd felt.

As the sensations receded, they were replaced by the quiet companionability of two souls in harmony. She sighed, glancing sidelong at Mr. Gallagher. How long would this interlude last?

How would she survive its end?

Chapter Nine

Try as he would, Reid couldn't get the memory of Miss Norton in his arms out of his mind. Almost every morning the two went fishing together, but no other opportunity presented itself in that realm. Miss Norton proved an apt pupil and was soon almost as competent as he with rod and reel.

He'd never had a female as a fishing companion and found her all that he could wish for in an angling partner. Together the two would return with a laden creel, well satisfied with their catch, knowing they would enjoy the fresh trout and salmon for dinner. Without any conscious consent, neither mentioned Miss Norton's participation in the fishing. His aunt and sister assumed the catch was solely his and the local gillie's. He didn't enlighten them and was glad Miss Norton kept silent, as well.

It wasn't in his nature to deceive. Yet, he sensed his aunt wouldn't approve of Miss Norton's having some recreation time to herself. He observed how demanding his aunt was whenever Miss Norton was with her.

Thankfully, his aunt depended more on Vera now, and the two spent a good part of the afternoon in the carriage making calls on the neighboring lairds. Reid avoided these calls as much as he could. Whenever he managed to remain behind, he usually invited Miss Norton on a hike. The hills behind the manor beckoned, and he told himself he was doing his own Christian duty by making sure Miss Norton got a real holiday.

He found himself wondering at the oddest moments of the day—reading a fishing journal or a volume from the library shelves, staring out on a misty yard, taking tea with his aunt—what it would feel like to have his arms about Miss Norton again.

Would it be as shocking to his senses? Or would the familiarity of being with her almost every day diminish the impact? The only sensation he could liken it to was the keen anticipation he experienced at the beginning of an archaeological dig, when the promise of uncovering some long-buried pottery of an ancient civilization faced him, but that excitement appeared monochromatic in comparison to what he was feeling now.

After Octavia had died, he'd never thought to experience these kinds of feelings for any woman. Perhaps that's why he'd avoided the company of women and buried his needs as deep as any ancient treasure.

But now he'd stare into space, his thumb and forefinger smoothing down his mustache, reliving the moment he'd held Miss Norton, until someone's voice would bring him back to the present and he'd start, and blurt out something about the weather.

It was during a rainy afternoon as he sat in a warm parlor, the peat fire glowing in the huge stone hearth, his aunt and sister entertaining a local gentlewoman and her daughter that he hit upon a perfect solution to his dilemma.

In a lull in the conversation, he ventured, "Do you ever hold any dances here locally?"

His aunt and sister stared at him as if he'd just asked if it snowed on the moon. Mrs. Campbell, their visitor, turned to him with delight. "We haven't had one in an age, but we do so love a dance, don't we, Priscilla?" She turned to her daughter, who had been silent until that moment.

The young lady blushed and nodded. "Oh, yes, Mama."

Reid's gaze drifted to Miss Norton who sat by a window embrasure, working on her embroidery as usual. She hadn't looked up during the exchange, and he wondered if she forswore dancing as some of the stricter evangelicals did. The dance plans would be for naught if that were the case. He braced himself and continued on, feeling like a plodder in the fine desert sand.

"We have a nice-size drawing room here." He consulted his aunt. "It would serve for a dance floor. What do you think?"

"I—well, I hadn't thought about it, but..." She turned to Vera. "What do you think, dear?"

Reid's sister clapped her hands together. "A dance is just the thing. There are some ever so agreeable families in the valley. I could write to Cecily, as well, and ask her to come up for the weekend. Theo could accompany her."

Aunt Millicent nodded her approval. "That's a wonderful idea. Now when should we hold this dance? Mrs. Campbell, you must help me draw up a list of the local lairds and their families to invite."

The women grew more animated in their talk. Reid rose, having no interest in the particulars of the dance. If Cecily Mason were to come, it would prove a tedious time. But he was determined to make himself agreeable if it meant an opportunity to hold Miss Norton in his arms once again. Like a scientist designing an experiment, he was single-minded in his effort to replicate the conditions.

He ambled over to the window embrasure and glanced down at Miss Norton's work, some sort of dark red tapestry.

"That's very intricate," he said.

She glanced up at him. "Thank you. It's…it's for a set of chair cushions for my parents."

"I see. Do you dance?"

She raised her head again. "Dance? I…"

He seemed to have taken her unawares. He smiled slightly, feeling suddenly like a nervous schoolboy. "Yes, dance…waltz, polka, quadrille…if my memory serves correctly. It has been some years since I hosted a dance."

Her cheeks were tinged a pretty pink. "It's been some years for me, as well…since I danced."

"I'm told it's one of those skills one doesn't forget."

"I'm…not certain."

The topic seemed to make her uncomfortable. He didn't blame her. It wasn't something he was easy conversing about, either. At least she hadn't said anything disapproving about dancing. He tried another tack. "Do you have any—" how to word it? "—party outfits?" She always dressed quite severely in plain, dark gowns, which was appropriate for a paid companion he supposed, though he thought it a pity, that one of her years and…complexion should have to dress like an elderly widow.

"Party outfits?" She made it sound as if the words were foreign to her.

Before he could explain further, his aunt's shrill voice interrupted them. "What are you two discussing? Reid, I need your help with this guest list."

He turned to the other ladies. "I was just asking Miss Norton if she danced."

"Miss Norton dance?" His sister's horrified laugh irritated him. "Miss Norton is Aunt Millicent's companion. She isn't paid to dance."

When had Vera become such a snob? "That doesn't mean she can't enjoy an evening's entertainment, does it?"

"Reid, don't be silly." His sister's voice took on that note he recognized whenever she took offense. "Now, come and help us invite some *suitable* guests."

He didn't argue further, knowing it wouldn't do Miss Norton any good. For some reason, he felt she wouldn't approve of his defense of her, either. With a murmured "excuse me," he moved away from her. He'd make sure she felt welcome at the dance, but he wouldn't do anything to draw attention to her.

Maddie sat perfectly still after Mr. Gallagher had moved away, her hands clutching the linen and needle, her head bent low over it. But her heart thudded with deafening rhythm in her chest.

He'd come expressly to ask her if she danced. Her face warmed in chagrin. He'd asked if she had any party dresses. She looked at the faded cloth of her skirt. For a man who didn't seem to take note of the beautifully dressed women around him, he had noticed how unsuitable her garments were for such an occasion.

The only fancy dress she had brought with her was a gown several years old, given to her by her first employer.

Maddie raised her eyes and looked across the room.

Mr. Reid sat with the ladies but spoke little. He seemed distracted. Probably thinking how he'd rather be hiking in the hills.

These last few days had been a paradise for her. Fishing trips in the early-morning hours, like being at the dawn of creation, everything untouched, unspoiled. Afternoon hikes through forest and hillside, over moor and meadow to stand far above the world.

She had never known such a wonderful companion. Quiet yet strong, sensitive to her every need, whether to stop and rest, or have a drink of water, or break for lunch. Her mind went back to that first morning when she'd landed the salmon. She'd been so happy to show him he hadn't brought her in vain, that she wouldn't be a millstone around his neck.

Somewhere, tucked deep down where no one and nothing could disturb it, was the memory of his arms around her. Enveloped, protected…cherished… The words rose unbidden.

Of course, she was sure he didn't harbor any of those feelings for her. She could never forget the ring he still wore on his left hand. But deep, where no one was privy to her thoughts, she could dream it was so.

Her feelings sank back down the next moment when she remembered his last question. Did she own something suitable for the dance?

Well, if she were expected to make an appearance at this dance, and if…her glance went once more to Mr. Gallagher…*if* Mr. Gallagher were to notice her, the old faille and crepeline would have to do. She had no alternative. Besides, Mr. Gallagher was used to seeing her in her everyday gowns. He wasn't prone to notice what a woman wore. She thought back to their first morning fishing and the close scrutiny he'd given her then. But that had been for strictly practical reasons.

Maddie sighed and poked her needle into the cloth. She'd best put all thoughts of balls and gowns out of her mind. Likely Lady Haversham—or Mrs. Walker—wouldn't permit her to attend.

The thought brought her no relief.

Scarcely a week later, Maddie stood at the head of the massive curved stairway in the manor's main hall. She touched the golden fringe along the pull-back drapery of her gown and swallowed. One last glance at the mirror in her room had not reassured her. She hadn't worn such formal attire in years. She brought a hand up to her throat, feeling almost naked.

The gold silk faille with the bronze underskirt in crepeline had been the height of fashion at one time. The low-cut square neckline with its narrow lace frill edging and tight cap sleeves felt inadequate. She wished she had a shawl to drape around her shoulders, but she'd had nothing appropriate.

She heard Lady Haversham from the drawing room. Maddie could hardly swallow from nerves, but knew she must join the family before the guests arrived. *Lord, be with me.* With that prayer, she finished descending the stairs.

The others were already gathered in the drawing room. A fire blazed in the stone fireplace against the cool evening.

"Madeleine, is that you?" Lady Haversham eyed her through a lorgnette. "Good heavens, where on earth did you get that gown?"

Maddie stiffened, crossing her arms as if to cover herself.

"What's wrong, my lady?" she managed with difficulty, feeling everyone's eyes on her. If only Mr. Gallagher didn't have to be among them.

Lady Haversham approached her, still examining her toilette through the glass. "Too many furbelows, for one thing." She walked behind her. "Doesn't suit you. Much too youthful for someone who's on the verge of thirty. You must begin to dress more soberly."

Maddie dearly wished she could sink into the floor beneath her, but the solid oak held firm. Her glance went across the room to Mrs. Walker in her plush burgundy velvet skirt and cream lace underskirt with its large appliquéd flowers in deep crimson. She must be at least Maddie's age, if not older.

Before Maddie could disappear into some corner of the room, Mr. Gallagher approached her and offered her his arm.

"I think she looks charming, Aunt Millicent." He smiled into her eyes, his blue ones offering warmth and support.

Maddie pressed her lips together, afraid they would tremble otherwise.

"Thank you," she said, the sounds coming out in a whisper, before she looked away.

He led her to a side table. "What can I get you to fortify you before this revelry begins?"

"A…a lemonade would be fine," she replied, hardly aware of what she was saying. He looked breathtakingly handsome in his black evening attire.

He stepped away from her and went to the sideboard. She fingered the lace at the edge of her bodice, feeling ridiculous. She touched her temple. Her hair was dressed differently, too, a few tendrils curled around her face and the rest drawn back loosely to the crown of her head, exposing more of her neck than she was accustomed to. Now, she wished she had a cap.

"Here you go." She started at the sound of Mr. Gallagher's voice.

She took the glass and napkin he held out for her and bit down on her lip to see her wrist shake. If Mr. Gallagher noticed, he didn't let on. He had turned away from her but remained standing beside her. She almost wished he would walk away. She felt humiliated and his presence only bespoke pity.

"Am I late?" A feminine voice floated from the doorway, and Maddie's heart sank at the sight of Mrs. Mason, who had made the journey from London the day before.

"Not at all, Cecily." Mrs. Walker gave her two airy pecks on the cheeks. "You look lovely."

"Indeed you do," Lady Haversham echoed.

Mrs. Mason remained in the doorway a moment longer, her confidence in direct contrast to Maddie's urge to hide.

Mrs. Walker nodded her approval. "Your gown is the latest fashion." The teal-blue gown with its puffy sleeves reaching to the elbows, its wider skirt, the bustle in back less prominent made Maddie feel all over again how dated her own was.

"Who are we awaiting, every laird in the region?" She smiled at her witticism, then slowly entered the room, as if to give everyone in it the chance to admire her.

Mrs. Walker laughed. "I suspect we shall be swarmed by every respectable family from here to Inverness."

Mrs. Mason stopped before Mr. Gallagher and eyed

his glass significantly. He asked her immediately what she would have.

"A sherry, if you please." As he moved away from them, Mrs. Mason glanced at Maddie's gown. With her lips pursed, she ran her eyes over its length but said nothing. Instead she turned to wait for Mr. Gallagher.

When he returned, she thanked him. "I vow, I had my doubts about coming all the way up here for merely a dance, but now I begin to feel recovered."

"I'm relieved to hear it."

Mrs. Walker came to stand with them. "I do hope you're not too tired to enjoy this evening's festivities."

"A nap has restored me, thank you." She raised her glass. "Here's to good food, good drink and good company." The others followed suit.

Maddie quietly moved away from them before they would notice her. She needn't have worried as Mrs. Walker began describing the local families to her friend.

The next moment, her three children trooped in with their nanny. They were clad in dressing gowns and slippers, their faces scrubbed and shiny.

Harry spoke for the group. "We've come to wish you good-night, Mama and Papa." Their father had traveled with Mrs. Mason to join his family for the weekend.

Maddie had to admire the way the children's manners had improved in the short while the nursemaid had been with them. Mr. Gallagher also spent a good portion of each day with them, taking them on horseback rides or organizing ball games out on the lawn.

"Good night, my darlings." Mrs. Walker bent down, offering each one her cheek for a kiss. Their father patted their heads as each one approached him.

Lisbeth reached up to put her arms around her mother's neck.

"You look ever so pretty, Mama."

"Thank you. Careful, sweetling, with Mama's coiffure."

"You smell good, too."

Her mother eased away from the girl's embrace. "That's because your mama is going to a ball."

Maddie felt a pang at the sight of the children's affection for their mother.

"Good night, Great-aunt Millicent and Uncle Reid," they chorused when they had finished bidding their parents good-night.

"Good night, children." Lady Haversham smiled regally. "Now, mind you get to bed on time and tomorrow you shall hear all about the ball."

Mr. Gallagher knelt down and gave them each a hug.

Soon the first guests arrived. Maddie forgot about her earlier discomfort as the hall filled to overflowing. The local gentry appeared a mixed bag, with titled dignitaries from Glasgow, Edinburgh and London mingling equally with the local lairds, whose pride came from their living in the area for many generations.

She wasn't formally introduced to anyone but when the orchestra began to play, she found herself asked onto the dance floor by a local laird named Duncan McGee. He appeared to be in his fifties, with steely gray hair and muttonchop whiskers. He wore a dark frock coat and kilt in a blue-and-green plaid.

After being led in a vigorous Highland jig around the dance floor, he didn't wait for her permission but took her hand and swung her around for another tune. Maddie hadn't danced in years, but she preferred dancing to standing or sitting along the sidelines, knowing no one there except Lady Haversham's family.

After the fifth or sixth dance—she'd lost count—she could hardly breathe and felt she would faint if she didn't sit down. She glanced at Mr. McGee's florid face, amazed at the man's stamina. Of course, he didn't wear a corset, she told herself.

"A fine pair we make, eh, lassie?" His gray eyes twinkled into hers as his rough palm squeezed her hand. She managed a wan smile, wondering where his wife was.

"I believe I'll sit this one out," she said.

He was ready to take her in his arms again but stopped and peered down at her. "Deen oot, are ye?"

When she managed to ascertain that he asked if she was "done out," she nodded. "Indeed."

"Well, coom along, then, we'll get you a wee dram. That'll fix ye up straightaway."

"If I may just sit this one out, I should be fine."

But he insisted on getting her some refreshment. She finally prevailed upon him to get her plain lemonade. He came back after a few moments with a glass of iced lemonade for her and a tumbler of whiskey for himself.

He took a healthy swallow and smacked his lips. "Finest malt in the land," he said with a wink. "Distilled right here along the Tay." He drained the glass and wiped his mouth with the back of his sleeve.

Maddie took a careful sip from her glass, wondering how she could excuse herself politely from this energetic gentleman.

He signaled a passing waiter. He placed the empty tumbler on the man's tray and took two more. "Best be prepared." He winked again. Before the waiter had moved more than a few paces away, McGee downed one of the glasses. He held the other one in his weathered hands between his knees and leaned forward.

Maddie inched back in her chair, away from the smell of the whiskey on his breath, her knees tightly locked, and wondered yet again where his wife might be.

"Ye hail from down south, do ye?"

"Yes, London."

"Bet yer happy to be up here where you can breathe some pure air."

She smiled. "Oh, yes. The air is very fresh here." She took another small sip and looked past the laird to the crowded room. She hadn't seen Mr. Gallagher since the music had begun. Perhaps she could excuse herself to check on Lady Haversham. She craned her neck, but didn't see the older lady, either. Reluctantly, she turned her attention back to the laird. "Are you family of the present owner of Taymouth Castle?" she asked, referring to the largest landowner of the region.

He scowled. "Ech, nay. I be of Clan Mackay."

Maddie glanced at his tartan. "Oh. I thought it was the Campbell pattern."

"Nay, lass." He smoothed the tartan over one knee. "The Mackay has the blue line, see. The Campbell is a broken black thread."

"Ah, yes." She noticed the difference in the two blue-and-green plaids.

He finished downing the third tumbler. Grabbing her by the wrist, her lemonade scarcely touched, he pulled her to her feet again. "That should do ye for the next round. Come along, lassie, the music's awastin'."

"Mr. McGee—" She barely managed to set her glass down before it spilled over her gown. Protesting against more dancing was useless. The man was either hard of hearing or willfully deaf to her weak protests.

Maddie's heart sank. The dance was a waltz, and she felt an aversion to being held in this stranger's embrace. But he held her close—too close—the rough wool of his coat chafing the exposed skin of her upper arms. She bit back a wince as one of his rugged shoes stepped on her slipper.

"Ouch." She pulled back but he didn't seem to notice. Her toes throbbed as he tugged her along to the music.

Suddenly a large hand clapped onto McGee's shoulder, separating him from Maddie. Her gaze traveled up the black-clad sleeve to Mr. Gallagher's forbidding features. "Excuse me, sir, but this dance was saved for me."

Reid set the laird firmly aside, making certain he didn't fall. Seeing the man hauling Miss Norton around, oblivious to her discomfort, had angered Reid beyond reason, and he was struggling inwardly not to cause a scene.

Reid had stayed away from the dance floor most of the evening, remaining in the billiard room after dancing an obligatory dance with his sister and enduring another with her talkative friend, Cecily. But finally, he'd returned to the great hall.

Not wanting to appear too anxious or eager, he'd begun a circular tour of the large room, his progress slowed by the crowd. His eyes scanned the dancers, in search of titian hair and a bronze-colored gown that complimented it so well.

He'd stopped in midstride, catching sight of Miss Norton before she disappeared behind another couple. He wove through the dancers as he made his way toward her.

She was held—crushed seemed a more accurate description—against—what was the fellow's name? McGee? Reid had met him earlier. Although Miss Norton smiled, her expression seemed strained. Her color was high. Then he caught a flash of pain in her features when the laird lurched against her. Reid pushed past the remaining couples and grasped McGee by the shoulder.

Reid disengaged Maddie's hand and enfolded it in his own. Her large tawny eyes went from alarm to relief. He frowned, taking in the sight of her flushed cheeks. "Are you all right?"

She nodded. "Only a bit of a headache."

He glanced around the crowded room. "It is infernally hot in here. Would you like to go outside for some air?"

"Yes…please…" She rewarded him with a grateful smile, a smile that never ceased to turn something around inside him. He stifled the desire to hold her in his arms, and instead, took her by the elbow and began negotiating a way out of the room.

When they finally gained the garden, he found her an empty bench. He remained standing and silent, giving her time to recover herself. In truth, he was afraid to look too closely at her. The first sight of her earlier in her evening gown had stunned him. There was no denying she was beautiful…and wholly feminine. The gown revealed a creamy neck and perfectly sculpted shoulders, slim bare arms, a small waist.

He swallowed, his mouth as dry as the Libyan Desert, and shifted his gaze off into the dark yard behind her. "Feel better?"

She nodded. "Much."

"It was pretty smoky in the billiard room and not much better in the hall."

She agreed. "It was getting harder to breathe."

He eased himself beside her on the bench and glanced sidelong at her. "Mr. McGee seemed to be holding you in a death grip."

A small laugh erupted from her, and he felt pleased to have made her laugh. "Yes, a little."

"Couldn't you escape him?"

"Well, he asked me to dance and then just kept dancing. He seemed not to hear anything I said. I didn't want to hurt his feelings."

"So, you risked being crushed by the drunken lout?"

"I… I kept hoping his wife would show up and claim him."

"I'm told the good laird has been a widower of some years and is in eager pursuit of a second Mrs. McGee."

Her smile died. "Oh."

"He's said to be worth quite a fortune." He eyed her in the dim light, wondering how she'd react to the information.

"I'm sorry I shan't be able to accommodate him."

He sensed a feeling of relief. "By the time we return, he'll probably have found himself another hapless young lady."

She made no reply. Dusk enfolded them and only muted sounds followed them from the ballroom. "You know you're really too nice for your own good."

She looked down at her gloved hands. "There is too much unkindness in the world as it is."

"I'll agree with you there. But many times people will interpret a person's kindness as weakness and take advantage of it."

Her gaze was steady and serious. "That's a chance

I'm willing to take. In the end, the Lord's love is stronger than any ill treatment I receive at an individual's hands."

Reid said nothing, not sure if he wholly agreed with her but admiring her all the more for her convictions. "It sounds like you're soon to have a birthday," he said instead, remembering his aunt's words to her earlier. He cleared his throat. "When is it to be, if you don't mind my asking?"

She looked away from him. "It hardly matters."

He'd probably done the unpardonable, broaching the subject of a woman's age. Nevertheless, he was curious, all the more so at her reticence. "You should at least have the day off."

"I feel as if I've had every day off since I came to Scotland." She half turned to him on the bench. "I want to thank you again for the holiday, Mr. Gallagher."

Even though the light was dim, Reid felt her smile radiate toward him. He was coming to know that smile well. It was wide and generous, always grateful, as if she was not used to receiving good things of people. The thought gave him pause. He stared at her in the gathering twilight, the notion growing in him that he wanted to make her birthday a special day.

His ears caught the strains of another waltz through the open doors, and his thoughts turned back to his earlier purpose. "Are you up to dancing one more dance? Perhaps if we dance out here, it won't be so uncomfortable?"

He waited, his breath held.

She looked at him. "I—"

He stood and held out his hand.

"Yes, I'm...quite recovered."

She placed her hand in his and stood.

He wrapped one hand around her slim waist, feeling the satiny texture of her gown. Her other hand came up to rest on his shoulder, her fingertips brushing his collar.

At last she was in his arms. He had to restrain himself from drawing her too close. After all those days of dreaming and imagining, he was finally reliving the experience. The memory had not exaggerated the reality. She felt fragile, like the most precious treasure. The cool air caressed them and the music floated out to them as they went around in time to the music. They could have been all alone in the world.

He had not held a woman in this manner since he'd danced with Octavia.

He wouldn't think of that. He refused to think beyond the moment. What was his intention in this folly? All he knew was that he had had to feel Miss Norton once more in his arms, to…what?

To see if the sensation he had felt some days ago had been real or imaginary. But now that he had succeeded…what would follow?

He glanced at her face to discover if she was feeling anything near to what he was feeling. But her eyes were focused somewhere over his shoulder. Back and forth, round and round they went, and he wished the music wouldn't end.

Because he knew he wouldn't allow himself another moment like this one. It was too dangerous. This woman threatened to destroy the carefully erected life he'd built for himself for the past decade. At the center of that life stood Octavia, his beloved wife, soul mate, the woman he was bound to love.

He took Miss Norton around again as the music came to its conclusion and then slowed as the last chord died out. Reluctantly he stopped and held her an instant longer. Their arms fell away from each other, and they stood like a pair of shy schoolchildren, with tentative smiles and awkward gazes.

Laughter and voices came through the open French doors as couples broke apart. "I—thank you." She murmured the words, her head bowed so he couldn't read her eyes. Then she was moving away before he could stop her. His every impulse wanted to follow her, but he restrained himself, watching the crown of her titian hair until it disappeared out of sight.

Maddie hurried away from Mr. Gallagher, skirting the crowded hall until finally finding an empty room where she could remain unseen. She put her hands up to her warm cheeks, glad of the darkness. The muffled strains of the orchestra reached her ears, and unconsciously she began to sway to its rhythm, reliving those moments in Mr. Gallagher's arms.

Even though she hadn't dared look into his eyes once during the dance, she had felt his gaze on her. She'd been afraid to raise her head, afraid he'd read what her eyes would convey to him—her yearning…and love.

She'd felt cherished in his arms, more cherished than she'd ever felt since she'd left home so many years ago. Since then she'd been a lonely pilgrim, in the employ of strangers, sometimes appreciated by them, sometimes not, but there had always been that wall of separation between employer and employee, that invisible line that couldn't be crossed.

What was it that was happening between Mr. Gallagher and her? Was she the only one experiencing it? Why had he asked her to dance—and such an intimate one? He could have asked her for a polka or quadrille, but he'd chosen the waltz. Was it only his innate sense of politeness, that sensitivity he displayed not only to her but to every human being he came in contact with?

She swallowed, afraid of the emotions he awoke in her. For if they weren't reciprocated, she was in for a nasty fall, far more devastating than what she'd felt when the only suitor she'd ever had had jilted her. She'd been only eighteen then. She made a small, strangled sound. If she'd thought herself brokenhearted then, what would she feel now that she was a woman, a woman who had been alone so many years, who knew the cold, hard ways of the world?

And if her feelings *were* reciprocated? No, it couldn't be. Mr. Gallagher had made it plain to her he loved his late wife. She remembered his words with chilling clarity. *I'm still married to her.* They'd rung a death knell to any hopes Maddie might have. And if there were any chance of her forgetting the words, the wedding band he wore was a fresh reminder every day of where his heart lay. And yet, the way he'd rescued her tonight and danced with her, his touch unmistakably tender...

Maddie shook her head in the darkness. She mustn't let her hopes rise, nor could she permit herself to give even a hint of her own feelings to Mr. Gallagher. She would on no account put him in an uncomfortable position. He'd been so kind to her already. She wouldn't make him feel that she had misinterpreted his generosity.

Oh, dear Lord, she prayed, *help me!* Only the Lord could give her the grace to accept the inevitable.

That evening, after Reid had prepared for bed, he went to his bedside table. Since the fishing episode he had kissed his wife's portrait as he'd done every night for the last decade, but it had felt hypocritical, as if for the first time in his life he had something to hide from her. He knew what an adulterer must feel who is trying to maintain an outwardly normal relation to his wife, but knows inwardly how false he is being.

He pulled down the covers and got into bed without glancing at his wife's photograph. But he felt its presence there in the dark as if she were looking at him with pity in her eyes, able to see and read into his very soul.

Without meaning to, he fingered the wedding band on his finger, slipping it up and down past his knuckle. He'd worn it since making his vows to Octavia that long-ago day. To love, honor and cherish her. Her death had released him from those vows. But since he felt responsible for her death, he'd never felt released. He owed her his allegiance. It was the least he could do to make amends for having cut down her life prematurely.

Maddie tossed and turned for hours before falling asleep. She lay in the dark, staring at the canopy above her and remembered being held in Mr. Gallagher's arms.

Her mind relived the dance. Once again, she couldn't help dreaming what it would be like if her love for Mr. Gallagher were reciprocated…if she could help him get over the pain and loneliness of a decade of widowhood.

Would she read something new in his eyes tomorrow—anything that let her know he was beginning to see her as a woman? Would she ever see his finger bare of the wedding band?

Chapter Ten

The next day, Maddie came into the breakfast room and saw only Mr. Gallagher seated there. She paused on the threshold, feeling a shyness come over her. How would he react upon seeing her?

He looked up and gave her his usual smile. "Good morning, Miss Norton. Sleep well?" His tone was pleasant, nothing strained or awkward in it.

She stifled a sense of disappointment and crossed the room to the sideboard. "Yes, thank you. And you?"

"Very well, thank you."

He continued eating, so she took a plate and served herself, chiding herself for getting herself all worked up about a simple dance. Was it a sign of an aging spinster when she began having delusions about a gentleman being attracted to her? She seated herself halfway down the table from him, unsure she could keep her own demeanor from betraying her. After a short blessing, she unfolded her napkin. When Mr. Gallagher lifted his coffee cup for a sip, Maddie couldn't help glancing at his hand.

Even down the length of the table she could distinguish the wedding band he still wore. If she needed any further proof that his feelings remained unchanged, the wedding band was irrefutable evidence.

His eyes met hers. "You're not too tired from last night's festivities?"

"No. I didn't go to bed too late." She strove to match his matter-of-fact tone.

"You never did tell me yesterday when your birthday is to be."

She blinked at him, surprised that he'd remembered the topic. She was foolish to make anything of it. "It—it's next Saturday."

"We were born a decade apart. I'll be celebrating my fortieth on the twenty-ninth."

She wondered how he'd celebrate. Before she could think of anything to say, he changed the subject. "We've been having quite a spate of good weather."

"Yes." She stirred a spoonful of sugar into her porridge, unused to the Scottish custom of unsweetened porridge.

"I've been thinking we should attempt Ben Lawers before the weather turns."

She paused. Had he said "we"? She cleared her throat. "You said you wanted to climb to the top."

"That's right. Do you still want to attempt it?" He grinned. "As a milestone to mark your thirtieth and my fortieth?"

The idea began to grow on her. To scale a mountain peak to mark her birthday would certainly be better than thinking of herself as being forever on the shelf. She nodded. "Yes." But what if she slowed him down? "That is if you still think I could—should...." She stopped, waiting for him to back out of his offer.

He shrugged. "It's up to you. I'm told it's anywhere from a five-to eight-hour hike there and back. We'd need to leave around dawn to return by midafternoon or a bit later."

She moistened her lips. He hadn't tried to get out of the invitation. Did that mean he really wanted her to go? His tone sounded noncommittal, yet, he was leaving it up to her. If he didn't want her, he certainly needn't have issued the invitation. He hadn't invited his own sister, for one thing. "Do you think Mrs. Walker would care to go along?"

"Vera? I should hope not. She'd probably expect me to provide a means of conveyance and stop every half hour."

"Yes, of course." He was paying her a compliment if he thought she would be little trouble. "When would you like to go?"

"I thought tomorrow, if you're sure you're sufficiently recovered from the dance by then. Vera mentioned something about taking Aunt Millicent to Aberfeldy. They should be gone till early evening. I don't think Aunt Millicent expects you to go along."

"No." It seemed perfect. She wiped her mouth with her napkin and set it down. "Then, yes, I should like to attempt the climb, if you're sure I won't hinder you."

"Good. We can leave around dawn, as I said." His tone conveyed no sign that her acceptance had either pleased or displeased him. "The gillie will accompany us. He knows the best trails from this side. I'll speak with him about what we need to take."

She nodded.

"There's one other thing...." He continued regarding her.

"Yes?" Was there something wrong? He was looking at her a bit strangely.

"It's just...your outfit."

She stared down at her starched blouse and dark skirt.

"You'll need suitable garments." He cleared his throat. "You certainly can't attempt a hike of that nature in a long skirt and—and—"

For the first time, she sensed his discomfort with the topic and took pity on him. "That's all right. I'm used to walking long distances in London."

"This is a lot different from walking the London streets. What you really need is a pair of...trousers—" His eyes shifted away from her.

She could feel the color stealing up to her cheeks and she remembered the previous time the topic had come up and he'd mentioned the word *bloomers*. But...was he talking about *gentleman's* trousers now?

He gave her no chance to reply, for which she was thankful. "I know it sounds shocking, but it's not as unusual as you might imagine. Women in India regularly wear loose silk trousers called pajamas. They're infinitely more practical than what western women wear in the name of fashion."

She bit her underlip, trying to assimilate what he was saying. She had been brought up with very strict ideas of what was proper and improper for a lady to wear.

"Chinese women, too," he was saying, but she hardly heard him, too concerned with what she was going to wear herself. Would this one detail keep her from accompanying Mr. Gallagher up the mountain?

"What do you suggest I wear? Those bloomers you mentioned the other day?" She strove to maintain her tone and gaze steady, despite the flush she could feel on her cheeks.

"Yes, precisely." He sounded relieved that the topic was settled. "Except... I don't know where you might procure a pair so quickly. Perhaps if we could just furnish you with a pair of borrowed trousers, a young boy's from here in the house?

"My mother would sometimes don a pair of men's trousers when she was painting a mural." He smiled, his expression reminiscing. "She painted a few on the walls of our rooms. We'd catch her gazing at a wall, and Father and I soon came to know that look. A few days later, we'd find her high on a stepladder, palette in hand. She'd borrow a pair of trousers from my father. She finally purchased a pair of her own, tired of having to cinch up the waist on a pair of Father's."

She couldn't help smiling at the picture she envisioned of this unusual, creative woman.

He rose from his chair. "So, I'll meet you at the stables at dawn then tomorrow. Wear comfortable boots, as well."

"I will," she promised. He was gone before she realized she didn't know what she would do about the trousers. What would Lady Haversham say? Her heart sank.

An hour later, when she went to her room to retrieve some thread for her needlework, she found a package had been delivered there and lay on her bed. She removed the brown paper and gasped when she saw a pair of corduroy trousers in it.

She unfolded them and stared. They looked worn but smelled clean as if freshly laundered. Gingerly she held them up to her waist, hardly able to imagine donning them. But they didn't seem too wide or long. Where had Mr. Gallagher found them for her? A stable boy's, most likely. Even a pair of suspenders was provided with them.

At tea she heard Mrs. Walker and Lady Haversham making plans to visit a family in Aberfeldy that had attended the dance. Maddie breathed a sigh of relief. She dearly hoped she and Mr. Gallagher returned before the two ladies came back from their visit.

It was still dark the next morning when Maddie came down the back stairs and headed for the stables. She felt strange walking with her legs encased in the soft thick material and was glad of the darkness. The trousers did feel warm, she admitted, in the cool air. She had also donned her warmest undergarments, a blouse, a warm jacket and the plaid.

Mr. Gallagher stood by the stable door with Ewane, the gillie, who was holding a pony's lead. They were to ride in the cart hitched to it, as far as the hamlet of Lawers a couple of miles along Loch Tay. From there they'd proceed northward along a track familiar to the gillie to the foot of the mountain.

"Good morning." She greeted each man with a brief nod, afraid of drawing too much attention to herself.

Mr. Gallagher gave her the once-over, bringing heat to her cheeks. "Good, I see the trousers fit." He turned abruptly back to Ewane. "I guess we're ready."

"Yes, sir." The gillie didn't seem to find her appearance in any way remarkable and she wondered if he was used to seeing tourists of every stripe.

Mr. Gallagher gave her a hand into the farm cart as the gillie took the reins. Maddie was glad of the semi-darkness as she climbed aboard. It felt too unnatural to have her shape so revealed by a pair of narrow trousers.

Once seated, though, with a blanket wrapped around her legs by Mr. Gallagher, she felt better. She soon forgot her appearance as they began their journey along the loch. White mists rose from it and birdsong erupted from the tree branches above them.

After a little while, Mr. Gallagher handed her an oatcake. "Hope that'll do for breakfast. There're plenty more if you get hungry." His white teeth flashed in a grin.

"Thank you, this will do fine." She munched quietly as the cart rattled along the dirt road.

The small hamlet was silent as they passed through it and took the narrow path away from the loch. The path soon disappeared into a grassy sheep track, which began to rise steadily northward. Alongside they heard the gurgle of a brook.

Ewane gestured to it with the stock of his whip. "Lawers Burn."

About three-quarters of an hour later they reached a small lake. Maddie gazed upward to the west and gasped. A massive peak loomed before her, the first glimmers of sun lightening its green surface.

"There she is," the gillie said, noticing her admiration. "Ben Lawers, the highest peak in the central Highlands." He turned to Mr. Gallagher. "We'll leave the cart here by Lochan nan Chat. There's a crofter nearby."

"Very good." The two men led the pony and cart toward a small thatch-roofed hut tucked away on one side of the small lake. Maddie waited, continuing to gaze up at the sloping mountain peak. Was she really going to ascend it today?

"Ready?" Mr. Gallagher asked when the two men returned a few minutes later.

She returned his smile, her excitement rising. "Ready as I'll ever be."

"Good, come along then."

The gillie led them through a stile and onto a stony farm track. She walked abreast of Mr. Gallagher, behind the gillie. Nobody spoke. Maddie didn't find the going hard as the slope rose gradually and was mostly grassy with only an occasional rock visible. Stone walls outlined some fields where sheep grazed. The air was cooler up here. She hugged the tartan shawl around her, glad of its warmth.

Mr. Gallagher lifted an eyebrow. "Cold?"

She shook her head. "Not at all. This plaid is very warm."

Once in a while they passed a heap of square stones. They looked too structured to have fallen that way naturally and she asked Ewane about them.

"Those be shielings. When I was a wee lad, we'd spend summers in them and bring our cattle up here to graze. That was afore the lairds began taking over all the land for sheep." The gillie kicked at the hard, stubby grass and spat. "They eat everythin' down to the dirt, leaven' the land fit for nothing but bracken to grow."

Once in a while they passed a shieling that still stood. Maddie spotted one in the distance, smoke rising from the center of the roof. A small, dark-haired child stood in the doorway, barefoot and ruddy cheeked. Maddie waved but he didn't respond.

"They be tenants, looking after the laird's sheep up here for the summer," the gillie said.

After a couple of hours' silent marching, they stopped to rest. The way was beginning to grow rockier and the grade steeper. The walking sticks they each carried came in handy.

Mr. Gallagher turned to her. "All right?"

"Yes." She was breathing deeply but had never felt more alive. She was also grateful for the trousers she was wearing. She'd become strangely accustomed to wearing them and they certainly made the climbing easier. She slipped a glance at Mr. Gallagher, another thing to be grateful to him for.

She surveyed the distance they'd come, shading her eyes from the rising sun. "My goodness." Below them lay thick dark green forest to the south and above it the grassy meadows they'd climbed. She could barely distinguish the thin curving line of the burn from where they'd started.

After a few more miles' march, Mr. Gallagher suggested they stop for lunch. She nodded. He turned to the gillie and exchanged a few words with him.

Maddie looked above her. The hill continued upward, but now the stubby green grass was giving way to craggy gray stones. They settled on some lichen-covered boulders and broke open the lunch packet of more bannocks, some fruit and flasks of tea. The gillie moved off a distance to eat his meal.

They ate in contented silence for a few minutes. Maddie felt as if she and Mr. Gallagher were all alone on top of the world.

"Are you still game to climb higher?"

She smiled at him, experiencing the most freedom she had in a long time. "That's what we came for, isn't it?"

"How're your shoes holding up?"

"Not a blister." She shook her head. "It's funny, when I was a young girl, I suffered quite a few bouts of illness. It seems I've grown quite hardy in old age."

"I wouldn't call thirty old age."

She blushed at the reference to how old she was to be in a few days. "It's not exactly youth. It's more the age of maturity," she said, attempting to make light of the fact.

"It appears youthful from my vantage, believe me."

He crumbled the remains of a bannock between his fingers. "What would you call turning forty?"

Her gaze traveled from his hand to his blue eyes watching her steadily. "A man's prime."

She was rewarded by the grin beneath his dark golden mustache and she felt a warmth spreading through her like the camphor oil her mother used to rub over her chest when she had suffered from congestion during her bouts of illness.

"Diplomatic answer."

"Truthful, nonetheless."

He said, "Excuse my impertinence, but I'm surprised you never married."

She was stunned by his bluntness for a moment. "I was almost engaged...once."

"What happened?" His voice was gentle, inviting confidences.

It all seemed so silly now. "The gentleman found out that I was obliged to work for a living." She shrugged. "He backed off before formally declaring himself. Who knows, maybe he never had any intention to."

Mr. Gallagher frowned. "If you believed he was going to, he must have taken things to a point where you would not have been unreasonable to expect him to. Courtship follows certain steps, and a man is no gentleman who raises a young lady's expectations without following through."

She looked away again, afraid of the sympathy in his voice and eyes. "It was so long ago, I can scarcely picture him. So it no longer matters."

The gillie walked over to them from where he'd been standing. "Excuse me, sir, we best be leavin' if we're to make it back afore nightfall."

"Right you are." Mr. Gallagher stood and they

stowed their things back into a pack, which he shouldered.

She glanced above them. "When will we be able to see Ben Lawers?"

The gillie pointed. "If we reach that rise there, we'll have a good view of Lawers and Ben Glas."

"And when we reach the summit of Ben Lawers, we'll be able to see the entire valley, Loch Tay and Glen Lyon to the north," added Mr. Gallagher.

"It sounds spectacular."

After that there was little distraction. The slopes became steeper. Maddie was glad of all the miles she'd walked in London. Even so, she was grateful to rest when they reached a forbidding line of crags. The air had a distinct chill to it.

They were silent, looking at the vast landscape all around them. Bluish-purple mountains strung out to the west and north of them across another valley. The valley they had come from lay to the south, the river scarcely visible between the smoke trails of clouds and thick forests. Maddie drew in her breath, seeing the vast lake connecting to the River Tay.

As if reading her thoughts, Mr. Gallagher said over her shoulder, "Loch Tay."

"It's beautiful, so blue against the forests."

He touched her lightly on the shoulder, directing her view to the opposite side. "On this side lies Glen Lyon." He turned to the gillie. "Isn't that right?"

"Aye. Glen Lyon, the bonniest glen in all Scotland. Thataway ye see Ben Lawers."

Maddie looked to where he pointed to the west and admired the mountain range, immediately distinguishing the grandest peak as Ben Lawers.

They soon recommenced walking, though the going

was much slower. Maddie was more grateful than ever for the trousers when she found herself forced to crawl on her hands and knees up narrow, rocky ridges.

"Best keep to this side o' the dike. There's a nasty hanging corrie up ahead," the gillie advised as he reached a narrow ridge and pointed to a hollowed-out portion of the mountainside.

Maddie edged closer to the dike. At the end of the stone barrier, the path leveled off somewhat and began to weave through jagged vertical crags. She had to focus all her thoughts on her steps. Tiny pebbles crunched under her boots and went rattling down the cliffs.

"Watch your step here." Mr. Gallagher held out a hand to her and she grasped it gratefully as they negotiated a tricky pass.

They reached a spot where another ridge joined the one they were on and stopped a few minutes to admire the view below. Mists floated between them and the valley.

"Almost to the summit," the gillie said with a motion of his walking stick.

Mr. Gallagher adjust the knapsack on his shoulder. "Come on then. The view is better from there."

They did no more talking, each one intent on maneuvering the steep rocky hillside. In places, they faced great mounds of boulders that they had to climb over. At others, they had to walk single file along narrow ridges.

Maddie climbed through a fissure in a large crag only to find herself on another treacherous course of boulders and sheer drop-offs. She'd taken a few steps when abruptly her ankle twisted under her. Before she could utter more than a cry, she was falling, slipping down the rocky slope, the smaller rocks falling with her.

"Miss Norton!" She heard Mr. Gallagher's shout above her but she could do nothing to stop her fall. Suddenly her head hit something sharp and the world went black.

Chapter Eleven

"Miss Norton!" Adrenaline coursed through Reid's body as he lunged for her, but he was too late. He watched her topple down the steep incline. A second later he was after her, scrambling down the rocky slope.

There was nothing for her to reach for. If she fell any farther, she'd be lost to them. "Miss Norton, I'm coming!" Trying to make haste and not lose his own footing, he worked his way down the rocky slope at an infuriatingly slow pace.

When he was able to turn around, he saw her lying still, her fall broken by a jutting rock. A new worry replaced his fear. He didn't like the way she looked so motionless. What if her neck was broken? Cold sweat erupted over his body, fear gripping his heart until he felt strangled by it.

When he reached her body, he hardly dared touch her. She'd lost consciousness and her face looked deathly pale. He wasn't aware of Ewane until he heard the other man's heavy breathing at his side. "Is she alive?"

Reid placed his fore and middle fingers at the base of her neck. Relief flooded him. "I feel a pulse." *Dear*

God, thank you. He looked above them. She'd fallen about thirty feet. "We've got to get her out of here."

"Aye. Trouble is there's naught around here to fashion a litter with."

Not a tree or twig graced the landscape this far up. "I'll just have to carry her."

"Aye." The older man nodded. "I'll help when you get winded. Best thing is to take her to the last shieling we passed mebbe half a mile back."

"Yes." Reid turned his attention to Miss Norton and frowned. She hadn't yet regained consciousness. He wished he had some of the smelling salts his aunt always had at her side.

Just then her eyes fluttered open and she stared at him. The tension began to ease from his frame. Never had he been so glad to see someone looking at him. "Miss Norton?" Would she know him?

Recognition lighted her eyes. "Mr. Gallagher." Her voice was a broken whisper. "What happened? I was—" She fell silent as if remembering the fall. She reached up a hand to the back of her head and winced as soon as she touched a spot on her skull.

"Easy there. You must have hit your head against this rock. It's the only thing that kept you from falling farther." He wondered whether she had suffered a concussion. It had to have caused quite a blow at the speed she'd fallen. But he voiced none of this.

"I'm going to have to help you get up the hillside."

She heaved a deep breath. "All right. Just give me a moment to catch my breath." Her voice sounded strained.

"First, let's make sure you've broken nothing. Try to move your limbs and tell me if you feel any pain anywhere other than your head."

She did as she was told. "Everything feels fine except my head."

"Good. Now, if you just lie still, I'm going to lift you in my arms to get you back up this slope."

Her eyes showed immediate alarm and she clutched at his forearm. "Oh, no, that won't be necessary. Truly, Mr. Gallagher."

He stilled her agitation with a touch to her hand. "We'll take it slowly. Just relax." He spoke as if to a child, still not liking how pale she looked. Gently, he placed one arm under her shoulders, trying to cushion her head, and the other under her knees. He focused on her as an injured person, and not a woman. How many times had he given similar aid to an injured man in the desert?

Bracing himself on one knee, he took a deep breath then lifted her up. She didn't weigh much, her form slim and delicate in his arms, but he knew it wouldn't be easy going. Ewane stayed at his side to catch him if his foot should slip.

One careful step at a time, Reid made his way back up the mountainside. When they reached the ridge, he only paused a moment to get his breath and ask, "How are you doing? Are you in any pain?"

"No. I'm fine. I just wish you'd let me walk."

"Don't exhaust yourself protesting over something that you have no say over." He gave her a slight smile to make light of the situation. Then he shifted her weight in his arms, and with a nod to Ewane, indicated he'd follow the gillie's lead.

The man turned and began the long trek back.

Miss Norton made no more protests. She was silent all the way back and Reid was afraid she must be in some discomfort. As hard as he tried, he couldn't help jostling her as he maneuvered past the crags and half slid down certain slopes.

He was getting winded but wouldn't let Ewane carry her when the older man offered to help shoulder the burden. If only Reid hadn't brought her up here. If only he'd listened to reason and kept her down below where she'd be safe. What had possessed him? Couldn't he see how fragile she was?

Ewane turned to him again. "Let me take her, lad."

Reid just shook his head, trying to keep from gasping for breath. Despite the cool air, his shirt was damp and he could feel the perspiration trickling down the sides of his face.

Miss Norton no longer insisted she try to walk and rested quietly against his chest. She still looked ghastly pale to him.

They had finally reached the grassy slopes when she suddenly pushed against his chest. "Please, let me down. I feel like I'm going to be sick."

He let her down as gently as he could. She scrambled away from him on her hands and knees and began to retch. He opened their pack to retrieve a bottle of water and a napkin, unable to keep the worry from his thoughts. It looked more and more as if she'd suffered a concussion.

He handed her the water and cloth. She took them from him, turning away again, and he felt bad for her, realizing she was probably feeling embarrassed in addition to being physically unwell.

"It's likely the knock on your head that's brought on the queasiness to your stomach," he said quietly when she'd finished washing off. He took the things from her and repacked the satchel. Ewane took it from him and shouldered it.

"We're not far from the shieling now, ma'am."

"Come on then. Let's go." Without meeting her gaze, Reid bent over Miss Norton once more and lifted her up, feeling awkward at the close contact. He'd wanted to feel her in his arms before, but not at this price. He wished he could make it easier for her but knew the most important thing was to get her to some sort of shelter.

"Are you feeling any better?" he asked, her soft hair rubbing his chin. Despite the difficult circumstances and the exhaustion he was feeling, he couldn't help being aware of her body curled so close to his, her head tucked under his.

He snapped his attention back to the trail. It wasn't the time or place to harbor such thoughts. If anything happened to Miss Norton he'd never forgive himself—

The realization brought him up short. Was he being punished for having had the kinds of thoughts about her he'd had lately? He should never have brought her to the Highlands.

First Octavia and now Miss Norton. If anyone deserved to die, it was he.

"There it be." The gillie pointed ahead of them far down the grassy slope.

Reid shut off the chaos in his mind and concentrated once again on the task at hand. First things first. There would be time enough later for self-recrimination.

Maddie remembered little of the next moments. After her initial distress at being such a burden to Mr. Gallagher, she felt too ill to think of anything much. Mr. Gallagher carried her so surely, she never once feared he'd drop her or lose his footing the way she so stupidly had.

She prayed for the Lord to give him the strength to carry her to wherever they were going. She knew she wasn't that light and no matter how much stronger or bigger he was, it was no easy task he'd undertaken. She could tell by his labored breathing and the damp patches on his shirt what an effort it was.

He'd been so kind and considerate, even when she'd been sick, as if he'd known exactly what she was going through.

She was hardly aware when they arrived at one of the small stone huts they'd passed earlier, until she heard the gillie conversing with someone in Gaelic. Then Mr. Gallagher let her down and she was finally able to try standing on her own two feet. She felt light-headed and clutched his arm. He immediately steadied her about her shoulders.

"We're going to stay here," he told her. "I just need you to crawl through the opening into the shieling. The opening is too low to walk through upright. Take your time."

"Stay here?" She didn't understand what he was saying.

"I'll explain once we have you inside."

"All right." She bent over to enter through the tiny square that served as a door into the hut. The space inside was high enough to stand in, but wasn't much bigger than a small room.

Mr. Gallagher appeared beside her in the hut. A woman led her to a crude bed, thin bedding over some wooden boards. Mr. Gallagher arranged some pillows behind her head and removed her boots before covering her with her own plaid and another blanket the woman brought him.

"Thank you, ma'am," he said, taking it from her.

He tucked it in around Maddie.

"I'm sorry to be so much trouble—"

"None of that, Miss Norton." His voice was low and soothing. "I just want to be sure you make it back down in one piece."

She met his earnest gaze and realized he was worried about her. She wished she could reach out and smooth the lines from his brow. Then she realized something worse than everything else that had occurred. "I kept you from reaching the top of Ben Lawers." She pressed her lips together, looking away from him. "I'm so sorry."

He shook his head. "It's been there thousands of years. It'll keep until we have a chance to have another go."

She swallowed. Once again he'd included her. Her eyes misted. She knew very well she would never have another opportunity for such an adventure. This holiday would soon be over. Mr. Gallagher would return to foreign soil. And she? She'd return to London and taking care of Lady Haversham. If Mr. Gallagher did return to the Highlands someday, it wouldn't be with Maddie.

Mr. Gallagher had turned back to the entrance of the hut and was conferring with the gillie. Maddie was thankful for having a moment to compose herself. She attributed her emotional state to the blow she'd received. The back of her head pained her and she felt more exhausted than if she had hiked all the way down herself. She brought her hand up to her skull only to find a large lump.

"You took a nasty fall." Mr. Gallagher had returned to her side and crouched beside the bed. "I've sent Ewane on down to let them know about the accident so no one will worry when we don't show up this afternoon."

"We…we're staying here?" Oh, dear, what was Lady Haversham going to say? Would Maddie lose her job?

He nodded. "I don't think you should attempt much movement for a while."

"I'm better, I assure you." She tried to sit up.

His hand immediately closed over her shoulder and held her back. "You might feel better, and I'm glad. But your head sustained some injury. You could have a concussion."

She stared at him. "Oh." She wasn't sure exactly what that was except that it meant a serious injury to one's head. She knotted her hands together. *Oh, Lord, forgive me for being so foolish, coming up here on some sort of adventure when my duty was by Lady Haversham's side. I didn't even tell her.*

"What's the matter?" Mr. Gallagher's blue eyes narrowed as if he could sense her agitation.

"I'm sorry for all the trouble," she whispered, this time unable to hide the quaver in her voice.

He covered her hands with his large one. "Steady there. Just be thankful you're alive and in one piece. When I saw you fall, it looked like you were going to roll all the way down to where we'd begun our trek this morning."

Her laugh sounded weak and watery to her own ears. He chucked her under the chin. "That's better."

"Will your—your aunt be very angry?"

"Don't worry about Aunt Millicent. I'll explain to her how foolhardy I was in dragging you up here."

"Oh, no. It wasn't your fault. Please don't take the blame."

"Shh. Worry is not good for head injuries." A gleam

of humor in his eyes belied his serious tone. He removed his hand from hers and adjusted the blanket around her. She kept her hands still, already missing the warmth of his touch.

The woman approached the bedside with a tin mug in her hands. "I brewed a bit o' mint tea for the lady."

Mr. Gallagher took the cup from her. "Thank you. That's just the thing."

With a quick bob of her head, the woman retreated. Two small children hovered behind her, staring at Maddie. She smiled at them and the youngest, a ruddy-faced girl of about six, smiled back.

"This might help settle your stomach," Mr. Gallagher said.

The words only reminded her of having been sick in front of him. She wrapped her hands around the cup, glad for the warmth against her cold hands.

"Careful you don't burn yourself."

She smiled at his attentiveness. "All right."

He readjusted the pillows so she could sit up higher then he left her, telling her he'd be just outside.

She sipped the tea slowly, afraid of upsetting her stomach further. At the other end of the room, the woman and children went about their tasks, stirring a pot on the open fire pit in the middle of the room, bringing in a pitcher of water from somewhere outside, setting a few meager utensils on a rough wooden table.

Outside she could hear the baaing of sheep. She sighed, taking another sip of her tea. Under other circumstances, she'd enjoy the cozy hut, which reminded her of some of the dwellings she'd been to with her parents outside of Jerusalem. Much different from her life in London with Lady Haversham.

Just when she started missing Mr. Gallagher's company, he came back in, accompanied by another man. Mr. Gallagher approached her bedside. "I've been talking to the crofter. This is his family. They're spending the summer up here to pasture the sheep on these meadows."

"I hope I'm not taking their bed."

"They are glad to offer you anything they have. He and his son will sleep outside. He says he does so on many a fine night. The woman and the little one will share the other bed."

"And you?" She could feel her face warm at the question.

"I'll catch a few winks outside, then I'll come in and rudely wake you up at some point."

She tried to discern if he was serious. "Why is that?"

"Just a precaution. If it is a concussion, you must be awakened regularly the first night."

"Why do you suppose it's necessary?"

"I haven't a clue. Head injuries can be tricky things, I'm told. I knew a chap once who fell from the pyramid at Saqqâra. He didn't even lose consciousness like you. Just said he saw stars. He got up right away and seemed fine, went back to work—" Reid stopped, realizing too late this wasn't the right story to be telling her at this time.

"What happened?"

He hesitated. "A few days later he keeled over, dead."

She drew in a sharp breath. "I'm sorry."

"Yes, so was I. He was a good man."

She was silent a moment and he wondered if she was worried about her own fate. But she sighed. "I'm glad, in that case, that I no longer live for myself."

Her calm tone intrigued him. "You don't worry about the future?"

"Not about my eventual end, if that's what you mean. I only worry if I feel I'm not in the Lord's will. I don't want to be like the man who was given only one talent and went and buried it instead of using it to multiply it."

He marveled at their different perspectives of multiplication. Did she feel she was using her talents buried alive at an old lady's side? "I'm sure the Lord is very pleased with what you're doing."

She turned away from him. "Yes, leaving my employer's side to traipse up a mountain in men's trousers. I'm sure He's very pleased indeed."

He clenched his hand to keep from reaching out and smoothing the hair from her brow. "I'm sure He's especially lenient with first-time offenders."

"You speak as if you think I never do anything wrong. Nothing could be further from the truth."

"No? I can't imagine you ever being naughty when you were a child. I bet you never disobeyed your parents like my niece and nephews for instance."

"I assure you I was as naughty as any child. Let's see… I remember once I wanted to go with my brothers to a fair, but I was always told I was too young, or too frail, or too something. This time I hid in the wagon and when they arrived, I sneaked out and tried to follow them. But then I got lost. I must have been five or six, like the little girl here." A smile warmed her tone. "Then I got so scared. I didn't think I'd ever be found or find my way back."

"Did you?" He drew a stool over and sat down, wanting to hear more of her story.

"After what seemed like hours, my brothers did find me. They were so angry. Of course, they were afraid of what they'd have to say to our parents if I hadn't been found."

They both chuckled.

"Well, if that's all you did as a child, your slate is very clean indeed."

Her hands knotted the blanket. "I wish it were so. But I'm afraid my shortcomings were a lot graver than mere disobedience." Her tone was so serious, he was afraid she would cause herself unnecessary distress.

"I hardly think you capable of committing any grievous offense."

She was silent a moment and he began to wonder what awful thing she imagined she had done. Fought with her siblings? Stolen a sweet?

"If I hadn't been so awfully weak as a child, my parents would undoubtedly still be following their calling on the mission field in Jerusalem."

He stared at her through the gathering gloom of the hut. "I hardly think you would be the cause of changing their life's work."

"It was because of my repeated illnesses that they were finally forced to come back to England."

Was that why she had undertaken such a life of servitude herself? To compensate for what she imagined she'd done to her parents? "I'm sure your parents felt it no sacrifice to do what was best for you."

"Yes, I always felt their unconditional love for me." She looked down at her fists. "Sometimes that made it harder to bear…knowing how much they'd done for me. I know if I'd been as healthy as my brothers, they would still be in the field."

He was beginning to understand the enormous burden she carried. "You don't know that. Life is too full of uncertainties, especially in a place as harsh as Palestine. It could just as easily have been one of your parents to have fallen sick."

She made no reply. But he felt her resistance to his argument. He knew well what it was to carry such guilt. Except in his own case, it was well-founded.

The crofter's wife approached them at that moment with a wooden bowl of porridge but Maddie hesitated. She looked at Mr. Gallagher. "I don't think I'd better eat anything yet. I'm not sure…" Her voice trailed off.

He turned to the woman. "Thank you, but I think all Miss Norton needs right now is some rest." He turned back to Maddie. "I'll leave you for a little while to do just that."

She nodded, grateful for his sensitivity. "Thank you."

She watched him walk away and sit with the family at their simple meal. With a sigh, she turned her back on them all and gazed at the rough stone slabs on the other side of her bed. She felt inordinately tired but not sleepy. The base of her head was throbbing. What a disaster. *Lord, please see us through this calamity. Help us to explain to Lady Haversham tomorrow. Deflect her anger from her nephew. If she would dismiss me, please help me find another position.* Tears filled her eyes once more. What a muddle. She mustn't give in to self-pity. She focused her prayers on her brothers and the lives they were touching, but it was hard to concentrate and she realized her words were sounding like nonsense.

She began reciting a psalm. Before she had finished it, she drifted off to sleep.

Reid made his way through the dark hut toward Miss Norton's bed, careful to bypass the other sleeping occupants.

He leaned over to touch her shoulder and paused, listening to her even breathing, noticing the way the slivers of moonlight offset her features. He pressed his fingertips to her shoulder, hating to wake her.

She didn't stir and he began to fear her sleep was too deep.

"Miss Norton," he whispered.

Her eyes opened. "Wha—"

"I'm sorry to wake you like this, but I wanted to make sure you were all right."

Her glance darted about her. "Where—?" She finally focused on him in the dark. "Mr. Gallagher."

He breathed a sigh of relief that she had recognized him. "Can you remember anything? Who are you?" he asked softly.

"Maddie," she whispered back immediately. "Maddie Norton." Then she thought a moment. "I…we…we were climbing… Ben Lawers, and I fell. I ruined it for you!" She turned stricken eyes to him.

"You ruined nothing," he said, her name resounding in his thoughts. *Maddie.* The name fit her. He pictured a carefree girl, vulnerable and tenderhearted. How he wanted to pull her to him and keep her safe.

But how could he keep anyone safe? He hadn't managed to keep Octavia safe.

"How am I doing?" He could hear the smile in Maddie's whispered voice through the dark.

"So far so good," he said, seating himself on the stool by her bed.

"You seem to know an awful lot about doctoring." Her voice was barely above a whisper.

"It comes in handy when one is miles from the nearest clinic. I've had to do my share of doctoring."

"In the desert?"

He nodded, then realizing she wouldn't be able to see him clearly in the dark, said, "Yes. Knowing how to dig out a bullet is always valuable. Setting a bone can be complicated but I know enough about making a splint until a proper physician can be had."

"How did you learn so much?"

Seeing she was wide-awake, and finding it better to keep her so awhile, he continued. "A doctor traveled in our company once and I watched him and asked a lot of questions. He said I made a good nurse. Taught me a lot of useful tricks, like waking a concussion victim in the night."

They sat quietly for some minutes. When he began to wonder if she had fallen asleep, she suddenly spoke. "Tell me about your wife."

He froze. Nobody ever asked him about Octavia, too respectful of his silence on the subject of his wife. He felt as if Miss Norton had intruded onto sacred ground. He shifted on the hard stool, making a conscious effort not to take offense, seeing Miss Norton's silhouette lying there in the dark, her eyes closed. She might not even be in her right mind, woken up in the middle of the night after suffering a concussion.

He cleared his throat, not sure where to begin. "She was a very special woman."

"How did you meet her?"

Her eyes remained closed and he found he didn't have the heart to rebuke her curiosity. "At a garden party. I had just come down from Oxford and my parents had thrown a large party. There was Octavia, at nineteen, as beautiful and fresh as one of my mother's just-opened roses." He couldn't help smiling in the dark, remembering the moment. "I was a blushing, stammering twenty-one-year-old. I don't know how I got through the introduction."

"I can't imagine you losing your poise. You seem so worldly and sure of yourself in every situation."

How little she knew of him. "Well, I assure you, I was none of that on this occasion. Not only did I stumble over her name, but later, as we were walking through a garden path, I tripped over a flagstone and went sprawling."

She laughed softly, and he chuckled at the memory of his most embarrassing moment. "What happened next?"

"By the time I managed to get on my knees, my best trousers torn, the palms of my hands scraped, I was planning to emigrate to India and never return to England, my humiliation was so great."

She stifled her laughter with a hand. "Oh, you poor dear! My own story pales in comparison."

Feeling something strange at the sound of the endearment on her lips, he went on with his story. "Well, thankfully, the situation improved. When I looked up, there she was, kneeling beside me, concern written all over her pretty face, begging me to tell her I was all right. I fell in love at first sight and haven't ever recovered from it."

He could feel her gazing at him through the dark.

"How soon before you were married?"

"A year later. Her father wanted her to wait until she reached her majority, but after a year of my constant presence at the house, he relented." He chuckled again. "So we enjoyed a decade together." He sighed. "Those were the happiest years of my life. We traveled a lot…until she fell ill. I don't remember an unpleasant moment with her."

"You never had children?"

Reid's lips firmed into a hard line, not expecting such a forthright question.

"I'm sorry, that was indelicate of me to ask."

His anger evaporated. How could she know? No one did. "No…we never did." He looked down at the outline of his folded hands, not ready to tell her about the circumstances of that subject. He'd never be ready to talk about that.

"That's the one thing I regret most about never marrying…not ever having children…." Her voice drifted off. "I would have loved to have been a mother…."

The words cut him to the quick. She'd have no idea how much.

She yawned. "I think it will be light soon. Do you think I'll survive the night if I go back to sleep now?"

He dragged his thoughts back to the present. She must be exhausted. "Yes, I believe so. Ewane will probably be up around noon with some help to carry you down the rest of the way." The words came out automatically, his tone steady, revealing nothing of the pain her words had reawakened in him.

"Surely I'll be able to walk by then."

"Not yet. You need to take it easy and let your head mend. Just for a few days at any rate or however long a real doctor recommends." He rose from the stool, feeling his stiff legs. His arms ached from the distance he'd carried Miss Norton.

"I'll catch a few more winks myself," he told her, although he wondered whether that would be possible, now that he'd awakened the past so thoroughly.

* * *

Maddie waited until she heard the sound of Mr. Gallagher's footsteps retreat. Only when she was sure he'd left the hut did she allow herself to react.

Although she'd made him believe she was ready to drop off again, in truth, sleep was the last thing on her mind.

She went over their conversation in her head. All Mr. Gallagher's words, his whole tone of voice when talking about his late wife, expressed complete devotion. Reid Gallagher still loved his first wife, as deeply and purely as on the day he'd first met her. Maddie stared dry eyed through the dark. With each word of his, every inflection of tenderness in his voice, she'd felt all her hopes snuffed out.

He'd been candid about his love. She had no reason to doubt it. No wonder he'd never remarried in all these years. No wonder he still wore his wedding band. No woman could ever hope to compete with such a sacred memory, least of all a penniless, aging spinster with nothing to recommend her—no connections, no looks and no charm—none of the attributes of Cecily Mason and any other lady his aunt and sister threw in his path.

Her future stretched before her, one colorless day drifting into another as she continued her servitude to Lady Haversham. Somehow she'd have to bury her growing feelings for her...employer. She hesitated over the word, which sounded too cold and formal for the man who'd carried her down the mountainside in his arms today and sat by her side and made her smile and in a matter of seconds had broken her heart so thoroughly....

What did one call that kind of person?

A man with whom one had fallen desperately, hope-
lessly in love?

*Dear Lord, don't let him know, never let him suspect
how I feel about him.*

Chapter Twelve

The next day the gillie, Ewane, arrived with another man. Feeling like someone feigning illness, Maddie protested against being carried all the way down to the glen in a litter, but Mr. Gallagher was adamant. She was not walking more than a few steps.

Now she lay on the litter, once again tucked into blankets by Mr. Gallagher, and felt its gentle sway. She bit her lip, stewing in her sense of powerlessness. She hadn't felt so helpless since she was a girl in the Holy Land, suffering bouts of illness. She remembered how she'd hindered her parents' work overseas, and now she had destroyed this man's climb to the summit. The comparison might seem ridiculous but Maddie couldn't help drawing the parallels as she watched his strong back at the front of her litter. He'd insisted on carrying one end of it.

They arrived back at the house by early evening. Both Lady Haversham and her niece stood at the front entry when Maddie was carried in.

Lady Haversham leaned on her cane and glared at Maddie. "What is the meaning of this? You caused me

the utmost worry yesterday. I couldn't sleep a wink the
whole night, isn't that so, Vera?"

"Yes, indeed. I had to sit up with her. Reid, where
in the world did you take off to with Miss Norton?"
She turned shocked eyes onto Maddie. "And Miss Norton, I'm amazed at you, sneaking off like that, leaving
your employ—"

Mr. Gallagher interrupted his sister. "That's enough,
Vera. Can't you see the woman is injured? Now, clear
the way, everyone," he told the hovering servants in a
stern voice.

Maddie sat up on the pallet, horrified at the accusations. "I can make it up the stairs on my own." Before Mr. Gallagher could stop her, she'd swung her
legs over the side. It was only in the shocked silence
that followed that she remembered her garments. She
swallowed, staring down at the trousers she still wore.

Lady Haversham's sharp intake of breath told Maddie all she needed to hear.

"Excuse me, my lady." She faltered then turned
and stumbled from the area, her only wish to disappear from the looks of disapproval all around her. She
clutched the stair rail, her legs feeling weak, but determined to mount the flight of steps.

She ignored Mr. Gallagher's "Miss Norton—" Instead of insisting on accompanying her, she heard him
give a sharp order to one of the maids, who hurried to
her side.

"Here, miss, take my arm and I'll help you to your
room."

"Thank you," she mumbled, hardly daring to look
the woman in the eyes.

By tomorrow she knew she'd be on a train heading
back to London, unemployed. She had no one to blame

but herself. Did all spinsters on the verge of turning thirty do such foolish things?

Reid refused to discuss Miss Norton with his aunt and sister until he'd sent for a doctor. Only then did he escort the two ladies into the library and shut the door behind them.

"Really, Aunt Millicent, did you have to light into the poor woman like that? Didn't you see she was injured?"

His aunt sat down in the wing chair and took deep, gasping breaths, one hand over her breast. "What did you expect me to do? You and the woman go missing yesterday and then I see her carried in on a stretcher, and her outfit!" She turned to Vera. "Did you ever see such a scandalous thing?"

At her niece's vigorous shake of the head, her attention returned to Reid. "Can you blame me? Here I thought Miss Norton was a respectable lady. I brought her to live under my roof." She closed her eyes and shuddered.

"Auntie, are you all right?" Vera asked. "Do you want me to get you your maid?"

"Give me a moment." Her voice was faint. "I've had such a shock."

Reid raked a hand through his hair, at a loss of how to deal with his aunt's hysteria. How long before the doctor arrived? Miss Norton had slept much of the way down, so he was more convinced than ever she had suffered a concussion. He wished he could go up and see how she was but was afraid that would only make things worse. If he'd known their entrance would cause such a disturbance, he'd have brought Miss Norton in through the back. Then he swore under his breath, disgusted at this subterfuge. He was tired of the way Maddie was treated—

"Haven't you heard a word I've said, Reid?" He swiveled around to face his aunt, who didn't look any too well herself.

"What?— Excuse me, Aunt Millicent, I'm simply concerned for Miss Norton. She suffered quite a blow to her head and I'm anxious for a doctor to see to her."

"A blow to her head? Whatever did you do to her? Oh, my goodness, my nerves can't take anymore—" His aunt began to fan herself.

"We were merely hiking up to the peak of Ben Lawers when she lost her footing and fell several feet. She hit her head on a rock and lost consciousness for a few moments."

His sister gasped. "Is she all right?"

"I don't know. I've known men to suffer less profound blows and be seriously injured. It can even prove fatal."

"But…but she's all right now, isn't she? She appeared fine," Vera insisted.

"She might *appear* fine, but we have no idea what internal injury might have befallen her. She could have a skull fracture, for all we know. I'm almost certain she suffered a concussion."

His aunt fanned herself more vigorously. "Oh, my heavens. How could you take her up there? I've suffered enough."

Vera went to her aunt. "There, Auntie, Reid is scaring us unnecessarily. He's used to talking to men and has forgotten the sensibility of ladies. I'm sure Miss Norton will be fine. Her color was good and she walked up the stairs herself."

"I must consider what is to be done once she is fully

recovered. I really can't have such behavior under my roof. Think of your children, Vera. What will Theo say?"

"Yes, I know. There'll be time enough to deal with Miss Norton once she is up again."

Reid stared at her. "Are you thinking of dismissing her, Aunt Millicent?"

"Reid, dear, consider my position. What were you thinking, taking an unmarried woman—my paid companion—up a mountaintop? How could you do such a thing?"

"I was thinking of her good. She spends most of her time cooped up in a stuffy house in London—"

"In my ample house in one of its best quarters—"

"You can hardly breathe the air in that city—"

Aunt Millicent closed her fan with a snap and tapped it against the chair arm. "Her behavior was improper, to say the least. What is everyone going to think?"

"I thought the fresh air would do her good—"

"Fresh air? Fresh air?" She waved the fan around her. "There's all kinds of fresh air around us."

Reid paced the room, frustrated. They were clearly talking at cross-purposes. "The poor lady is as pale as a sheet and suffers headaches."

"Nonsense. She's as strong as a horse and gets out on plenty of my errands. And how do you know so much about her, anyway?"

Reid stopped. "She works for me, too, or don't you remember Uncle George's collection?"

"I should never have agreed to that arrangement. I regret ever hiring the woman. Well, she won't be with me much longer, I can tell you that."

Reid's resolve hardened. He'd done Miss Norton

enough harm. "If you dismiss her, I'll hire her to work with me at the British Museum."

Suddenly Aunt Millicent slumped forward. "Oh, Reid, I feel...it's my...heart...it's just tripping. Help me!"

Reid and his sister were at her chair instantly. "What is it? What can I get you? Where are your pills?"

"Ring for Mad—for my maid," she amended, clutching her chest.

The maid, when she arrived, immediately got her one of her pills and handed it to her with a glass of water. "There, ma'am, that should fix you up."

Vera rose to look out the window. "I wonder if the doctor has arrived. He can take a look at you, Auntie."

"Yes, please," Aunt Millicent whispered, lying back against the chair now, her breathing steadier.

Reid headed for the door. "I'll go see." He felt torn between worry for Miss Norton and causing his aunt further upset. Her attack of nerves seemed almost too convenient, but he couldn't doubt it. He'd done enough damage as it was already.

Women! He was better off returning to the desert and the company of men. He knew how to deal with them there.

The doctor confirmed that Miss Norton had indeed suffered a concussion and was to take it easy over the next several days. He gave Lady Haversham a sedative with instructions to the others not to worry her with anything.

By midafternoon the next day, when Lady Haversham was sitting up in her bed, her niece came to share tea with her.

"How is that woman?" was Lady Haversham's first

question after replying to Vera's inquiry over her own health.

Vera made a moue of distaste. "I've seen neither hide nor hair of her. Hiding out in her room, it seems."

"What are we to do? I don't like it, not at all. You saw the way Reid blew up at me over her."

"I know, Auntie. I agree the situation is of concern." She tapped her teacup with a fingernail, looking at her aunt with troubled eyes. "But do you really think Reid would give a woman like that a second glance… I mean, with *serious* intentions?"

Lady Haversham firmed her lips. "I wouldn't have thought so until yesterday. But remember how he was with Octavia? One look and he fell hard for her. What if he were to do so with this…this creature?" She shuddered.

Vera gave an incredulous laugh. "Miss Norton and Octavia? Why, the two are nothing alike. What does Miss Norton have to offer? Oh, I grant you, she's passably attractive, but she's no longer young, she comes from who knows where. She's a *paid* companion, for goodness' sake!"

"Nevertheless, she's wily," Aunt Millicent reminded her. "She has insinuated herself as an assistant to poor Reid. It's all my fault for allowing her to work some hours with him on your uncle George's artifacts. To think of her closeted alone with Reid. The poor man has been beguiled."

"Yes… I see."

Lady Haversham squeezed her niece's hand. "Don't forget, you and Reid are my only heirs. Miss Norton is no fool. She's looking out for her future." Her eyes hardened. "I won't have some gold-digging servant get her claws into my nephew who's too gullible to know he's being taken in. I told Reid I'd dismiss her, and I meant it."

"You must be careful, Aunt Millicent. You heard what Reid said about hiring her himself."

"Oh, don't even mention that! I won't have it!"

"Yes, I know. I like it as little as you do, but we need to consider things carefully. We wouldn't want to precipitate anything."

Her aunt regarded her niece. "What do you suggest, then? I can't have her under my roof anymore."

"Perhaps it's better to have her where you can keep an eye on her…keep her so busy she'll have no time to be in Reid's company."

Her aunt considered and slowly nodded. "I see your point, my dear." She gave a deep sigh, lying against the pillow. "I shall have to think about your suggestion."

"Well, there's no undue rush. The woman has to convalesce awhile, it seems, according to the doctor."

Her aunt's look soured once again. "Yes. She certainly arranged that conveniently."

"Don't fret, Aunt Millicent. As long as she's confined to her room, Reid can't see her, either."

"Yes, there is that. It will give us time, too, to decide on our course."

Maddie awoke on her birthday feeling every one of her thirty years.

After washing and dressing, she examined herself in the mirror—an activity she wasn't in the habit of doing. She didn't look any different. No gray threads running through her hair yet, but it was only a matter of time.

She swung away from the glass. Enough of that nonsense. At least the pain in her head had subsided. The doctor had explained to her that her brain had been jolted around a bit and was most likely a bit bruised. "Best to let it settle and heal," he'd said with a final snap of his bag after instructing her to take it easy and to indulge in no strenuous activities for at least a week.

She didn't see the family until dinner. She'd spent most of the intervening days in her room, having her meals sent up. It wasn't that she was afraid of confronting Lady Haversham, but neither had she felt up to facing an immediate dismissal without references. She had no doubt that was what awaited her as soon as she saw her employer.

She'd also not seen Mr. Gallagher. Her feelings there were more complicated. She had received a brief note from him, delivered by a maid. He urged her to rest and take it easy. She wondered if he, too, thought it best that she stay out of his aunt's way for a few days. Torn between desiring to see his dear face and afraid of depending on him too much, she'd finally kept to her room in order to avoid him, as well.

Maddie had packed most of her few belongings. Now she stood a second, hearing the murmur of voices in the dining room, telling her the others were already assembled.

She opened the door and immediately they all fell silent. Everyone around the table turned to look at her.

Lady Haversham held her fork aloft. "You've decided to grace us with your company, I see." Not waiting for Maddie's reply, she turned away and continued eating.

"Yes, my lady." Maddie stepped to her place. A footman came immediately to pull out her chair. "Thank you."

"Good afternoon, Miss Norton." Maddie turned to greet Mr. Gallagher, who stood. She returned his smile with a tentative one of her own. At least he did not regret their outing to Ben Lawers. "It's good to see you up and about again."

She took her seat. "Thank you."

Lady Haversham turned her attention to Maddie again. "I can't say *I* have fully recovered. I have suffered countless lost hours of sleep and a terrible strain to my heart on your account."

Maddie's smile disappeared. "I'm sorry for any—"

Mr. Gallagher set his fork down with a clatter. "Now, Aunt Millicent, do we really need to begin our meal in this manner? We've been over this already."

"You are right, dear boy. This is not the time nor the place for what I have to say."

Whatever appetite Maddie had had upon entering the room shriveled up and she shook her head at the tray of sliced meat the footman held before her. Instead she took a sip of the crystal goblet of water.

Lady Haversham turned to her nephew. "Reid, I'm told there's a beautiful castle we really must see. I do hope you can accompany us before we leave."

Maddie's heart sank, not wanting to be reminded of having to leave Scotland.

"Just let me know when you'd like to visit, Aunt Millicent, and I'll arrange an outing."

"Thank you, my dear." Lady Haversham sighed. "It's hard to imagine that by next week it will be time to return to London. Poor Cecily Mason was desolate to have to depart so soon."

"I, for one, look forward to our return," Vera said. "Not that I haven't enjoyed this holiday, but there's something about the vigor of city life I miss."

"It's a pity Theo couldn't stay longer," Lady Haversham said.

"Yes, another reason I must return. I'm sure my poor husband is pining."

Maddie sighed. What would it be like when they returned to London? Would Maddie ever see Mr. Gallagher again? Where would she go? She could only count on her unpaid wages.

"Aren't you hungry?"

She lifted her head at Mr. Gallagher's sharp tone.

"Not too much, I'm afraid." Her stomach already felt twisted in knots.

Lady Haversham looked at her fork. "This lamb is delicious, so tender and well seasoned. The cook has outdone herself with the new potatoes and peas. What a shame to have it go to waste."

Mr. Gallagher motioned for the footman to pass Maddie another platter. "If you want something lighter, we can have them bring in some of the potato-and-leek soup from the first course."

"No, this is fine, thank you." She took some of the vegetables offered her, determined to make an effort to eat, if only to please Mr. Gallagher. She could see he was trying hard to be agreeable to everyone and at the same time shield her from his aunt's barbs.

Finally, the dishes were cleared away and the dessert plates brought in. Mrs. Walker's three children marched into the room, their nursemaid accompanying them.

Harry came up to his uncle, his face eager. "Are we in time, Uncle Reid?"

"Just in time." He placed a finger to his lips. "Hush, now."

The boy nodded vigorously. All three children seated themselves at the foot of the table, at the place where their nursemaid indicated.

Lady Haversham smiled at them from the opposite end of the table. "What brings all of you here?"

"A surprise!" her oldest nephew answered, barely able to keep his excitement contained.

Before she could react, a maid appeared in the doorway carrying an enormous round cake topped by dozens of lit candles. Amidst the children's chorus of "Happy Birthday," she headed toward Maddie.

Maddie's hands flew to her cheeks, unable to believe what was happening.

The maid smiled and set the cake before her. "Happy birthday, miss."

"Th-thank you." Maddie hardly knew what to say. The children clapped, and she noticed Mr. Gallagher clapping, as well. She looked around her in question, but both Lady Haversham and her niece seemed as surprised as she. Maddie's gaze landed on Mr. Gallagher who gave her a small nod of acknowledgment.

Before she could decide if he'd been responsible for her surprise party, the butler brought her a tray of wrapped packages. "Oh, my, what's all this?"

Lisbeth stood up. "Happy birthday, Miss Norton. The presents are from us—and Uncle Reid."

Her gaze flew once more to Mr. Gallagher. He shrugged. "Just a small token to celebrate this special day."

"Oh, my." It was almost too much to absorb. She stole a look at Lady Haversham, and her joy evaporated when she saw the woman's pursed lips.

"Aren't you going to blow out your candles, Miss Norton?"

"Oh—yes!" She looked from Lisbeth's shining face to the candles which had burned down at least halfway.

"As I recall, today you're officially an old maid."

At the acid tone, Maddie turned to her employer, surprised by how much the words hurt. "Yes, your memory serves you well." She drew a deep breath, ready to extinguish the candles.

"Make a wish first!"

She stopped immediately. "Of course." She edged back and closed her eyes. The only thing she could think of was to wish that she'd always remember this moment, and the warm light shining in Mr. Gallagher's eyes, later…when the way got lonelier.

Then she opened her eyes and blew out the candles. There seemed to be so many candles, but she didn't stop to count them. At that moment it didn't matter how old she was. She felt she was once again eighteen.

The maid removed the cake from in front of her and proceeded to cut it. Meanwhile the children clamored until she opened their gifts. She saw at once which ones were theirs. They were clumsily wrapped in brown paper with colorful string and ribbons.

Timmy leaned toward her. "That one's from me."

"Sit straight," his mother admonished.

Maddie took her time opening it, relishing the act. Inside was a yo-yo, which she recognized as Timmy's own. She looked at him with a smile.

"That's my favorite one. You can have it now."

"Thank you, Timmy. It's very kind of you to part with your favorite yo-yo."

Harry grabbed a thin parcel "Mine next, mine next!"

"Goodness, Harry, where are your manners, reaching across the table like that!" Lady Haversham scolded.

"Thank you, Harry." Maddie smiled at the boy, taking the package from him.

Inside she found a folded paper. Spreading it flat, she saw a picture he'd painted with his watercolors.

"That's Ben Lawers from Loch Tay. And that's you falling down the hill."

Maddie looked more closely at the drawing. Sure enough, a sticklike figure was tumbling backward down a crudely drawn mountainside. She laughed. "Indeed it is. I'm glad I didn't fall quite so far." She looked across at Mr. Gallagher and met his smile. She handed the painting to him.

He looked at it, amusement lighting his blue eyes. "So it is. I agree with Miss Norton. It's a good thing she didn't fall quite such a distance. But you were very accurate. It certainly seemed as if she'd fallen that far the other day."

Lisbeth handed Maddie her parcel with a shy smile.

"Thank you, dear." She found one of the young girl's hair ribbons neatly rolled up in the small parcel. "It's beautiful," she said, fingering the blue satin ribbon.

"It will look very pretty against Miss Norton's hair," Mr. Gallagher told his niece.

Lisbeth looked pleased.

Maddie felt herself blush. A glance at the other two women at the table caused her to quickly put the ribbon back in its wrapping and gather the packages together.

"Miss Norton, you forgot your biggest present." Harry reached across the table and handed her the neatest looking package.

If she'd had any doubts whom it was from, Mr. Gallagher's next words dispelled them. "Many happy returns."

She lifted her gaze to meet his. "Thank you." His answering smile was so warm, she felt her heart squeeze with tenderness. How was she to manage without him?

"Aren't you going to open it, Miss Norton?" Timmy piped in.

Mr. Gallagher gave a slight nod. "Go ahead."

She wished she could take his gift up to her room and open it in private. Her fingers trembled as she untied the bow of the wide ribbon holding together the wrapping paper. She laid it on the table and parted the paper.

"Oh!" Inside lay a leather-bound book. She turned it toward its spine and read the golden letters: *The Poems and Songs of Robert Burns.* She opened the book and leafed through the gilt-edged pages, before looking toward Mr. Gallagher. "Thank you. It's beautiful."

"Just a small token to mark your day…as well as your holiday in the Highlands."

"Yes." How apt his gift. She would always remember her holiday in the Highlands.

"You'll find his poem 'The Birks of Aberfeldy' in there. It's said he was inspired by the burn that runs through the town."

"We must visit it, then," Vera said.

He turned his attention away from Maddie. "Yes, we could make an excursion there."

Maddie continued paging through the beautiful Moroccan bound edition, the voices around her fading as she read scraps of poetry. Already she was pondering what she could give Mr. Gallagher on his birthday. She hadn't much to spend, and was mindful of what would be proper for a lady to give a gentleman that wasn't too personal. But she wanted him to have something to remember her by once he was far away in the desert….

After they'd eaten their cake, Lady Haversham rose from the table. "Miss Norton, please attend me in my room."

"Yes, my lady."

Feeling the hour of reckoning had come, Maddie gathered her gifts and followed her employer.

"I'll not say I'm happy with your conduct, Madeleine. You behaved with the utmost lack of decorum. Never forget your father is a respected curate—in a small parish, to be sure, but respected, nonetheless. If you're not thinking of yourself, at least think of him and his reputation among his flock.

"With this in view, I shall overlook your conduct this time. But, I warn you, I shall not be so merciful the next time. You must respect the office of your employment here."

Maddie bit her lip to keep from protesting. Her cheeks grew red. She could hardly believe the older woman would drag her father into the conversation. What had Maddie done? She couldn't fathom that a hike in the Scottish Highlands would be seen as such a wicked thing. "Yes, my lady," she finally managed in a quiet tone. "It won't happen again."

"I realize the fault is not entirely yours. I have spoken to my nephew and made him see that conventions here in England cannot be ignored, regardless of what type of civilization—or lack of it—he is accustomed to in the Middle East."

"Yes, my lady." She was still grappling with understanding what terrible crime she had committed, but now she felt doubly bad on Mr. Gallagher's behalf. He shouldn't have to endure his aunt's reprimand for offering Maddie an experience in the out-of-doors.

"Now, you may sit with me awhile and read to me from Dr. Hickey's sermons. I suggest you turn to the one on the 'wages of sin.' I believe it was found in the previous chapter."

"Yes, my lady." Maddie fetched the heavy tome and took a seat.

Three-quarters of an hour later, Maddie finally exited Lady Haversham's room, the stinging words of the sermon reverberating.

She made it back to her room, her mind slightly dazed. How had her life gotten so topsy-turvy in a few short weeks? She'd always prided herself on her decorum, her conduct at all times above reproach in the households where she'd worked.

She collapsed on the chair at the writing desk, bringing her palms up to her cheeks, which still felt warm at the reprimand. At least Lady Haversham had not dismissed her. Maddie tried to feel grateful, but at the moment all she wanted was to give her employer a few choice words and leave, never looking back.

The thought of never seeing Mr. Gallagher again stopped her. He'd been nothing but kindness itself. She closed her eyes and fisted her hands against her cheeks, trying to stem the emotions that flooded her at the thought of this gentleman, so different from any she had ever met.

A wave of despair assailed her whenever she thought of the future without him. *Lord, forgive me for getting distracted with such worldly thoughts. Help me keep focused on the ultimate goal.* She repeated the words of scripture that had always sustained her in the past.

Let us lay aside every weight, and the sin which doth so easily beset us, and let us run with patience the race that is set before us, looking unto Jesus

the author and finisher of our faith; who for the
joy that was set before him endured the cross...

She must remember her Lord's sacrifice to prevent
herself from falling into self-pity. She opened her Bible
that sat on the desk and retrieved her brother Todd's letter, which she had received the day after her fall. She
unfolded the much-creased pages.

The letter was dated over a month ago and, except
for the topmost note, was stained and smudged.

Dearest Maddie,
As you can see, I began the first part of this letter
over two months ago. Much has happened since
then. I have just returned to King's Town, where
your last four letters awaited me. They were a
most welcome sight, believe me, like a little bit
of home right here in West Africa.
I was delayed upriver due to many things. Praise
God, I was finally able to journey to the remote
village of Oku Ban. Many had warned against
going there, the tribes being known for cannibal-
ism and aggressive warfare. But God is faithful.
He protected me and the small group accompanying me.

His letter went on to describe all the things they
had experienced during their time in that village, the
drunkenness among the tribesmen, the fevers and the
fighting between tribes.

Oh, Maddie, if you could have seen the illness
and filth among those people, your heart would

have wept. The supplies you sent on the last
steamer were well used, believe me.

Never doubt, dear sister, that your sacrifice is
seen and appreciated. I know you'd join me here
in a moment if you could. The greatest breakthrough came when the chief accepted Jesus as
his savior. Glory to God!

I was further delayed because I, too, fell ill with
fever. It lasted some weeks, but praise God, He
has brought me through to continue with my task
here.

Don't forget we all run a race and until the Lord
summons us home, we must do everything He
calls us to do to finish our course....

Maddie looked up from the paper, the tears dampening her cheeks. Her brother's words had done her good.
She must gird her loins, the way the Lord exhorted Job
to do. There was too little time to sit around and feel
sorry for oneself when so many souls were perishing.

She took out her handkerchief and wiped her eyes.
Enough weeping for today. With God's grace she would
continue in Lady Haversham's employment, under the
woman's authority, knowing that through her obedi-
ence, a greater good would come about.

As to her feelings for Mr. Gallagher, she would have
to entrust them to the Lord and depend upon Him to
see her through any heartbreak.

Chapter Thirteen

Regret and relief warred within Reid when he left the Highlands. He didn't wish to cause his aunt any further distress or Miss Norton any more tension with her employer. He had no patience with the intrigues of women—and with his sister and aunt in league, he feared Miss Norton was at a distinct disadvantage.

Although he'd promised his aunt he'd find Miss Norton employment at the museum should she dismiss Maddie, Reid wasn't certain how well he could keep that promise. All the employees there were male and highly specialized in their field.

But more than these concerns was the deeper fear of being unable to contain his own growing feelings for Miss Norton. During the week of her convalescence it had been a daily struggle for Reid to treat her with simple courtesy and friendliness, when what he really wanted was to take her in his arms and hold her.

He would never forgive himself if he raised Miss Norton's expectations and then was unable to offer her anything more than friendship—and a temporary one at that—until he returned to Egypt.

He remembered her story of the suitor of her youth,

already despising a man who would lead a young lady on and then not make her an offer of marriage. Worthless cad...

Yet, what more could Reid, himself, offer her? He could never permit himself happiness with another woman—not when he had been responsible for curtailing Octavia's life. Miss Norton's fall on Ben Lawers had been a rude awakening for him. He was not to be trusted with a woman's well-being. If he had proved such a terrible husband to Octavia in London, how could he possibly protect Maddie in a place like the desert?

His thoughts went round and round in this vein, coming up with no solution. One thing was certain. He would be unable to return to London and the working relationship he'd developed with Maddie. Ever since she'd spoken her name, he'd been unable to think of her as anything but "Maddie."

It would be impossible to have her at his side each day without... Well, he refused to let his thoughts go down that road.

He sighed. He'd just have to hire a new assistant. One of those earnest young chaps at the museum. Yes, that was the only solution. He'd been foolish to propose this arrangement to Maddie in the first place.

The day after they arrived back in London, his aunt made the decision easier for him when she called him into her parlor.

"Reid, I really cannot spare Miss Norton to work with you any longer. What strength I had has waned considerably, and I need her at my side."

Reid glanced at his aunt in surprise. "Did the trip to Scotland leave you worse off?"

"Yes and no." She fiddled with her jade necklace.

"It certainly was a nice change, and I had a lovely time with both you and Vera. But the trip has exhausted me. You don't realize how I am getting on in years."

"I'm sorry. I know it was a long trip."

"You meant well in planning it for us. I'll always be grateful for it. But now I must take it easy. The heat in London leaves me feeling drained."

Reid looked away from her, knowing the news he was about to deliver wouldn't be welcome. He leaned forward and braced his elbows on his knees. "I've received word that the British have wrapped up their investigation and so I hope I'll soon be able to return to the Sinai."

"Oh, no…" Her head fell against the chair back. "I had so hoped you were home for good this time."

"I know." He tried to smile. "But you know my life is there."

She shook her head. "You and your uncle both yearned for adventure always." She sighed. "Ah well, at least I have your sister and her family."

"Yes." He coughed before continuing. "As I explained to you when I first undertook the task of Uncle George's artifacts, it's too much for one individual. My time back in England is limited."

Before he could continue, his aunt held up her hand. "I have given it considerable thought, and I've decided if you can bring in an assistant—someone who is quiet and will not disturb the household's routine—then I will not oppose it."

Reid smiled in relief. "I'm sure I can find someone to fit your requirements. In fact, I know just the chap. I'll have to talk to him and to the curator of the museum to see if his services could be spared for a few hours each day. It would help enormously." He didn't allow himself to think how much he'd miss Miss Norton's quiet, capable presence. Life had taught him that all good things came to an end, including his time with Maddie—Miss Norton. Soon, he'd be gone himself.

"Very well, I shall welcome him when he comes."

Reid rose. "Good then. I'll let you know as soon as I've arranged things."

"Your sister is planning a party for your birthday."

He frowned. "I'm not used to paying much attention to the date anymore."

"That may be so in Egypt, but here you're among family and we'd like to recognize this special day. After all, you're turning forty."

"You needn't remind me."

"There's no reason to feel down about it. Forty is a man's prime. You should be proud of your accomplishments. Not many men can boast of all you've done."

Wanting to end the subject, he moved toward the door. "Well, just let me know Vera's plans. I need to return to the museum." He hadn't seen Miss Norton since he'd walked in and wondered where she was. His aunt had said nothing, and Reid wasn't about to ask her.

As he was leaving the house, he spotted Miss Norton crossing the square, Lilah leading on her leash. He stopped and waited for her, telling himself it was just courtesy that made him want to greet her.

It had only been a day since their return, but he found himself taking in every inch of her appearance. Her cheeks were flushed in the heat of the noonday, and wispy strands of her hair that had escaped the thick roll at the nape of her neck framed her face. He had to clench his hands to keep from reaching out to touch one. "Good afternoon."

She gave him a smile, and he was struck afresh by

her beautiful pink-tinged complexion. "Hello, Mr. Gallagher."

"Have you come from a ways?"

"I've just been walking Lilah, as well as coming from the apothecary's for your aunt." She indicated a small parcel.

He frowned. "It's quite a warm day for such a walk. Don't overdo it."

The color in her cheeks deepened. "I'm sure my head is all healed."

He cleared his throat. "I was talking to my aunt about…" He hesitated. How would she take the news? Disappointed or relieved? "About our working arrangement."

"Yes?" She looked at him, her clear tawny eyes watching him.

"My aunt has agreed to an assistant from outside, from the museum, that is."

"Oh." He couldn't read anything from her expression. Her gaze remained steady.

"I realize how much strain the work put on you, having to divide your time between my aunt's needs and mine. I hate to lose you as an able assistant, but I think this will relieve you somewhat."

"I see." He wished he could know what she really meant with the two words.

"I'm going to the museum now, to try to arrange something with a fellow I know there. He's quite knowledgeable on Egyptian antiquities…." Impatient with himself for fumbling for words, he touched his fingers to his hat. "Well, it's good seeing you back to normal again. Good day."

"Good day, Mr. Gallagher." She looked away from him and continued up the steps. He hurried to open the door for her and she passed through without looking at him.

He remained looking at the door after it had shut, feeling both irritated and annoyed without knowing why. Had he expected Miss Norton to weep at his announcement? He must be thankful she had taken the news so coolly. It proved her heart wasn't yet touched.

Not as his was beginning to be. After so long a slumber, it was proving a painful awakening.

Maddie removed her hat and hurried to deliver the medicine she'd gone to fetch for Lady Haversham. She stood while her employer inspected the bottle and asked her a host of questions.

Finally she was able to excuse herself. She escaped to her room, glad to have a few minutes to herself before she'd have to attend Lady Haversham again.

So, the bright spot of her days in London was to be snuffed out. Perhaps it was better this way.

Maddie went to her sewing basket and removed the needlepoint project she was working on. Better to keep her mind busy. She'd temporarily put aside the chair cushions to make this bookmark. She could only work on it while she was alone, but it was small so she was sure she'd have it done in time for Mr. Gallagher's birthday.

She held the marker away from her a moment. It was coming along nicely. She liked the colors she'd chosen, blue and maroon, suitably masculine, yet the bright gold letters kept it from being too somber. It was an appropriate gift, she decided. Not too familiar, useful, small, so he could easily carry it with him on his travels—and the message was her own way of making it personal and memorable....

* * *

Maddie wasn't able to wish Mr. Gallagher a happy birthday on the day because she didn't see him at all. His sister organized a party for him and Lady Haversham ordered her carriage to convey her, but didn't invite Maddie along, taking her maid instead.

After considering what to do with her small gift, Maddie decided to have it sent to Mr. Gallagher's lodgings. She penned a short note and wrapped up her gift and gave it to a footman with instructions to have it delivered to the Travellers Club.

She tried returning to the chair cushions, but found it hard to concentrate. Finally she put on her hat and went out, deciding a long walk was the best way to clear the cobwebs from her mind. A short interlude of her life was over, and she mustn't dwell on it overmuch.

Reid returned to the Travellers that evening after having spent the day at his sister's among a gaggle of friends and acquaintances of hers. He'd known many in his younger days, but shared little in common with them now. So much senseless chatter...

The tight collar chafed at his neck and his frock coat was stiff and uncomfortable.

The porter bowed to him in the quiet foyer of the club. "Good evening, Mr. Gallagher."

"Good evening, John."

"You received a telegram, sir. And here is your mail."

"Thank you." He took the envelopes handed to him, wondering what the wire was about. Was it his travel orders?

Before he could open it, a voice hailed him. He looked up to see Cyril striding across the lobby. "I say, old man, where have you been?"

"Scotland."

"Ah, yes, you told me you were heading up there." Cyril reached him and the two shook hands. "You look fit. The holiday must have agreed with you."

Reid nodded, releasing his friend's hand. "Yes, it was very pleasant."

"Get any fishing done?"

"Yes, quite a bit. I also got in some hiking." He remembered Maddie walking at his side, never tiring, never complaining.

"Have you tried the latest sport? I daresay you haven't had a chance to, being in the desert."

"Which sport are you referring to?"

"Why, cycling! You must have noticed everyone in London is pedaling around."

Reid thought about the number of bicycles he had seen since he'd been in London. "Yes, I suppose there are a few."

"A few? Thousands, I'd say. Since they came out with the pneumatic tires, it's a national pastime. Have you never been on one?"

Reid shook his head.

"You must. It's a great sport."

"I think I'm a little old for a new sport."

"Nonsense. My wife and I just learned this spring. We go all over the countryside when the weather is nice." He clapped Reid on the back. "Come on out, and I'll set you up. You'll be pedaling all over in London in no time." Without giving Reid a chance to refuse, he asked, "So, how much longer are you in London anyway?"

"Hopefully, not much longer. In fact—" Remembering the telegram he'd just received, he tapped it. "I believe this might be the good news I've been wait-ing for."

"You haven't opened it?"

"No, I was about to when you hailed me."

"Well, don't let me keep you. Go ahead."

Reid slit open the envelope and read the few words in a matter of seconds. He looked up to find his friend's gaze on him.

"Well, what is it? You look mighty puzzled for news you've been expecting."

He handed the paper across to his friend.

Cyril's bearded face split open in a grin. "By golly, you're to be awarded a knighthood by order of the Queen!" The next second he pumped Reid's hand. "Congratulations, old man! Splendid, I say." He shook his head. "Who would have thought picking about in old ruins would have been of more value to Her Majesty's kingdom than making filthy lucre in trade!"

"I can hardly believe it." Reid felt overwhelmed with the news. "I didn't expect…anything like this…."

"Oh, you'll get used to the honor. Well deserved, by what you've told me. Think how you've enriched the British Museum for future generations." He took up the telegram again. "It says here an official letter will follow with details for the ceremony. I hope you'll invite me to attend."

Reid was hardly listening. A knighthood. Like his Uncle George. He smiled. His uncle would have been proud.

Cyril stepped away from him. "Well, I'd better get to the train station. It's been wonderful seeing you again, old man. I'm serious about the invitation. Why not come out this weekend?"

Reid thought about it a moment. It might not be a bad thing to get away for a few days. He needed to gain some perspective on things. Being in Scotland in such close company with his family…and with Miss Norton—he admitted the latter only reluctantly—had thrown him off balance. It was not too late to rectify things. His uncle's artifacts could wait. If they'd waited this long, they could wait a few more days. With that uncharacteristic attitude, he nodded to his friend. "All right, if you're sure your wife won't mind a stranger in your midst."

"Of course not. She's a wonderful hostess." After giving him instructions for the railway, Cyril bid him good-night.

Reid headed up to his room. Only then did he remember the rest of his mail. He flipped through the small stack. The bottom one caught his eye because it was a bit thicker than the rest. That and the neat script on the outside, which looked very familiar.

He opened the flap. A folded sheet of notepaper slipped out, but he ignored that as he spied the richly colored object that came out with it. A bookmark, he saw immediately, its gold silken tassel identifying it.

It was beautifully worked, minute stitches filling in every space, the colors reminiscent of an Islamic mosaic—in hues of blues and purples. He narrowed his eyes at the letters in gothic script. "Wherever I wander, wherever I rove, / The hills of the Highlands for ever I love."

He recognized the words of Burns's poem and was immediately transported to that day on the mountains, before Maddie's accident.

He unfolded the paper that accompanied it.

Dear Mr. Gallagher, Just a small token for your birthday. I shall always be grateful for the won-

derful holiday in the Highlands. May the Lord
bless you. Yours truly, Madeleine Norton

Maddie's small, yet beautiful gift was just what he'd
needed on this day marking his fortieth year. She'd
understood. It touched him more than all the expensive gifts of shirts, ties, tiepins and waistcoats he'd received that afternoon. If he could have spent this day
with anyone, she would have been the perfect companion, he realized, remembering his contentment during
their fishing expeditions, her eager interest in all his
conversations, her wide smile of pleasure. She would
understand what he was feeling today.

He rubbed his thumb across the silken threads, feeling tears smarting his eyes. Hastily he wiped at the corners of his eyes, dismayed by his reaction.

He most certainly needed to get away for a while
and get things in perspective. He would not, *would not,*
be disloyal to his wife's memory. Her death would not
have been in vain.

Maddie heard that Mr. Gallagher had gone away for
the weekend. Hardly having adjusted to the fact that
she only saw him briefly now when he came in to work
in the library, she swallowed her disappointment that
she wouldn't see him at all for a while.

She was surprised therefore when she received a
note in the mail addressed to her. It was postmarked the
day after his birthday. She unfolded the piece of paper.

Dear Miss Norton, I was touched by your beautiful gift. Please accept my sincerest thanks for
your time and thoughtfulness. Sincerely, Reid
Gallagher

Maddie tried not to feel disappointment at the stiff, formal words. They sounded so unlike the man she'd come to know on holiday in the rugged outdoors of Scotland. With a sigh, she folded the note back up and replaced it in the envelope, knowing she'd keep it even though there was nothing special she could glean from it, nothing to comfort her in future days. Had he no inkling of the love she'd poured into every stitch of the needlepoint? She'd tried to express through her own note what was in her heart without burdening him with the full force of her feelings for him.

Hearing Lady Haversham's bell, she tucked the envelope inside her Bible and headed to answer her employer's summons.

Reid returned from his weekend more glad to be back in London than he'd ever imagined possible.

He was pedaling his brand-new bicycle along the London street, on his way to his aunt's, wondering how soon he'd run into Miss Norton. He knew he'd gone away to try to get his feelings under control, but all he'd done while he'd been away was think of her.

He glanced down at the bicycle, the one reason he was glad he'd gone away. He was grateful now that Cyril had insisted he try out the sport. After a few false starts he'd gotten the hang of balancing on the two-wheeled contraption that had come a long way from its early days of one giant forewheel and two small rear ones, a tricycle a person needed assistance to mount.

After mastering the technique of riding, Reid had hardly been off it during the weekend. Cyril and his wife belonged to a cycling club and the two took excursions near their home every weekend. Reid had enjoyed their Sunday-afternoon tour all around the western suburbs of London. The bicycle made the miles go by in minutes.

He'd decided then and there to purchase his own bicycle and use it to get around London while he was there. When he returned to Egypt, he'd have it shipped to Cairo for when he was in the city.

Now he pedaled to his aunt's house, having arranged to meet the new assistant there at ten o'clock. As he turned the corner into Belgrave Square, he spotted Miss Norton heading from the opposite direction, Lilah tugging at her leash, and tried to suppress the joy that welled up in his chest at the sight of her.

Seeing Miss Norton walking behind the terrier, Reid felt his remaining discipline evaporate like raindrops in the sun. He also felt ashamed of the curt little thank-you note he'd sent her. What a coward he was.

He pedaled past his aunt's front door until he came to a stop before Miss Norton. Her hand flew to her cheek. "Mr. Gallagher!"

He grinned at her surprise, more glad than he could imagine at seeing her. "What do you think?"

She eyed the bicycle. "I didn't know you cycled."

"I didn't. I just learned this weekend."

"So fast? How is it possible?"

He got off the bike and pushed it alongside her. "It's really not difficult. I went to visit a friend and he prevailed upon me to give it a try. He wouldn't listen to any arguments that I was too old a dog to learn new tricks."

"Oh, no, you're not too old at all—" She stopped short at her words. "What a beautiful bicycle. Is it yours?"

He looked at her closely, trying to figure out why she'd interrupted herself. Did she mean it that she didn't consider him too old? "Yes," he said, trying to follow her change of topic, when his mind was reliving holding her in his arms during their dance together…helping her bring in the salmon…. He cleared his throat. "I just bought it. Would you like to give it a try?"

She stopped. "Me? Oh, goodness, no, I couldn't possibly—"

"Why not? I did."

"I couldn't learn."

"Of course you could. I thought it would be difficult but it's not. It would help you, having a bicycle, with all the errands you run for my aunt. Look how flushed you are in this heat. You could ride for twice the distance you walk now in a quarter of the time—"

She bit her lip.

"You'll see how easy it is to learn." Not giving her a chance to refuse, and not questioning his own motives, he hammered on, "I'll come by tomorrow morning and take you…let's see, what about the Green Park? There's plenty of room there and not many people will be out early."

They had reached the front door. "I don't know… I'm not in your aunt's best books right now. I don't know what she'd think."

"She won't fire you."

She frowned at him. "How do you know that?"

He grinned at her again. "I told her if she dismissed you, I'd hire you full-time at the museum."

Her tawny eyes grew large. "You said that?"

He nodded. "When she was being unreasonable about your fall at Ben Lawers."

"You stopped her from dismissing me?"

He felt his own face flush at her awed tone and regretted having repeated his rash promise.

"Oh, she just threatened to. I don't think she was serious."

"I don't know about that. She was rather angry at me."

"Anyway, cycling is very different from climbing Ben Lawers. Lots of ladies are doing it. I'll talk to her."

She bit her lip again. Before she could continue refusing, he reached over and opened the door for her. "It's settled. Meet me here at eight tomorrow morning."

She said nothing in reply but entered the house. He decided not to press her. He'd just have to wait and see if she showed up. She disappeared from sight, and he continued on to the back. He still wasn't sure what, if anything, he'd tell his aunt. There could be nothing wrong in teaching Miss Norton to cycle. He'd see about renting a bicycle before tomorrow.

Feeling curiously lighthearted as he hadn't since before the accident on Ben Lawers, Reid stowed his bicycle and headed for the library ready to confront the artifacts.

Chapter Fourteen

Maddie waited nervously on the front stoop the next morning. Lady Haversham hadn't said a word about the cycling last evening, so Maddie had no idea what Mr. Gallagher had told her.

She relived his words from yesterday. He'd have hired her if Lady Haversham had dismissed her! The same warmth welled up in her heart as it did every time she thought of his words.

She spied him cycling toward her, and watched in amazement to see him balancing another bicycle with his left hand. He'd brought her her own bicycle!

"Good morning," he said with a smile, coming to a stop in front of the house. She walked down to meet him. How on earth was she going to get on that high seat in her skirts? She'd worn her shortest and loosest skirt, yet…

"Good morning," she replied, eyeing the bicycle doubtfully.

He got off his own bicycle. "Here, take your bike and walk it along. We'll go to the Green Park on foot."

"All right." She went to the other bike and placed her hands on the handlebars as she saw him do. Together they left the square and headed for the large park, which was only a few blocks away.

"Beautiful morning, isn't it?" He turned to her with a smile when they'd gone a little ways.

"Yes." She felt lost in his blue gaze and was hardly aware of what kind of day it was.

When they passed through the tall wrought iron gates of the park, Mr. Gallagher scanned the area. "Let's head down this way where there's no one walking about."

They left a few nursemaids pushing prams and made their way to the empty path he indicated.

"All right, the first thing is to mount. I'll hold the bicycle so you won't fall. Once you begin to pedal, it'll stand by itself, you'll see."

She didn't like the idea of sitting up there on two thin wheels. She looked at the bicycle, then at Mr. Gallagher. "How can I maintain my balance?"

"Once the wheels are moving, the bicycle won't tip over. Just look straight ahead and pedal. Oh, and when you do want to stop, you push the pedals backward, and they brake."

She tried to keep it all straight in her head, envisioning herself falling on her face in worse shape than her fall off Ben Lawers.

He was eyeing her skirts again. "I do wish you'd get yourself a pair of bloomers. My friend's wife had a pair."

She smoothed down her skirt. "Maybe this isn't such a good idea."

"Well, I have seen ladies cycling in skirts. Come on, up you go."

Not wanting to appear a coward in front of him, she took a deep breath and asked for God's mercy. Once mounted, she gripped the handlebars until her knuckles hurt. Mr. Gallagher's larger hand covered her left one, his other holding the bike steady at the back of the seat. She felt herself teetering on the two large, narrow wheels.

"All right, I'm going to walk with you while you pedal. I won't let go until you've got the idea."

"A-all right."

They began to move and the pedals turned under her feet.

"Keep the steering wheel steady. That's it."

She tried to do as he said. She couldn't imagine being able to keep the bike upright if he should let go. He began jogging alongside her.

"You've got it," he said. The bicycle began to keep a straighter course. The path sloped downward slightly. Suddenly she was pedaling on her own. She wasn't sure quite when he had let go, but the bicycle was going by itself. The wind was blowing past her.

"That's right, just keep pedaling!" She heard his shout behind her.

Then she panicked and began to move the handlebars. The wheels wobbled. She gave a small scream as the bike tilted to one side. She put out her foot. Her skirts began to tangle with the pedal but finally she had her foot on solid ground and managed to keep the bike upright. Her heart was pounding with fear.

Mr. Gallagher ran up to her, a wide smile on his face. He clapped her on the back. "You did it!"

She was panting, more from the fear than her exertion. She looked at him in amazement, only then remembering how she had been riding for a while on her own. "I did, didn't I? Oh, my goodness, I can't believe it."

"Let's try it again."

Her heart sank. "I don't know…" She gazed at the level path before her. "There's no slope here. That's probably all that kept me upright."

"Then let's go back there. This time, don't move the handlebars so. Just keep a steady course when you reach the bottom."

"What if I want to stop? I almost fell off this time."

"You'll learn to ease to a stop then put one foot down the way you did." As he spoke, he led her back to where she'd started.

Her fear grew that he'd make her do it on her own this time. "Will you take hold of the bicycle again, please?"

"Of course. I won't let go until I see you've got your balance."

Once again, she mounted the bike and waited for him to grip it firmly. This time she concentrated on keeping the handlebars steady. She prayed for the Lord's direction. She was praying so hard she didn't even notice when Mr. Gallagher removed his hold. Before she knew it she reached the end of the slope and kept going.

Steady, Maddie, keep the wheel straight, she told herself. To her amazement, the bike didn't fall over but kept going. Once again, when she started to think about it, her balance faltered but this time she kept her head and was able to bring the bike to a less abrupt standstill.

Mr. Gallagher ran up to her again. "Well done, Miss Norton."

She beamed at him, breathing heavily. "I can hardly believe it. It's a wonderful feeling, like sailing through the air."

He smiled at her. "Precisely. I wasn't convinced,

either, until I tried it. Come on, let's fetch my bicycle and we can try it again."

They spent the next hour practicing. Every time she got back up on the bicycle, she felt a little more confident of not falling off. By the end of an hour, they were able to circle the park. Her only moments of fear came when they had to pass a pedestrian or nursemaid with a pram. Maddie usually came to a full stop and let the person pass before daring to get back on the path.

When they left, Mr. Gallagher persuaded her to bicycle back. She was afraid of the horse-and-buggy traffic so they walked their bikes across the busiest street near the park, and remounted them on the quieter side streets.

They put their bicycles away in the mews behind the back garden. "We'll do it again tomorrow morning," he told her.

"Is the second bicycle yours?"

"I rented it for you. You can use it this week and then we'll see about getting you your own."

"Oh, Mr. Gallagher, I couldn't possibly purchase one."

He rubbed a spot of dry mud off the front bar of one of the bicycles. "You wouldn't have to. I'm thinking of purchasing another to leave here in England and taking this one with me when I go back to Cairo. You could keep mine for me until I return."

The thought of his leaving took away any pleasure his words would otherwise have given her of entrusting his bicycle to her keeping. "I see."

"You wouldn't mind looking after it, would you?" His blue eyes searched hers.

"No, of course not."

They walked through the garden together. At the

back door, she turned to him, her fingers threaded to-gether. "Well, I'd better go see about walking Lilah before she makes a mess in the house."

"And I'd better see if my new assistant has arrived." He cleared his throat, looking away from her. "Listen, I meant to tell you how much your gift meant to me."

"Oh—" She flushed, remembering her puny gift. "That was nothing, just a small token—"

"No, it wasn't nothing. It was a beautiful piece of workmanship."

She warmed at the praise. "Nothing like an artifact."

He was looking at her so intently. "No, the same. Both are works of art. It was a very appropriate line of verse you chose, as well."

"I've enjoyed the poems very much. That one seemed...fitting."

"Very. It was just the antidote I needed for the vague melancholy that hit me as the day wore on."

Maddie couldn't look away from his steady gaze. Had he experienced the same kinds of thoughts she had on her birthday? It didn't seem possible. His life was too full. "I'm glad you liked it then. It wasn't much—"

"It was a great deal."

"I imagined you surrounded by a crowd of acquain-tances on your birthday."

"I was and yet I felt quite alone. When I got back to my rooms, your gift was just the lift I needed. It took me back to Scotland."

Her stomach fluttered, and she averted her eyes from his steady blue gaze. "I'm glad I could be part of your day in some small way then," she whispered.

"So am I."

Without daring to look at him to read what was in

his eyes, Maddie opened the door to the corridor behind her. "Well, I—I'd better run along."

"Yes." He didn't move and she could feel his gaze still resting on her.

She finally forced herself to take a step away from him. They heard Lilah's bark somewhere on the ground floor. "Oh, dear, Lilah's getting restless. Thank you for the cycling lesson, Mr. Gallagher." With a quick curtsy, she turned and hurried down the corridor.

"Miss Norton—"

She whirled around at the sound of his voice. "Yes?"

He held up his hand. "Until tomorrow."

A few idyllic mornings followed. Mr. Gallagher was always on time and the two spent the next hour cycling first along the quieter routes of Hyde Park, and then down to Chelsea. One morning they pedaled all the way to the embankment where they rested a while gazing out over the Thames and across to Battersea Park.

It was only by chance, while attending to Lady Haversham in the parlor, that Maddie heard of the great honor about to be bestowed upon Mr. Gallagher. "I've told him he must have all new stationery ordered. Sir Reid Gallagher, what a fine ring it has," Mrs. Walker said to her aunt.

Sir Reid Gallagher. So, he was to be knighted.

Mr. Gallagher's sister continued with a sound of disbelief. "He said it wasn't necessary. What was he to do with fine stationery in the desert? Can you believe that?"

Lady Haversham shook her head. "I don't know how he comes upon such outlandish ideas. Well, the ceremony is in a few nights. I wish I could be there, but alas, it would be too much for me."

"Yes, I know. But Theo and I shall be in attendance. Oh, I've ordered the most beautiful gown, an emerald satin embroidered in glacé silk. It features the new puffed sleeves. I had it copied from *La Mode Illustrée....*"

Maddie listened intently but nothing more was said about Mr. Gallagher. She sat in awe of his impending knighthood. He hadn't said a word to her about it. But of course, why should he tell her anything of his personal affairs?

Her heart warmed, though, at the thought of the honor. If anyone deserved such recognition from the Crown, it was Mr. Gallagher. How she wished she could be there to see him knighted by the Queen.

Should she say something to him about it? Offer him her congratulations? Perhaps when they went cycling tomorrow morning. But the fact that he hadn't told her meant he didn't want her to know. Perhaps he was just being modest. From all she'd gotten to know of him, she understood how little outward distinctions meant to him.

She decided not to say anything unless he gave her any indication of the upcoming ceremony.

The next two days it rained and Maddie didn't see Mr. Gallagher at all. She knew he came by to work in the library with his new assistant, but she was kept so busy by Lady Haversham that she had no opportunity to see him at all.

Reid made an impatient sound as he nicked himself a second time with his razor. What was wrong with him this afternoon?

He dabbed at the blood with a washcloth, then paused at the knock on his door.

"Come in."

Cyril's head appeared around the doorway. "Just popped in to see how you're getting on before the big event." His friend sauntered in, dressed in black tailcoat, his thick hair plastered down with macassar oil. "Goodness, man, aren't you ready?"

Reid turned back to the mirror over the basin, dressed in shirtsleeves. "Almost, if I don't leave my face a road map of cuts."

"Why don't you have a valet?"

"I travel light," he answered shortly, concentrating once more on his razor. Finally, with a last swipe to his jaw, he rinsed the remaining soap off his face and toweled it dry.

Cyril lifted a book off his nightstand and flipped through it. Reid struggled to attach the starched white wing collar to his shirt. His fingers felt twice their normal size on the small buttons.

"Pretty bookmark," remarked Cyril. "Quite lovely, in fact. Picked it up while you were in Scotland?"

"Er—no." He looked at himself in the mirror and took each end of the tie in his hands. "It was a gift."

Cyril raised an eyebrow. "Very nice. Have to ask my wife to fashion me something like this." He noticed Reid's task. "Good gracious, man, you're making a hash of that tie. Here, let me."

His friend took the white ribbon from his fingers. "My wife always does mine." In a few deft movements, he managed a presentable bow. Patting down the points of Reid's turndown collar, he stepped back. "There, that should do it. You really need to get yourself a valet, or at least a wife." With a chuckle he retrieved Reid's coat on a chair and helped him on with it. "Ready? You

don't want to be late for the Queen. The way it's raining, the streets are jammed."

Reid tugged at the shirtsleeves under the coat
sleeves. Why was he feeling so on edge? Could a
knighthood bring him to this state of nerves? He wasn't
the kind of person to let things get to him, much less
ceremonial nonsense.

Or was it because he hadn't been able to talk to Maddie in so many days? She didn't even know what he'd
be going through this evening. What would she think
of it? Would it matter to her at all? Would she think
this was just a worldly vanity?

Cyril clapped him on the back. "Relax, old fellow.
It's not as if you're going to the gallows."

He smiled at his friend's attempt at humor. "It certainly feels like it at the moment." He paused. "Listen,
I promised my aunt I'd stop in before I left for the ceremony. She's not up to attending, herself."

"Capital idea. I haven't seen Lady Haversham in
an age."

Reid hesitated. He'd really been hoping to catch a
glimpse of Maddie at his aunt's, and he felt awkward
enough as it was. It seemed his aunt kept Maddie hidden away these days. "Why don't you—uh—meet me
at the palace? You'll see Vera and Theo there."

"If you'd prefer. We'll wait for you there then. Don't
be long. Remember the traffic."

"Yes, I'll be only a few minutes behind you."

The two left Reid's room. At the entrance to the
club, they parted. Reid hailed a hansom, thinking of
the coming few hours. What he really needed was to
see and talk to Maddie. He tapped a finger against his
knee, wondering how to manage that if she wasn't sitting with his aunt. And if she was, how to see her alone?

He needed to—what? Talk to her? He glanced out the rain-streaked carriage window, trying to analyze the longing he'd felt since the last time they'd gone cycling together. He'd be happy with just a few moments in her quiet presence. That would rectify everything.

Maddie opened the door to the parlor to fetch her needlework.

She stopped short at the sight of Mr. Gallagher. She hadn't seen him in three days, but it seemed longer. She certainly hadn't expected to see him tonight. She knew it was the day of his knighthood.

He turned at the sound of the door and her breath caught. Never had she seen him so distinguished looking, not even the night of the dance in Scotland. He wore an elegant black tailcoat and trousers, a gleaming white shirtfront and low-cut, black silk waistcoat and bow tie. His blond hair was combed meticulously, making it shimmer. "Miss Norton."

Her hand went to her chest, as if to quiet its heartbeat. "I'm sorry… I didn't know anyone was in here. Have you come to see Lady Haversham?"

"Uh—yes."

She moistened her lips, unable to tear her gaze away from him. She should excuse herself. He was here to see Lady Haversham. This was his big night. "I… I'll leave you then."

"No." He cleared his throat. "That is, won't you stay a moment?"

She hesitated, knowing Lady Haversham wouldn't be pleased to find her alone with her nephew. Maddie hadn't missed the fact that Lady Haversham excluded Maddie from any occasion on which Mr. Gallagher visited his aunt.

Finally, she took a few more steps into the room, deciding she would at least offer Mr. Gallagher her best wishes. "I haven't had a chance to congratulate you."

He quirked an eyebrow. "You've heard?"

She nodded with a tentative smile.

"The ceremony is this evening at Buckingham Palace."

"It's quite an honor."

He made a gesture. "Yes. I don't know as I deserve it, but the Crown seems to think I've done them a service with my work in antiquities."

"Oh, yes!" she added.

When he said nothing, she said, "Your aunt must be very proud of you."

"Yes…" He gave a slight smile. "I'm sorry my Uncle George isn't around to give me some advice. He received a knighthood, as well."

"I'm sure he'd have been very proud." She moved farther into the room. "Is the ceremony…very long?"

"I don't know. It depends on how many are being honored, I suppose. My aunt won't be attending, so I thought I'd stop by and see her before going on to Buckingham."

"Of course, how thoughtful of you. I know she'll be gratified to see you dressed so elegantly—" She stopped, feeling herself begin to redden.

He made a motion of dismissal about his appearance. "She rarely has that privilege…those things are important to her…" He ended, his gaze shifting away from her. "Have you ever met the Queen?"

"No. I saw her during the Jubilee a few years ago, but it was from quite far off. She was riding by in an open carriage."

He turned away from her and began fiddling with a pile of sheet music on the top of the piano.

"Have you ever met her?" she said after a moment.

"No… I never have…" He tapped the piano top, still looking away from Maddie. He seemed distracted, and she wondered if she should leave.

Instead, she approached the instrument. "Are you nervous? About the knighthood, I mean?"

"Yes… I suppose…a bit." He coughed. "It's a silly thing really." He fidgeted some more with the sheet music, realigning it into a neat pile.

Maddie took a few steps closer to him, trying to decide what she could say to ease his mind.

He swung around and he seemed surprised to see her standing so close. "Oh—"

"I'm sorry—" They both began to speak at once and just as quickly fell silent.

Suddenly the atmosphere between them was charged. Maddie couldn't move although courtesy dictated she take a step back if she stood this close to a person. He, too, seemed unable to move. Before she could command herself to breathe again, he reached out and touched a loose strand of her hair by her temple.

Her lips parted as she stared at him. He seemed fascinated by the lock. His gaze shifted to her lips. Maddie found her own glance going to his lips and she wondered what his thick mustache felt like. Was it soft or bristly?

Before she could stop the absurd direction of her thoughts, he was leaning toward her.

His lips touched hers. A kiss as soft as a breath…

She felt the earth crumbling beneath her like grains of sand loosening until nothing was left but a tiny pinnacle directly under her toes. Then that, too, was gone and she would have fallen if his hands hadn't come up to hold her.

He pressed his lips more firmly to hers, the soft hairs of his mustache brushing her skin. She sighed, lifting her arms to his waist, her fingertips touching the soft wool of his jacket. The strength of his back seemed to emanate through the material, as her arms encircled him.

His kiss deepened and she was lost in the touch and scent of him. Sandalwood…the softness of his lips… the rough-smooth feel of his shaved skin…the thickness of his mustache.

The next instant empty air met her as he took a step back. She would have lost her balance if she hadn't reached out and found the solid piano beside her.

He half turned from her, his hand covering his mouth and jaw. "I beg your pardon. I—please forgive me for taking such liberties—"

Maddie was too stunned by what had just happened to take in his words.

He turned his back fully to her. "I'm sorry… I don't know what I was thinking—" He seemed to be collecting himself.

Her head swung around at the sound of the door. "Ah, there you are, Reid. Why didn't you tell me you'd arrived? How elegant you look." Lady Haversham frowned at Maddie. "I didn't know you were here, Madeleine." Her eyes went from Maddie to Mr. Gallagher. "Is there something you need?"

Maddie pressed her lips together, her heart feeling as if it had been yanked from her and now was trying to find a way to retreat back into herself away from harm. "I w-was ju-just on my way out." She glanced at Mr. Gallagher but he hadn't looked at her once since breaking their embrace. She didn't know how she managed to reach the door. Her fingers gripped the knob as if it was her only hold on reality. At last she was able to close the door behind her, softly but firmly. She brought her fingers up to her mouth. Had she just dreamed his kiss? It had been over so quickly she wondered if she'd just conjured it up from some deep-seated desire. The lingering scent of his cologne was her only evidence that it had been no dream.

Oh, Lord, what happened? Was it wrong of him to kiss me? Was it wrong of me to kiss him back? She clutched her chest, feeling a pain so deep at his rejection of their kiss. What was she to do now? How could she ever face him again, having revealed her own feelings so fully when he'd so obviously repudiated their kiss?

What had he done? Reid got through his interview with his aunt somehow, thankful she'd probably attribute his lack of coherency to his nerves before the ceremony.

He hurried from her house and remounted the awaiting cab, cursing himself once more. What had he done? Had he gone mad? Kissing Miss Norton! He no longer dared call her Maddie. That kind of liberty meant only one of two things: either he had no respect for her or the complete opposite—he meant to ask for her hand in marriage. The former was certainly not true, and the latter…was impossible.

He rubbed his jaw in frustration, wishing he could undo the last quarter of an hour, at the same time craving another moment in Miss Norton's company. He remembered being mesmerized by the look of her rosy, half-parted lips, feeling all restraints in him snap at the sound of her soft intake of breath.

What was worse was her look of shock when he abruptly drew away from her, the sheen of tears in her eyes the more he'd heaped a pile of inept apologies on her. He could murder himself for having taken advantage of her sympathetic nature. She probably thought him the most insensitive, worthless scoundrel and she'd be right in her estimation.

She deserved at least a decent explanation from him. Could he bring himself to do that? Not having had to bare his heart before anyone for so long, he didn't know if he was capable of it.

The investiture ceremony, which should have been a high point in his career, went by in an indistinct haze as his mind kept reliving what had occurred in his aunt's parlor just previously. Reid knelt before the old Queen and scarcely felt the blade of the sword as she touched him lightly on each shoulder. He went through the motions, barely aware of the usher leading him away into the courtyard where a photographer took pictures of him and his family. He automatically shook hands with all those who congratulated him. Afterward, they all went to his sister's where a crowd of well-wishers gathered.

At last it was over, and he was able to return to his room. He lay on his bed, in his shirtsleeves and trousers, his head pillowed under his arms, thinking only of Maddie. How was it possible to care for another woman the way he'd cared for Octavia so many years ago?

He turned on his side, away from Octavia's photograph, but even so, her soft features reproached his back. The recriminations became unbearable until he could no longer stand them but was forced to get up and walk to the French windows that led to a narrow balcony. He stood, leaning his head in his hands against the stone railing, condemnation weighing against him like an avalanche.

When Mr. Gallagher had left, Maddie found herself summoned once more, this time to Lady Haversham's sitting room.

The older lady was standing, her walking stick planted into the carpet beside her. "What have you to say for yourself, Miss Norton?" The woman's pale blue eyes glittered at her in outrage.

"I'm not sure what you mean, my lady."

Lady Haversham stamped the stick into the carpet. "Don't be impertinent with me, pretending no knowledge of what I saw in the parlor."

"Saw in the parlor?" Maddie repeated in a faint voice. Could she have seen? Maddie was certain she hadn't heard the sound of a door until after Mr. Gallagher had moved away from her.

"You were obviously waiting to have a private interview with my nephew." She narrowed her eyes at Maddie. "Don't think I haven't seen what you've been up to. Insinuating yourself into his company. A lonely widower." She gave a dry bark of a laugh. "You thought he was easy prey, didn't you?"

"No, my lady, of course not—"

Lady Haversham took a few steps toward her, brandishing her walking stick at her. "I'll not have it, do you hear me? You think you can finagle my fortune for yourself by bamboozling my nephew with your wiles. Parading around in a pair of trousers, pretending to fall in the Highlands so you could stay out all night with him—"

Maddie fell back. "How could you think such a thing?"

The old lady narrowed her eyes at her. "I've been watching you. With your quiet ways, pretending to be such an innocent. I should never have brought you into my house, you brazen hussy—"

Lady Haversham began to tremble. Suddenly the cane fell from her hands. "My salts—"

"Yes, my lady." Maddie rushed to her side and helped her into her wing chair then fumbled for her smelling salts.

Lady Haversham looked deathly pale beneath her rouged cheeks. She revived slightly with the ammoniac. "I'm warning you, Madeleine, if you don't desist with your designs on my nephew, you shall regret it." Her eyes bulged. Maddie, fearful for her health, only nodded.

"Shall I ring for your physician?"

"I'll cut him out of my will! I shall name Vera my sole beneficiary. Do you hear me?" Her shaky voice rose with each threat.

"Yes, my lady." Maddie's alarm grew at the woman's pallor.

"I swear it. I shall summon my solicitor immediately."

"Yes, my lady. Let me call Dr. Aldwin." She rose and hurried away to summon the doctor and Lady Haversham's maid.

What had she done? Had she caused Lady Haversham irreparable harm? Maddie paced outside Mrs. Haversham's room while the doctor examined her.

Lord, don't take her in this condition. I pray for your mercy for her. Show her the truth, that she needn't fear anything from me, that I'm not after her wealth, that

I haven't done anything underhanded with her great-nephew. Maddie wrung her hands, anguished at the rage she'd seen in the old lady's eyes. *Don't let her depart with unforgiveness in her heart. Have mercy on her soul...*

She swung around when she heard the doorknob turn. "How is she, Doctor?"

Dr. Aldwin shifted his bag to his other hand as he closed the door softly behind him. "She'll be all right, I expect, by tomorrow. I gave her a sedative. She gets a little too excited about things no matter how much I tell her to take it easy."

She breathed a sigh of relief, her hands clasped in front of her. "She was very upset with me, I'm afraid."

The old doctor patted her arm. "I wouldn't worry too much about it. Just keep out of her way until tomorrow. Bessie is in there and can attend to her tonight."

After the doctor had left, Maddie felt too restless to go to her room. She was tempted to take her—Mr. Gallagher's, she corrected—bicycle out, but was afraid to leave the house in case there was another emergency with Lady Haversham. She finally settled in the parlor with her Bible. But that room held no peace. All she could think of was what had occurred there earlier.

Could Mr. Gallagher really feel something for her? Once again, Maddie touched her lips, reliving the feel and scent of him so close to her. How she longed to be held by him again.

He'd pulled back so quickly. What had passed through his mind? Was it because of his wife? Remembering his words about her and his tenderness toward her, Maddie realized it must indeed be his love for his deceased wife that had stopped Mr. Gallagher. She hated the thought that she was causing him pain.

She hugged herself now, feeling bereft without Mr. Gallagher's warm smile and kind words. If she'd thought she'd miss him before, what would it be like now that she'd tasted his kiss and had an inkling of what he might be feeling for her?

Reid knew he had to see Maddie again and explain why he couldn't—why *they* couldn't—

Early the next morning, he stood at his aunt's front door and rang the bell, his palms sweaty. The maid who let him in told him that his aunt was still abed and that Miss Norton had gone out with Lilah earlier and as far as she knew wasn't back yet.

"Thank you. I'll just wait in the front parlor."

He stood in the bay window, watching the street through the filmy lace curtain, his stomach clenched in knots. He'd hardly slept. This morning he'd looked a long time at his dear Octavia's portrait. Was it to engrave her in his mind before facing Maddie?

He finally spied Miss Norton turning down the street, the dog trotting along in front of her on its short legs. Reid's heart twisted at the sight of Miss Norton's fresh features, her pert hat scarcely hiding the beautiful shade of her hair. He watched her approach the house and when he heard the front door opening, he went to the entrance of the parlor.

She was crouched beside the dog, undoing its leash. "There now, Lilah, hold still while I take this off you—" She looked up at the sound of the door.

"Good morning, Miss Norton."

She rose slowly, letting the dog scamper away, its nails clicking on the uncarpeted portions of the floor. "Good morning, Mr. Gallagher." She looked as serious as he felt.

"May I—" He coughed then began again, "May I speak to you?"

She glanced down the corridor toward the interior of the house. "I'm…not sure. Lady Haversham was unwell last evening."

What was the matter with Aunt Millicent now? "Just for a moment. I'll go see my aunt directly we're through."

She bit her lip then with a slight bow of her head assented.

He held the door open as she walked past him into the parlor. He closed the door quietly behind him.

"I…" How could he begin? Where could he begin? "I wanted to apologize for my conduct yesterday."

Her gaze slid away from his. "There's no need, Mr. Gallagher."

He took a step closer to her, and he noticed she took a step back. Was she as reluctant as he to rekindle the… attraction he was feeling for her? Part of him was relieved. Perhaps this would make it easier for what he had to say. "There's every need. I want you to know I'm not in the habit of forcing myself upon ladies—"

"Please, Mr. Gallagher! There's no need. You needn't say anything more." She half turned away from him as if the whole topic were distasteful to her.

The last thing he wanted was to upset her further. "I'll make this as brief as possible, Miss Norton. Just hear me out, please."

She bowed her head and he had to strain to hear her words. "Very well."

He cleared his throat. "As I said, I'm not in the habit of forcing my attentions upon a lady—any lady. I can only blame my behavior on having been in the rough company of men too long. I—" he stopped, feeling ex-

ceedingly awkward "—I've grown very fond of you."
His face grew warm. "I would never have kissed you
otherwise. It's just that—" he ran a hand through his
hair "—that I'm not ready to enter into…into…that
kind of…of union with another woman…not after my…
wife…" His voice cracked on the last words.

"I'm sorry, Mr. Gallagher." Her soft voice came to
him after a few seconds. "I don't wish to cause you any
pain. I know you cared—continue to care—for your
late wife. I would do nothing to come between you
and…your memory of her."

"Thank you, Madd—Miss Norton," he amended,
checking himself in time.

They were silent for another moment before her
voice came to him hesitatingly. "You've mourned your
dear wife a long time."

"I'll never mourn her long enough!"

They stared at each other, and in her shocked gaze,
he realized he owed her the truth. He took a deep breath
and forced himself to continue. "Since it was I who
caused her death." In the stillness that followed, he
could scarcely believe what he'd admitted. Miss Norton looked even more stunned. He gave a weary smile.
"You find that hard to believe? It's true."

She took a step toward him. "Of course you didn't
do any such thing. Many people feel a sense of guilt
when a loved one passes away."

Reid collapsed into the nearest chair, feeling utterly
old and exhausted. "Octavia died of the influenza…
complicated by a…miscarriage.

"Oh no!" Her voice was full of sympathy.

He forced himself to continue. "Nobody knew she
was with child but myself…and her physician." The
words, even now, ten years later, were so hard to utter,

as if saying them brought back every scream of agony when the baby came too soon. And the bleeding…so much blood. Nothing he could do could stanch it. "She might have survived the influenza if she hadn't been so weakened by the early months of pregnancy."

Now that he'd begun, he felt compelled to finish, speaking of things he'd never voiced aloud. "She was always afraid of having children. Her mother had died in childbirth, so it was understandable. It was I who wanted to start a family."

Miss Norton drew up a chair close to him. "Please, Mr. Gallagher, you needn't tell me. I understand."

He leaned forward, no longer seeing Maddie, but Octavia in those last agonizing hours. He gripped his hands together, bracing himself to go on. "At first I was patient. As I told you, we traveled a good deal. But…as the years went by, I yearned for children to make our union complete. I began to pressure my wife more. It wasn't natural *not* to have children. As she neared her thirtieth birthday, it was as if I panicked a bit, thinking that soon she'd be too old to have children. I became more insistent. I'd spoken to our physician, and he'd confirmed my fears that it became more and more dangerous for a woman to have children—particularly her first—the older she became."

He bowed his head, finding it harder to go on. "Eventually I wore down her resistance. She would face childbirth out of love for me. And I would get what I wanted because I'd known how to use someone's love to get my way. I sometimes wonder whether love really exists or is it all an excuse to manipulate a person to one's will?"

"Oh, no, Mr. Gallagher, love does exist! You must believe that." Her expression radiated only kindness.

"God loves us and He's given us the capacity to love, even when it means sacrifice."

He nodded. "Octavia certainly sacrificed out of her love for me."

"But you mustn't ever believe you didn't love her. Your desire for a family was no evil. You didn't set out to make your wife feel guilty. Your desire was natural."

He looked away from the compassion in her eyes. He didn't deserve her understanding.

"She got terribly sick—morning sickness they call it—she could hardly keep anything down. But still, she'd bravely insist on accompanying me whenever I lectured. It was after one of these lectures, that she… collapsed."

He passed a hand over his eyes, reliving those days. "I called our physician at once, and he diagnosed the influenza. There were several cases that winter. She must have contracted it at one of the crowded lecture halls. The physician would have been optimistic, with Octavia's youth, but he said her weakened condition… because of the morning sickness…"

He forced himself to continue. "After some days, she started bleeding…. I tried to stop it…." His hands kneaded the cloth at his knees, his head bowed low. He wanted to stop talking about it, thinking about it, but he couldn't. It was as if he were unburdening a great weight he'd carried so long by himself. "There was nothing the doctor could do, he said. I tried to save her but I couldn't. She slipped away from me. She was so cold, so pale. I tried to warm her, but I couldn't do anything." His voice had grown hoarse. He looked across at Maddie, hardly noticing the tears filling her eyes. He wished he could weep, but no tears came. He'd cried all the tears he had in him a decade ago and in the years following.

Maybe the harsh desert air had dried up everything inside him.

Miss Norton reached over and covered his hands with hers. "Don't distress yourself, Mr. Gallagher. You mustn't speak anymore of it. It wasn't your fault, please believe that."

But she was wrong. It *had* been his fault. And nothing he could ever do would change the fact. If he hadn't worn down her resistance…he'd used every argument, every logical reasoning, every cajolement… His very reason had overcome her illogical fears…except they hadn't been so illogical. They'd been very real fears.

His selfish desire for a family had been his young wife's death sentence. He didn't deserve to be happy again.

Chapter Fifteen

When Maddie saw that nothing she said would comfort Mr. Gallagher, and that her presence only seemed to cause him more anguish, she finally left, her heart breaking at the revelation.

She went up to her room, climbing the stairs slowly, wishing with all her heart she could help Mr. Gallagher accept the forgiveness he sought. She could only pray for him and…leave his aunt's side.

She'd resolved on that course the night before and would hand in her resignation as soon as Lady Haversham awoke. In the meantime, Maddie could write her letter and begin packing.

She sat at her desk and bowed her head, asking for the Lord's wisdom. Then she took up her pen and a sheet of notepaper.

Dear Lady Haversham,
It is with a heavy heart I tender my resignation as your companion. Please understand it is with no admission of guilt at your charges that I feel it best we terminate the conditions of my employment, but rather to ease your mind. I'm sorry if

you misinterpreted my actions or behavior in relation to your great-nephew. My conduct with Mr.
Gallagher has been above reproach. I have never
sought his attentions, nor has he forced his upon
me, in any way.

She paused at this last sentence. Searching her heart,
she knew it was truthful in essence. Mr. Gallagher's
words and conduct this morning showed clearly that he
did not wish to pursue anything with her. And he certainly had not forced himself upon her. She had been
a willing recipient to her own folly and grief.

She continued.

That said, I would rather leave your household
than be the source of any anxiety for you. I wish
you and your family all God's blessings and happiness. Please forgive me for any upset I may have
inadvertently caused you.

Yours sincerely, Madeleine Norton

She folded the paper, placed it in an envelope and
sealed it. Then she wrote Lady Haversham's name on
it. Maddie would either give it to her in person or have
her maid deliver it for her.

Feeling a weight lifted from her shoulders, although
a heavier one weighed on her heart at the thought of
never seeing Mr. Gallagher's dear face again, or of not
being able to assuage his secret grief, she rose and went
to dig out her portmanteau.

After being told his aunt was still sleeping, Reid
spent a miserable morning working among the artifacts
in the library. No longer were the lifeless relics of the

ancient past enough to make him forget everything else. His enthusiasm now was merely to keep up appearances before the young man working attentively by his side.

In the afternoon Reid spent a while at his aunt's bedside. She looked pale and haggard and complained of a general malaise.

"My dear Reid, this is why you must reconsider your decision to go back to Egypt. I feel myself getting weaker every day. I don't know how much longer I'm good for on this earth."

He held her hand. "Don't talk such rubbish. I'm sure you'll outlast me."

"Oh dear no. You must be here to oversee my affairs. You and Vera are my heirs, you know."

He shifted on his chair, unable to give her the reassurance she sought. In an effort to lighten her mood, he said, "Uncle George's collection is coming along very well. I'm working with my new assistant to write everything up in a catalog that I can present to the college."

She gave him a wan smile. "I knew you'd know what to do with all his treasures. Your Uncle George would have been so proud of you with your knighthood." She patted his hand and closed her eyes.

"I don't want to tire you. Would you like me to call Miss Norton for you?" Part of him longed to see Miss Norton again. What was the point after telling her he wanted nothing to do with her? He would only hurt her more.

"No, not that woman. I want Bessie."

He rose, troubled by his aunt's reaction to Maddie's name. "All right, I'll fetch her."

On his way out, he looked around for Miss Norton, but didn't see her anywhere. It was for the best, he reasoned, placing his hat on his head before walking out.

He left by the back to get his bicycle from the mews. Once on the walkway in the garden, he couldn't help one last glance at the upper-story windows, wondering if she was behind one of them.

When he got to the shed, he felt a pang at the sight of the second bicycle, remembering the rides he'd enjoyed with Miss Norton. Were they never to be repeated? Obviously not. She'd take no pleasure in a man's company who had treated her so shabbily.

When Maddie heard that Lady Haversham was still feeling under the weather, she decided not to aggravate the elderly woman with her presence. The letter could wait one more day.

After packing most of her things, Maddie left the house. On the spur of the moment, she decided to take her bicycle out. Mr. Gallagher's bicycle was not there. She wondered whether he still wanted her to take care of this second one when he left England. Clearly not, if she wouldn't be in his aunt's employ.

She pedaled the bicycle away from the square, not sure where she would go, only knowing she wanted to be away from Belgrave Square. If only she could flee somewhere far, far away. The bicycle ride was the next best thing. She ended up going through Hyde Park all the way to Kensington Gardens. By the time she returned to the house, it was late afternoon, and she felt somewhat better. After she'd put the bike away, she entered the quiet house and took the back stairs up. As she came onto the landing, she heard a male voice. Thinking it might be Mr. Gallagher, she stopped short, unwilling to upset him further with her presence.

But it wasn't Mr. Gallagher. She recognized the voice as that of Lady Haversham's solicitor. Mattie's heart thumped in fear. Had she made good on her threat so soon? She could hardly believe Lady Haversham would cut her only nephew out of her will. Oh, why hadn't Maddie given her the letter earlier? Would it do any good now? It *must*.

She'd ask the maid to deliver it to Lady Haversham as soon as possible. Maybe it wasn't too late to help Mr. Gallagher.

Reid arrived at his aunt's early the next morning. He wanted the time alone in the library to collect his thoughts before having to face his assistant.

Collect his thoughts…or catch a glimpse of Miss Norton? He'd thought his confession the day before— things he'd spoken of to no one in a decade—would somehow eradicate his feelings for Miss Norton. Surely, she would want nothing to do with him now. Why then did he still long to see her?

He parked his bicycle alongside Miss Norton's, remembering the miserable night he'd spent. How had he made such a mess of things so quickly? If only he hadn't kissed her like that—

He went immediately to the library. But once there, he found it hard to settle down to work. He stood every few moments and walked around, stopping at a window and glancing out, or picking up an artifact, realizing after a few seconds he wasn't studying it at all, but picturing Maddie's face.

Finally, he stepped out of the library. All was quiet. Where could Miss Norton be? Would she already have left to walk Lilah? Was she even up yet? Breakfasting? He decided to check the breakfast room. No one was there but a maid, picking up dishes from the sideboard.

He stepped back at the sight of her, but she'd already turned around.

"Good morning, sir. I was just clearing things. Would you like some breakfast? I can bring you a fresh plate of ham and eggs."

"No, thank you."

"A pot of tea, then? Or coffee?"

"No, thank you. I'll ring for something later from the library."

"Very good, sir." She curtsied then left the room with a tray.

After hesitating a few more seconds, he exited the room, as well. Where else could he look? He walked toward the main staircase with no clear plan in mind. Just as he looked up, debating whether to go up or not, Miss Norton appeared around the curve of the staircase.

She stopped short. For a second, he thought she'd retreat. But she said, "Mr. Gallagher."

"Good morning, Miss Norton." How he wanted to bound up the stairs and grab her up in his arms.

"Do you need anything?" Her quiet voice was all business. They might never have been sitting together in the parlor a day ago, he breaking down.

He cleared his throat. "No."

"Lady Haversham is still abed, I believe. I—I haven't seen her myself." This was the first sign she gave of nervousness.

He realized he couldn't be honest with her. The only reason he was standing at the bottom of the stairs was to catch a sight of her. Now, all he could do was feast his eyes, knowing that's all he would do.

They both turned at the sound of running feet on the stairs above Miss Norton.

"Oh, miss," Lady Haversham's personal maid came

to a panting halt. "Oh, miss, please, come quickly. It's her ladyship. I don't know what's wrong with her. She can't move!"

Reid didn't wait to hear more. He took the stairs two at a time, Miss Norton already ahead of him. Together they entered his aunt's room.

His aunt was lying on her bed, her nightcap still on. Reid bent over her. "What's wrong, Aunt Millicent?"

She gasped, struggling to get each word out. "I... I don't...know. Can't seem...to move..."

Reid noticed then how stiffly she lay. Miss Norton had reached her other side and laid a hand on her forehead. "I'll have Dr. Aldwin fetched. I'm sure he'll put you to rights."

Reid took hold of his aunt's hand but it lay inert in his. He tried not to think the dire word *apoplexy*.

By the time the doctor left he had confirmed the dreaded suspicion. Indeed, Lady Haversham had suffered a stroke. Maddie didn't leave her bedside, but tried all she could to make her comfortable.

A few hours later, Mrs. Walker arrived. After a whispered consultation with Mr. Gallagher in the corridor, she hurried to her aunt's bedside.

"Dearest Auntie," she said, taking the woman's hand in both of hers. "I came as soon as I heard. You poor dear."

Lady Haversham tried to utter something but only unintelligible sounds came out. Her condition had worsened over the last few hours. What little mobility she had had earlier in the morning was gone, and she was completely paralyzed.

Maddie rose and excused herself though no one took

notice of her. When she entered the hallway, she was surprised to see Mr. Gallagher still there.

"I was hoping I'd see you," he began at once. "I wanted to let you know I'm going by the doctor's now to inquire about hiring some nursing help."

"Oh." She hadn't considered that, thinking she'd assume that duty. Then she remembered she was no longer employed by Lady Haversham. But perhaps no one else was aware of the fact? It didn't matter. She knew she couldn't leave her employer until…well, not in this state. "Very well, Mr. Gallagher," she finally replied.

"Good then. If you don't mind looking after her until we can get some full-time help, I would greatly appreciate it."

"Of course I wouldn't mind. Anything I can do—"

He brought his hand up to her shoulder and squeezed it before quickly dropping it away. "Thank you. I knew I could count on you." His blue eyes looked keenly into hers for a few seconds, and she wished she could reach out to offer him comfort, but he turned and entered his aunt's bedroom before she could say anything more.

In the days that followed, Maddie could hardly think of anything but Lady Haversham. Watching the poor woman struggle to speak, Maddie's heart went out to her. The only sounds which came out of her mouth were gurgles, and Maddie tried to soothe her, seeing that the woman's efforts only aggravated and exhausted her.

If only there was a way to communicate. She tried getting Lady Haversham to clasp her hand, but it lay inert. Finally Maddie thought of something. "My lady, can you blink your eyes?"

After a second, Lady Haversham's eyelids moved slowly but surely.

Maddie pressed her hand. "That's excellent. If you

blink once, let that be for 'yes,' and if you blink twice, let that mean 'no.' Do you think you can manage that?" She watched the woman's eyes intently.

Lady Haversham blinked once.

"Wonderful. Now, let me try to figure out what you'd like. Are you thirsty?"

One blink. "Would you like a sip of water?"

Another blink. "Very good." Maddie placed a bolster behind her head and with difficulty managed to prop her up enough for her to take a few sips from a glass. "There, that's better, isn't it?"

She noticed Lady Haversham's agitation when she began to sputter something.

"What is it? Did I hurt you?"

Two blinks. "Do you want to lie back?" Two blinks. Maddie pursed her lips, trying to think what else she might want. "Are you too warm?" Two blinks. "Are you cold?" Two blinks.

Maddie straightened the covers and sat back down on the chair beside the bed. "Would you like me to read you some Scriptures?"

The pale blue eyes stared right at her, as if imploring her. One blink.

"Very good. Let me get my Bible." It was beside her on the nightstand. "Would you like to hear something from the Psalms?"

One blink. Maddie leafed through them until coming to the twenty-third one. "'The Lord is my shepherd, I shall not want…'"

When she'd finished, she asked, "Would you like me to read some more?" One blink.

Maddie found another. "'God is our refuge and strength, a very present help in trouble…'" Then she flipped further. She began reading Psalm 112. She got to the tenth verse, "'The wicked shall see it, and be grieved; he shall gnash with his teeth, and melt away: the desire of the wicked shall perish.'"

Lady Haversham began to whimper again. "What is it, my lady? Shall I stop reading?" Two blinks. More whimpering. Maddie pressed her lips together. Perhaps that last verse had been too harsh. She flipped over to a more soothing psalm. "'Oh give thanks unto the Lord; for he is good: because his mercy endureth forever…'"

But Lady Haversham's agitation continued. "Lady Haversham, I don't understand. I know you want to say something, but I'm afraid I remain in ignorance. You must be patient with me. Would you like me to send for your maid?"

Two blinks. "For Mrs. Walker?" Two blinks. She swallowed. "For Mr. Gallagher?" Two blinks. "Do you wish to tell me something?" One blink. "All right. Is it about the Scriptures?"

One blink. "Did you like that last psalm?" Lady Haversham didn't react. "Was it the one before that? Let's see…" Maddie turned the pages back. "Psalm 112. 'Praise ye the Lord. Blessed is the man that feareth the Lord.'" A hesitation then one blink.

"Would you like me to read it again?" One blink. "Very well, I shall read it again." When she reached the tenth verse, once again, Lady Haversham made noises in her throat. Maddie reread the verse slowly. "'The wicked shall see it, and be grieved…the desire of the wicked shall perish.'" She looked up to Lady Haversham. "Is that the verse that particularly interested you?" One blink. Maddie reread the verse to herself, puzzling over it. She looked back at Lady Haversham who was eyeing her, as if waiting for her to draw some conclusion.

"Is there someone who has harmed you, Lady Haversham?" Then it dawned on her. "Do you think it is I who wished you harm?"

Two rapid blinks. Maddie breathed a sigh of relief. "I'm glad, my lady. Did you receive the note I wrote you?" One blink. "I wrote the truth. I truly didn't mean to come between you and your nephew in any way. In fact, I would be gone from here by now, if you hadn't… hadn't fallen ill."

Lady Haversham began to moan. "What is it, my lady? Are you in pain?" One blink. Then two.

"Shall I move you a bit?" Maddie half rose from her chair but Lady Haversham began to whimper again. Maddie sat back down and reread the verse slowly. When she next looked up, she saw in alarm that the old lady's eyes had watered and two tears were running down her wrinkled cheeks.

"Oh, dear, you mustn't be upset." She got a handkerchief and dabbed at the tears. "Why don't I let you rest a little? I'll read to you some more later."

Lady Haversham closed her eyes and Maddie rose with some relief.

The following days were similar. Both Lady Haversham's niece and Mr. Gallagher spent some time sitting with her, but the bulk of the time was shared between the nurses Mr. Gallagher had hired and Maddie. Each time Maddie attended Lady Haversham, the woman wanted her to read from the Scriptures. Each time Maddie read something dealing with wickedness, sin or forgiveness, Lady Haversham became overwrought. Maddie began to understand that Lady Haversham had something weighing on her heart.

Maddie reassured her by reading texts from the gospels about the forgiveness offered through Jesus Christ.

But Lady Haversham's obvious frustration only increased, and Maddie could see it wore her down.

Mr. Gallagher came into the sickroom every day. The first time, Maddie immediately stood, ready to leave at once, but he motioned her to remain where she was. He took a seat on the opposite side of Lady Haversham's bed.

He held one of the old lady's hands in his and smiled at her. "Good morning, Aunt Millie, how are you doing today?" He then proceeded to tell her about the work in the library.

He didn't stay long. When Maddie left the room, Mr. Gallagher was waiting for her. "Miss Norton—"

She stopped in the corridor, her heart pounding anew each time she was near him. No matter how hard she tried, she couldn't forget the feel of his lips against hers. Her glance strayed to his mustache, remembering the feel of it. Quickly, she looked back at his eyes, and found them searching hers.

"I just wanted to thank you again for being so patient with Aunt Millicent."

"You don't have to thank me, Mr. Gallagher."

"She seems to want you near her."

"Perhaps it's because we've developed a simple method of communicating." She explained the way of having Lady Haversham respond by blinking.

"That's ingenious. I must put it into practice and explain it to Vera." He sighed. "It must be so frustrating for her not being able to speak or move."

She nodded. "I believe something weighs on her heart." She hesitated, but seeing Mr. Gallagher waiting, she continued. "Perhaps if you summoned her minister, he might be able to pray with her, perhaps offer her the solace she needs."

"Of course. I should have thought of it myself." He shook his head. "It's times like these that we realize how unimportant everything else we've put our energies to is, and there's only one thing of lasting value." He looked at her gravely. "You seem to have known that all along."

"Please don't credit me with anything out of the ordinary." She gave a slight smile. "I was raised by a curate, remember."

He nodded, and she sensed the short interview was over. "I shall contact Reverend Steele straightaway."

"Yes, thank you." With a quick bow of her head, she entered the room, glad they'd managed to achieve something of their former friendship, yet sensing still an invisible and insurmountable barrier.

When Reverend Steele had visited Lady Haversham, the vicar told Maddie and Mr. Gallagher, "I agree with Miss Norton that Lady Haversham is not at peace, but I'm afraid I couldn't get anything more specific than that." He patted Maddie's hand. "I suggest you continue sitting with her and the Lord will illuminate you concerning this."

"Yes, sir." She only hoped he was right. She'd been praying steadily for Lady Haversham, but had felt no breakthrough.

The days passed slowly. The house was even more quiet than usual. Mrs. Walker's children were not permitted to visit. Only Lilah was allowed by the lady's side. The little dog seemed to understand her mistress's condition and spent most of her time curled up at the foot of Lady Haversham's bed.

All Maddie could do was pray for Lady Haversham. She knew the prognosis was virtually hopeless, so she asked the Lord that if Lady Haversham were not to recover that He would give her peace and take her unto Himself. As she was meditating over one of the Scriptures that seemed to cause Lady Haversham agitation, it occurred to Maddie that perhaps Lady Haversham wished to ask for God's forgiveness. Perhaps she regretted her fury toward Maddie that last evening before her stroke. Lady Haversham only seemed to exhibit her distress in Maddie's presence.

Seated at Lady Haversham's bedside the next day, her Bible on her lap, Maddie began, "My lady, pardon me if I'm being impertinent, but do you wish to ask God's forgiveness for your own sins?"

Lady Haversham looked at her intently and blinked once. Maddie swallowed and braced herself to continue.

"Very well. Remember the Lord says in His word that if we ask forgiveness He is faithful and just to forgive us our sins. You may just pray along with me in your heart." She bowed her head. "Dear Heavenly Father, I come before you asking for forgiveness for my sins. I ask for the cleansing blood of Jesus Christ to wash away all my iniquity. I accept His atoning work on my behalf."

She paused and watched Lady Haversham. The elderly lady had closed her eyes and was mumbling, but they weren't sounds of agitation but rather as if she was praying along. Satisfied that Lady Haversham had been able to pray, Maddie continued. "Now, would you like to ask someone in particular for his forgiveness?" Immediately the lady's eyes opened and she blinked. "One of your family members?"

Two blinks. "One of the servants?" Two blinks. "One of your friends?" Two blinks. "An acquaintance?" Two blinks. Having eliminated all the more obvious,

Maddie finally dared asked, "Would you like to ask my forgiveness for anything?"

Immediately the lady blinked once. Maddie's heart began to pound, surprised that she'd been correct, and humbled to realize the Lord was working in Lady Haversham's heart. She took one of the lady's limp hands in her own. "Please know that there is nothing to forgive. I don't feel you have wronged me in any way."

Lady Haversham began to whimper and Maddie squeezed her hand. "Let me continue, my lady. I do forgive you, for whatever you wish. If there's any way you feel you have wronged me, know that I *do* forgive you. I love you with the love of our Savior, Jesus Christ, and hold nothing in my heart against you. Please believe me."

The lady's eyes filled with tears. Maddie tried to soothe her, and when at last the lady appeared at peace, Maddie gave her a sleeping draft that the doctor had left prepared.

After that time, Maddie noticed Lady Haversham grew quieter as the days wore on. All she seemed interested in was hearing the Scriptures read.

Finally one morning, the maid summoned Maddie to tell her Lady Haversham had passed away in her sleep.

Maddie could only breathe a prayer of thanks that her ladyship's suffering had ended. She wondered how Mr. Gallagher and Mrs. Walker would receive the news.

They soon arrived and Maddie could tell little from Mr. Gallagher's closed expression. Mrs. Walker immediately began to cry. Maddie left Mr. Gallagher to comfort his sister.

She went to her room and knelt by her bed. Although sad for the sake of the lady's relatives, Maddie felt a deeper, inner joy knowing Lady Haversham had been at peace with her Maker. She gave the Lord thanks for having used her to communicate the Savior's love to her employer. All the petty offenses disappeared in the greater work the Lord had wrought in Lady Haversham's life.

With a sigh, Maddie rose. She should repack the belongings she'd unpacked during Lady Haversham's illness. She decided to remain until everything had been arranged for Lady Haversham's funeral and then she would tell Mr. Gallagher she was leaving. Perhaps she could ask him for a character reference. She would have to obtain a new position and didn't know how long that might take. In the meantime, she'd need her last wages to get a room somewhere.

Maddie paced her room, trying not to think too far ahead. She must trust in the Lord to see her through to a new assignment.

She made every effort not to think of Mr. Gallagher and what he would say when she told him she was leaving. He'd seemed so kind and gentle since his aunt's stroke. Would he miss Maddie at all? Would he wish her to stay? But what reason could there be for her to stay?

She had been, after all, only an employee of his aunt's. At the demise of her former employer, she had been expected to leave right away.

Mrs. Walker certainly wouldn't welcome her any longer than necessary. The woman had never treated Maddie with more than bare civility.

Maddie sighed as she closed up her portmanteau. Once she knew where she was going, she would leave her forwarding address.

If Mr. Gallagher needed her for anything, then he would know where to find her. She tried not to let a spurt of hope rise from that decision. Let the Lord's will be done, she repeated to herself, as she'd trained herself to do all her adult life.

Between funeral preparations and wrapping up the work on the artifacts, Reid hardly had a moment to consider the future. All he knew was that with the passing of his aunt, an era had passed.

For so long, whenever he'd returned to England, she had been his main family contact. Even though Vera was his only sibling, Reid had felt himself growing further and further apart from her each time he'd come back. He resolved to rectify that, if only for the sake of his nephews and niece. He'd become reacquainted with them over the short holiday in Scotland, and he'd be sorry to lose that once he returned to Egypt.

Egypt. He knew he could return as soon as he and Vera decided what would be done with Aunt Millie's estate. The reading of the will was the next day, but he expected no surprise there. He and Vera were his aunt's only heirs. It would just be a matter of hearing about all her charities, helping the servants with references, deciding if the house was to be shut up or sold.

He had no strong opinion either way and would leave it up to Vera. She was sure to have something to say.

The only issue of any importance was the one he shied away from, but it remained like a big nebulous cloud in the center of his thoughts.

Maddie Norton.

How could he bear to leave her behind when it came time to sail for Cairo?

And how could he suggest a future with her when he would never expose her to the dangers and rigors of such a harsh place as Egypt? If he couldn't protect his own wife in her native England, what could he do overseas with someone who, by her own admission, had been weak and frail as a girl?

He sighed, coming to no conclusion, preferring to shove the issue to the back of his mind as he did each time he glimpsed Maddie's face in his comings and goings to and from his aunt's residence.

Chapter Sixteen

Maddie attended Lady Haversham's funeral and remained afterward to help serve the many people who came to the house.

The next day, the solicitor called everyone to assemble in the parlor for the reading of the will. Maddie sat in the rear with the servants. She would have preferred not to attend. She was too new an employee to receive anything, unlike the rest of the servants, but the solicitor had insisted all household employees be present.

As the lawyer's voice droned on, Maddie's attention wandered. She glanced at the back of Mr. Gallagher's head from time to time. He sat with his sister and brother-in-law near the front. She'd hardly exchanged any conversation with him since his aunt's death, and those few words had only concerned his aunt.

The lawyer finally began with the bequests. He mentioned the gift of the artifacts to the University College with the stipulation of her great-nephew as overseer. A few other charities received generous gifts.

Maddie breathed a prayer of thanksgiving when she heard of Mr. Gallagher's trusteeship. It must mean that

Lady Haversham had not made good her threat to disinherit her great-nephew, after all.

As expected, a long list of legacies followed to each and every servant in Lady Haversham's employ. Lady Haversham had not overlooked even the lowliest scullery maid, who received five pounds. Maddie glanced over to the young girl, whose smile showed her appreciation. Suddenly Maddie started up, hearing her own name.

"…to my paid companion, Madeleine Norton, who has only been in my employ since April last, I leave nothing. For she has proven herself a conniving, deceitful woman and if I die prematurely, it is likely due in great part to her."

Gasps and murmurs broke out. Maddie felt the room spin around her. She grasped the edge of her chair to steady herself. What was happening? Was this some terrible nightmare?

She suddenly found Mr. Gallagher at her side. "Don't pay attention to those words. They were clearly the words of a senile old woman."

Maddie struggled to rise, and his strong hands helped her.

Mrs. Walker appeared at her brother's side. "Make her leave this house immediately!" Her eyes narrowed at Maddie. "How dare you cause my aunt such pain? Because of you, sh…sh…she's gone—" Her voice broke at the last words. Her husband came up to her and put his arm around her, gently leading her away from Maddie.

Again, Maddie tried to pull herself away from Mr. Gallagher, but he held her firmly. "Don't listen to her, Miss Norton. Vera's just overcome with her grief. She doesn't mean what she's saying."

There was no recrimination in his eyes or tone. Maddie's lips trembled in gratitude, and she was afraid she would break down in front of him, in front of everyone in the crowded parlor.

Mr. Gallagher's attention was diverted to the lawyer as the elderly man approached them. "What kind of nonsense is this in my aunt's will? How could you permit such vile language in a legal document?"

The lawyer responded in a quiet tone and Mr. Gallagher in a louder one. Maddie realized how everyone in the room was staring at her. She would have fallen down in shame if Mr. Gallagher's hand had not held her. But she knew she mustn't make things more difficult for him. She managed to slip from his grasp while he was disputing with the solicitor.

"Wait, Maddie—"

But she only shook her head and fled the parlor. When she reached the solitude of her room, the thoughts came. How could Lady Haversham have done such a horrible thing to her? Did she hate her that much? Maddie's tears flowed freely now, as she blindly began to collect her last belongings. At all costs, she must be gone from this house before anything else happened. She should have left when Lady Haversham first charged her unfairly with deceitful behavior.

But would her ladyship have died forgiven of her sins if Maddie had not been there? The question brought her up short and she dropped the shawl she held in her hands. *Forgive me, Lord.* Had the Lord kept her deliberately, because He knew Lady Haversham would not have died in peace if she had continued angry at Maddie, no matter how unjustly?

Was Maddie's call to serve the Lord only valid when it was convenient for her to serve Him? Was her commitment to help in her brothers' missionary work only paying the Lord lip service? Maddie felt more shame as the questions rose in her mind. She'd always prided herself on her unwavering commitment to the work overseas, not minding whatever deprivation she must suffer if it meant she could send more material help to the field.

But was she able to suffer shame on her Lord's behalf? It was much more difficult to be reviled by those around her than to live without luxuries. She remembered the stares of everyone downstairs. They'd looked at her as if she'd murdered Lady Haversham.

Yet, if she hadn't remained by the lady's side— Maddie thought about Lady Haversham's agitation during those days before her death. She had known what awaited Maddie.

Maddie sank down onto the bed, staggered by the realization. Lady Haversham had known no peace until she had obtained Maddie's forgiveness. Maddie bit her lip as something else occurred to her. It had been easy to forgive her then when it had seemed only a blanket forgiveness for little slights. But now, could she forgive a woman who was gone but who had left Maddie an awful legacy of shame to live with?

A knock interrupted her thoughts. Likely the housekeeper demanding she leave the premises immediately. Maddie rose slowly, hating to have to face accusing eyes.

Mr. Gallagher stood there. She covered her mouth. What must he think of her?

"Please don't—" He held his hand out as if afraid she'd close the door on him. "May I speak with you for a moment?"

She tried to compose herself. "Let me assure you, Mr. Gallagher, I'll be gone within a few minutes—"

"No! I haven't come to ask you to leave. Please stay as long as you need." He cleared his throat. "First of all, let me apologize for that unforgivable statement in my aunt's will. I don't know what she must have been thinking. The lawyer tells me she only recently rewrote her will, making no changes, except to insert that terrible statement. He assures me she had a legal right to do so, but it means nothing."

She shook her head, still unable to compose herself.

"Please, Maddie, hear me out—"

He'd called her by her first name for the second time. Her hand gripped the doorknob, her heart warmed by the fact that he hadn't condemned her.

"May I…come in?" At her nod, he entered the room, his eyes never leaving her face. Once more, he cleared his throat. "I—that is, you must marry me. You must see that."

She stared at him, too stunned by his words. That was the last thing she'd expected to hear. *He wanted to marry her.* He ran a hand through his hair, leaving it in disarray. How she ached to smooth it down for him. "You see the necessity of it. My sister is threatening legal action."

No…she realized, his meaning becoming clear. Her heart plummeted from the leap it had taken. He felt he *had* to marry her.

"I appreciate your concern, Mr. Gallagher." She was amazed at how calm her voice came out. "But you needn't feel you must marry me."

"Vera is alleging you somehow brought about my aunt's death."

She'd thought it couldn't get any worse. "How can that be?"

"I know it's nonsense, but she will twist the words in the will around and have a magistrate investigate. It could get messy. If you're my wife, she wouldn't dare bring any legal charges against you."

"Oh, Mr. Gallagher, I didn't do anything to your aunt, please believe me. Please tell your sister that."

"I know that. I saw how you soothed her in the end. She would have known no peace if you hadn't been at her side, demonstrating a devotion she didn't deserve. I've told Vera all these things and will continue to do so. But she's distraught. There's no telling what she'll do in this state."

He took a step toward her.

"So you see the necessity. If Vera knows you are to be my wife, she won't make a public scandal, no matter what she may think in private."

Maddie shook her head, unable to get any words out. Did he really think she would marry him just to save herself?

"You must consider this rationally. It's the only thing that will stop my sister."

"Please don't mention marriage anymore."

His brows drew together as if in irritation. Before he could wear her down with further arguments, she drew herself up. "I'm not afraid of what Mrs. Walker might do. I know I didn't do anything to harm your aunt. My conscience is clear on that score."

"I know it is, but you don't understand the damage this might do to your reputation."

"Not with those who matter to me."

His blue eyes looked into hers offering her his full conviction in her honesty. "I know. But with all those who don't know you—it can affect your chances for future employment...."

She knew his words were accurate, and she had no idea what she would do in that event. But she wouldn't marry without his love, and he had said no word of his affections. "I appreciate your kindness to me, Mr. Gallagher, but you needn't marry me out of fear for my future."

"Miss Norton, I must insist you look at this more sensibly. You don't know my sister when she gets a notion into her head."

"I appreciate your warning."

He let out a frustrated breath. "You mustn't be so stubborn, Miss Norton. You don't want to end up in the street, with no prospects for employment—"

"I'm not a charity case, Mr. Gallagher."

He drew back. She hadn't meant to speak so sharply, but if she didn't stop him, she was afraid he'd weaken her resolve. And her principles were all she had left.

This time it was he who took a step back. "I never suggested you were, Miss Norton. Please forgive me if my proposal was unwelcome to you." His stiff tone broke Maddie's resistance even further, but she knew she mustn't give in to the tempting idea of accepting his well-intentioned proposal.

"There is nothing to forgive. You only wished to protect me." She stood quietly by the door until, with no further word, he left the room.

Reid stalked away from his aunt's house, too angry to sit in a cab. Women could be the most infuriating creatures on the face of the earth, beginning with his late aunt, continuing with his sister and ending with Miss Norton. Her behavior topped them all.

How had things come to this pass? He could not understand what had possessed his aunt to insert such a ludicrous statement into her last will and testament. Probably some fit of pique over something as minor as Maddie not having treated Lilah with all the care Aunt Millicent expected. She'd probably gotten over it by the next day and hadn't gotten around to changing things. She might not even have thought about it anymore. Or the stroke had prevented her from making any other changes. Reid thought back over his conversation with the solicitor. He had been called in the day before Aunt Millicent's stroke.

Reid's pace slowed, trying to remember what might have set his aunt off at that time. He stopped in the middle of the pavement, remembering his kiss with Miss Norton. Could Aunt Millicent have witnessed it? She had walked in on them—not in the very act, but soon enough after that Reid was hardly aware of what he was saying. Could Aunt Millicent have suspected something?

It hardly seemed possible, but his aunt was an inquisitive woman—and very protective of her relatives. Who could tell what had gotten into her head. She'd probably mentioned it to Vera, and between the two of them, who knew what they'd cooked up. He'd have to confront Vera with it. His mind recoiled at the thought of having to reveal any of his own feelings to his sister.

He came back full circle to the original reason for his exasperation, still flabbergasted at Miss Norton's reaction to his proposal of marriage.

Instead of gratefully accepting his offer, she'd refused him! He recommenced his rapid stride. Of all the high-handed, proud reactions. Against his better judgment, he'd been willing to betray Octavia's memory, to expose Miss Norton to countless dangers and risks overseas, in order to save her reputation…only to be told she wasn't a charity case!

Women! The sooner he was back in Egypt the better. But he couldn't leave Miss Norton to the mercy of the courts. He'd have to strangle some sense into Vera if it was the last thing he did.

He wasn't put to so drastic a measure. The next day, before Vera could call the local magistrate, Aunt Millicent's personal maid discovered a letter Miss Norton had written to her before the stroke.

Reid reread the letter of resignation, which the maid handed him, then passed it to his sister. "I think this proves for once and for all Aunt Millicent's judgment was clouded by an unfounded prejudice against Miss Norton."

"This letter proves nothing at all, unless to show Miss Norton did have some designs on you."

He turned from his sister in disgust. "For goodness' sake, will you face the facts? Aunt Millicent began fabricating a supposed attraction between Miss Norton and me. The fact is the two of us were working closely together. I admire and respect Miss Norton highly, but that doesn't mean I was going to run off with her!"

Vera came up to him and gazed into his eyes. "Are you sure, Reid? It's been a long time since… Octavia passed away. I know it must be lonely for you. You're in a vulnerable position if a woman comes along and pretends a kindness and sympathy that might perhaps not be sincere—"

He gave a bark of laughter. "Like Cecily, for instance."

"She's someone from our own class, your equal in

every way. She doesn't have to pretend something she doesn't feel."

His jaw hardened. "Miss Norton is as much a lady as you, Vera."

"That may be, but her position in society is nothing to be compared to ours. Really, Reid, Miss Norton is a paid companion. Her folks are as poor as church mice from what I understand."

"That's enough. Her good name has already been libeled by our aunt. I won't have her further ill-treated by our family."

"I'll do anything to protect you, Reid."

He exhaled in frustration. "Can't you see the poor woman was already willing to give up her job for my sake? What more do you want of her?"

"I want to be certain she didn't do anything to upset Aunt Millicent to precipitate her collapse."

"Listen, Vera. For your information, I proposed marriage to Miss Norton the day I heard Aunt Millicent's cruel insinuations read to everyone under this roof." At his sister's shocked expression he continued, his tone deliberately quiet. "*She* turned me down."

Vera's mouth dropped open.

"Yes, you heard me. So much for your accusation of self-interest. So, I'll say this only once, Vera. Desist with your ridiculous threat to call in a magistrate to investigate Miss Norton's behavior toward our aunt, or I'll do everything in my power to force my suit with Miss Norton."

Vera's mouth snapped shut and she turned away as if in a daze. "Oh, Reid, I had no idea you'd go so far. I'm sorry." She turned stricken eyes back to him. "Did you…care very much for her?"

He looked away from her. "It doesn't matter what my feelings were. I wasn't going to stand back and see her treated so unjustly."

"I see. I misjudged Miss Norton then. She is an honorable woman."

Reid left her then. He hadn't seen Miss Norton since the day before. All he knew now was he wanted to see Maddie, to offer her his help in any way she might need. He realized his anger at her refusal had been his own wounded pride, but he still worried about her situation. If she refused to marry him, there must still be some way to get her to accept his help, perhaps with finding a new position.

He stopped a young footman. "Could you please tell Miss Norton I'd like to see her?"

"I'm sorry, sir. She's gone." At the look in Reid's eyes, he added, "Didn't you know, sir?"

"No. Gone where?"

"Don't rightly know, sir. She left with all her bags— or bag, I should say. Would you like me to find out?"

"Yes, please do." He paced the entry hall as he awaited a reply. After a few minutes, Mrs. Reeves, the housekeeper appeared.

"Good afternoon, Mr. Gallagher."

He nodded. "When did Miss Norton leave precisely?"

She pursed her lips, thinking. "Why just after the reading of the will." She looked down as if embarrassed.

He hesitated, hating to have to ask, but needing to know. "How was she?"

"She didn't let on much about her feelings, if that's what you mean, sir, but I could see she felt she could no longer lodge here." She cleared her throat softly behind her hand. "I must say I understood her position."

"Yes, quite. Can you please tell me where she has moved to?"

She pursed her lips. "I couldn't tell you, sir."

He suppressed his impatience. "What do you mean?"

"I mean I don't know, sir." She hesitated. "I'm not sure if she herself knew precisely where she was going to and she left no forwarding address."

If the floor had shifted beneath him a few minutes ago, now he felt a fear growing in him as great as when he'd seen his wife begin to bleed. He tried one more avenue, knowing instinctively the futility of the inquiry. "Perhaps someone else in the house would know? Or perhaps she has been in touch with another servant since she left?"

"I can look into it, sir."

"Yes, please do. I'll wait in the library."

"Very well, sir. Would you like me to bring you some tea?"

"No, thank you. Just fetch me the moment you know something."

It wasn't long before his suspicions were confirmed. Maddie had told no one where she was going. He then proceeded to ask if anyone knew her family's address. No one knew.

His panic mounted as the day waned. He racked his brain, trying to remember if she'd ever told him anything that would help him find her now.

He finally notified Vera of what had happened. All she could add was that she believed Maddie's parents hailed from Wiltshire. He ransacked his aunt's desk, searching for any correspondence from Maddie, but all he found were receipts of the salary payments his aunt had made to her, a paltry sum paid quarterly. That presented a new worry. Had Maddie been paid her last earnings? If so, had she already sent everything to her parents and missionaries as she was accustomed to? Where would she go? How was she going to live? Finding nothing else useful, Reid finally enlisted the housekeeper's help, as well as that of Aunt Millicent's personal maid, to search his aunt's bedroom and sitting room.

At last he found a letter from an acquaintance of his aunt's, recommending Maddie for the position of companion. Attached to it was a letter from Maddie herself. A pang stabbed him when he recognized her neat script. At the heading was a London street address. He clutched the letter, half crumpling it in his fist, the first tide of relief washing over him. Could Maddie have gone back to this location?

He left the house and hailed a cab, praying the whole way. The address turned out to be a modest boarding-house in a respectable middle-class neighborhood near Paddington.

But once he rang the bell and spoke to the landlady, he obtained no new information. The lady vaguely re-membered Maddie, a quiet woman who had only stayed a few days with her. No, she had left no forwarding address.

Reid's shoulders slumped. He turned away, view-ing the setting sun over the buildings, thinking only of what Maddie was doing, alone in London, with lit-tle money, no references. Where would she go? What would she do? He dearly hoped she would seek refuge with her parents. But would she? She *must*. It would be the logical thing while she was seeking new employment. But how successful would she be, without his aunt's reference?

Maddie blotted the short note and reread it one last time.

Dearest Mother and Father,
This is to let you know I am safe and well. I have left the residence of Lady Haversham following her demise. The poor lady had a stroke, which left her immobile. I can only thank the Lord that He granted me His grace to minister to her in her last days. She died in peace, having found mercy in her Savior.
I am presently seeking new employment. I have enclosed no return address. Please don't be concerned over this fact. I do not wish to be contacted by anyone from my last place of employment. It is possible you would be requested to provide some information on my whereabouts by someone from Mrs. Haversham's family.

Maddie bit the edge of her pen, wondering if she was being presumptuous that Mr. Gallagher would try to find her. In any case, she couldn't run the risk. She continued reading.

I don't want you to be in a position where you would be forced to conceal something that it is not in your nature to conceal. Please be assured I have done nothing wrong or of which I am ashamed. Only know I endured a painful ex-

perience at the end of my term with Lady Haversham and would prefer to put it behind me.
As soon as I find new work and a more permanent living situation, I will send you my address
as well as some money. I trust it will be soon.
Please don't worry. The Lord is watching out for
me and I am not in want of anything.
Your loving daughter, Maddie

With a sigh and final glance over the letter, she
folded it up and placed it in an envelope. She would
post it tomorrow when she went out again in search of
employment.

She slumped over the scarred, uneven table at which
she sat. Her search had been unfruitful in the week since
she'd left Lady Haversham's residence. All the reputable
employment agencies she'd contacted frowned upon the
fact that she could provide no references from her last
place of employment. Because her last two positions had
been found through informal arrangements of someone
recommending her for the position, Maddie had no record with any of these agencies. She'd also scanned the
newspapers every day for positions, but nothing suitable
had appeared. She had no experience as a nursemaid or
nanny, and knew that those, too, required impeccable
references. She had tried applying for seamstress positions at a few places, but unsuccessfully.

She didn't know how much longer her scant savings
would last. She bit her lip, knowing she mustn't dwell
on the issue, reminding herself of the words in James:

The trying of your faith worketh patience. But let
patience have her perfect work, that ye may be
perfect and entire, wanting nothing.

She sighed again and rose to prepare for bed, not looking too closely at her surroundings. They were ruder than anything she'd ever faced, even as a child in their humble dwelling in Jerusalem. She'd found the least expensive room she could find, but it came at the cost of dirt and squalor. Street noises continued far into the night and began again early in the morning. Thankfully, her third floor room was high enough that she didn't fear sleeping with her tiny window open. Otherwise she'd suffocate in the heat and stale odor of the narrow room, which barely had space enough for a bed, a chair and table. Only a few nails on the back of the door were available to hang clothes, but she'd left most of her belongings in her portmanteau, the only clean place in the room. She wished she'd brought her own sheets. The stained and musty-smelling ones on the lumpy mattress were distasteful.

When she'd finished her few preparations, she climbed into bed. These moments were the only ones in the day she permitted her mind to dwell on things that had no future.

She knew she'd done the right thing in leaving Lady Haversham's household when she had. Mr. Gallagher's gallant proposal proved he was much too honorable a gentleman not to leap to her defense against the awful accusations in Mrs. Haversham's will and his sister's threat to bring legal action against Maddie.

Maddie had never been so touched in her life as when Mr. Gallagher had told her they must marry. No matter that the request hadn't been attended by all the romantic avowals of love a woman longs to hear. Maddie knew how much more special this man's proposal was in light of his still-strong feelings for his wife, as well as Maddie's own inferior social situation to his. She'd never thought about his financial position before. He certainly seemed to be respectably off in his own right, but now, with his aunt's inheritance, he must indeed be a wealthy man. As well as a knight, she reminded herself. What need had he to look Maddie's way, except out of pity? But Maddie valued the pity that had prompted his proposal. How different Mr. Gallagher's conduct from that of her former beau. He'd been a handsome, charming young gentleman. At least she'd thought him a gentleman, but now with the experience of time, she realized what a shallow, self-centered young man he was to have led her on and dropped her the way he had.

Mr. Gallagher had proven a true gentleman from the moment he'd met her. Maddie turned on her side, resting on her arm. Knowing him now the way she did, she had the strong suspicion he'd continue wearing down her resistance, insisting she marry him in some noble effort to save her from the magistrates. She smiled in the growing gloom of her room, touched by his gallantry.

She'd left because deep down she didn't know how long she'd be able to resist him if he kept on trying to offer her his protection. What a shallow woman she'd prove to be if she married a man only to provide herself with material security.

No, she would never do that to him. She loved him too much to ruin his life...the way she had ruined her parents'.

She turned onto her back and looked up at the cracked, stained ceiling. This was the moment she permitted herself to dream. As she lay in the sweltering heat, she could ignore the shouts from down below in the street, she could forget the dingy sheets she lay between and whatever critters inhabited the mattress under her and dream about what it would have been like to be married to Reid Gallagher and live in far-off Egypt.... Only in the darkness did she permit herself to weave a hundred dreams of that life, where she would be busy with the Lord's commission and Reid would be uncovering the secrets of the past....

Chapter Seventeen

Reid couldn't concentrate on anything. In the fortnight since Maddie had left, he'd hired a private detective and spent just about every waking hour scouring the streets of London himself. But Maddie was nowhere to be found. In the city of over three million, it was as if she was one particle of sand in the vast desert.

The only progress the detective had made was in locating Maddie's parents. Reid took the train out to the village they lived in in the west of England. They were a very nice elderly couple and treated Reid with warmth. They had only heard once from their daughter, they told him, but they had no idea of her whereabouts. Her letter had been postmarked London, but she might have moved elsewhere if she'd found a situation as she intended.

Reid had found a lot of common ground with them. Maddie's father was a scholar on Biblical archaeology, and the two spoke about Reid's work, as well as Mr. Norton's time in Jerusalem.

"Your daughter proved an able assistant to me in cataloging an extensive collection of my late uncle's," he said, in order to explain his association with Maddie.

Mr. Norton smiled. "She has always had an interest in the Middle East. It's a pity she was never able to return."

"She told me it was due to her frequent ill health as a young girl that you were forced to return."

"It is true she was frequently ill," Mrs. Norton said, "but it wasn't the only reason we decided to return to England."

"That's right," Mr. Norton added. "You see, it was about that same time that this curacy fell open and I was asked to take it. The church here had fallen upon hard times and was on the verge of closing its doors. It's a poor community." He turned to his wife and patted her hand. "We spent some time in prayer about it, but the Lord confirmed it to both of us—" he tapped his chest "—in here, where it counts, that it was His will that we return from the mission field and make this community our mission field. We haven't ever regretted the decision. The church is thriving and, not too long ago, the Lord sent me a young assistant who is showing much promise to take over when I start slowing down." He smiled a gentle smile, which reminded Reid of Maddie.

Reid spent as much time with them as he dared to spare, learning of Maddie's young life. He thanked her parents for their time, and Mr. Norton accompanied him back to the small train station. The two men shook hands when Reid's train pulled in.

Mr. Norton released Reid's hand. "I hope you find her."

Reid nodded, unsmiling. "I do, too."

He returned that night to his room at the Travellers Club. A fitting place for him, a traveler, except the name no longer appealed to him. He no longer wanted to be a mere nomad, passing through a city with no roots anywhere. He longed for a home and wife and children.

When he entered his quiet room, the street sounds muffled by its thick walls and drapes, everything in order, it only augmented the hole he felt in his heart. He took off his jacket and loosened his tie before going to sit on his bed.

He took up his wife's portrait and stared at it a long time. Octavia's face smiled lifelessly back at him. How long he'd acted as if she were still alive. Of course, his love for her had never died, but she would always be what she was now, a lifeless image in a portrait…not a living, breathing, warm woman. As he'd done with everything in his life, he was living in the past.

He sighed heavily. "I'm sorry. I'm sorry, but I can't live without her. I need to find her. Please forgive me." He bowed his head. "I never meant to cause you harm, to betray your memory with another woman. I'm so sorry, but I need her. Please forgive me…"

After a moment, he continued, "please forgive me, Lord." The portrait fell to his lap. "Let me find Maddie, please. Show me where she is. Oh, God, protect her, wherever she is. I'm so sorry I hurt her." What a blunder he'd made of his proposal. No wonder she'd gone away. He'd be lucky if she ever wanted to see him again.

He'd already endured untold agonies imagining the worst possible scenarios of her alone in London. He realized he'd rather chance the risk of losing her at his side than never see her again.

He continued praying for Maddie, as if her unerring faith had infused his own heart in his hour of need. What a fool he'd been! Why hadn't he ever told her he loved her?

* * *

Early the next morning, a footman handed Reid a note just as he was leaving his room. It was from the private detective.

> Good news. Come to my office as soon as you receive this.
> Sam Abbot.

His hopes soared. Had the detective found her?

Barely fifteen minutes later, Reid walked into the man's office.

Abbot stood at once from his desk, his checked jacket and trousers calling attention in the somber office. "Mr. Gallagher, we've hit the jackpot." He held out a crumpled piece of paper to Reid.

Reid's hand shook as he read it. It listed a street.

"She has a room there."

Reid eyed him. "You're certain?" They'd followed false leads before.

The man gave him a satisfied look. "As certain as my granny's name is Jane. It took me a while, but I scoured every neighborhood, every boardinghouse. I knew if she hadn't left London, I'd find her. All it takes is persistence. One by one, I tracked them down."

"Thank you, Mr. Abbot. I'll go there at once. If she's there, I'll come by your office and settle with you this afternoon, including the bonus I promised you if you located her within a month."

"She'll be there, all right, or my name's not Sam Abbot."

Reid checked the address again, thanked the detective and went for a cab.

* * *

Maddie left the rooming house to begin her weary trek through the city once again. She gave the warped door a second yank to get it to close properly then turned toward the pavement.

"Maddie."

She froze.

Was she dreaming? There, a few feet from her, stood Mr. Gallagher, as devastatingly handsome as the first time she'd seen him, his blue eyes piercing into hers.

Her first impulse was to run to him. Then she remembered. He only pitied her. She must flee before she broke down in front of him. Where could she go? She began pushing through the crowd, away from him. She didn't feel strong enough to resist his noble intentions.

"Maddie, wait!" She quickened her step, but too many people stood in front of her. In a moment she felt a strong hand clasp her shoulder and she was forced to face him.

Her heart constricted at the sight of his dear face. His eyes looked tired, the lines around his mouth deepened. "Maddie, why did you run away from me?" His quiet tone sounded hurt.

"Please, Mr. Gallagher, you shouldn't have come—"

"Why are you afraid of me, Maddie?"

She shook her head and tried to speak but couldn't. She raised a hand to her mouth to hide its trembling and finally turned away.

"Why didn't you come to me?"

She looked down at her feet, too ashamed to look him in the eye. Why did he have to see her like this?

"We have to talk. Is there somewhere we can go?"

She wanted to weep at the concern in his tone. "Please," she whispered.

"Maddie, trust me."

She raised her eyes to him and felt her resolve slipping. She'd tried so hard to give him up. But there he stood, so solid and sure. How could she ever say no to him? She took a deep breath. She'd hear him out. She owed him that much, but she must remain strong. She *must.* "All right." She led him back to the boardinghouse, hating the thought of taking him there, but knowing of nowhere else.

The door stuck as usual. Before she could give it an additional shove, Mr. Gallagher put his greater strength to it and held it open for her. She slipped past him and led him into a dingy side parlor.

Murky sunshine only highlighted the years of grime on the upholstery and carpet. She didn't offer him a seat nor did he take one. He removed his hat and held it in his hands. "I saw your parents."

Her gaze flew up to his. "You did? When?" The next second, she asked, "Did they tell you where I was?" No, how could they? They didn't know.

He shook his head. "They said they didn't know."

"No…they didn't."

He cleared his throat. "You needn't have run away. We found the letter you wrote to my aunt just before her stroke. It convinced my sister you had no ulterior motives. She's sorry she misjudged your character."

Maddie's back straightened. "I didn't run away out of guilt or fear—" She stopped, afraid she'd give away the real reason.

"I know you didn't."

She remained silent, feeling the fear grow in her.

"Your parents send their love. They're concerned about you."

"You didn't tell them anything—"

"What could I tell them? You disappeared. I merely said you were my assistant, as well as my aunt's companion."

She stared at him, wondering what her parents had thought of him.

"I think your parents understood the real reason I was there looking for you."

"The real reason?" She waited, hardly breathing.

His gaze remained steady. "That I love you."

Her lower lip began to tremble again and she bit down on it. "Don't, Mr. Gallagher. Pl-please don't say anything more. You don't owe me anything."

"I owe you a great deal. You gave me back hope and life and such a deep sense of happiness. You helped restore my faith and feel young again."

Her eyes filled with tears so she could no longer see him in front of her. "You mustn't speak like that." Overcome, she sniffled, turning away from him. "I'm not worthy—"

He approached her and took her wrist in his hand, forcing her back though she held her face away from him. "Why? What are you afraid you'd do to me?" As he spoke, he rubbed the inside of her wrist with his thumb. "What are you afraid of if you married me? Other than making me the happiest man on earth?"

"I'm not g-good enough f-for you. Look what your aunt said about m-me."

"My aunt was a selfish old woman—"

"You mustn't speak ill of her—" She could hardly think for the feel of his thumb pad against her skin.

"Marry me, Maddie, and come back with me to Egypt. You've always wanted to go back to the Middle East. Come with me." His soft voice wore down her control. How could she fight him reasonably when he stood so near, his touch and low tone hypnotizing her?

"I'd only ruin it for you the way I did for my parents," she whispered, knowing she must persuade him any way she could.

"Your parents told me they didn't come back because of you."

Maddie stared up at him.

"They said the Lord led them to the curacy your father now holds. They said they prayed long and hard about it and felt it was the Lord's will for them to return to that village in England."

Maddie pondered his words. She knew her father had been content in the village where they'd lived upon their return. Why would her father say such a thing to a stranger unless it were true?

Mr. Gallagher offered her his handkerchief, a large white square of finest cotton. She took it and wiped her nose and eyes.

Before she knew what he was doing, he leaned toward her, until his face was almost touching hers. "Marry me, Maddie...and don't make me go through the agony you put me through in the last fortnight." As he spoke, his lips skimmed her temple and cheek, his mustache brushing her skin.

"Agony?"

He nodded, his cheek grazing hers. "I've searched high and low for you. I couldn't rest until I saw your face and held you in my arms."

"How did you...find me?"

"I hired a detective."

She drew back from him, unable to believe what she was hearing. Did he care that much about her? She tried again, though her voice sounded wavering to her ears. "I'd hold you back—"

"How could you when you give my work meaning? These last couple of months with you have made me realize how little it all means if I have no one to share it with. You've reminded me there's something greater than my little, self-protected world. You've given me hope." He fell silent and touched his lips to her cheek, raining soft kisses along her jaw, not stopping until he'd reached the corner of her lips.

Before she lost all reason, she asked the hardest question of all "What...about your wife?"

He drew away a fraction and she was sure this was the end of his proposal. But he held her gently by the shoulders. "I loved Octavia very much, but you've shown me it was time to let her go. She's gone and I think I've finally laid her to rest." His blue eyes searched hers. "Can you forgive an old fool for not realizing until you left me how much I love you?"

"You loved your wife."

"And now I love you. You showed me my heart hadn't died with Octavia. Maddie, marry me because I can't live without you—" He stopped in midsentence. "Oh, I can, literally. I can survive, as you well know, just as you can without me. But I'll only be existing the way I've done since Octavia died. I know we have eternity, but I don't want to miss the chance to enjoy your company in the here and now as long as the Lord gives us."

He touched her cheek with his fingertip and stroked it softly. "Marry me, Maddie. Don't let me turn into one of those fussy old bachelors who snaps at his servants and can't remember where he put his reading glasses and when they point them out at his side, he'll never admit it's his failing memory that's at fault." As he saw the humor begin to lighten her eyes, he pressed on, "Don't let that terrible fate befall me. I need you, Maddie. I'm desperately in love with you and can't imagine not seeing your beautiful face beside mine each morning."

Her cheeks heated, no doubt turning a bright shade of pink. He continued his caresses with his fingertips.

"Why didn't you tell me any of this the first time you proposed to me?"

"Perhaps I didn't want to admit it, even to myself."

She appeared to consider his words. Seconds passed, in which she seemed to be weighing his words, determining their authenticity, and Reid was reminded of himself when he studied an artifact. Was it genuine or a cleverly masked fake? And now his own words were being weighed in the balance. He could feel the thud of his heart, pounding loudly in fear.

She glanced at his left hand still resting on her shoulder. His ring finger was bare, the paler skin where his wedding band had sat so many years making its absence all the more evident.

She stared back at Reid. He nodded, telling her with his eyes that he had finally relinquished this most tangible sign of his first marriage.

Seconds passed. She moistened her lips. "Perhaps I should rethink my refusal. I wouldn't want to subject you to such a miserable fate."

He hardly understood the first part of her words, but by the end, he discerned the humor warming her tawny eyes.

He pulled her to him and her hand came up to his chest. "What are you doing?"

"Exacting my revenge." He lowered his face down to hers.

"For what?"

"For putting me through an agonizing fortnight."

"Oh." His lips touched hers and he was relieved she made no more move to stop him.

He scowled at her rosy face. "Is that all you have to say?"

"Was it so very bad?" She touched his cheek.

"It was in direct proportion to the pleasure I shall exact from you now," he murmured between light kisses to her mouth.

"I see. Will it be so very bad for me?"

"Let's just say Aunt Millicent would find it most inappropriate—" he touched her lips again "—indeed."

"It sounds dreadful," she breathed against him as her arms came up to wrap themselves around his neck. Then she was unable to speak anymore.

He kissed her long and deeply, his senses reveling in the taste and touch and scent of her.

After a few minutes, she broke away from him. "I'm sorry that I caused you any pain. I thought loving you meant I had to give you up."

He lifted her chin with his fingertip. "Never run from me again. You almost killed me with worry."

"I'm so sorry."

"You should have come to me."

She smiled. "I will the next time."

"There'd better not be a next time," he growled.

She laughed softly.

He drew a deep breath, separating himself from her only far enough to say what he meant to say. "Now that you are sufficiently penitent, permit me to rephrase the question I put to you so inelegantly after that dreadful reading of my aunt's will."

Her eyes clouded at this reminder and she would have looked away if he'd permitted it, but he cradled her face between his hands. He cleared his throat. "Maddie, will you marry me? I love you with all my heart and soul and breath."

The warmth that began in her beautiful eyes spread to her mouth as she smiled. "I will indeed, for I think I have loved you since the first day I met you at Lady Haversham's."

"I'm sorry it took me so much longer."

"Oh, Reid, you'll never know how grateful I was that day you offered me your protection." She hugged him fast. "You are the most wonderful man!"

He laughed in response. "Just keep thinking that for the rest of your life."

"That won't be difficult."

"I like hearing my name on your lips, by the way."

"Reid," she repeated softly, her color heightened. "How I love you and thank God for bringing you into my life."

"As do I." His smile met hers as he leaned in until she was a blur and he closed his eyes and kissed her again.

Epilogue

Cairo, Egypt 1900

Reid felt the deep sense of satisfaction that coming home always gave him. He led the donkey by the reins as he approached the large whitewashed palazzo he called home. The words on the brass plate by the door, The Good Shepherd Orphanage, announced the dual function of the building.

The Cairo sun was low in the sky, washing the front of the building in its golden light. The air resounded with the muezzin's call to prayer. A servant boy exited the building. Spotting Reid, his face broke out in a smile.

"Sir Gallagher!" Quickly he came and took the reins from Reid and led the donkey toward the stable in the back. Reid entered through the heavy front doors. He came to a tiled courtyard filled with orange trees. A fountain tinkled in the middle. Children's voices could be heard from there and above in the galleries.

He smiled as he saw Maddie among the group of children. She was blindfolded, her arms stretched outward. The children screamed in laughter, jumping around her, just out of reach.

Over the years, she'd gained a lot of confidence around children. When he'd first brought Maddie to the Middle East, she'd proved a willing and able partner, not only donning men's trousers once again when she'd worked alongside him on archaeological digs in the field, but also the roomier, more comfortable Arab and Turkish garb.

Cairo under the British was a city of many races and religions. He and Maddie had purchased a large house in the Coptic quarter of the city. With the birth of their first child, she had blossomed into the mother she was meant to be. Reid had remained in Cairo then, helping to establish a museum to house the antiquities. Soon after, he and Maddie had received their first foundling, a homeless boy. Over the years, other children were left with them.

Now, ten years since they'd married, he and Maddie had three children of their own, and twenty additional children who called this place home.

"Papa Reid!" a child's voice cried out, spying him. He motioned the boy with a finger to his lips to be silent. The boy understood at once. With a conspiratorial smile, he accompanied Reid as he approached Maddie.

The crowd of children fell silent at his signal, their faces alight with anticipation.

Reid positioned himself close enough to Maddie to let her catch him. Her hands landed on his front, and she stopped immediately. "Reid?"

The next moment she whipped off her scarf and broke into a joyous smile. Before he could do more than return her smile, he was bombarded by several children's bodies flinging themselves around his legs and waist. "Papa Reid! Papa Reid!" He looked over the children's heads at the elegant woman in front of him.

Maddie had changed little in their ten years together. Still as slim as when he'd met her, her tawny hair was hardly touched by gray, but best of all, she had the warmest smile in the world.

Slowly, the children parted as he took a step toward her. Her arms wrapped around his neck as he took her in a bear hug.

She looked up at him, giving him the smile he'd dreamed of in the desert. "Welcome home, dearest."

"Hello, Maddie. I've missed you."

His own firstborn son came running up. "Papa!"

"Alex!" He gave the blond-haired eight-year-old a tight hug. Then he turned to his five-year-old daughter, Pippa, who was pulling at his arm. Last of all, their Egyptian nurse brought their youngest, two-year-old Troy, for him to hold. He raised him high in the air amidst his giggles.

"Papa." The toddler's chubby hands came up to play with Reid's hair.

Reid put the child on his shoulders as he gave his attention back to his wife.

Together, the group walked toward the house, Reid and Maddie arm in arm. His darling Pippa, her hair as tawny as her mother's, her eyes as blue as his, clung to his free hand and chattered all the way. His oldest son walked alongside his mother. Reid gave him a special wink, promising they'd have that "man-to-man" time alone later.

Reid squeezed Maddie's shoulder. She met his look. These days, as director of the orphanage, she ran a staff of people and never turned a child away. Best of all, her life reflected the gospel she preached—feeding the hungry, clothing the naked, visiting the prisoner.

He was proud of his wife and never ceased thanking God for giving him this opportunity to love again. Maddie had taught him over the years to open his heart and not to be afraid to give of himself. With each child they welcomed, they risked their hearts. With the Lord's love sustaining them, they never refused the call to love.

* * * * *

*Evicted from her home, Joanna Nelson and her two
children seek refuge on the harsh Montana plains—
which leads her to rancher Aidan McKaslin's property.
When outside forces threaten their blossoming
friendship, Aidan decides to take action. Can he
convince Joanna to bind herself to him permanently or
will it drive her away forever?*

Read on for a sneak preview of
High Country Bride *by Jillian Hart!*

"Where are you going to go?"

His tone was flat, his jaw tensed, as if he was still
fighting his temper. His blue eyes glanced past her to
where the children were going about their chore.

"I don't know." Her throat went dry. Her tongue felt
thick as she answered. She trembled, not from fear of
him—she truly didn't believe he would strike her—but
from the unknown.

Of being forced to take the frightening step off the
only safe spot she'd found since she'd lost Pa's house.

When you were homeless, everything seemed so
fragile, so easily off balance. It was a big, unkind world
for a woman alone with her children. She had no one to
protect her. No one to care. The truth was, Joanna had
never had those things in her husband. How could she

expect them from any stranger? Especially this man she hardly knew, who seemed harsh, cold and hard-hearted?

And, worse, what if he brought in the law?

"Let me guess. If you leave here, you don't know where you're going and you have no money to get there with?"

She nodded. "Yes, sir."

"Then get you and your kids into the wagon. I'll hitch up your horses for you." His eyes were cold and yet not unfeeling as he fastened his gaze on hers. "I have a shanty out back of my house that no one's living in. You can stay there for the night."

"What?" She stumbled back, and the solid wood of the tailgate bit into the small of her back. "But—"

"There will be no argument," he snapped, interrupting her. "None at all. I buried a wife and son years ago, what was most precious to me, and to see you and them neglected like this—with no one to care…" His jaw clenched again, and his eyes were no longer cold.

Joanna didn't think she'd ever seen anything sadder than Aiden McKaslin standing there in the slanting rays of the setting sun.

Without another word, he turned on his heel and walked away, melting into the thick shadows of the summer evening.

Don't miss
High Country Bride *by Jillian Hart,*
available October 2018.

www.LoveInspired.com

Copyright © 2018 by Jill Strickler

LIHEXP89584

Love Inspired®

Save $1.00

on the purchase of ANY
Love Inspired® book.

Available wherever books are sold, including most bookstores, supermarkets, drugstores and discount stores.

Save $1.00

on the purchase of ANY Love Inspired® book.

Coupon valid until October 31, 2018.
Redeemable at participating retail outlets in the U.S. and Canada only.
Limit one coupon per customer.

52615896

Canadian Retailers: Harlequin Enterprises Limited will pay the face value of this coupon plus 10.25¢ if submitted by customer for this product only. Any other use constitutes fraud. Coupon is nonassignable. Void if taxed, prohibited or restricted by law. Consumer must pay any government taxes. Void if copied. Inmar Promotional Services ("IPS") customers submit coupons and proof of sales to Harlequin Enterprises Limited, P.O. Box 31000, Scarborough, ON M1R 0E7, Canada. Non-IPS retailer—for reimbursement submit coupons and proof of sales directly to Harlequin Enterprises Limited, Retail Marketing Department, Bay Adelaide Centre, East Tower, 22 Adelaide Street West, 40th Floor, Toronto, Ontario M5H 4E3, Canada.

5 65373 00076 2   (8100)0 12379

U.S. Retailers: Harlequin Enterprises Limited will pay the face value of this coupon plus 8¢ if submitted by customer for this product only. Any other use constitutes fraud. Coupon is nonassignable. Void if taxed, prohibited or restricted by law. Consumer must pay any government taxes. Void if copied. For reimbursement submit coupons and proof of sales directly to Harlequin Enterprises, Ltd 482, NCH Marketing Services, P.O. Box 880001, El Paso, TX 88588-0001, U.S.A. Cash value 1/100 cents.

® and ™ are trademarks owned and used by the trademark owner and/or its licensee.
© 2018 Harlequin Enterprises Limited

LICOUP89584

SPECIAL EXCERPT FROM

Love Inspired®

*When Amos Burkholder steps in to help the
Miller family, he soon discovers that middle daughter
Deborah disappears for hours at a time.
Where does she go?*

Read on for a sneak preview of
Courting Her Secret Heart *by Mary Davis,
available September 2018 from Love Inspired!*

Amos Burkholder looked out over the Millers' fields to be plowed in the spring. He couldn't help but think of them as partly his. Of course, they weren't his fields, and he might not even be here to do the plowing and the planting. But if he was, he would take pride in that work.

Bartholomew Miller appreciated everything he did around the farm, so Amos worked harder than he ever had at home.

Bartholomew had never had a son to help him with all the work around the farm. How had he run this place without sons?

But on the flip side, Amos's *mutter* had been alone doing the house chores, cooking, cleaning and laundry for six men. How did she do it without help?

On the far side of one of the fields, a woman emerged from a bare stand of sycamore trees nestled next to a pond. She walked across the field.

The woman came closer and closer.

Deborah.

Where did she go all the time? She had disappeared every day this week and would be gone for hours. He was about to find out.

With her head down, she didn't see him approaching. He stepped directly into her path a few yards in front of her. When it looked as though she might literally run into him, he cleared his throat.

She halted a foot away. She was so startled to see him there, she appeared to lose her balance. Her arms swung out to keep herself upright.

LIEXP0818

He reached out and took hold of her upper arms to stop her from tumbling to the ground. "Whoa there."

She gasped. "I'm sorry. I didn't see you."

"Where have you been all day?"

"What? Nowhere." She tried to pull free of his grip, but he held fast.

He shook his head. "You've been somewhere. You've left every day this week and been gone for most of the day."

"I—I went for a walk."

"Where? Ohio?"

"We have a pond just over there. I like to sit and watch the ducks. It's a nice place to think and be alone. You should go sometime."

"I did. Today. You weren't there."

Her self-satisfied expression fell. "I was for a while, then I walked farther."

He sensed there was more to her absence than a walk. "Where?"

"Why do you care?"

"With your *vater* laid up, I'm responsible for everyone on this farm."

"I'm fine. I can take care of myself. May I go now?"

He didn't want to let her go but did. "I don't want you to leave the farm without telling me where you're going."

"Are you serious?"

He gave her his serious look.

She huffed and strode away.

Where did she go every day? He had wanted to follow her, but he realized it was none of his business. But curiosity pushed hard on him. He still might follow her if she didn't obey. Just to see. Just to watch her from a distance. Just to know her secret.

Something inside him feared for her. Feared she would walk out across this field and never return. Feared her secret would consume them both. She was a mystery.

A mystery he was drawn to solve.

Don't miss
Courting Her Secret Heart *by Mary Davis,*
available September 2018 wherever
Love Inspired® books and ebooks are sold.

www.LoveInspired.com

Copyright © 2018 by Mary Davis

LIEXP0818

Looking for inspiration in tales
of hope, faith and heartfelt romance?

Check out **Love Inspired**® and
Love Inspired® **Suspense** books!

New books available every month!

CONNECT WITH US AT:

Facebook.com/groups/HarlequinConnection

Facebook.com/HarlequinBooks

Twitter.com/HarlequinBooks

Instagram.com/HarlequinBooks

Pinterest.com/HarlequinBooks

ReaderService.com

LIGENRE2018R2

Love Inspired®

**Inspirational Romance to
Warm Your Heart and Soul**

Join our social communities to connect
with other readers who share your love!

Sign up for the Love Inspired newsletter
at **www.LoveInspired.com** to be the
first to find out about upcoming titles,
special promotions and exclusive content.

CONNECT WITH US AT:

Harlequin.com/Community

 Facebook.com/LoveInspiredBooks

 Twitter.com/LoveInspiredBks